Reckoning

Reckoning

A Valentine Shepherd Novel

SHANA FIGUEROA

FOREVER
YOURS

New York   Boston

Copyright © 2017 by Shana S. Figueroa
Excerpt from *Vengeance* copyright © 2016 by Shana S. Figueroa

Cover Illustration by Craig White
Cover design by Scott Silvestro

Cover copyright © 2017 by Hachette Book Group, Inc.

Forever
Hachette Book Group
1290 Avenue of the Americas, New York, NY 10104
forever-romance.com
twitter.com/foreverromance

First Trade Paperback (Print-on-Demand) and Ebook Edition: July 2017

Forever is an imprint of Grand Central Publishing. The Forever name and logo are trademarks of Hachette Book Group, Inc.

The publisher is not responsible for websites (or their content) that are not owned by the publisher.

The Hachette Speakers Bureau provides a wide range of authors for speaking events. To find out more, go to www.hachettespeakersbureau.com or call (866) 376-6591.

Library of Congress Cataloging-in-Publication Data has been applied for.

ISBNs: 978-1-4555-6751-5 (trade paperback, print-on-demand),
978-1-4555-4013-6 (ebook)

*To my brothers and sisters in arms at the
Security Assistance Office in Afghanistan, who
fought for a better world while giving me
ample writing material on how to be a hero.*

Prologue

When Kat lifted her head up from between Stacey's thighs, she said in a tone not unlike one might use to remark on the weather, "We're going back to Seattle."

"What?" Stacey panted, still catching her breath from the explosion of bliss that had seized her only a moment ago.

"I said we're going back to Seattle."

"You mean a city in *France* called Seattle, right?"

Kat crawled forward, flipping her lustrous blond hair over her shoulder as she lay down next to Stacey. "Why do you care if we go back?"

"Come on, you know why I care." Stacey hadn't been back to her hometown in almost five years, not since her former best friend dumped her for a rich piece of ass. Even that might not have been a deal-breaker—chicks before dicks, after all—but for the fact that her "friend" had used knowledge of the future to save her life…and then never told her. Never gave her an option to choose if she wanted to defy fate or not, or to come to terms with whatever that decision might have been. She should be dead. She *was* dead. How many times had the universe killed her, only to have its will thwarted by a woman who fucks to see the future?

Stacey wasn't one to hold a grudge, but…okay, she held a grudge. She had her own hot piece of ass now, her own soul mate, a reason for living even though she wasn't supposed to be alive. Kat made room in her hectic life for Stacey, had brought her girlfriend into the fold so they could be together. For over five years they'd been a team, doing odd jobs for Kat's employers, an organization Stacey knew only as Northwalk. Kat admitted she had blood relations with the top echelon of the group—their leader was her mother—but they weren't close, and only communicated when business required it. Stacey and Kat had traveled the world together, occasionally doing something as grand as stealing a piece of fine art from a wealthy asshole (Kat excelled at the honeypot con), or something as simple as picking up a person's mail. Maybe fate had decreed she and Kat should be together, too.

Now they lay in a ridiculously fancy hotel room in a posh resort on the French Riviera, and Kat wanted to go back to goddamn Seattle, where it had all begun. The place she'd run away from, the place where she'd *died*, and where the person she had trusted the most, who'd lied to her for years, still lived.

"So what if you run into her?" Kat skimmed a finger along Stacey's sweaty collarbone, working her usual magic. It wasn't a coincidence Kat dropped this bombshell in the middle of their lovemaking. Sex was her greatest weapon and she wasn't afraid to use it, even against her own girlfriend. "You don't owe her an explanation."

"I know that," Stacey snapped. "But she owes *me* one, and she'll dance around it instead, all, 'I did what I thought was right,' and 'I knew you wouldn't take it well, blah, blah, blah.'" She pushed herself to the head of the four-post bed and hugged her knees. "You know Seattle sucks this time of year. Cold and rainy doesn't inspire holiday cheer. I never had a white Christmas growing up, not once."

"You won't have a white Christmas here, either."

"The white sands of the Mediterranean are close enough." She sighed. "Why do we have to go back?"

"Something big is about to go down."

Stacey cringed. Shit. This was what she'd been hired for, but still she had hoped this day would be much farther into the future. She didn't know or care what Northwalk's ultimate goals were, as long as she and Kat could be together. Her gaze raked over their five-star hotel room, the midafternoon sun glinting off bay windows framing an azure sky, Kat's naked, tanned body coiled across the white bedspread. Paradise—like she'd *died* and gone to heaven. She shuddered, thinking of all she was about to lose. "But *why* do we have to go back?"

Kat sat up. She put a hand on Stacey's arm and squeezed reassuringly. Then her grip tightened, until her fingers dug into her girlfriend's flesh. Stacey yelped and tried to pull her arm away, but Kat held it fast. She was stronger than she looked; quicker, too. And meaner.

What was Kat doing? Her ice blue eyes cut into Stacey's with a ferocious intensity Stacey had never seen before.

"We need to go because Cassandra says it has to be now," Kat said, her voice pitch-black velvet. "*And I want my goddamn inheritance.*"

* * *

You will walk up the stairs until you reach the eighteenth floor. You'll use the security badge you procured from your lover to exit the stairwell and gain access to the inner offices. If you stay flush with the outer walls, you'll avoid the cameras. After you reach the executive suites, you will spot a conference room under construction. You will find a cluster of boxes filled with nails and other construction supplies in the corner of the room.

That is where you will plant the bomb.

Obey my divine will, as you, my child, are my agent of flesh, commanded to break apart the ebony fox and red raven. Love me as I love you, and fear me as they will fear you.

Chapter One

Valentine Shepherd sat cross-legged on her son's squat bed, gritting her teeth as she watched Simon dig through a pile of brightly colored books with cardboard pages and huge fonts. The kids' room sported an abundance of short bookcases, but still they had too many books to fit, the excess strewn across the floor as miniature mountains of knowledge. Like father, like son.

"Just pick one, Simon."

He kept rooting. Val took a deep breath and tried to control her annoyance. It was already an hour past the twin's usual bedtime, as they'd insisted on "helping" her bake a batch of gingersnaps for the holiday cookie exchange between her group of playdate moms—well, mostly nannies—the following day. As she juggled cookie trays, they decided to have a raw egg fight in the living room. She'd ordered them upstairs, then cleaned up the slimy mess. Toby, their Jack Russell terrier, helped by licking egg yolks off the walls. Then he puked them up onto the carpet. At that point, she'd smelled the cookies burning.

"Just pick one, Simon."

After a minute he snatched up a book he liked, sprinted back to Val, and dropped it into her lap.

Val read the cover. "*The Night Before Christmas.* Appropriate enough."

Simon launched himself onto the bed and snuggled up to his mother. He beamed up at her, beautiful hazel eyes with starbursts of emerald green at their centers radiating the pure love of a devoted four-year-old. Val's irritation ebbed, her love for her children an aloe that always soothed her most frayed nerves. She ruffled his blond hair and kissed his head.

"Lydia, come on," Val called out.

A moment later her daughter wandered into the room, head down and eyes glued to a tablet computer.

"Turn that off. It's time for a story, then bed."

Lydia looked up and pushed black hair out of her big gray eyes. "But Mommy," she whined. She turned the tablet toward Val. Flashing stars danced across the screen; some kind of numbers game. "I almost have the high score."

"That's great, honey. Turn it off."

Lydia's delicate pink lips curled into a pout, then she pressed the power button until the screen went black. She dropped it on top of a book pile and curled up next to Val, opposite her brother.

"Okay." God, finally. "*The Night Before Christmas*, here we go..." Val flipped to the first page. "'Twas the night before Christmas, when all through the house—'"

"How does Santa get down the chimney?" Simon asked.

"It's a trade secret."

"Santa's not real," Lydia told Simon in her usual serious tone.

"Lydia!" Val frowned at her daughter.

Simon's lips trembled and he looked at his mother with big doe eyes.

"Of course Santa's real," she said to Simon. "In a way. He lives in our hearts." She smiled at her son, and his wounded innocence turned to confusion. It was good enough. "Okay, so where were we…" She cleared her throat and tried to read with the practiced animation Max was so good at when he usually did this. Her exhaustion made it a hard sell. "'Twas the night before Christmas, when all through the house, not a creature was stirring, not even—'"

"When's Daddy coming home?" Lydia asked.

"In two days."

Simon: "Where is he?"

"Fort Lauderdale. That's in Florida, America's flaccid wang." Val cracked a smile. They wouldn't know what that meant for years. There was no shame in enjoying a dirty inside joke with herself. Reminded her that she technically still belonged to the adult world despite being consumed by the daily grind of four-year-old affairs. She took her small pleasures wherever she could get them.

Lydia and Simon peered around their mother and at each other. Their eyes widened and misted over with a glaze Val recognized, the one that sent a cold chill racing up her spine.

Simon said, "Daddy was in Florida—"

"But he's not there now," Lydia finished.

Val swallowed hard. She wished they wouldn't do this. More than wished—she *prayed to God* they wouldn't do this. She'd hoped the twins had escaped the curse that afflicted her and Max, but since their verbal skills had exploded over the last six months, it was becoming clearer by the day they hadn't. They knew things they shouldn't, and they didn't need to be in a trance to see it, like Max and Val—they were *Alphas*, like Cassandra, the woman in white she'd seen only in her visions. Other parents expressed amazement at how *advanced* Lydia and Simon were, sometimes through teeth clenched together in jealousy at their own child's implied inferiority.

But what made them special made them vulnerable. *They* would be coming for her children. Maybe someday soon. Sten Ander, her sometimes enemy/sometimes ally, had told her they called themselves Northwalk. They owned Cassandra, and they wanted Simon and Lydia as well. She would burn down the world before she let her children be stolen from her.

Val began again, her throat suddenly dry and sapped of the meager enthusiasm she'd worked to channel a minute ago. "'Twas the night before Christmas, when all through the house—'"

"Daddy reads it better," Simon said.

"Well, Daddy's not here, so do you want me to read the story or not?"

Simon nodded, resigned to his fate of a subpar book reading. A long sigh escaped Val's chest. She flipped through the book and cringed at the walls of text. *Ten pages of this?* She didn't remember the poem being so long.

"'Twas the night before Christmas, when all through the house, not a creature was stirring, not even a mouse…' Except Santa was there! He spread gifts everywhere for all the good little boys and girls, and when he left, he said, 'Merry Christmas to all, and to all a good night!'" Val snapped the book shut.

Lydia frowned. "That's not what it said."

"That's the abridged version. And since when do you know how to read?"

"I've always known how to read."

"Jesus Christ," Val muttered to herself. To Lydia: "Don't tell anyone else that." She clapped her hands. "Time for bed. Chop, chop."

Lydia scrambled off Simon's bed and slipped into her own, kitty-cornered to Simon's in the same room. Val tucked them in with hugs and kisses.

"I love you, my beautiful babies," she said as she held Simon's tiny body against hers, then Lydia's. "Love, love, *love* you."

"We love you, too, Mommy," Simon said as Val walked to the doorway. "And Nana."

She froze. "Who?"

"Nana," Lydia answered. "She's the best grandma ever."

They didn't have a Nana...Well, technically they did, but she might as well be dead. Val hadn't seen or heard from her mother in almost thirty years—until recently, that was. To choose not to have contact with your own children for decades, even after one of them took her own life...she was certainly *not* the best Nana ever. The kids must be referring to someone else. Maybe one of their friends' grandmothers. That must be it.

Val flipped off the light, a constellation of blue stars from a nightlight making slow circles across the ceiling as she shut the door. It was nothing. She didn't want to see her mother again anyway. She couldn't even remember what the woman looked like. All she could recall was red hair like Val's—probably gray now—and the acrid odor of the menthol cigarettes her mother liked to smoke. And her mom's eyes, the same steely blue as Val's, that crinkled at the edges every time she laughed. And her mom's voice, shrill and frantic as she screamed about the injustice of the Gulf War. And she remembered the feel of cold hardwood on her knees as she knelt at the foot of her bed, praying for her mother to return. What kind of person abandons their own children? How could she—

Val leaned against the hallway's wall and blinked back tears. She was working herself up over nothing. Who knew what the twins really saw? They didn't know themselves half the time—a blessing for their poor four-year-old minds. Her own children would grow up with a loving mother and father, and that was all that mattered.

Nana wasn't real. Her mother was dead to her. Or might as well have been.

Val pushed herself off the wall in the hallway, took a deep breath, and fought the urge to walk straight to her bedroom and read *the letter* again. No, she wouldn't let it distract her. She had more important things to do, good-mother things. Instead she made her nightly round through the condo: first the kitchen, then the indoor pool and surrounding patio, then the living room, the study, the den, each bathroom, and ending at the guest room—checking all the guns she'd hidden out of the children's reach but within her own. For when *they* came. She and Max had enjoyed a crazy-conspiracy dry spell since the twins had been born, but it couldn't last forever. With all the effort Max and Val's tormentors had put into bringing the two of them together, it was only a matter of time until they resurfaced to resume their torture. This time, she'd be prepared.

Rounds completed, she considered watching some TV, maybe the *Real Housewives of Something*, to numb her mind. But if she stumbled on a news report involving Delilah Barrister, Seattle's ex-mayor and Washington State's newest Congresswoman, she was already pissed enough she might punch the television. It'd taken a massive amount of willpower to resist going after the woman who'd murdered Val's fiancé and manipulated Val into killing Delilah's husband, the late, terrible Norman Barrister, in order to fuel her political ambitions and assist Northwalk in forcing Val and Max together to create their special children. But Val had left Delilah alone to rule Seattle and climb the political ladder, because her family's lives depended on it. Delilah had proven she was capable of killing anyone to get what she wanted. The fate of poor Zach, the teenaged hacker who'd helped Val almost nail Delilah and had "committed suicide" for his trouble, still gave her nightmares. She wouldn't put her family in danger of a similar situation, even if it meant backing off her enemy—for now. Delilah would get hers someday. Val *fucking swore it*.

Yep, no TV tonight. She went to the laundry room and collected warm clothes from the dryer, carried the load to her bedroom, and dumped it on the mattress. She stared at the pile for a moment. Goddamn laundry. There were many techniques a person could use to fold a four-year-old's underwear, though she'd been told by another stay-at-home mom only one was correct. If she didn't fold the clothes now, they'd wrinkle, and she'd get disapproving looks from the other mothers in her kids' play group. What a tragedy. Her hands balled into and out of fists. Dammit. Of all the ways she could be torturing herself at that moment, she could think of at least one better than laundry. Turning her back on the pile, she made a beeline to her nightstand, yanked open the drawer, and took out a worn envelope.

Val stared hard at the letter gripped between her fingers, an unassuming piece of mail holding only one piece of paper and sliced open along the top. It was just a rectangle of white with her address scrawled on the front in loopy cursive, ordinary to anyone but Val. What normal person sent personal letters via snail mail these days? Her eyes traced the path of those handwritten letters and cut between her name in the center and the sender's in the corner—Danielle Shepherd.

She'd read the short letter dozens of times. *Sorry I haven't*

*kept in touch, it's a long story, I'd love to tell you all about it,
can I come visit?* Could her long-lost mother come visit? Was
she serious? Silence for over thirty years and now she wanted
to reconnect? Did Danielle's sudden interest in Val's life have
something to do with her new, rich husband? Or the conspiracy
that surrounded their lives, lurking out of sight, haunting her
dreams and her visions, waiting for the right moment to close in
on them? Be nice if she could get a second opinion from someone else, a real friend maybe, but the last one she had took off
after Val imploded a few years ago. She hadn't connected with
any of the other rich, stuck-up moms and their nannies in her
kids' play group, and they weren't interested in connecting with
her. She and Max were tabloid fodder with a salacious history,
after all, though they'd kept a fairly low profile since the Lucien
Christophe nightmare five years ago. Maybe she should put out
a personal ad: *Looking for a no-frills, down-to-earth, big-hearted
bestie with a bohemian streak who likes to watch bad movies, solve
mysteries, and can keep a secret.* Yeah, right. There was no replac-
ing Stacey.

Val would never let a stranger into their home, because that's
what Danielle was…but the twins had *seen* her, *knew* her—

Val froze when she realized someone was standing right behind her.

Chapter Two

An arm wrapped around her waist. In a flash she dropped the letter, seized the wrist, and cocked it hard to the side. Half a second later she smelled the delectable aroma of bay rum aftershave, and her grip slackened.

"Ow," Max said, though he slipped his other arm around her waist.

She took a deep breath and tried to slow her heart, jackhammering with the spike of adrenaline she would've used to fight. "Jesus, Max, I could've killed you."

"I know, my love." His lips touched her neck and he mumbled into her skin, "But you didn't. Thanks."

Val leaned her head back, exposed more of her neck for him. With each kiss, she felt her foul mood lifting, a warm, erotic blanket wrapping around her. "I thought your conference didn't end for another couple days."

"It was boring. I left early." His hands drifted underneath her sweatshirt and slid up her rib cage, onto the mounds of her breasts, where his fingers took turns gliding over her nipples. Horny bastard. She bit her lip and smiled.

"The board will be angry you played hooky from yet another financial conference. They might consider firing you, for real this time."

He laughed. "God no. If they had the stones to do it, I might be worried. I'd have to find another hobby." His hands stopped their sensuous path across her chest; one slipped out of her sweatshirt and picked up the letter she'd dropped on the bed. "Second thoughts?"

"No." She sighed. "I don't know. The kids...saw her. I assume it was her anyway. They said, 'We love Nana.'"

He rested his head on her shoulder and hugged her from behind. It was meant to be comforting; in almost any other situation, it would've worked. "That's good, right? Maybe you should give her a chance."

"Because you've had such good luck trusting your family?"

She felt his breath catch for half a second and immediately regretted her words. Even alluding to his horribly abusive father was a low blow. Sometimes she wished she considered and dissected her words more before she spoke, like Max did. "I'm sorry," she said to him.

He kissed her cheek—apology accepted. "I wish I had the chance to reconnect with my mother, is all I'm saying. But I know the circumstances are different—your mom had a choice, and mine didn't. Do whatever you're comfortable with."

How could he be so sensible about family after the nightmare that was his childhood? Well, she *was* tired of staring at the letter and wondering what could be. "I guess I could ask her to stay for a couple weeks. If it gets weird or she asks for money, I'll kick her out."

Max chuckled. "There's my mushy-hearted wife."

Dropping Danielle's letter on the nightstand, he lifted her

gingerbread batter–stained sweater over her head and tossed it to the side. Val's skin prickled where his fine dress shirt and thousand-dollar suit vest pressed against the bare skin of her back. He pulled out the elastic band holding her strawberry-colored hair in a messy ponytail, and it spilled across her bare shoulder in loose waves.

"I'm sure it'll be fine," he said as wound her hair around his hand, then gently pushed her head down until her naked torso lay atop the bed's foot.

"It'll be a disaster," she muttered into the comforter, her mouth beginning to water in anticipation of what he'd do next.

Max leaned over her, his clothed chest against her bare back. He wedged his hands between her skin and the sheets, slid his fingers across her breasts and down to her hips as he made a trail of agonizingly slow kisses along her spine. "If you're nervous, I could stay home. Quit my job. We could do this all day."

"We could *not* do this all day." But God, she wished they could. He eased her sweatpants and panties off, dragging her socks and slippers along with them, until she lay half on, half off the bed, completely nude. "If you stayed home, you'd be even more bored, but also exhausted—"

She gasped when he reached between her legs and caressed her clitoris, already wet for him. He leaned over her again and kissed the back of her neck, his fingers stoking a fire in her belly that threatened to immolate her when they'd barely begun. She hadn't even seen his face yet since he'd returned, but she didn't need to. She knew him—his scent, his taste, his touch, his voice, his walk, his thoughts, his past, his secrets, his everything. He was a collage of everything good and a little bad in the world, all the most interesting parts, as if brought to life by some force that made him just for her, and she for him.

He whispered, though his voice was clear with his lips against her ear. "I'll do the dishes, you'll take out the garbage. We'll sneak away, once, maybe twice a day—"

A long sigh flowed from her lips. She clutched the sheets as all rational thought fled her mind.

"And fuck our brains out."

Oh, that sounded nice. His chest slid up and down her back, his breath burning her neck in rhythmic puffs. His tongue flicked her ear. A moan rushed from her chest and out her mouth in a gush of lust. He excelled at pleasing the woman before himself, using everything he had besides his own manhood to delay his own climax and the trance that followed, which seemed like a strange sexual dysfunction to anyone who didn't understand what they could do. Already she was close to falling over the edge into one of her visions, but this was the best part—the act of lovemaking. At its most primitive level, her body craved the finale, but her mind begged to stay in this moment, with Max. Yet he excited every inch of her flesh with his touch, pulling her further toward the climax as she fought with herself to remain in the present.

"Yes…I'd like that," she said, breathless. "Every day—"

In a blink, her cheek left the mattress when he lifted her upright, his hand stoking the fire between her legs into an inferno. She leaned back against him, her moans growing into screams she couldn't control as the passion inside her grew unbearable. With his free hand, he turned her head toward him and smothered her mouth with his, muffling her cries—*can't* wake the kids—and the taste of him was enough to send her over the edge—

"Get up!" Sten yells in my face as sirens blare all around us. "Goddammit, Shepherd, GET UP!"

I struggle to stand but my legs won't hold my weight. Blood trickles down my forehead and into my eyes. I can't get up.

Sten is frantic. He pulls on my arm but can't drag me far. He's limping. Specs of blood splatter the body armor he's wearing.

"Get up—" Sten's head jerks sideways as a bullet strikes his temple.

Blur.

Max grabs fistfuls of clothes from a dresser drawer and shoves them into a duffle bag.

"Fine, just run away," I say, my voice shaking. I tremble with rage, and there are tears on my cheeks. I don't know why. "Run away like you always do."

"I can't do this anymore," he says. His face is haggard and his eyes are red like he's been crying, too, though his anger has overwhelmed his sadness. "We're never going to find her. They will always be one step ahead, and I can't…I can't." His voice chokes up. "I'm sure that, wherever she is, they're treating her well." He zips up his bag.

"You fucking coward," I say. "Get out and don't come back!"

He brushes past me, wiping tears from his eyes.

"When I find her, I'll tell her Daddy gave up!"

Like cigarette smoke, the image faded. After a second of confusion, Val realized she'd been moved to the bed, onto her side with her naked chest pressed against Max's clothed one. He propped his head up on one hand while his other hand stroked her shoulder.

"You okay?" he asked. He knew her visions were generally

awful, filled by and large with predictions of future death and mayhem. The less traditional methods of copulation offered less intense prophesies, though; why, neither of them knew. But the ecstasy of being intimate with him far outweighed the unpleasantness of what should have been an orgasm but was instead some strange "anatomical abnormality," as Max called it, that caused them trouble to no end. Since she and Max made love often enough to make Dr. Ruth blush, she'd learned to process the visions with a more objective eye, like a detective observing a crime scene. She could change what she saw, after all. They were only glimpses of what could be.

"I'm okay." Val didn't always tell Max about what she saw, and he didn't press. She preferred to come to grips with the visions before filling Max in on anything she thought he needed to know. She definitely preferred he not know that Sten still haunted her future, even though she hadn't had any contact with the dirty cop in over five years. Some things it was better her husband didn't know.

Val sat up. "And no, we can't both stay home."

"Why not?"

"Because you'd get bored, and you know it." She shimmied to the foot of the bed and began unlacing his wingtips.

He leaned back and folded his arms behind his head as she popped off his shoes. "Come with me, then. We can travel together."

"What am I supposed to do with the kids while you're in meetings all day?" She unbuttoned his pants, pulled them off, and let them drop to the floor. "They behave for you. Not for me."

Max chuckled. "They get *that* from you." He watched her slide his underwear down his legs and toss it away so he lay naked from the waist down. She crawled over the bed, back to his side, and grasped his hard cock. She enjoyed the firmness and warmth in her hand, the way it slid up and down her palm with ease, the ridges rolling over her fingers, the wetness at the tip. It was the definition of his manhood as well as his vulnerability, the source of his curse, and the thing she wanted most at that moment. Leaning down, she took it into her mouth and gave it one long, delicious suck. A faint moan escaped his chest. Just a taste of him wouldn't do. They'd been apart for three days, after all.

"I know what you need," he said as if he could read her mind, his eyes dark and heavy.

She straddled his waist and guided his cock until their flesh was joined. He let out a soft sigh, the rising and falling of his chest growing faster as she rocked her hips into his. At the same time, she popped open the buttons of his suit vest. "What do I need?"

His fingers burned a path up her thighs. "A nanny."

"This again? Max, please. I don't need help."

"Yes you do."

She worked the buttons of his dress shirt free and ran her hands along the tight folds of his abs, up his meaty pecs, and through the small patch of black chest hair. Not an ounce of fat cushioned his lean torso. Oh, not to have suffered the bodily consequences of squeezing out two children. Even after three years of consistent exercise, she still couldn't get rid of the small hill of flesh below her belly button, or get her breasts to fit comfortably into her pre-pregnancy bras. Strangely, he seemed to want her even more in her plumped state.

Val leaned down and kissed the center of his chest, right above his heart. "I *don't* need a nanny," she said, kissing her way up to his ear. "We're getting along just fine." Sitting up, she loosened his tie and slipped it around her own neck, letting the blue silk drape between her breasts. "We're already bringing one virtual stranger into our home. Another who's not even related is out of the question." The children had never been out of either Max or Val's sight. Leaving them alone with anyone else was too dangerous. "No one can be trusted. *No one*."

Max grabbed her wrists. Looking down, she saw her hands had balled into fists. "Relax, Val. They're not going to bother us again. If they still wanted our kids, they would've taken them by now. Lucien gave them what they wanted. It's over."

Lucien *might* have given Northwalk Val's eggs and Max's sperm so the evil cabal could make their own Alpha child, which was still horrific if true. But her continued visions of her and Max fighting over their lost child told her there was at least a chance Northwalk hadn't succeeded. Max thought it was over because that's what he wanted to believe, but she didn't buy it for a second. She was about to say so, like she always did, when he pulled her down to him with his tie, kissing her slow and deep, his lips lingering on hers—his way of changing the subject, like *he* always did.

"'The lady doth protest too much, methinks.'"

"Don't quote Shakespeare at me, or whatever the hell that was."

"*Hamlet*, Act Three."

"Whatever, nerd. I'm not protesting, I'm stating a fact. The vast majority of the parenting world gets by without nannies. We can, too."

He sat up. "We *can*, but you're obviously not enjoying yourself anymore."

She pushed the shirt down over his strong shoulders so he could slip out of it. "I'm enjoying myself right now."

"And if I hadn't come home tonight, you'd be anxious about the letter, folding laundry, and going to bed early," he said as he shrugged the fabric off. "I think *you're* the one who's bored and dying to get out of the house. We can't watch them forever, Val. Eventually we'll have to leave them with someone else." Finally as naked as her save the tie around her neck, he grasped the flesh of her back and pulled her chest to his face, nuzzling the skin between her breasts. "I'm tired of arguing about it. We're getting a nanny."

His lips fluttered against her nipple, then moved up her shoulder and across her collarbone. Val rested her cheek against his wavy black hair and cradled his head in her arms, holding on to him as he moved through her. She loved this part, when his lust overcame his other senses and he lost himself in her, free for a sweet moment of his always-churning mind while his body devoured hers. Thank God she could give him this, something beautiful and safe, somewhere he felt loved and unburdened by his past, a place he could lose himself in pure joy.

With a grunt like a wild animal, he flipped her onto her back, hitched her legs up, and drove into her. Max stared into her eyes with his gorgeous hazel ones, a frenzy of passion and love flowing from him into her until she matched his hysteria. She wet his lips, his jaw, his ear, and his neck with a continuous line of desperate kisses.

"Don't stop," she breathed against the furnace of his mouth, clutching his firm, smooth ass. "Don't stop."

The fever in his eyes grew. She saw him try to hold on as she had tried when he'd made love to her with his hand, until he lost the sweet battle. He shuddered before his eyes drifted closed, his taut body going slack on top of hers as he slipped into the trance of a prophetic vision. Barely a second later she fell over the edge with him—

I'm standing on the balcony of Max's old house, the balcony where he threw his father to his death. The sky is overcast, the water is black. All the glass is cracked and trash is strewn everywhere. At my feet I see a weathered newspaper with a headline that reads: "President Barrister Declares War." Before I can check the date or read the article, the brightest light I've ever seen bursts in the sky and mushrooms upward. I hear and feel a rumbling that grows louder, shattering the glass around me, until a shockwave hits and I'm engulfed in flames.

Blur.

"It's really not that bad," Sten says as he walks a lap around our cheap hotel room.

"Yes it is." Wearing only a bra and panties, I pick up a half-empty bottle of whiskey from the floor and take a long drink. "Yes it is."

Sten rolls his eyes. "Here we go with your goddamn hysterics again."

I ignore him to concentrate on drinking the liquor as quickly as possible. I bet if I focus on breathing through my nose, I can shotgun it—

Sten grabs my arm and yanks the bottle from my lips. "Stop it. It's not that bad."

"Maybe you can live like a slave, but I can't."

I must have hit a nerve, because anger flares behind his eyes. His grip around my wrist tightens until the pain becomes too much and the whiskey bottle drops from my hand, thudding against the stained carpet at our feet. I whimper but refuse to ask him to stop. I'll let him kill me if he wants. I almost wish he would.

He seizes my other wrist and slams me down on the bed,

the mattress groaning underneath the force. Pain jolts through me from deep cuts and bruises all over my body.

"I never took you for a quitter, Shepherd," he says, his mouth about an inch from mine. "There are ways to resist. At the very least I thought you'd want to have one more quality meeting with your mother. Your efforts so far have been frankly pathetic."

Angry tears leak down my cheeks. I want to spit in his face, but I want release more. I can't think.

"Show me where they are." I stare hard into his black eyes. The fire's still there, but the anger's been replaced with something else—hunger. "Show me."

He knocks my wrists against the mattress as if the act will make them stay there, then drops to the foot of the bed and rips my underwear off. I close my eyes, empty my mind, and think of nothing as he unbuttons his jeans, hitches my legs around his waist, and shows me what it's like to truly use sex as a weapon.

Blur.

A middle-aged woman's gray eyes widen as she stares down the barrel of a gun in disbelief. Her red hair, streaked with gray, frames a delicate face lined around the eyes and mouth with age. "You don't understand—"

BOOM BOOM BOOM. Three shots to the chest. She collapses to the ground and spits up blood for a moment before going still.

Val gasped as if she herself had been shot. She blinked, trying to push the last image out of her mind, but it refused to go quietly. It wasn't real. It couldn't be real. That woman couldn't be—

"Val?" Max touched her face, and she flinched as her

thoughts snapped back to the present. "What's wrong?"

"I think—" She buried her face in his neck, relishing the feel of his skin against hers as she concentrated on slowing the hammering of her heart. "I think I saw—" Steel blue eyes. Red hair cut in a long bob, streaked with gray. And she'd smelled menthols, the kind Danielle Shepherd liked to smoke.

Val met Max's concerned eyes and choked out, "I think I saw my mother being murdered."

Chapter Three

Her vision settled it—if she was going to have any time to investigate and prevent her mother's future murder, they needed a damn nanny.

"Let me start by saying you have excellent references, Jamal," Val said to the man sitting across from her in the living room interviewing for the nanny job, "but they don't say anything about your self-defense capabilities."

Jamal's warm, broad smile fell a hair. "My…what?"

"Self-defense. Hand-to-hand combat, weapon skills, firearms training. Those things."

"Um, I don't have any of that." He ran his hands along the pleats of his pressed slacks without looking down, then let out an awkward chuckle. "It's never been necessary, at least not for any of my previous clients. But I am certified in Montessori education techniques, can cook a wide range of healthy meals to accommodate any gluten-intolerant, diabetic, or allergic needs, am fluent in French, German, and Japanese—"

"But do you think you could learn to shoot a gun?"

"I—hmm…" Jamal's lips tightened and he looked off to the side of Val as if seriously considering her question. At least he was open to the possibility and didn't freak and run like the other people she'd interviewed so far. If they were going to get a nanny, then the least that third wheel could do was provide a little protection if the conspiracy that'd consumed their lives a few years ago resurfaced again. Based on her visions, she knew it was only a matter of time.

"I could learn," Jamal said, "though I'd really prefer not to. Guns and children don't mix."

Val scoffed. Damn, he was like all the others. He'd seemed so reasonable a moment ago. "Yeah, well, sometimes you don't have a choice when shit goes down—*Gah!*"

Val jerked backward when Lydia came out of nowhere. With an ice cream cone in one hand, she sprinted between her mother and Jamal while wearing a child-size life vest over a bathing suit covered in pink dolphins.

"When shit goes down!" Lydia yelled over her shoulder.

Val shot up. "Don't talk like that! And you cannot take that ice cream into the pool!"

Lydia came to a hard stop, ran back, and threw her arms around Val. "Sorry, Mommy," she said in her cutest voice, and Val almost forgot about the cone still in her hand until she dropped it on the coffee table and ran off again.

Val let out a long, exasperated sigh as the ice cream melted into a white puddle of goop, probably permanently staining whatever expensive wood constituted the table. "Goddammit."

"Goddammit!" Simon's voice came from behind her. She turned to see her son clad in his own blue dolphin shorts and life vest, riding piggyback on Max while Toby followed close behind. Her husband wore only boxers. Great. Well, it was better than his usual outfit for their indoor pool—his birthday suit.

"Don't say the things Mommy says," Val said. "Come on, we've talked about this."

Simon answered by giggling and taking a big lick of his own cone. Val winced as ice cream dripped onto the carpet. Another mess to clean up.

Jamal rose and extended a hand toward the duo. "Hello, Mr. Carressa, I'm Jamal. Pleasure to meet you."

Max thrust his hip out so he could meet Jamal in an awkward handshake while keeping a hold on Simon. She saw the nanny candidate glance at the brilliant aquamarine fractal tattoos on Max's inner forearms, one of the Julia set—which represented her, something about "chaotic perturbations" or whatever—and the other of the twin dragon—which obviously represented their children. He'd gotten them years before he'd even met her; an important glimpse of his future, now his reality. "Hey there," Max said. "She hasn't scared you away yet?"

"No sir," Jamal said with a polite, lying smile. "This has been one of the more, uh, interesting interviews I've had, but I figured as much—not to say I expected you to be bad people or anything, I didn't mean it like that—"

"But you expected us to be *weirdos*, right?" Val said. Just what she needed—another goddamn person judging them while having no idea who they were or what they'd been through.

"No, no, of course not," Jamal stammered at the same time Max said, "Val…"

"Local celebrities stalked by trouble? People who, for some inexplicable reason, leave a trail of shit behind them wherever they go? You know what? Everything you've heard is true. We're chaos magnets. Nannies who can't handle that need not apply—"

"*Val*," Max said, his lips pressed into a tight frown. "Language." He looked at Jamal and grinned, slipping on the mask she recognized as the one he used to put people at ease when intimidated by either his good looks, wealth, status, or abrasive wife. Someone had to tell it like it was. "She hasn't had her coffee today. Ran out this morning. Nothing personal. It was great to meet you, Jamal." He turned toward Val, mouthed *Be nice*, then tromped off with Simon to join Lydia.

"Be nice, Mommy!" Simon hollered on their way out.

Even her own children were against her. She gritted her teeth and forced a smile at Jamal. He stood dumbfounded, his mouth hanging open a crack.

"Well, thanks for coming by, Jamal. Any questions for me?"

"Um…oh, uh—" He reached into his pocket and pulled out a handkerchief, then flailed it at her until she realized he wanted her to turn around. Val did so, and felt a delicate dabbing at her back.

She craned her head to see behind her. "What are you—" When the dabbing stopped, she faced him and saw smears of ice cream on the hanky. Lydia must've left them there during their hug. "Thanks," she said.

He used the rest of his handkerchief to scoop up the white goop and cone from the coffee table. After wiping his fingers off on his slacks, he held his hand out to her and gave her a warm smile. "It was a pleasure to meet you and your family, Mrs. Carressa."

It was still *Shepherd*, actually, but…Was he taking that ice cream cone home with him? And did he just address her with respect, and not fear and contempt? She felt her rigid frown loosen until she returned his warm smile. "It was nice meeting you, too. When can you start?"

* * *

Max smeared peanut butter on a piece of bread, pulled it in half, and gave one piece to each twin where they sat at the kitchen table. "Got one you like yet?" he asked Val as he made himself his own slice of peanut butter bread.

She tapped a pen against her notebook, filled with old pages of hand-drawn clues she had seen in her visions when she'd been a private investigator. These days it held grocery lists, to-do items, cookie recipes, and now the names of every potential nanny she'd interviewed and the pros and cons of each. "I liked the last guy. There's one more to interview today; she'll be here in twenty minutes. Maybe she'll be a Krav Maga expert or something."

"Fingers crossed," Max mumbled through a mouth full of peanut butter. "I'm hoping for a hot blonde myself."

Val shot him a cross between a smile and a sneer. "Me, too."

Max nearly choking on his food as he chuckled, then glanced at the kids. They nibbled their snack, blissfully ignorant of their parents' lewd joke. Simon and Lydia weren't quite all-knowing—yet.

She let the pen drop next to her scribbled note: *None will carry gun.* "This is pointless. These people don't know what they're getting themselves into. We should just hire a bodyguard and teach him how to do arts and crafts with the kids."

"It'll be fine, Val." Max shoved the last bit of his bread into his mouth.

"It will *not* be fine. What if I pick a bad nanny? What if letting my"—it felt odd to say the two words together, almost painful—"*my mother* visit is a mistake? What if I can't stop what's going to happen to her? What if Northwalk shows up again and we're not here?"

Max walked around the marble kitchen island separating them, wrapped his arms around her waist, and pulled her close. "It will be *fine*. They're not coming back. Even if worse comes to worst, we can handle it. I've got you and you've got me, remember?"

He touched his forehead to hers. She leaned in for a kiss and tasted the peanut butter on his lips, relaxing in his embrace and losing herself for a moment in him.

Lydia interrupted their private moment. "The wife is here," she said to no one in particular.

Val pulled her lips away from Max's to look at her daughter. "Who?"

The intercom to the door buzzed. It must've been the last nanny. Val wasn't exactly a paragon of manners, but showing up to an appointment twenty minutes early seemed unusually anal retentive. Nannies with sticks up their asses need not apply, either. And why would Lydia call her "the wife"? She'd need to have another talk with the kids about not announcing future events right before they happened; it got the wrong kind of attention, and also freaked people out.

"I'll get it," Val said. "Almost done for today, thank God."

Max asked, "Want me to sit with you on this one?"

She cocked an eyebrow at his naked torso, a towel wrapped around his waist. "Yeah, no. The last thing we need is Mary Poppins telling the tabloids you exposed yourself to her. Get the kids dressed, will you? And keep them out of the living room, for Christ's sake."

"Will do, boss." He kissed her, then herded the kids out of the kitchen. They stampeded up the stairs like squealing baby elephants, leaving the first floor to Val and the final nanny.

In the front hallway, Val hit the intercom button that connected to the gate enclosing their condo complex and buzzed in Donna from the Seattle Premiere Nanny Agency. When Val answered the door, however, it wasn't Donna who stood in the threshold.

Chapter Four

Lacy Zephyr?" Val said as much to remind herself as imply a question.

Lacy returned Val's gaze with a cold, uneasy determination, her knee-length white cashmere coat, fur hat, and Prada handbag clutched between tan leather gloves giving her the look of a haute Russian princess, or maybe Santa Claus's high-maintenance mistress. Lacy's bright red, surgically plumped lips pressed together in a tight frown as she lifted her chin under Val's confused stare, somehow managing to look down at Val even though she stood a couple inches shorter.

"Why are you pretending to be a nanny?"

Lacy sniffed. "I heard you were getting one, *finally*," she said, her big mouth twitching on the last word into a split-second sneer.

Val didn't know Lacy well, having only met her a couple times at Carressa Industries functions. Her husband, Aaron Zephyr, worked for the company as a financial analyst or something. Rumor had it her father had connections to organized crime, though officially he ran a lucrative construction business. Based on their two-sentence conversation so far, if she got any more acquainted with Lacy, the woman might end up with an even fatter lip. "So you're role-playing as my nanny for shits and grins?"

"I didn't want to announce my presence. I'd like to talk to you privately." She craned her neck to look past Val, scanning for any witnesses. "Alone."

"I know what 'privately' means."

A crash followed by peals of laughter came from above them. Lacy flinched, and intense anxiety peeked through the cracks of her icy façade. So she didn't want Max to know she was there. Interesting.

"He's upstairs," Val said. She stepped aside and held the door open. Might as well hear what secret the woman had to spill. "We can discuss your nanny credentials in the study—by that, I mean *privately*."

Lacy's gaze cut past Val again, looking for Max one last time. Finally satisfied the coast was clear, she stepped into the hallway. Val led Lacy to the study, a comfortable room lined floor to ceiling with books, almost all of which came from her husband's vast collection. An old-school chalkboard on wheels hugged the corner, equations and strings of numbers in Max's handwriting scrawled on the top half, stick figures and crude children's drawings on the bottom half. Val sat on one of the soft leather couches and motioned for Lacy to join her. Lacy took a seat at the opposite end, removing a headless Barbie doll from a pillow with her thumb and forefinger like the toy was a piece of rotting flesh before sitting her butt down. Val crossed her legs and bounced her foot in the air while Lacy sat rigid, purse in her lap like a shield, still in her full winter getup.

Val smiled, enjoying Lacy's prissy discomfort with a lived-in house a little more than a mature adult should. "So, Lacy, what can I do you for?"

After a long pause where it seemed Lacy might wordlessly get up and leave, she said, "You used to be a private investigator, right?"

"Yeah." Everybody knew that. Her and Max's bizarre adventures while she'd been a PI were national news. Hell, if Lacy knew through the bored-housewives-of-King-County grapevine that Val was interviewing nannies today, then she knew all about Val's past.

"Does that mean you don't do it now?"

Ah, so *that* was her angle. "Do you want me to look into something for you?"

"Not if you don't do it anymore."

"I'm…considering going back to work. What is it you want investigated?"

Lacy eyed the exit, considering her last chance to bail before the point of no return. When she looked at Val again, the cold determination had returned, along with the anxiety. "I think my husband's having an affair."

That was it? Val tried to hide her disappointment at being presented with such a mundane problem. Of course he was having an affair. All those moneyed types did—except Max. He loved her—and his balls—too much for that.

Flexing her old PI muscles a bit, Val asked the first of her standard set of questions. "Have you asked him if he's having an affair?"

Lacy gasped. "Of course not!"

"Maybe you should ask him."

"I can't just *ask* him. He won't be honest."

The standard response. Val could point out a lack of honesty and communication in their relationship was likely the source of their marital problems, but that wasn't how one landed a client. Lacy didn't seem like the introspective type anyway.

"What makes you think he's having an affair?"

Lacy forced the words out as if they caused her physical pain. "For the last three months he's been coming home late—much later than normal anyway—reeking of booze and cigars, and women's perfume. He says the senior guys at the company have started going to this exclusive smoking lounge after hours for client meetings, but…he's acting differently. He's distant." Her eyes misted over. "He barely looks at me anymore."

Damn, now Val felt a little shitty for turning Lacy's screws earlier. If her husband was in love with another woman and drifting away, Val would've been a bitch to be around, too.

Lacy sniffed and pushed back her tears. "If he's having an affair, I want pictures. I need leverage. I'll take every penny that no-good son of a bitch bastard has." Spittle flew from her mouth as she hissed, "We'll see how horny he is when I threaten to send his mother pictures of her perfect son getting his pipes cleaned by a ten-dollar whore. He thinks he can fuck around on me? *Me?* My father built half this city—"

"I get it, Lacy." Val leaned back a hair. Lacy's vindictiveness could also have been a small speed bump in their happy marriage. "Why don't you ask your father to set Aaron straight? I hear he can be persuasive."

"I thought about it, but Daddy would…overreact."

Made sense. Wanting someone punished for their transgressions didn't mean you wanted them dead. There was one thing, though, that Val didn't understand. "Why are you coming to me with this? There are plenty of active PIs who'd be happy to look into your husband's dirty laundry."

"I thought, maybe…" She bit her lip. "These 'work meetings' Aaron's always having…I thought maybe your husband went, too."

Val lifted an eyebrow. "He's never mentioned it—"

"But he knows about them. He must."

"So you want me to pump Max for info."

"No private investigator I hired off the street would have that kind of insider access. It's a good place to start, isn't it?"

She was right about that. But if Max knew about these back-room meetings, he would've told Val about it. Probably. In any case, he never came home late reeking of booze and women's perfume…though he was smart enough to get the stink off him before returning to her—oh, come on. She was letting paranoia get to her again. Maybe this case wasn't such a good idea after all. Secret clubs, free-flowing booze and sex, rich men behaving badly…sounded too much like the Blue Serpent cult for her taste. Finally, her life was mostly stable, mostly normal. Mostly happy. Except for the deep desire for vengeance that still burned inside her like a decades-old subterranean fire. But she'd be damned if she let it consume her again.

"I'll pay you, of course." Lacy pulled a manila envelope from her purse and held it out to Val. "Two thousand dollars, cash. I don't know what you charge for expenses, but I can get you more if you need it. It's also for your *discretion*, to keep this matter between us."

Val almost laughed. Being married to Max, the last thing in the world she needed was money. If she were to take on another case, it'd either be for a noble cause or to kill her boredom. Paranoia about another Blue Serpent nightmare aside, a case of a philandering husband seemed simple enough. Low-threat. An easy chance to learn how to be a PI again, so she could work up to investigating her mother's future murder.

"Keep your money." Taking a page from her husband's playbook, she said, "I'll take a favor instead."

Lacy's brow knotted as she withdrew the money. "What kind of favor?"

"I don't know yet. I'll tell you when I think of something." A little deal-with-the-Devil-ish, though Lacy could take comfort there were a lot worse people than Val to be indebted to.

"Okay," Lacy said, though her brow stayed knotted. "But the terms still stand. I expect discretion. My reputation—"

"Sure, Lacy. God forbid anyone should know you're a human being."

Lacy sniffed again like she smelled a fart, then stood. She sent a furtive glance to the ceiling. "Is there a back way out of here?"

"No, but I'll make sure the coast is clear."

Val walked ahead of Lacy to the stairs. Muffled stomps from above told her Max still kept the twins occupied, or maybe the other way around. Either way, Lacy wouldn't have to face the shame of locking eyes with someone who knew she'd stooped to hiring a PI to spy on her husband's roaming dick.

Lacy hurried after Val to the front door. She stopped in the threshold and addressed Val a final time. "When will I hear from you again?"

"When I find something worth telling you—good or bad." Could be Lacy's husband told her the truth and wasn't fucking around. Unlikely, but possible.

Lacy's lips puckered a hair—she didn't hold out much hope for good news, either—but she nodded and left without looking back.

"That was quick," Val heard Max say behind her. She turned

and saw him pulling on a V-neck sweater at the foot of the stairs, hair still wet from a shower. "Good nanny or bad nanny?"

"Neither, actually. Where are the kids?"

"Upstairs reading to each other. Pretty impressive you taught them how to read. Our nanny will have to be good to match that."

"I didn't teach them how to read."

"Oh." He frowned, though it was more of a contemplative frown than a disturbed frown. The oddness of their children didn't faze him nearly as much as it did Val. He was confident if they provided their kids with a safe, loving environment—something he never had growing up—it would be good enough to keep evil at bay. To say she didn't share his confidence would be an understatement.

"If that wasn't a nanny, who was it?"

Val smirked. "Destiny."

Chapter Five

Val sat at the foot of the bed, sipping coffee and watching Max futz with a tie in front of the bedroom mirror. From the first floor, Lydia's laughter reached them through their closed door. Hopefully that meant the kids were already warming up to Jamal.

"You've never heard of a group of guys who go to a secret smoking room or possible sex club after work, have you?" she asked.

Max's hands stopped. He looked at her through the mirror, an eyebrow cocked. "You're kidding, right?"

"Is that a no?"

"Yes, that's a no."

Thank God. She probably wasn't dealing with an evil sex-slash-faith-healing cult again. Chances seemed slim anyway.

He continued knotting the purple silk around his neck. "Is this related to Lacy Zephyr's visit a couple days ago?"

"Maybe. Yes." She'd told him Lacy came by, but had kept the details to herself out of respect for her first client in about half a decade. Now she realized she couldn't get Max's help without bringing him fully onboard. She'd tried keeping him in the dark once before, during her investigation into Blue Serpent; it had turned out disastrously for them both. The specter of Lacy's disapproval could take comfort that Max was good at keeping secrets. "How well do you know her husband?"

"Aaron? Not well. I see him at meetings sometimes."

"So you don't know what he does in his spare time, say, after work?"

"No idea."

She regarded him over the rim of her mug, drumming her fingers on the sides of the ceramic.

Max straightened his tie, glanced at her in the mirror, and frowned. "Don't even ask."

"Please?"

"No. Aaron and I aren't friends."

"But you could be." Lord knows he could use more friends. Of course, he could say the same thing about her, especially since Stacey took off five years ago for destinations unknown, but this wasn't about her.

"I'm not palling up with someone I barely know just to find out what he does after work."

"Okay, fine." She took another slurp of her coffee. "Could you at least find out what his schedule looks like over the next week or so?"

Shoving the end of the tie under his vest, he turned to face her and shook his head.

"Then I'll have to spend all day and night staking him out. Don't know how long that'll go on for. When my mom comes to visit in a couple days, you've got it covered, right?"

Max's gorgeous hazel eyes drilled into her, his lips tightened in a half smile. Hot damn, never had bemused frustration looked so sexy. She loved twisting his screws just to get that look.

"To state the obvious, you are manipulative," he said as he snatched his suit coat off a loveseat in the corner and slipped it on. "I'll see what I can do, all right?"

She jumped up and kissed him, careful not to slop coffee on his suit. "Thanks. You can punish me later."

"You bet I will." He slapped her ass and seized her lips with his, kissing her with such force, she thought he might throw her on the bed and make love to her right then. When his kiss turned her insides to liquid and she started pulling at his belt buckle, a feverish desperation for him burning in her belly, he pulled away, stepped past her, and bounced down the stairs.

She gasped, the void where he used to be like a splash of cold water to her face. "Tease," she called after him.

He snickered the rest of the way to the first floor. Yeah, real fucking funny. She'd make him pay for that. He wouldn't be getting any sleep tonight, that's for damn sure.

After Val composed herself, she followed Max downstairs and into the living room. Sitting cross-legged on the shag rug at the foot of the couch, Jamal did something with a pack of cards that the kids found riveting.

"Getting acclimated all right?" Max asked Jamal as he threw on his heavy overcoat.

"Yes, sir." Jamal flashed a broad smile. "Your kids are wonderful."

"I think so, too, though I might be biased. And call me Max." He cocked his head toward his wife. "And call her Val, no matter what she tells you. See you tonight, kids. Be good for Jamal."

The twins ran to him and threw their tiny bodies into their father's arms, nearly knocking him over with their youthful vigor. After he returned their hugs, he gave Val a chaste kiss free of the heat from a moment ago, one safe for their audience.

"Love you," he said, then whispered in her ear, "Be nice," before scratching the dog behind the ears and leaving through a door in the kitchen that led down to the carport. Toby sat and whined at the door, like he did every morning.

Val stood unmoving for a moment with her hands on her hips, alone with Jamal and the kids. Jamal sat back down on the rug and resumed his card game—some kind of matching thing—while pretending not to notice the glare she fixed on him. Despite the fact she'd hired him and he'd done nothing wrong *so far*, every instinct told her to kick him out. They already had one stranger—her long-lost mother—on the way to squat in her home for who knew how long. Why deal with two? But she could already hear Max's disembodied voice of reason—*That's exactly why we need a nanny. You need help with the kids, your mother will demand even more of your attention, and a job outside the home will keep you sane.*

Well, Jamal was going to be here all the time now, doing the things she usually did, so she'd better get used to it. Her wristwatch showed ten past eight, a little early to run the errand she had planned. What to do, what to do…

She spotted a neat stack of envelopes on the kitchen counter and frowned at Jamal. "Did you handle our mail?"

"I brought it in. It's part of my job description."

She didn't remember that detail, but whatever. None of it looked opened, and in any case, most of it was junk. There was, however, one piece that looked like a personal letter with her name handwritten on it, no return address. Another one of those damn things. Since she'd become moderately well known, she started receiving fan mail and hate mail in equal measures from people who incorrectly assumed she cared what they thought of her. The missing return address suggested this piece belonged to the latter group. She should toss it, though it could be something from her mother again, who also wrote letters by hand. Or something from Delilah, who had a history of sending her mail with no return address.

She ripped it open and read it, just in case:

Valentine,

You have the name of a saint, yet you are not that blessed thing. We all have paths to follow, a purpose, and you disrupt that purpose. I ask you to stop, for the sake of your soul. HE is not pleased with you. When glass and steel rain down from above, know it was meant to be, and is only the beginning.

Huh. A little on the weird side, but short and not a rape or death threat, so fairly tame by hateful troll standards. It definitely wasn't from Delilah; not her style. She crumpled it up and spiked it into the trash, pissed she'd wasted her precious time—well, not so precious anymore. Not with her *substitute* at hand. What was she supposed to do now, stare at this guy all day? Investigating her mother's future murder, and Lacy's husband when Max returned with Aaron Zephyr's schedule, probably wouldn't actually take more than a few hours a day at most. She didn't want to leave the kids for any longer than necessary anyway. Yet they'd hired Jamal for his morning-to-evening babysitting services.

Val forced herself to relax. "I need to run an errand," she

said, though it came out a little bitchier than she'd intended. She tried to tone the hostility down. "Are you…going to be okay here with them? Alone?"

"Yes, ma'am—Val—uh, ma'am."

She took a step toward the door, then turned back. "You've got everything you need, right? Their nap schedules, their favorite books, their lunch and snack foods—"

"Yes, I've got it. I wrote it all down," he said in a gently reassuring tone. She'd need to get used to that voice, and train herself not to mistake it for condescension.

"And it's *one* snack before lunch. Don't let them trick you into giving them an entire package of Oreos. They're more clever than you might think."

"Oreos on lockdown. Clear as crystal."

"You remember all the codes for the locks and alarms on the house, right?"

"Uh-huh."

"And you've got my number if you need anything?"

"I sure do."

She nodded, walked to the living room's threshold, stopped, and turned again. "Don't let anyone in here who isn't Max or me, no matter who they say they are. I mean it."

Jamal smiled again—he did that a lot, maybe because he had nice teeth—though a hint of uncertainty tainted his friendly gaze. Probably wondering what the hell he'd gotten himself into. "Yes, ma'—Val. I won't let anyone in."

"No one."

"Got it. No one's coming through that front door, not on my watch."

She should've left then; instead, she stared at him until a bead of sweat trickled down his temple.

Simon broke the standoff. "We'll be fine, Mommy. Go talk to the cop."

Val softened a bit at that. If Simon knew he and his sister would be fine, then they'd be fine. As long as she didn't inadvertently change the future, what he'd seen would come to pass. Val embraced them both in long hugs, kissing their foreheads. She thought they might cry when she left; they didn't. They knew they'd see her again soon. Still, when Val walked to the door leading down to the carport and grasped the doorknob, she saw her hand shaking. She'd never forgive herself if something happened to her babies while she left them with an overpriced babysitter. Would they really be safe without her? They'd have to be. Max was right—she couldn't be with them all the time. She'd have to trust other people eventually, and that time was now. God help Jamal if he screwed it up, though.

Swallowing back a lump in her throat, Val forced herself forward, away from her children, into her car, out of the house, and back into the world she'd been hiding from for over five years. Tendrils from its black underbelly would likely rise up and try to seize her again. But there was no way around it if she wanted any chance to save her mother.

Time to go see the cop.

Chapter Six

Sten Ander still lived in the same boring middle-class apartment complex in Tacoma she remembered. Beige vinyl siding, fresh asphalt from the previous summer's repaving, and bedraggled Christmas decorations hanging from small second- and third-story decks made the place indistinguishable from every other batch of apartments within a twenty-mile radius. Which was exactly why Sten lived there. He liked to blend in—lots of people did—though he excelled at it despite the fact there was nothing ordinary about him. His world was deception, and she was about to waltz back into it—a mistake for sure, but one she couldn't avoid.

Val spotted his car in its assigned spot. He worked the evening shift on the Seattle Police Department vice squad. Her guess he'd still be home in the midmorning looked correct. Climbing the stairs to his apartment, she felt an uncomfortable sense of déjà vu as memories of their sordid affair from years ago crept back. Max wouldn't be happy to know she paid a visit to the man who tried to kill him twice. Even less happy to learn she'd slept with Sten a handful of times in a misguided and self-destructive bid to learn how to better control her ability. For reasons she didn't understand, he could focus her visions in a way no one else could, not even Max. Though their twisted relationship had occurred when she and Max weren't together, it was better for everyone, really, if Max never knew. Visiting Sten now, she poked the hornet's nest that'd stayed dormant for almost half a decade. But she needed answers about her mother that only he could provide. With any luck, the hornets would stay asleep. It was a small poke, after all.

Val reached Sten's apartment door, took a deep breath, and knocked. She tapped her foot and waited for the better part of a minute. Maybe he wasn't home after all. Damn, she'd have to find another opportunity to come back—

The door rattled, then swung open. Sten stood in the threshold, scruffy and bare-chested, one arm braced against the jam while his other hand rubbed sleep from his eyes. Before she could stop herself, her gaze drifted down from his well-defined pecs, bulging biceps, over a toned, flat stomach, and ending at a pair of unbuttoned jeans sagging off his hips. Oh yeah, she almost forgot—he'd been good in bed. Very good. Not as good as Max in the looks or sex departments, but a close second—

For God's sake, Val, stop that!

She blinked and forced her eyes back to his dark, heavy ones, praying he hadn't noticed her ogling him like a juicy piece of meat. Why the hell did he answer the door half-naked anyway? It was *December*, for Christ's sake. Knowing him, he probably did it to mess with her and faked the just-woken-up shtick. He always did love mind games. Fucking Sten.

"Hoooleee shit," he said, his voice rasping with the roughness of a hard night. "Valentine Shepherd. The world's about to end, isn't it?"

She cocked an eyebrow. Let the games begin. "Any day now. Did I ever tell you I have a recurring vision of Delilah Barrister becoming president and nuking the world?"

"Crazy bitch would do something like that." He leaned against the doorjam and ran a hand through his brown hair as if still rousing himself from sleep. His pants looked like they might slip off at any moment. What a goddamn actor. Anything to distract her.

"Are you still Delilah's slave?"

His eyes popped open and he stood up straight, folding his arms across his chest. "I was never her *slave*." *Now* he was awake. Very few things bothered Sten, but his indentured servitude to Northwalk and their associates, such as Delilah, happened to be one of them. "Listen, I'd love to exchange passive-aggressive witty banter with you all day, but I've got places to be. If you're in the mood for a quick fuck, come on in. Marriage gets stale, I understand."

Val rolled her eyes. Same old Sten. "No, I don't want a quick fuck, but yes, I'd like to come in."

He turned and walked back into his apartment, leaving the door ajar so she could enter. Closing it behind her, Val was struck by the emptiness of his place—nothing on the walls, no knickknacks on the shelves. Not that she expected Sten to have any interior decorating sense, but she didn't recall his bachelor pad being quite so bare. Walking into his living room and the adjoining tiny kitchen with beer cans piled on the counter, she spotted a couple stacked cardboard boxes and made the connection.

"You're moving," she said.

"Affirmative." He padded to the kitchen on bare feet and flicked on the coffeepot to heat up black liquid already in it—yesterday's brew. Damn, that was gross, even for him.

"Where?"

Walking to the living room, he tapped a cigarette out of a carton lying on his coffee table. "East," he said as he lit the cigarette, took a long drag, then sat down on the sofa and propped his feet on the table.

How far east? Across the city? The country? Back to Asia? Five years ago, he'd implied he grew up an orphaned child soldier in Chechnya. Northwalk had picked him up off the street, groomed him to kill for them, then dropped him into American society to be their inside man, employed as a cop while doing odd jobs at their behest. So he'd said anyway. He'd always been evasive about his past—about everything really—so she couldn't take anything he told her without a huge grain of salt. She stopped herself from asking where he was moving, though; she didn't want to sound too interested. Despite the fact she hadn't seen Sten in years, she realized she liked knowing he was around, within reach. In case of emergency. Once upon a time, he'd insisted they were partners in the fight against Northwalk. *Partners* was putting it strongly; more like he was willing to be her ally under certain circumstances. She'd take anyone she could get.

"Found a better job?"

"No." The word snapped from his mouth with a sharpness she hadn't expected. She'd hit on another sensitive topic. Usually he wasn't so testy. She studied him for a moment, curious. Sten met her gaze and let her look him over without flinching away. Last time she saw him, he'd perfected the art of smarmy cool with glimpses of the human being underneath few and far between.

Stretched out before her now, he looked leaner than she remembered, tauter. Tense. New creases dashed out from the corners of his eyes. Whatever he'd been up to these last few years, life hadn't been easy on him. Now his handlers were making him move, and he wasn't pleased about it.

As she studied him, he studied her. She felt his gaze as if he were pawing her with his bare hands, down and up the length of her body until resting on her face again to trace the outline of her features with his eyes. Val tried not to squirm under his scrutiny; she'd started it, after all. Sten said he had places to be, yet he seemed content to sit there and stare at her for the rest of the morning.

Dammit, she shouldn't have come. Already things were getting weird. But he was the only person she knew who might have answers.

"Do you—" Val shook her head. There was no way to ask that didn't sound strange. Might as well come right out with it so she could get back to her kids. "Do you know my mother?"

He squinted at her as if confused. After a pause, he said, "Biblically?"

"*Goddammit*, Sten—"

"If this is the start of a joke, you're not telling it very well. Needs more levity."

"Can I assume that means no?"

He scratched at the stubble on his chin, cocking his head like he might actually be giving her question some serious thought. "Are we talking about the woman who abandoned you when you were a kid?"

Val nodded. So he remembered. She'd told him about her mother years ago, when they'd served in the Army together and briefly dated. Should she be touched or disturbed he recalled long-ago details from her life? She went with both.

"Why do you think I know her?"

Sighing, she knew her only hope of getting a straight answer out of him relied on the truth, no matter how much it might compromise her. She still had no idea where his true loyalties lay at that particular moment. "I had a vision where you told me, 'There are ways to resist. I thought you'd want to see your mother one last time,' or something like that. Then I saw her being shot and killed."

"Huh. What were we doing while we had this conversation in the future?"

His slight smile told her he knew she didn't want to answer, so of course he would dig. "I don't know exactly. We were in a hotel room"—Sten smirked—"*hiding* from something, I think. We were upset. Nothing sexual happened between us, if you're wondering." Except for the last part of her vision. He didn't need to know about that, though.

Sten tapped cigarette ashes into a soda can, then lounged backward as he took another drag. "Wow. It's almost like we're meant to be together."

"Jesus, Sten, do you know her or not?"

He played with the cigarette, rolling it between his fingers as he seemed to consider every possible way he could answer. Finally, he said, "No."

Great. Assuming he wasn't lying, he wouldn't be any help solving her mother's future murder. At least she wouldn't need to see him again anytime soon. Silver lining.

When she turned to leave, he said, "But I know someone who might."

Val stopped and faced him again. "Really."

"If your mom's got any connection to this fucked-up freak show you and I find ourselves forced to perform in, my contact would know. She's closer to the top of the food chain. She sees things us peons don't."

So he wanted to help after all. Thankful and wary at the same time, she stopped herself from cringing and asked, "What do you want in return?"

"Just your gratitude." He pressed his lips into a tight smile, amused by his own bullshit. "One friend helping out another."

In other words, he expected a favor. They'd played this tit-for-tat game before, and it had ended in blood—she'd unintentionally murdered a man she'd never met at Sten's urging, and he'd jailed and killed her rapists. As his last gift to her, he'd rid the world of Lucien Christophe, the medical genius and pure evil behind the Blue Serpent cult. She would always owe Sten for that. It wasn't only their prior relationship that kept her uncomfortable around him; her debt to him weighed on her as well. And he knew it.

Val swallowed hard. She didn't want to play this game again, but what else could she do? No matter what happened, she wouldn't kill for him. Nor could he have her body, despite what her visions suggested. They *weren't* partners. "Yeah, well, if you find out anything, let me know."

"Uh-huh." He rose and walked back to the kitchen, poured the now-hot black sludge into a coffee mug, and took a long slurp. "You know, you can come by anytime if you need to hit something again. I think I'm in the mood to hit something, too."

Val's jaw clenched. They'd fallen into bed the first time during a spasm of anger she'd taken out on him while drunk, punctuated by some swift punches to his face. But that wasn't all he meant. At the time, she'd asked him to help her take down Delilah and Northwalk; he'd refused, saying the time wasn't right. Now he was "in the mood to hit something"—he was ready to fight. Whatever he'd been doing for Northwalk for umpteen years, he'd had enough and wanted out.

What's more, he wanted to punish them. And so did she. She could practically *taste* their blood in her mouth. It was the tie that bound them, a pitch-black thread wrapped around their souls, pulling them together as surely as the white thread that connected her to Max. The years-long, simmering fire of vengeance grew in her, her cheeks heating up at just the thought of finally making those bastards pay. With Sten's help, they could kill all of Northwalk—

No. If she went down that road, she put her family in danger.

It's not worth it, Val. You've been good this long, and Northwalk and Delilah have left you, Max, and your children alone. Don't throw it away.

But she *could* get vengeance now, if she wanted.

Aw, shit. Bile rising in her throat, Val turned and left without looking back—not that it mattered. She'd see him again soon. There was no avoiding it now. She'd poked the hornet's nest—including the long-buried one inside her—and they'd all begun to wake up.

Chapter Seven

Sitting at his work desk, Max flipped through half a dozen college-ruled papers filled top to bottom, front and back, with handwritten numbers. Spotting a familiar sequence, he pulled a page from the group and circled a string of digits—a Laplace transform; specifically, a probability distribution. Right before the transform, he recognized the vector equation that symbolized the Standard & Poor's 500 Stock Market Index, then eight numbers he remembered from a previous vision which represented Boston Scientific. Would the company's stock be going up soon? He scanned to the end of the transform—probability of one, so yes. By how much? The next number—seventeen percent. Max grabbed another numbers-laden page off the desk. Already marred with circles, exes, and arrows, he'd scrawled "Jackson Instruments" on the top. He compared this one with the Boston Scientific. Yup, his initial guess had been correct—

"You're going to the shareholders' meeting tomorrow, right?"

He looked up as Michael Beauford, CFO of Carressa Industries, stepped into his office. The older man's craggy face wrinkled even more when he narrowed his eyes at Max. "Don't start with excuses why you won't be there, buddy boy."

Max let his gaze drop back to his papers. "I'm extremely busy," he lied. He had enough information from his most recent visions with Val to dispense nuggets of financial wisdom through the New Year. While pretending to work hard deciphering the markets for information he already had, he'd quietly begun tinkering with software code, trying to write a computer program that could guess the future on par with his visions. The damn thing wasn't even close yet, but it kept him busy. At a minimum, he could point to the program if anyone started asking serious questions about how he could be so accurate. He slipped in a wrong prediction every once in a while to throw possible accounting sleuths off his scent—even wrote a program for that, too, to make it look more random.

When he had his fill of coding, he would spend the rest of the day setting up and pulling down backdoor accounts to anonymously funnel money to charities. All told, he wasn't *extremely* busy, but he stayed busy enough puttering around the office doing things he liked, with no one to harass or antagonize him as his father had. In truth, he was the happiest he'd ever been. For the first time in his life, he enjoyed going to work.

Except for the goddamn meetings.

Michael scoffed, and Max looked up again to see him fold his arms over his chest as he fixed Max with one of his disapproving-dad stares. Time for a lecture. "For God's sake, Max, you're the *majority shareholder*. You can't keep skipping these things. Sell your shares if you don't like it. And why do we keep having this conversation?"

"Because you won't accept reality." If he sold his shares, he'd have a boss again. He'd killed the last one in a fit of rage. Sure, that last boss had been his horrible child-molesting father, which made it unlikely to ever happen again, but still. He'd rather not take the chance.

Max tapped his index fingers on the two number-covered sheets of paper. "Boston Scientific is about to acquire Jackson Instruments. Their stock will rise seventeen percent. Suggest to the board we buy into Boston Scientific. I don't need to be there for that."

Michael's eyes flicked to the papers, his face falling into a deep frown. He knew what Max could do, but still couldn't quite accept it despite indisputable evidence. Did he still think Max was crazy? That'd be some serious cognitive dissonance if he did, since Max had never been wrong. Whatever Michael thought, he'd kept Max's secret and hadn't recommitted the "unstable, spoiled rich man-child" to the psych ward—a moniker Max knew most members of the board called him behind his back, among worse things. In fact, Michael was the only one who didn't treat him like a freak; ironic, given Michael was the only one who knew Max really *was* a freak.

Michael flinched with effort to look away from the impossible numbers. He sat down across from Max, his usual jovial smile returning. "How's the new nanny?"

"He seems nice enough. I like him. Val might murder him, though, just to be safe."

Michael chuckled. "It's always like that at first. Gracie and I had nannies as soon as the kids were born, and she'd still twist her knickers in a bunch anytime the rug-rats were out of her sight for more than a few hours. Even now she worries if more than a week goes by and they don't call. They're in their thirties, for Pete's sake. *Pfft*, mothers."

"Val's got reasons to be paranoid." Max chewed his thumb and looked past Michael. She had her reasons, but they weren't rational. Northwalk had left them alone for five years, when at any time the powerful cabal could have easily waltzed into the condo with guns blazing, grabbed the twins, and disappeared forever. But they hadn't, so they must have gotten what they wanted from somewhere else. Seemed logical enough to him. In any case, his family couldn't live in a fortress, or make their curses go away. Lucien might have developed a cure, but his research had disappeared when he died, probably reclaimed by the people who controlled him. All Max and Val could do was provide Simon and Lydia with the best home possible and shower them with love, which was more than his father ever did for him—

"Why don't you bring the family over for dinner tonight?" Michael asked, interrupting Max's train of thought. "Gracie's making some new health crap from a recipe she found online. Don't make me suffer alone."

"Maybe. Josephine might come by this evening with her new boyfriend. She wants us to meet him, so I guess it's serious this time."

"Bring her, too. And a shotgun. That's what big brothers are supposed to do, you know—scare the bejesus out of their little sister's boyfriends."

Max smiled as he gathered his papers back into a neat stack. "I think she can take care of herself."

"That's not the *point*. Christ, Max, you're hopeless." Michael stood. "See you tonight at seven—and at the shareholders' meeting tomorrow, dammit." After a finger-point for emphasis, he left.

Max shook his head and fired up the shredder behind his desk. Were other surrogate dads this much of a pain in the ass? He lowered one page into the rotating blades, destroying evidence that might lead to uncomfortable questions in case of an audit, then looked at his watch—ten to twelve. Good chance Aaron Zephyr had gone to lunch by now. If he swung by his office, Max could believably express "surprise" to find the analyst gone, then ask his secretary for his schedule to set up a meeting later. That should give Val something to chew on for a little while anyway.

Max lowered another paper into the shredder. Would she really stake Aaron out if he didn't give her the schedule? Probably not with her mother in town in just a couple days, but Val tended toward the unpredictable, one of the many things he loved about her—

Wait—what is this? He jerked the half-eaten page out of the shredder to stare at the numbers again. One-two-seven, one-two-seven, one-two-seven, repeated throughout the page. He grabbed an intact paper off his desk. There it was again—one-two-seven, embedded throughout the page. How could he have missed this? He spread out the pages, placing them side by side. After he'd circled every instance of the one-two-seven sequence, he leaned back and took them all in as a whole, looking for a pattern or a numeric cypher.

Then he saw it. Rearranging the pages and accounting for both fronts and backs, the placement of the numbers actually spelled out a word—most of a word, since he'd shredded a page: N-E-V-E-R-M-O-.

Nevermore. As in, "Quoth the Raven 'Nevermore,'" from "The Raven" by Edgar Allan Poe. What in the hell could that mean? Max almost laughed; the numbers told the future, but his subconscious interpreted them in the strangest ways sometimes. One-two-seven. Nevermore. He guessed it meant something bad. More than that, he had no idea.

Max sighed and dropped the rest of the papers into the shredder. Look out for one-two-seven. Like he didn't have enough to worry about.

Chapter Eight

"Max! So nice to see you!" Aaron's secretary, Marge, gave Max a bright smile when he approached her desk. After his father's stern leadership, it had taken a while to convince employees to call him Max instead of Mr. Carressa. In fact, though he kept a low profile, everyone but the board of directors seemed to like him. Since he'd successfully avoided a scandal for several years, the board had grudgingly let him assume a more obvious role again, even allowing him to publicly represent the company on occasion.

"You, too, Marge. Grandson graduated from college yet?" Thanks to his better-than-average memory, Max could remember a lot about people. He liked hearing about their average, comfortable lives. For the first time in his life, he got to experience it himself with Val and the kids, and he loved it.

Shaking her head, Marge said, "That lazy bag of bones is determined to live out the rest of his life in my basement. Fat chance of that happening, since I'm three times as old as him. Millennials. What're you gonna do, right?"

Max grinned. "I'm sure I'll have to shove my kids out the door one day, too." He was sure he wouldn't, not with his unique family circumstances, but he sympathized anyway. Marge smiled back and her eyes glazed over in that way women sometimes did when they looked at him—*mooning* would be the best way to describe it. He forced himself not to squirm; the attention always made him uncomfortable.

"Is Aaron in?"

"I'm sorry, you just missed him," she said, like he knew she would. "He'll be back around two, though. Would you like to talk to him then?"

"Actually, I need to leave early today. Can you send me his schedule for the rest of the week? I'll give it to Nadine and she can set up an office call for later."

"Sure can, Max—oh, there he is now!"

Max tried not to cringe as he turned to see Aaron walking toward him. Aaron stopped at his desk and gave Max a quizzical smile.

"Hey there, Max. Haven't seen you in a while. What brings you over here?"

Marge answered, "He came to talk to you. I told him you were out, but I guess not quite. Perfect timing!"

"I left my wallet on my desk," Aaron said. "Had to come back for it. What did you want to talk about?"

Max gritted his teeth for a second. He should've thought this through better. "I wanted to talk to you about the shareholders' meeting tomorrow. Run some ideas I had by an objective party before bringing them up to the board, see how they'll play."

"Really?" Aaron's mouth split into an eager grin, eyes wide like he couldn't believe his luck. "I didn't know financial geniuses needed second opinions, but I'd be honored to be your sounding board. Before I realized I had no money, I was heading out to lunch. Why don't you join me?"

Max gritted his teeth again. Having a private lunch date with Aaron was exactly the last thing he wanted to do, but hell if he could think of a way to decline that wasn't suspicious or rude.

He forced himself to smile. "I'd love to."

* * *

Max knew next to nothing about Aaron or his wife. Sitting across from the analyst at the dim sum restaurant, music from a traditional Cantonese pipa wafting through air thick with the smell of steam and soy sauce, he hastened to sum up the man through quick glances. About Max's age, Aaron kept his blond hair close-cropped despite his receding hairline, a refreshingly honest choice over the full head shave or the comb-over many middle-aged men adopted to hide the march of time. Though a slight gut pulled at the buttons of his dress shirt, he looked fit, not from a targeted exercise regimen but from playing sports he enjoyed, like basketball or squash. Team sports. A man with lots of friends, regular blue-collar types, Max guessed, in contrast to his posh wife. What drew Aaron and Lacy together, two apparent opposites, Max could only speculate. A secret connection maybe. He could relate to that.

Aaron shoved a pork dumpling in his mouth and smiled at Max, cheeks puffed with food. He regarded Max with a touch of amazement, as if he was dining with a celebrity. Max repressed an eye roll. This was why he didn't like eating out.

After Aaron swallowed, he said, "So, you wanted to run some ideas by me?"

"Uh, yes." Max poked at his shrimp noodle roll. "I think the company should branch out a little more into the medical market, maybe buy into Boston Scientific. But it's only a hunch. I don't think the board will go for it without a more compelling reason than my gut feeling."

Rubbing his chin, Aaron nodded. "Boston Scientific's got growth potential for sure. They've been sluggish the last couple quarters, but that could mean they're gearing up for something big. Anything's possible." Aaron slapped Max's arm; Max flinched at the sudden contact. "I've got a secret for you, dude. Most market analysis is gut feeling. You've got a better handle on it than the rest of us number monkeys. If even *you* can't figure it out, then I sure as hell can't help you."

"Oh. Sorry to crash your lunch for nothing."

"Nah, I'm grateful honestly. I'd originally planned to read a couple earnings reports and grab a salad while wishing I was eating Chinese. This is way better. Lacy's been on my case to lose the spare tire." He patted his stomach. "I bet you don't have that problem."

"You'd be surprised."

Aaron cocked an eyebrow. "Valentine's on your case for being fat? *You?*"

"Well, not about weight. Other things."

"Like what?"

Max squirmed in his seat. He'd already said too much to someone he barely knew. "Eh, you know. We argued about getting a nanny."

Aaron nodded. "She didn't want one, right?"

"No, she didn't."

"I can tell. She's the kind of person who thinks she can do everything herself and doesn't want any help, even if she needs it."

How the hell did he guess that? Max had exchanged more words with Aaron in the last few minutes than all of their previous interactions combined. He wasn't *stalking* Max, was he? No, more likely he was a true *people person*, the thing Max pretended to be in polite company.

"Those kind of folks are tough nuts to crack," Aaron went on. "Iron-willed, but also unyielding. My sister's like that. Royal pain in the ass, but I love her."

Max nodded. Aaron was right, of course. Though Max cared a lot about other people, he always kept them at arm's length. If he got to know *them*, they'd get to know *him*, and that always ended badly—Michael and Val being notable exceptions. An open book who truly related to people…that sounded like his deceased half brother, Robby. For the first time in a long while, Max felt out of his depth. "So what do you do when your sister insists on doing things the hard way?"

"What *can* you do? I just let her. Either she learns, or she doesn't. Well, you know. Your dad was kind of like that. Iron-fist type. Got results, but not a lot of friends."

"*He* didn't get results. He bullied other people to get results for him."

Why had he said that? He flinched when he noticed he'd been rapping his chopsticks against his soy sauce dish with such force the dark liquid had slopped over the side and seeped into the white tablecloth. Forcing his hand to be still, he took a slow breath and tried to regain his composure. "But I'm sure your sister's not like that."

Aaron regarded Max with a new softness, a guy who knew he'd accidentally hit on a touchy topic. "Not that bad, no." Compassion tinged his words. Or maybe pity. Goddammit. Max didn't need anybody's fucking pity. "I don't tell many people this, but when I was a teenager, my dad went to prison for embezzlement. It's still a sore spot in our family. Other kids made fun of me, Mom cried all the time, that sort of thing. A real bummer."

"That's…unfortunate." Max would've said he was sorry, but he knew how empty those words were. Throat suddenly dry, he gulped down a mouthful of water. "Did you ever reconcile with him?"

"Nope. He died in prison. Heart attack. But life goes on, whether you like it or not. You never really get over it; you just accept it. There's a whole field of psychology about acceptance—probably developed by people who've never experienced serious setbacks, they've just *heard* about it." He snickered. "However it's supposed to go, I think I'm in a good place now."

So was Max…wasn't he? Again he forced his hand to stop fiddling with the chopsticks. Any shrink would say he needed therapy—probably a lifetime of it—but if he told them about his condition, they'd diagnose him as delusional, maybe even prescribe antipsychotic meds. Aaron managed to be a fully functioning, healthy adult despite his past trauma, without therapy. If he could do it, Max could, too.

Aaron glanced at his watch. "Damn, I need to get back. Meeting at one thirty." He leaned toward Max. "There's this place I like to blow off steam after work, if you'd like to join me. Or don't. Either way is cool."

Oh yes, this was the information Val wanted. He'd nearly forgotten his original reason for dining with Aaron. "I've got a thing tonight, but I might drop by for a bit if I get out of work early enough. Where is it?"

"Union Street in downtown Seattle. Place called Jones's. It's a nice bar, very chill. I'll send you the address, and maybe I'll see you there."

"Sure, maybe," Max said, surprised he meant it. Aaron wasn't such a bad guy. Perhaps cultivating a friendship would be good. He already felt better having talked to Aaron, whatever that meant.

After paying the bill, Max rode with Aaron back to the Thornton Building, which housed Carressa Industries head-quarters. Without the convenience of valet service like Max enjoyed, Aaron parked in a garage across the street and the two walked toward work.

"Shit, I'm gonna be late," Aaron said as he quickened his step.

Max checked the time—1:26 p.m. From behind him, a crow swooped forward and landed on the awning of the building's glass entryway. The bird fluffed its feathers and tapped its foot on the overhang—just like in Poe's famous poem.

Nevermore…

"Wait." Max grabbed Aaron's arm, stopping them both in the middle of the street.

Aaron looked between Max and the building. "Why?"

A car cruised to a halt and honked at them as Max looked at his watch again. It rolled over to 1:27 p.m.

One-two-seven. Nevermore.

"Just wait," Max said. "Something's not right—"

An explosion ripped open the floors above them, cutting off Max's words in a shower of glass and steel.

Chapter Nine

Breathe in, breathe out. Max repeated the mantra to himself as he sat hunched over on the curb across from the Thornton Building. Every fire truck and ambulance in the city swarmed the street, emergency personnel crisscrossing his vision as red and white blurs trying to manage the chaos. He coughed; dust from the explosion still polluted the air. He felt sick.

He'd known it would happen, but failed to correctly interpret the signs until it was too late. His ability wasn't well tuned to danger. It cared about money. Money, money, money. How many people died because he'd done nothing? Medics still carted injured victims and cloth-draped bodies away—

"It could've been an accident, like a busted gas pipe or something," Aaron said yet again from where he paced a few feet away.

Max closed his eyes and rubbed the bridge of his nose. "Maybe," he muttered. He had no idea.

"I mean, there's no way someone did this on purpose. Why would they? What's Carressa Industries ever done to anyone? Maybe some anticapitalism nutjob…"

Max swallowed hard, his throat dry again. Carressa Industries wasn't malevolent, but its founder had been. An old enemy could have decided now was a good time to extract some long-overdue justice by hurting innocent bystanders. Why not? Dean Price, Max's real father, had done it. Lester Carressa, the monster he'd thought was his father until Val exposed the truth, would've done the same. Of course, the forces of fate conspired to save him again—the person least deserving of such mercy. God, those poor people…

Breathe in, breathe out—

He jerked when he felt something on his shoulder. For an irrational second he thought it was the raven; it was only Aaron's hand.

"You saved me," the analyst said as he stared down at Max with wet eyes. "I don't know how, but you knew what would happen and you saved me."

A spike of panic quickened his heart. "No, no, I didn't know." The police already hated him. Hell, they'd tried to kill him *twice*. Aaron's fawning over how Max "saved" him using mysterious prior knowledge of the explosion would surely rile up the cops again. "It was only a feeling. A bad shrimp dumpling."

"I still owe you my life—"

"Max!"

Val's voice reached him over the din of chaos. He jumped up and saw her push her way past a throng of reporters, then she burst through a police cordon and sprinted into his arms.

"Thank God, thank God," she said, her head buried in his chest. "I heard over the radio. I thought it might've been you."

It should have been me.

She looked up at him. "Are you all right?"

"I'm fine." Even to his own ears, his voice sounded robotic.

Physically, I'm fine, his tone implied, but he couldn't help it. It was an accurate expression of how he felt: numb.

Val understood. She took his hands in hers. "Can we go?"

He'd already given a short, unhelpful statement to the police. They'd asked Max and Aaron to stick around for further questioning, just in case, but he wasn't obligated to obey. He didn't linger at the cops' behest.

"Michael hasn't come out yet," he said. The robot voice was gone, replaced with something desperate from deep in his chest. "No one will tell me if he's one of the injured, or d—" The last word stuck in his throat, and it was only with every scrap of energy he had that he kept his composure. He glanced at the reporters straining against the cordon, their cameras swiveling between him and the carnage. Leeches.

Val nodded, a familiar steel in her eyes that matched their color. "Wait here."

Her hands slipped out of his, and she marched over to a clutch of ambulances where EMTs gave first aid to people with minor injuries. She exchanged words with a couple medics, who frowned at her and shook their heads, then she moved on to a third, who finally nodded about something. Barely three minutes after she'd told him to wait, she trotted back to Max, her lips in a tight downturn. She put a hand on his arm.

Oh God, he shouldn't have asked.

"Michael's been injured," she said. "They won't tell me how badly."

He felt the blood leave his face. Why couldn't it have been him?

"I'm sorry," Aaron said beside him with what sounded like genuine sorrow. "I know you guys are close."

How would he know? That's right, Aaron was a people person. The fact that he'd noticed Max and Michael's relationship and seemed to care that it was in danger made Max like him even more.

"They took him to Harborview Hospital," Val said. "We can go there if you want—"

"Yes. Let's go now."

* * *

With Val close behind, Max hustled past a wall of reporters and walked into a chaotic emergency room lobby packed with family members on the verge of panic. He scanned the room for a nurse or doctor or anyone who might have information on Michael until his eyes landed on Gracie, Michael's wife. Seeing her face creased with weeping as she leaned against another woman—a good friend maybe—he approached slowly. Maybe she didn't want to talk to him, the lucky survivor *again*.

When he was close enough to touch her, she finally noticed him. She embraced him in a hug.

"Oh, Max," she said, breathing a sigh of relief over his shoulder. "I'm so glad you're okay."

To hell with him. He wasn't the one brought in on a stretcher. "How's Michael?" he asked.

She pulled back and fresh tears filled her eyes. "He's in surgery now, but still with us. They don't know if they can save his arm, though."

Save his arm? But he was alive. At least he was alive. There was that. Good news. He blinked as the room began to slew a little, voices muffling.

"I'll stay until he's out of surgery."

Gracie gave his shoulder a tender squeeze. "No, please, don't stay here just for that. The doctors say he'll be under the knife for hours. You need to go home and rest. Be with your own family. I'll give you a call as soon as I know more."

But Michael's my family, too, he didn't say. Instead, he muttered, "Okay," and after a kiss on the cheek from Gracie, he walked away, stiff as a corpse.

* * *

When they got home, Jamal had already put the kids to bed. From the doorway of the children's bedroom, Max watched Lydia and Simon sleep. Val laid her head on his shoulder and wrapped her arms around his chest like a warm, full-body brace holding him up. The kids slept safe in their beds, unaware of the pain others suffered at that moment, children just like them who'd lost a mother or father that day—

"Son of a bitch, *that letter!*" Val said out of nowhere before letting go of him and disappearing down the stairs.

He closed the door to shield the twins from any more random outbursts, then shuffled to the master bathroom and splashed water on his face. He felt sick again. His left hand twitched against the porcelain, wanting to open the medicine cabinet and fish out his long-gone bottle of OxyContin. The craving came rarely; stress seemed to trigger it. Like a phantom limb, it would itch ferociously for an agonizing few seconds until he reminded himself it wasn't there anymore and it faded away, but never quite gone for good. Only waiting. Something about a permanent rewiring of the brain, he'd read somewhere.

Val appeared in the bathroom doorway holding a wrinkled letter in her hand, food stains smeared down the back as if it'd spent some time in the trash. "This letter came in the mail today. There's a line in it that says, 'When glass and steel rain down from above, know it was meant to be, and is only the beginning.' Glass and steel raining down—like the explosion!"

Max let out a long sigh. Shit, this again? *Again?* No. Absolutely *not*. It wasn't another conspiracy. It wasn't another Delilah Barrister, or Lucien Christophe, or Sten Ander, or Northwalk, or whoever the hell. They'd left Max and Val alone for five years. They got what they wanted the last time around—Val's eggs, his sperm—and they weren't coming back. "It doesn't mean anything."

She gawked at him. "Of course it means something—"

"Any crazy person can string vague phrases together and claim it's a prophecy. That's how psychic scams and cults work. It means nothing." He walked past her and into their bedroom, ignoring her incredulous stare.

"Max, you know what we can do—"

"Yes, I know." He yanked at his tie until the knot around his throat loosened. This bullshit wouldn't swallow their lives again. They had too much to lose.

"You know what we've been through—"

"I know!" He ripped off the silk noose and threw it on the ground. "I know! Why would they come back now? Why blow up a building? What was that supposed to accomplish? I thought they wanted us alive—"

"To reproduce. But we already did that. Now maybe—maybe they want us out of the way, so they can take our children."

"They don't need ours. They can make their own with what Lucien gave them. And why bomb a whole building full of random people? Why not just storm into our condo and take Lydia and Simon?"

"Because we'd see it."

He scoffed. "There are a million different ways—"

"Their Alpha sees everything, but our kids can, too. They tried to kill you, Max."

"It wasn't them. It makes no sense. Everything is not a fucking conspiracy! Why can't you be happy with what we have and let it go?"

Her lips became a tight line, her eyes icy. "I *am* happy with what we have. But we can't ignore this. What if this person strikes again? What if this is the person who kills my mother? He wrote the explosion was just the beginning. He *tried to kill you.*"

"Then give the letter to the police. Let them handle it."

"The criminal justice system can't be trusted to do shit. You know that. If I don't find out who did this, no one will."

"No. *No.*" Enunciatng every word, he growled, "Let someone else handle it. We need you here."

"Really?" She scoffed. "I thought that was what Jamal was for now."

"Don't even start with the goddamn nanny. What are you going to investigate anyway? You're not a bomb expert. And it could have been an accident. A random gas leak. Sometimes bad things happen for no reason."

"That's what you said when you were trying to convince me you didn't kill you father."

Max's breath caught and he stared her down. She would bring that up *now?* She might as well have spit in his face. Val met his glare with an unspoken challenge of her own, and he felt his face heating up, his teeth grinding. He was getting angry. Very angry. He needed to leave.

He turned away from her and stomped out the door, flew down the stairs and out of the condo, slamming the door to the carport as he left. Let her wonder what he was thinking. Let her obsess over a fucking letter. Let her check all the locks and the goddamn guns she kept hidden around the condo, muttering to herself about how *they* were coming for the children at any moment, like a modern-day Miss Havisham haunting the bowels of their home. Let her do it without him.

Lost in the labyrinth of his own thoughts, he drove aimlessly for at least an hour, streetlamps and Christmas lights streaking by like stains against the surrounding darkness. Old habits must have taken over—how else to explain why he found himself in front of his old sex club, the Red Raven in Moonlight? Of course, it wasn't his anymore; he'd sold it shortly after he met Val, leaving behind a part of his life he didn't care to return to. Yet there he was. Though it wasn't the Red Raven anymore.

It was Jones's. Aaron's bar.

Chapter Ten

What were the chances Aaron suggested this place at lunch, knowing Max had previously owned it? Relatively low; the media never mentioned the Red Raven, and he'd taken precautions to hide his connection to the club. And Aaron didn't seem like a mind games kind of guy. Most likely an interesting coincidence.

Or invisible puppeteers pulling his strings again.

Screw it, a coincidence was what it was. He should go somewhere else.

Well, what did it hurt to take a look? Have a beer, check out the new drapes. In any case, he needed a drink. His hands still shook from his fight with Val.

After he handed his car off to a valet, he stood in front of the door for a moment. It was still painted red, though a neon sign announcing the bar's name replaced the single lightbulb that'd been there before. His gut told him to try the back entrance he used when he owned the place, but of course, that was absurd. If the club's latest owners had turned the Red Raven into an upscale bar as Aaron claimed, then being seen there shouldn't raise eyebrows. Nor should the barrier to entry be as daunting. He turned the handle; the door swung open, no invitation necessary. Okay.

The hallway that served as the preamble to the club was better lit than he remembered, less a tunnel to dark desires than a primer for relaxation after a hard day's work. Smooth jazz and cigar smoke wafted down the hallway, growing stronger until he reached the second threshold that led into the main seating area. The layout looked about the same as his old club. An expansive bar stocked with nearly every kind of alcohol known to man, classily displayed on backlit glass shelving, flanked clusters of tables. The motif, however, eschewed bold reds and blacks for warm browns and burgundies.

The place was busy, but not packed. He caught a few stares as he walked to the bar and ordered a vodka on the rocks, though people had the manners to smile politely and look away when he noticed, as opposed to openly gawking. It was an upscale crowd, after all. He shotgunned his drink, ordered another, then sipped it as he walked the periphery of the room, passing by the corridor that used to lead to the erotic stage show. Now he heard live jazz music, ostensibly performed by fully clothed musicians. He would have checked had he not been more intrigued by the second corridor off the bar. An ornate oak door blocked that part of the club. Abutting the door, a man big enough to be a bouncer yet dressed in a manager's suit stood waiting behind a counter.

"Happy holidays," the bouncer said when Max approached. "Members only beyond this point, sir."

Max eyed the door, a sliver of dim light peeking through from underneath. "What's back there?"

"Private rooms with individualized hosting services."

"Any available now?"

The bouncer poked at a tablet computer with his thick finger. "Yes, sir. But you have to be a member. There's a vetting process, and a fee."

"Do you know who I am?"

With a slight smile, the bouncer said, "Yes, Mr. Carressa."

"So bill me."

The big man's smile widened and he beckoned Max forward. "Right this way, sir."

Max followed him through the oak door and into what used to be the hallway to his private sex rooms, now private lounges. Could be they still served the same purpose; one never knew in these kinds of places. He'd find out soon enough, though he didn't intend to partake of anything salacious. His curiosity needed sating. Above all, he needed a distraction from his racing thoughts.

The new owners had removed the windows that allowed visual access into each room, turning the hallway into a mosaic of glass tile bricks. Oak doors broke up the hallway, each leading to a private lounge. Some of the doors stood cracked open a bit, and though Max would soon have a room of his own, he glanced in the ones he passed and noticed different themes—French colonial, Japanese contemporary, ancient Chinese. He slowed as they passed one room dedicated to imperialist Russia, wondering if the books he spotted on a shelf in the corner could be early editions from the Golden Age of Russian literature. He stepped as close as he could without sticking his head completely into someone else's private room, almost able to discern the book titles—

"You made it."

Max's gaze cut to the source of the words—Aaron Zephyr.

The analyst lounged in an oversized leather loveseat, a highball in hand, his coat and tie tossed over the back of a matching leather couch a couple feet away. At Aaron's side, a beautiful woman in a black pencil skirt and white silk blouse sat on the thick arm of the loveseat, pale yellow hair falling across her shoulders in carefully controlled waves. The tips of her stiletto shoes grazed the shag rug as her bare legs dangled off the side, her lips in a slight curl that was almost a smile, but not quite. Even though the two weren't touching, Max got the distinct feeling he'd stumbled upon something he shouldn't be seeing.

"I'm sorry," Max said, "I didn't realize…I'll be leaving—"

"No, come in, come in!" Aaron waved Max inside. He cocked his head at the woman. "We were just talking. She's my hostess. Max, Eleanor; Eleanor, Max."

A name Edgar Allan Poe could appreciate. *Quaff, oh quaff this kind nepenthe and forget this lost Lenore.* The way she perched beside Aaron, though, she might have been the raven, there to pronounce his fate. Max had always been partial to ravens.

He nodded at Eleanor but didn't smile. He wasn't in the mood for pleasantries. She didn't smile at him, either; her lips stayed locked in that almost-smile, as if she worked to hold back some secret mirth. Instead, she regarded him with a mysterious intensity that made it impossible for him not to stare back.

"I have to admit I didn't expect you to come," Aaron said. "I hope you didn't feel obligated."

"No, not that." Max took a small step inside. "I wanted to go somewhere…comfortable. I haven't been here in a long time."

Eleanor rose and walked to him, silent and graceful like a Gothic ghost. He didn't think the tight skirt she wore had pockets, but she produced a marijuana cigarette from somewhere and gave it to him without a word. She knew what he wanted somehow. A lighter came next, and she fired up the joint as he held it to his lips, flames licking the tip as he took a long drag. All the while her emerald eyes never left his, and he caught himself wondering how many women he'd met in his life who were as beautiful as the creature in front of him. Kitty, wherever she was, Abby probably, and Val—of course Val.

He shouldn't be thinking this. He took a step back, putting some distance between himself and Eleanor. He'd walked farther into the room than he thought. This weed must be the good stuff; already he felt a little light-headed.

"This is my new favorite place," Aaron said as Eleanor returned to her perch on the loveseat's arm. She rested a hand on the back of his neck and began massaging his muscles in slow circles. He closed his eyes and let his shoulders drop in quiet ecstasy. "Pricey, but you can't beat the service. Lots of the guys come here after work. I'm surprised you've never heard of it."

"I've been avoiding this area of town."

"It's Seattle's best-kept secret." He opened his eyes to slits and glanced at the couch, head still bowed as Eleanor caressed his skin. "Wanna sit down?"

Max shook his head.

"You sure? She gives killer back rubs."

He shook his head again. Just the idea of her touching him made his neck itch, as if her hands were already there. He moved his gaze to the books in the corner, but still felt her eyes on him even as she serviced Aaron. Why did she keep staring at him? What did she want? Surely she had access to lots of wealthy men. Max wasn't special in that regard.

For that matter, what did *he* want? What was he doing there? He'd already satisfied his curiosity over what had become of his old haunt, yet there he still stood, rooted to the floor of some-one else's private room, spacy and sullen, vodka in one hand and a joint in the other.

Survivor's guilt, they called it. Someone would say that.

A trill sounded from Aaron's pant leg. He stirred from the lethargy Eleanor's neck rub had put him in, pulling his cell phone from his pocket.

"Shit, Lacy." He sighed and stood, looking back and forth between Max and Eleanor, not wanting an audience for his im-minent argument with his wife. But as Max turned to leave, he said, "No, no, you stay here, relax when you feel like it. This'll only take a minute." He snorted on his way out the door. "*Now* she cares if I'm alive…"

For a moment Max watched the empty spot in the doorway Aaron had disappeared through, unable to will himself to leave despite having no good reason to stay. He would finish his drink and his joint, then leave—if he felt sober enough to drive. If not, he'd have no choice but to hang around a little longer. Sure, he could always call a cab, but he didn't want to leave his car…

When he turned away from the door, he found Eleanor standing in front of him again, her svelte body only a couple feet from his, on the cusp of too close.

"You were at the Thornton Building when the bomb went off," she said.

Exactly what he didn't want to talk about. He puffed on his cigarette, trying to ease his nerves. "The police don't know yet if it was a bomb. Could have been a gas leak."

"The news reports keep mentioning a bomb. I guess they think it makes a better story than an accident." She cocked her head. "Did you find it disturbing?"

Did he *what*? "Why would you ask me that?"

"You've been through a lot, according to your biographies."

"*Unauthorized* biographies."

One corner of her deep-red lips turned up, that perpetual grin she'd been fending off finally breaking through. "I see now there's some truth in them."

He let out a mirthless laugh as he blew smoke in the air. "After speaking fifty-two words to me in your entire life, you can tell I'm heartless and unconcerned with the suffering of others?"

"Of course not. I meant the opposite. Death and mayhem follow you around. It can harden a person, make them cynical and uncaring. But you're not like that."

"You don't know anything about me."

"I do. Let me show you."

She took a step closer—definitely too close now—and shifted her weight so the curve of her body from her shoulders to her ankles made a smooth arc. A glint of gold brought his attention to a tiny cross suspended from a thin necklace nestled between her breasts. The heat of arousal rose up his neck, along with anger. What was she—a hooker? A modern-day courtesan? Simply an opportunistic waitress? This woman could have any man she wanted. Hell, she already had Aaron. Why was she messing with him?

He took a step back. "No thank you."

If anything, he expected an angry outburst at being spurned, not the hearty laugh she gave him instead. He had no idea what was so funny. "God has a purpose for us all, and we must walk that path even when it's difficult and painful. Some people call it acceptance. Embrace what's come before and accept what will be."

Now he knew where Aaron got his psychology lessons, couched in a sermon. "I've embraced everything I need, thanks.

The rest I've let go. If you've read my biographies, you'd know that."

"Then why are you here, at your old club?"

He coughed on his joint, the smoke stuck in his throat for a moment. Shit, she knew. How? She must have told Aaron, or vice versa, to get him there. Why? So she could hit on him, then blackmail him if he took the bait? No, that scenario required too many coincidences to be premeditated. But she knew about him somehow, more than she could have gleaned from an Internet search. An undercover reporter maybe.

The clinking of ice caught his attention, and he looked down to see his hand shaking, rattling the cubes in his glass. Before he could order the tremors to stop, Eleanor cupped his hand in hers, a move so forward, he didn't know how to react.

"I forgive you," she said, "for killing your father."

Max felt the blood leave his face. She didn't know. She was guessing. Fucking with him. Nobody but Val, and maybe Delilah Barrister, knew the truth. And he didn't need the forgiveness of someone he'd known for all of ten minutes. Lester Carressa deserved to be thrown off his balcony. He'd been a terrible human being who had earned a much worse fate than what he ultimately got.

Of course, people could say the same thing about Max.

Why was he still there? Why was he still talking to this woman?

Max jerked his hand out of her grasp. He dropped the joint into his glass, the glass onto an end table, and finally stormed out of the room and out of the club like he should have done the second he set foot inside the place. This was why he usually stayed away from the past—demons lurked everywhere.

* * *

All was dark and quiet when he returned to the condo a little after midnight. Val was sleeping soundly on her side of the bed, an indistinct hill in the sliver of moon that shone through the blind slats. Without turning on any lights, he shed his clothes, letting them drop to the ground where he stood until nothing remained. He slid into bed next to his wife, inching closer until his chest pressed against her back. He nuzzled her neck; her hair smelled like apples, her skin like cucumbers and melon. Touching his lips to her warm flesh, he tasted the salt of the ocean where they were married, the vanilla of the milk they'd fed their newborn children, the wine they'd drunk to celebrate their first wedding anniversary. Everything good in his life was tied to her, an angel fallen from heaven for him, cursed to endure the worst of the world by his side because he couldn't do it without her.

When he wrapped his arm around her waist, he felt her turn to face him, awake after all.

"I'm sorry," she whispered.

He ran his fingertips across her cheek, caressing the contours he couldn't see but knew well, and his lips met hers in a long, deep kiss. Movements heavy and lethargic in the dark, she gave herself to him, surrendering to his needs as he moved around her, slipping off her panties and her T-shirt, until the full length of her bare body pressed up against his. Her legs yielded to him and he pushed inside her, surging in and out like the heartbeat of the ocean against the shore. Their rhythmic breathing, like the breaking of waves, was the only thing he could hear. He wanted to think of nothing but her warmth and wetness, but of course he thought of everything instead—all those poor people who died, more injured in the hospital, Michael's mangled arm, Val's insistence on putting herself in danger yet again, his children's inherited curse, murdering his own father and escaping punishment, Aaron's mistress who tormented him with her forgiveness. His lips never stopped moving against Val's mouth, her face, her neck, anywhere he could reach. He tasted the salt of his own tears as they rolled off his cheeks and fell into her hair and across her skin.

God, he loved her. He loved her with everything he had. He'd come close to losing her so many times, every second he touched her, he thought it might be his last.

Any other night he would have pleasured her first, but on this night a selfish desperation seized him, a singular, passionate agony that needed release only she could give. With a final crash, the waves broke through him and his life spilled out—

31415926535897932384626433832795028841971693
99375105820974944592307816406286208998628034
82534211706798214808651328230664709384460955
05822317253594081284811174502841027019385211
05559644622948954930381964428810975665933446
12847564823378678316527120190914564856692346
03486104543266482133936072602491412737245870
06606315588174881520920962829254091715364367
89259036001133053054882046652138414695194151
16094330572703657595919530921861173819326117
93105118548074462379962749567351885752724891
22793818301194912983367336244065664308602139
49463952247371907021798609437027705392171762
93176752384674818467669405132000568127145263
56082778577134275778960917363717872146844090
12249534301465495853710507922796892589235420

1995611212902196086403441815981362977447713—

The red raven flies high above the numbers, her crimson feathers glinting in the light of an unseen moon. She swoops down and skims her claw between one row of digits, clips another in half with her beak. Wild and free, she ascends and dives again, sleek body held aloft with lustrous wings she commands to beat against the wind. Down she comes, one claw extended, ready to snap the numbers in two, when a dog-like beast with ragged yellow fur leaps out of the darkness and snatches the raven in its jaws. The raven caws until the beast cuts off her screams with gnashing teeth, grinding, swallowing, until the raven is gone. The yellow hyena grins, fur bristling up its back as a cackle rises from its bloody mouth—

Max gasped as his mind snapped back to the present. Val lay underneath him, quiet and calm. His head rested on her chest, rising and falling with her deep breathing as her fingers made slow tracks through his hair. Blinking away tears continuing to well in his eyes, he took a haggard breath.

What had happened? Ever since he learned to exert some measure of control over his ability, he'd only seen numbers, and occasionally the red raven.

Now, the yellow hyena. A beast, coming for Val.

For the rest of the night he stared into the darkness and listened to her heartbeat, painfully aware he wasn't the one who could change the future. What he saw was destiny.

Chapter Eleven

Stacey leaned against a support pillar on the first floor of the empty forest mansion, watching as Kat talked to a heavyset older man in a white-collar suit despite the blue-collar roughness of his face. Temporarily abandoned construction supplies and equipment littered the floor, ready to be picked up again once Kat finished surveying the progress on the extensive renovations she'd ordered almost six months ago. She laid a silver briefcase on the ground and popped the latches open.

"It's one hundred and fifty thousand dollars, Mr. Rodgers," she said to the man standing opposite her. "You can count it if you want."

Rodgers hoisted his slacks up and squatted over the briefcase, riffling through the money with his thick fingers. "I'm not sure if this'll be enough to finish the job as quickly as you'd like."

"It's not what I'd like, it's what *must* happen. The schedule takes priority. Money won't be a problem."

A cocked eyebrow betrayed his doubt, but he snapped the case shut and lifted it as he stood. "Okay." He looked Kat up and down—ogled, more like it. Men always did that, like they assumed she wore a tight pantsuit with strappy heels just for them. Actually, she *did* wear it just for them, the better to convince horny marks to do things they might otherwise not be too keen on doing. And it worked, most of the time. Hell, it worked on Stacey.

"I'll be in touch," Rodgers said. He gave Stacey a courtesy nod on his way out.

When he'd gone, Kat walked a slow lap around the giant room, a musty smell still in the air from when the place had sat empty for years after the real estate crash.

"Why here?" Stacey asked as she moved toward the exit, hoping Kat would follow. "A penthouse suite in a high-rise hotel would have worked just as well, and wouldn't take as much effort to set up."

Kat shook her head. "We need a hardened location. It's easier to move construction equipment in and out of here. There isn't another house for miles."

"And Northwalk needs specially built accommodations because…"

"We have a lot of enemies. And we've had…bad luck with hotels. The council likes to stay at places where they can effectively hide in style."

Stacey crossed her arms and frowned at Kat. There was more. There was always more. She waited for it…

"And Cassandra said it has to be here."

Of course. Whatever that bitch wanted, she got. Stacey had never met her, but according to Kat, the woman was taking a slow boat to Crazytown, making strange demands and spewing predictions about the future no one could fully understand anymore. But she was the only Alpha left in the world—a seer who could see *all* of the future, not just glimpses of it during sex—and Northwalk did whatever she said, determined to squeeze every second of usefulness out of her before they had to put her into retirement, or however these things worked.

"So it's not a coincidence this is the place where Val lives. And there was just an explosion where her husband happens to work."

"Northwalk doesn't do coincidences."

Stacey swallowed hard. "Are you saying they had something to do with the bombing?"

Though the news said a terrorist group she'd never heard of claimed responsibility, she couldn't be certain. Kat herself had planted at least one bomb Stacey knew of, though no one had died in that instance. Of the little she knew about Northwalk, she was sure it wasn't run by nice people. But the organization had never forced her and Kat to do anything truly terrible…yet. Was that about to change? Would she still be on board with that?

"No," Kat replied without hesitation. "I meant all things are connected. Northwalk chose this location because the distraction of the bombing provides good cover while they do their business."

Stacey had no idea if Kat told the truth. They'd been together for five years, and she still couldn't tell.

She eyed the exit again. To hell with this. Whatever Kat had to do, Stacey would wait for her in a hotel room. It wouldn't be the first time. Before she could stomp out, Kat sauntered over and put an arm around her waist.

"Baby, calm down," Kat said in her silkiest voice, the one she reserved for her toughest marks. "All we need to do is set the stage for Northwalk, let them do their thing for a few days, then we're done. We'll be gone by the New Year, I promise."

"And then you get your inheritance?"

"Exactly. My parents step down from their roles in the North-walk executive council, and we step up. Then we go wherever we want, just you and me."

Stacey never thought she'd marry rich—or marry *anyone*, for that matter—but the prospect excited her beyond reason. To never have to worry about money, to be able to go anywhere in the world anytime you wanted with the person of your dreams...sounded a lot like Val's fabulous fucking life. Why couldn't she have the same thing?

Kat kissed her, and in that moment she believed Kat told her the truth.

An hour later, they sat in a café on the waterfront, finishing lunch as they watched seagulls through the glass diving for fish. A waiter came by with a dessert menu. Normally Stacey skipped the sweet stuff, but she needed a little pick-me-up. She hated being back, and she hated the holidays.

"Anything without peppermint," she said to the waiter.

He nodded and left, probably to go fetch some disgusting fruitcake. Damn, she should have been more specific.

"Not a mint fan?" a man said behind her, a voice she immediately recognized. "Now I know why your breath always smells bad."

Goddamn Sten Ander strolled up to their table and took a chair next to Stacey and across from Kat. Where the hell had he come from?

"Morning, ladies." He snatched a dinner roll from Stacey's plate, ripped a piece off, and threw it in his mouth. "How are my two favorite lesbians?"

"Busy," Kat replied with her usual cold, calm demeanor, completely unfazed by Sten's sudden appearance.

"What the hell are you doing here?" Stacey said with all the venom she could get away with and not make a scene in the middle of the restaurant.

"A little bird told me you were in town." He kept throwing bits of bread in his mouth, like a duck feeding itself. "Thought I'd say hi, Merry Christmas, Happy Festivus, et cetera."

Kat smirked. "You always were sentimental."

Maybe Kat didn't mind amusing him, but Stacey did. "Beat it, Sten. Us lesbians are trying to eat here."

"You don't have to be rude," he said with fake offense. "But fine, I'll admit to an ulterior motive. Your masters told me to pass on the news if Valentine Shepherd contacted me again. You know, in exchange for sparing my miserable life, and then making it even more miserable."

"Come on, Sten," Kat said, "You *did* kill Lucien Christophe when they explicitly told you not to. What did you think would happen?"

"I don't know. I'm impulsive. Everyone knows that. Anyway, she came to see me a couple days ago."

Stacey sat up in her chair. "What did she want?" Certainly not to rekindle their frenemies-with-benefits relationship. She and Max were still together, right? It would've been big gossip column news if they broke up, and she'd never known Val to be the cheating type.

"Wanted to know if I knew her mom. Had a vision involving *La Madre Shepherd*, thought it might be connected to our friends on high."

Holy shit, Val's mother was back in her life? Since when? What did it mean? Val must be going through a tidal wave of emotions, confronting the woman who abandoned her as a child while also trying to make amends. She could probably use a friend to lean on right now, someone like Stacey *had* been. Sure, she had Max, but Stacey wasn't too angry to realize it wasn't the same.

"I've never met the woman." Sten looked at Kat. "Have you?"

Kat took a long, deliberate sip of water. The silence at their table stretched for several seconds.

Shit, Kat *did* know Val's mom. That must be part of the reason why they were back in Seattle. She'd lied through omission to Stacey *again*. That bitch—

"No," Kat said with confidence as she set her glass down. "Why would I know her?"

"You and her mom arriving in town at the same time—"

"Is an interesting coincidence."

Except Northwalk doesn't do coincidences.

Sten pressed his lips together in a tight smile like he smelled bullshit—the same thing Stacey smelled.

Kat rolled her eyes at him and Stacey, surprised for some reason that they didn't believe her. "If I wanted to send in a mole to get close to Valentine, I'd secure the father, not the mother. They're still on decent terms and she'd be less suspicious of him." She gave them a practiced laugh. "In either case, what's the point, hmm? What would Northwalk's end game be? You tell me."

Kat was right about Val's father—because Stacey had told her. Pillow talk. A chill grew from the pit of Stacey's stomach and moved up her back until the hairs on her neck rose. It was the sensation, she realized, that one got when they became aware they just might have, possibly, made a terrible mistake.

Sten and Kat held each other's gaze, engaged in a tense, word-less conversation only two long-time associates could manage, trying to ferret out the other's true motives while keeping outsiders—that would be Stacey—in the dark.

After what felt like an eternity, Sten grabbed another uneaten roll and stood, his swagger returning. He nodded at Stacey. "Ma'am," he said in a parody of Southern charm. To Kat, he added, "Claire. May we both eat shit and die."

Kat flinched at the use of her real name, the first time her aloof demeanor had slipped during their entire conversation. Actually, it might've been the first time her control had slipped in *months*. She glared at him as he walked away, then her gaze cut back to Stacey, a rare hint of unease in her eyes.

She's worried I heard too much.

Stacey almost laughed. Sten could stir the pot like a pro, maybe even better than Kat. But just because she recognized what he was doing didn't mean it hadn't worked.

Kat smiled and put a reassuring hand on Stacey's forearm. "We've got time today. Let's walk through Pike Place Market like we used to."

"Sure," Stacey said, unable to think of a good reason to say no. Why not relive old times, pretend things hadn't changed? It was better than stewing by herself.

Though she didn't *have* to spend all her time with Kat. Maybe reconnecting with Val wasn't such a bad idea after all.

* * *

You will walk quickly away from the crowd, snaking through a group of mourners who choke the exit. You'll descend a narrow staircase and find yourself in the bowels of the church, an area with a simple kitchen in the corner and cheap tables set up throughout, the kind of place where flock members cook meals for the homeless and host Narcotics Anonymous meet-

ings. Quiet and cloaked in darkness, this is where you will start the fire.

Walk behind a pillar, then around a corner, into a pantry with a single lit lightbulb hanging from the ceiling. An old man will be there, rummaging through the food. Picking what he wants to take for himself. He pretends to volunteer his services to the church so he may gain access to its bounty. He steals holy trinkets he thinks he can sell, tidings left unattended. He's a leech in my world, a shame on my earth.

You'll announce yourself. The man will spin around and slam into the pantry's shelves, knocking food to the floor. He'll sputter, embarrassed he's been caught and struggling to think of a lie to save himself. Then his face will turn red, and he'll begin gasping for air. I will slow his heart, disrupt its beating. He'll yank a bottle of pills from his pocket and paw at the cap, desperate to get it open.

You will take his pills away. He'll fight with you, but his strength will quickly wane until he collapses to the floor, rasping and clawing at his chest.

Look into his eyes and watch as I slowly extinguish the light there. What I gave him once, I take away. Careful not to leave fingerprints, you'll pour a jar of cooking oil to the floor, then let it drop and shatter next to the dead man. You will take the cigarette pack from his pocket, use his lighter to light one, and lay it near his hand, atop the oil. Do this for me, and the distance between the ebony fox and the red raven will grow.

Chapter Twelve

Danielle Shepherd looked just as she had in Val's vision, when she'd been shot to death by an unknown assailant. Of course, she wasn't dead yet, but looking at her mother sitting at the kitchen table still gave Val the sensation she'd stumbled upon a ghost.

"What a nice home you have," Danielle said for the fifth time since she'd arrived a couple hours ago.

Max stepped forward from where he'd been leaning on the kitchen island and motioned toward the mug she clutched in her hands. "Can I get you more coffee?"

Normally the nanny would've done that—did nannies do that?—but after a quick meet-and-greet, Val had ordered Jamal to keep the kids busy in the study while she and Max vetted the virtual stranger whom she'd stupidly invited into her home based solely on their blood relation.

"That would be nice, thank you. And please call me Dani."

Max grinned and took Dani's mug, though Val recognized the smile as one he used to placate people; it didn't touch his eyes. He wasn't in a good mood, hadn't been since the explosion three days ago. Today was also the day of the memorial service for the people that died, eight in all. He'd be expected to say a few words.

Jesus, now was not a good time for this visit.

"How long have you been living here?" Dani asked as Max placed her refilled cup on the table and took a seat.

"Five years." Val glanced at Max. "Six for him. He lived here before me. It's his place, really."

Max frowned at that—*it's* our *place, Val*, she could almost hear him thinking—but she ignored him. Her fingers drummed the table's surface. How long were they going to keep up this small talk?

Dani took a deep breath and stared into the depths of her coffee. As if sensing Val's growing frustration, she said, "I guess we should talk about where I've been."

Understatement of the year. "Yes, we should do that."

"It was hard for me, with two kids. Well, you know."

"No, I don't know," Val snapped. "I love my children."

"Of course. So did I—so *do* I. But you have money, and a nanny…"

Why did she have to bring up the fucking nanny? Val clenched her jaw, holding back a yelling fit. This woman knew nothing—*nothing*—about her life. Maybe now would be a good time to tell her to leave.

Dani shrank a little from her daughter's icy glare. "I had…I don't know what it's called these days. People talk about it more now, but they didn't then. It was, you know, embarrassing. It's still embarrassing. I guess you'd call it…the correct term these days is…some kind of mental illness."

"Like what?"

She sighed, fidgeting in her chair. It was obviously an uncomfortable subject for her, but Val needed to hear it. "People have told me bipolar disorder, and manic depression with paranoid delusions, I think. The diagnosis changes sometimes, depending on who I talk to." She looked at Val and frowned, knowing Val expected her to go on. "I couldn't stay. There was too much wrong with the world. So I went to Canada and just…wandered around a bit. Found myself in different jobs, different shelters. Then I came back to the States and wandered some more, in and out of hospitals, trying to hold down jobs. I went on and off medicine, but nothing really worked until recently.

"I've been staying with some people, and they helped me recover. A lot. You could say they healed me—my soul." Her eyes turned weirdly cold for half a second, then in a blink softened. "I feel like the fog is lifting for the first time in years. It's made me realize that I need to make amends with my past, apologize to the people I've hurt—especially you. So that's what I'm trying to do."

A sob ripped from her chest. She hunched over the table and cried into her coffee. Max patted her back, offering comfort. Val just stared. Did Dani tell the truth? Or did she invent this literal sob story? She certainly seemed sincere. Real tears flowed from her eyes, and she had the twitchy, uncertain demeanor of someone possibly battling a mental illness. Val had seen enough of it to recognize the signs.

But maybe that was the point. This could all be an act. Val didn't want to care until she was certain.

Max stopped patting Dani's back to glance at his watch. He looked at Val. "We need to go."

Now was her last chance to tell her mother to leave. Otherwise, this woman—a stranger in every sense but blood—would be alone with her kids…and the nanny, technically, but he hadn't learned to use a gun yet, so they might as well be alone.

Val put her hands in her lap and clenched her fists. Her mother back from the "dead," remorseful and wanting to spend time with her…it was everything she'd wanted as a lonely, awkward kid growing up with a strange ability she didn't understand. She hadn't asked her mother about it yet, if Dani could do it, too. How could she? She'd never know if she kicked her mom out now, nor could she leave Dani to a fate of being shot to death.

"We'll be back in a couple hours," Val told Dani. "You can set up your things in the guest room on the first floor. Jamal will help you with anything you need until we get back."

Dani wiped her eyes and smiled. "Thank you, pumpkin."

Val winced. *Don't call me that.* She stood with Max, and they put on heavy black overcoats to match their funeral attire.

Before they left, she stopped by the study, where the kids practiced writing their ABCs on the chalkboard while Jamal looked on from the couch. She pulled him aside. "We're going to the memorial service now, and my mother will be here, getting settled in her room, I assume."

Jamal nodded mildly. He probably thought he was used to family drama.

"Listen, I don't"—she glanced at the kids and lowered her voice—"I don't really know anything about her. She could want money, she could try to steal things, she could be looking for a story to sell to the press." She looked at her children again, and Jamal followed her gaze. "I don't care about any of that shit. Keep the children safe. That's your only job." Her eyes cut back to him. "Understand?"

"Yes, ma'am," he said, quiet but confident. He hadn't been

with them long, but he'd spent enough hours with Simon and Lydia to notice by now they were *special*, even if he couldn't quite put his finger on why. At least he seemed to be getting used to her family's oddness. He'd stopped sweating every time she talked to him anyway.

"Good-bye, kids." She knelt down to hug both children at the same time, one in each arm. "Daddy and I will be back soon."

"Can we talk to Nana?" Simon asked.

"You can talk to her, but only when Jamal is with you." Knowing they'd sneak away if the mood hit them, she added, "I mean it." In a whisper: "Don't tell her what you *see*. She won't understand. It could scare her. We don't want to frighten Nana, do we?"

They'd already gotten this lecture concerning Jamal and anyone else they spent more than a few minutes with, but they were only four years old. Did they really understand that Nana wasn't any different yet?

Probably not. But she was about to be late to a funeral she couldn't skip. Her ambiguous, useless warning would have to do.

Chapter Thirteen

Courtesy of Carressa Industries, a black service sedan chauffeured Max and Val to the Saint James Cathedral. It was easier than driving themselves, hassling with parking, and being assaulted by reporters. Sitting side by side, Max stared out the window while Val raked her eyes over the mysterious letter that had predicted the blast. The curve of the handwriting was angular but steady and neat. Not obviously male or female. A capitalized "HE" and mention of saving her soul—some kind of religious thing. Anger at Val for disrupting a vague purpose.

Did this person know what she could do? What Max and her children could also do? The circle of people who knew about her ability was extremely small. If that person had plans to hurt her family, she had to find them first. And kill them.

Max was right—she wasn't a bomb expert. But she was an expert on fucked-up people. Why send her a letter with a bunch of crazy, ambiguous threats? Someone who wanted to be found, that's who. Someone who would leave clues for her to follow, if she searched hard enough. A group of religious zealots in Africa had taken responsibility for the bombing, but this letter offered proof that they lied. The real bomber was still out there, taunting her.

Val looked up when the sedan slowed to fight thick traffic a few blocks away from the cathedral. Chewing on his thumb, Max glanced at her, the wheels of his incredible mind churning behind his eyes. His gaze flicked to the paper in her lap, then he crossed his arms, frowned, and resumed staring out the window.

He still thought she was overreacting, that it was nothing and Northwalk wasn't coming back. The bombing and the letter weren't *logical* to him. Hadn't he learned anything from their six years together?

She jabbed a finger at the paper. "When are you going to take this seriously?"

"I'll take it seriously when it becomes a serious problem," he replied without meeting her eyes. "Your mother seems nice. I can set her up with a doctor's visit and medication if she still needs it."

"Fine. Ignore it until it goes away." She refolded the letter and shoved it in her coat pocket. "That's worked so well for you in the past."

His head snapped toward her. "What are we supposed to do, Val? You have one vague letter to go off of. If you think it's so important, give it to the police."

"You know I would if I could—"

"Would you?"

She flinched. "Of course I would. That's why I have to look into this. You're right—maybe it wasn't Northwalk. But someone tried to kill you, and they'll probably try again. You and the kids always come first, you know that."

He looked away again, lips a tight line, nostrils flared with anger he worked to keep from bursting to the surface. He didn't believe her. How could he even entertain the idea that she cared more about a case than she did her own husband and children? Did he really think she could be as callous as her own mother and dump them for something shinier?

Now she felt her own blood pressure rising. They silently seethed at each other for a minute until the chauffeur parked in front of the cathedral and opened the door for them. Max slid out first and held his hand out to her, not too angry to be polite. People were watching, cameras snapping. Had to keep up appearances.

She kept her head down as they hustled past reporters, the chilled air bringing tears to her eyes. Through the heavy double doors of the cathedral's entrance, a mass of somber people greeted them, families and coworkers of the victims. Max shook hands and offered hushed words of condolences while Val stood by his side and said nothing. He was better at this kind of thing than she was. Anyway, she hated funerals; they always reminded her of her sister's suicide. No use wallowing in those painful memories.

Val scanned the crowd and spotted Aaron and Lacy Zephyr sitting toward the middle of the church, chatting with a couple in the pew behind them. When Aaron saw Max, he rose, snaked through the crowd, and embraced Max in that handshake-hug thing men did. To Val's surprise, her husband didn't recoil from the overly friendly gesture; in fact, he seemed to welcome it. Were they friends now? Enduring trauma together could bring people closer than they'd normally be otherwise; she knew that much. Still seemed weird.

Eventually Max made his way to the front, Val trailing after, and took a seat a couple rows away from the altar. Others squished in around them until every available sitting space was taken and latecomers were forced to stand around the periphery, clogging up the aisles. Organ music wafted through the cavernous cathedral. Val looked around once more as the thick crowd fell silent and priests began their slow march to the altar. No way all these people were friends and family of the deceased. Rubberneckers and reporters must have snuck in.

The bomber could be here. Criminals who caused *scenes*, like arsonists and ritual killers, often enjoyed reveling in their handiwork.

Max elbowed her, and for a moment she thought he would chastise her for staring suspiciously at people in mourning. Instead, he cocked his head a hair to the side, motioning at something behind him as discreetly as possible.

"She's here," he whispered.

"Who?"

"The woman Lacy thinks Aaron's having an affair with. The blonde twelve rows back."

Val turned to get a good look at Aaron's possible mistress, ignoring Max's elbow jabbing at her obvious gawking. She spotted her immediately—a gorgeous woman with pale yellow hair and full red lips, impeccably dressed in a black silky thing that looked designer. The woman bore a notable, if not striking, resemblance to Lacy. Men were so predictable.

"What the hell is she doing here?" Val asked Max as the priests started to talk about God's plan.

"I have no idea. Maybe she had relations with one of the people who died. The bar she works at is popular with some of the board members and company managers. Seems I'm the only person who didn't know about it. Her name's Eleanor."

Her gaze cut to Aaron, sitting on the other side of the aisle.

If he noticed his paramour crashing the funeral, he did a damn good job of hiding it. His arm around his wife, his attention never wavered from the ceremony unfolding in front of him.

At the priest's direction, everyone lowered their heads to pray. Max bowed but his eyes stayed open. Irrespective of his allegiance to logic and skepticism, too many unanswered prayers had killed his faith. Val mimicked him, head lowered and eyes open, though she pretended to lean into Max's shoulder so she could stealthily watch Eleanor. Pulling her phone out of her pocket, Val raised it just a hair over the back of the pew and snapped a picture. The woman prayed with what seemed like genuine enthusiasm, her lips mouthing the priest's words while her face contorted into a mask of divine rapture. A true believer. That must be nice, to be so certain of your place in the world that you had a powerful friend looking out for you and a purpose—

We all have paths to follow, a purpose, and you disrupt that purpose.

The letter. Electricity ran up Val's spine. Did Eleanor write the letter? Did she plant the bomb? *Why?* Why would she do either of those things? Had they crossed paths before? Val didn't remember ever meeting the woman. Maybe she'd somehow discovered that Lacy had hired Val to look into Aaron's roaming dick. No, that had nothing to do with the letter. Probably not. Did it?

Max would say she was being paranoid—and he'd be right. But just because she was paranoid didn't mean she was wrong.

With her head still bowed, Eleanor opened her eyes and looked straight at Val.

It IS her, Val's gut screamed.

A second later, the prayer ended and everyone's attention went back to the priests up front.

She gripped her husband's arm tight. "Max, it's her," she whispered. "Eleanor's the one who—"

Max stood, pulling his arm out of her grasp with him. He'd been called to the front, she realized, to give a eulogy on behalf of the company. He scooted out of the pew and walked to a podium beside the altar.

Max began, "For those of you who don't know me"—light laughter drifted through the crowd—"I'm Maxwell Carressa, the office janitor." More laughter. "Through my duties sweeping floors and taking out trash, I often get to know people from afar, get an objective perspective of what they're like when they think no one's looking. I can tell you without a doubt that May Salander, Corey O'Leere, Annie Norman, Nihan Shah, Shweeta Sestahn, Marshall Ambrose, DeShawn Joy, and Johanne Sans were not only hard workers critical to the company's success, they were good people…"

As Max went on, Val's gaze cut to Eleanor. She looked engrossed in the eulogy. Giving public speeches was something Max had become good at through his time on the philanthropy circuit. He didn't even need notes. Eleanor watched him speak with a slight smile on her angelic face, a grin that looked almost devious. She plotted something.

The crowd laughed again. Val looked to the front to see Max pantomiming pouring a cup of coffee with his pinky finger in the air. Something about how one of the victims was a dainty coffee drinker.

"There are so many sides to people we never see," he said. "No one is just an analyst, or an accountant, or a wife, or a mother, or a tough guy. If we're truly lucky, the people we love and care about will share with us the sides of their personality they don't often show, the sides they might be embarrassed by or ashamed of. The things that make them unique. The things that make us love them, and the reason why it hurts when they're gone."

Val looked back at Eleanor through a sea of sad faces, some smiling, some sobbing.

She was gone.

What the hell? Val swiveled around in her seat for any sign of Eleanor. She couldn't have gone far, not in this crowd. Then she saw it—a flash of yellow in the back of the church, pushing through a group of standing mourners toward an exit. Leaving in a hurry.

Val started to get up, stopped, and looked at Max. He'd be pissed if she left in the middle of the service.

"We can try to pluck meaning from the fog, and note that it's not the years of our life but the life in our years that count—"

If she didn't go now, she'd lose Eleanor. The woman could be planting another bomb.

"But it's not so easy when life is cut short for such a terrible reason."

Val stood and forced her way out of the pew, muttering apologies as she went.

"In my infinite wisdom as the office janitor, all I can say is, in the end, our love is all we really have. It's the only thing that will never die. And so May, Corey, Annie, Nihan, Shweeta, Marshall, DeShawn, and Johanne live forever. Thank you."

The sounds of hundreds of hands clapping filled the cathedral. Val used the opportunity to move faster, shoving her way through the crowd she'd seen Eleanor disappear through, until she reached a side exit. Unlocked, the door opened into a corridor that ended at an egress point, with a stairwell branching off it that led down.

Outside or down? She went with her gut—down.

Val descended the stairs at a quick trot, unsure what she'd find in the old church. A dark, open space greeted her when she got to the bottom, and instinctively she reached for her gun—she hadn't brought it, of course. Damn.

Muffled sounds from the cathedral above drifted down through the ceiling; otherwise, all was quiet. She walked forward, then paused for a moment so her eyes could adjust to the dark. Round dining tables spread out across the room, adjacent to a long, thin counter. Some kind of soup kitchen. A potpourri of processed food aromas lingered in the air, along with the smell of…something burning?

She crossed the gauntlet of tables, cringing as her heels clicked against the hardwood floor. There'd be no sneaking up on Eleanor if she had, in fact, come this way.

A faint light caught her eye. She followed the glow past a support column, around a corner, and into a food pantry. Beneath a single harsh lightbulb hanging from the ceiling, an old man laid crumpled on the floor. His eyes bulged out of his face, mouth locked in a silent scream. One still hand clutched at his chest while the other reached for a pill bottle lying just out of his reach. Flames grew on the floor next to him, a blaze from what looked like a cigarette dropped on top of a pool of oil about to explode into an inferno.

Val ran for an extinguisher and blasted the fire, killing it before it had the chance to grow and engulf the church. Breathing hard and thankful she'd averted what would have been a horrible disaster, she dropped the extinguisher and put two fingers to the man's neck, feeling for a pulse. Though she'd hoped there might be a chance to help him, she confirmed what was obvious—he was dead.

Looking at the pattern of oil she'd extinguished, Val took a

step back and gasped—the oil was in the shape of a smiley face.
This wasn't a coincidence—it was Eleanor. Val didn't know how
or why, but she was certain. First, the woman threatened her
family, then tried to kill Max in the explosion. Now she taunted
them, leaving more dead bodies in her wake in some kind of sick
game. It wasn't Northwalk after all—it was a crazy stalker threatening Val's husband and children. Eleanor must be the one who
would to kill Val's mother.

She implored a God she wasn't sure existed; if he did, this was
the best place to reach him: *God help me stop that evil bitch.*

Chapter Fourteen

Val was right—Max was *pissed*.

After an ambulance came to retrieve the old man's body, they spent most of the ride home in a tense silence. Val explained to him what happened, but he responded with one-word answers—when he responded at all—until she gave up trying to talk to him. He drummed his fingers on his knees as he clenched his jaw, obviously itching for a fight but holding it in. Not in front of the driver.

When they got home, he marched straight to their bedroom and slammed the door behind him. After confirming nothing eventful happened at home in their absence, Val dismissed Jamal, ushered the kids to bed, fed the dog, and ensured that her mother was settled in the guest bedroom for the night. Then she followed Max upstairs, sucking in a deep breath before facing the full wrath of whatever he'd been holding in during their car ride home.

His clothes were already scattered across the floor, shed in a frenzy. She heard running water in the bathroom and the whisks of a toothbrush. As she shimmied off her dress, he came stomping out. Pretending to ignore her, he threw back the comforter on their bed as if he intended to turn in early.

Val sighed. "Max, I'm sor—"

"What the hell were you thinking?" he spat. "We were at a *funeral*, Val. A *goddamn funeral!* Everyone saw you just get up and leave!"

"I stopped a fire that could've burned down the entire church."

"Alarms would have gone off. The fire department would've shown up before it became serious."

"Oh, I'm sorry. I should have let everyone possibly die in a horrible fire so I didn't embarrass you."

"You only discovered that fire because you were chasing after somebody in a fit of paranoia, which everybody got to witness firsthand."

"Since when do you give a shit what other people think?"

"I give a shit that eight people died, and their friends and family were there to mourn them, and instead of a loving tribute to their memories, they got to watch *you* run off in the middle of the service."

"Nobody cared what I was doing."

"*I* cared!" He jabbed a thumb at his chest. "I needed you beside me and you were gone!"

She scoffed. "You needed the arm candy? What am I, Lacy Zephyr now? A prop to hang your doting husband costume on?"

His frown turned into a snarl, then he shook his head. "You know what? Forget it." He jumped into bed, jamming his feet under the covers as he turned away from her. "Just fucking forget it. Do what you want."

"I *found a body*, Max! I know she killed him. I know she tried to set the church on fire."

He threw off the comforter and leapt to his feet again. "How? How do you know that?"

"I saw Eleanor walk over there right before he died, so obviously—"

"You saw her walk in that general direction, where about a dozen other people also happened to be. And how did she kill him? Scare him to death? Because the man clearly died of a heart attack while stealing food and smoking in the basement, dropping his cigarette in the process. And why would Eleanor try to burn the church down? What's the point?"

Val threw up her hands. "I don't know, Max! I don't know how or why she did it! But I know it was her! She's taunting us! She tried to kill you. She'll try to kill my mother. Why can't you believe me?"

"Because I...I—" His words hitched, and he looked away for a moment before meeting her eyes again, fear muting his anger. "I saw something in a vision. Not the numbers, or the red raven. It was a...a beast...a monster, like a hyena...a yellow hyena. And it—" He took a trembling breath. "It ate the raven."

"You think Eleanor is the yellow hyena?"

Shaking his head, he said, "I don't know what to think."

"If she is the hyena, that's all the more reason for me to kill her before she kills me, or you, or my mother, or anyone else."

His anger flared back, eyes wide and fists balled. "Are you crazy? Stay *away* from her, Val! She'll hurt you. She'll hurt us."

"I can't sit here and do nothing. Last time I tried that, Lucien Christophe almost killed you."

"We can leave. We can move away—"

"I am not running. I'll kill her first. I might not be able to kill

Delilah or Northwalk, but if it's the last thing I ever do in this world, *I will fucking kill her.*"

Max clenched his eyes shut and grabbed his head as if it might explode. His voice quivered. "I can't do this again—"

"Then *help me*. I need to know what she's going to do. What she's planning. Show me." She threw off the rest of her clothes until she stood naked before him. "I can stop her from hurting us. I can fight for our future. I just need to see it."

His eyes drifted open as his hands fell to his sides. "You want to use me to confront the woman who will kill you?"

"It's our best option. You said it yourself—all we have to go off of is the letter, and that's not enough. The police won't believe us, and they can't be trusted anyway. We need a plan."

A shadow fell across his face, a specific kind of darkness she hadn't seen in him before. Something akin to despair and disappointment. Whatever he felt, it was a small price to pay to keep their family safe. Why couldn't he see that?

"You want to use me?" he said, a dangerous edge to his voice. He yanked off his underwear and walked around the bed that separated them until he stood toe to toe with her, looming over her as he radiated an angry, frightening heat.

She forced herself not to back away. This was what she'd wanted, after all.

"Fine," he said, "*Use* me."

He grabbed her arm and shoved her onto the bed. She gasped when he gripped her legs and flipped her onto her stomach, then pinned her down with his own naked body. A shiver ran up her spine despite the warmth of her husband's flesh pressed to hers.

He'd never hurt her. He couldn't. *He wouldn't.*

"What do you want to see, huh?" he said, his words dark and caustic, sandpaper to her ears. He rubbed his body against hers in a rough cadence, and she felt him hardening at the small of her back, willing himself into arousal. "Do you wanna see me dying? The children dying? The world on fire?"

Tears stung her eyes. She didn't want it to be like this, but she didn't have a choice. "I need to see what Eleanor's going to do next. I need to stop her. I need to protect you and the children. I need to save my mother."

"Sure you do. Of course you do."

She yelped when he jerked her hips up, forcing her to her hands and knees. He slammed into her from behind and thrust like a jackhammer, like a piece of equipment. Or a robot.

"Look into the future, Val," he rasped. "Watch this woman kill you, if that's what you want to see."

It was what she wanted to see. Only by seeing it could she stop it. That's how their curse worked. He knew that.

She reached behind her and clutched his hard thigh as it slapped against her skin. "Harder, Max. Please." Sweat exploded over her skin. She needed what only he could give. The climax, the vision. Answers. Vengeance. "*Please.*"

He gave her what she wanted, hard, fast, and unrelenting, without his usual soft caresses, without kisses, without whispers of love in her ear. It didn't matter. What she needed now was the purely physical reaction. Flesh on flesh. If she concentrated, she could make it. She could make it. *She could make it—*

A middle-aged man with a sprawling bald spot atop his head screams as the floor collapses beneath him. He's weightless for a terrifying second until his body slams into the ground below. A chunk of cement falls on top of him, then another, and another.

Blur.

A woman sails through the air, reaching for anything to stop her fall, but everything's falling. There's nothing to grab. She makes contact with the floor below, so hard she bounces once before landing in a heap.

Blur.

Blood leaks out an Asian man's mouth as he lies amid ruins made of rock and Christmas lights, his eyes searching for something before they glaze over and stare at nothing.

Blur.

From between the cracks in a pile of debris, Rudolph's nose blinks. Somehow the tiny light, attached to a buried person's sweater, hasn't broken. It might be the only thing that hasn't.

Blur.

Simon looks at me with tear-filled eyes. "Help me, Mommy! Please help me!"

"I'm coming, Simon! Hang on. I'm coming!"

Blur.

Max lies in a hospital bed, tubes protruding from his body. A machine beeps in the background. His face is waxen where it's not covered in black bruises, his body limp, his eyes closed. A gasbag pushes air into his lungs.

"There was a lot of cranial hemorrhaging," one doctor tells another at the foot of Max's bed. "I'm not sure if he'll wake up—"

Blur.

"Don't be sad, Mommy," Lydia says. "I'll always love you. Daddy, too. If you love us, we're never really gone. We'll live forever."

Blur.

Dani's steel blue eyes widen as she stares down the barrel of a gun in disbelief. Her red hair, streaked with gray, frames

*a delicate face lined around the eyes and mouth with age.
"Don't do this, please." Her lips tremble. "I have something to
live for now. You don't understand—"*

*BOOM BOOM BOOM. Three shots to the chest. She col-
lapses to the ground and spits up blood for a moment before
going still.*

Blur.

"No!" I scream. "No! No! No!"

"You wanted to see."

*A woman in a white A-line skirt with a matching satin
blouse stands next to a wall of glass, silky black hair cascad-
ing over her shoulders. We stand in what looks like an office
in an enormous house, except there are no books or furniture
other than a simple glass desk and a couple sleek steel chairs.
Through a window on the opposite wall, I see an evergreen
forest.*

*Who is she?...I remember now—Cassandra. This
woman is Cassandra, Northwalk's Alpha.*

*"No!" I say. "I want to see them live! I want to know how
to save them."*

*"There are infinite ways," Cassandra says with a breathy
English accent. "The choice is what you are willing to sacrifice."*

"Everything."

"Your love or your anger?"

*I should sacrifice my anger, if that's what she means. That
would be the right thing to do. "But...I need my anger. It
gives me strength. I need to protect my family. If love means
doing nothing...I can't."*

*"Then this is your choice: amidst a sea of blood will stand
the ebony fox and the crimson wolf. Kill the wolf."*

"What does that mean? What—"

The scene evaporated. Cassandra again. Val had only talked to the mysterious woman once before, when she and Max first made love in the boathouse six years ago. All she wanted to know was how to keep her family safe, but all she'd seen was their suffering. Though she had a chance if she killed the wolf…whatever that meant. It was better than nothing. If Max had seen Eleanor as a yellow hyena, who was the wolf? The last cryptic advice Cassandra gave Val ended up saving her life.

Kill the wolf.

Lying facedown on the mattress, Val pushed herself up onto her forearms and blinked as her eyes adjusted to the room's light.

"Max?"

Every time she could remember, he'd been with her when she awoke from her trance, to comfort her if she needed it or to talk about what she'd seen. She did the same for him.

Now he was gone.

* * *

Max flipped on the shower faucet and let the water course down his skin, so hot it nearly scalded him. With both hands, he braced himself against the stall's wall and tried unsuccessfully to catch his breath.

Had he just assaulted his own wife? It almost felt like he did, the brutality of it. But she'd asked for it, she'd wanted him to…

Jesus, what have I done?

He didn't know what came over him. When she said she wanted to *use* him, memories of his father had boiled up from the places he'd buried them and tried to ignore, and he'd…he'd lost it. Lost control of the darkness inside him. He gave her what she wanted in the worst possible way.

All they had to do was leave. She was the one who could change the future. If they left, just avoided the yellow hyena—whether it was Eleanor or something else—and let the police handle the bomber, they'd be safe. They could stay together as one happy family, the way they were before. But she was too wrapped up in solving the world's problems to consider the simplest, best solution. She said she wanted to protect him, her mother, and the children, but he knew better. Val wanted payback for Robby's murder, for her rape five years ago, for the hell the people who pulled the strings had put them through. She wanted someone, anyone, to pay. She wanted blood. He couldn't help her this time.

He shut the water off and toweled down, calmer and more collected than when he'd rushed in, though the core of him still shook. The memory of what he'd just done felt like an oil stain on his soul. Taking a deep breath, he walked back into the bedroom, prepared to apologize.

Val sat at the foot of the bed, frantically writing in the notebook she used to record her visions. She didn't look upset at all. She'd wanted a glimpse of the future, and she didn't care how she got it. Vengeance was all she wanted.

Max slipped on a T-shirt and a pair of pajama bottoms while Val scratched away at her book. When he grabbed his pillow, she looked up.

"What are you doing?"

"I'm sleeping in the study tonight," he muttered.

"But…but Max, I saw Cassandra this time, and she said—"

He turned and walked away. He didn't care what the crazy

lady in white said. What he cared about was *her*. If she couldn't be bothered to care about her own well-being or the effect it had on her family, then there was no use talking.

As he trudged down the hallway, he heard, "Daddy?"

Max spotted Simon in the doorway of his room, his tiny body silhouetted by the starry nightlight illuminating the ceiling.

"What is it?" Max knelt next to his son. He put a tender hand on Simon's shoulder.

"Are you and Mommy fighting?"

"Um…we had a disagreement, but it's okay. Everything's fine. Go back to bed."

"Don't fight. If you do, the wolf wins."

Max frowned. Another one of the kid's cryptic premonitions. He could tell Val about it, but it would just fuel her wrath, and he didn't want to talk anymore. A child shouldn't be burdened with a curse even worse than what Max and Val had, but what could they do? Only Lucien had a cure, and he took it to his grave.

"We'll be fine, Simon. Go back to sleep, okay?" Max ushered his son to bed, shushed him so he didn't wake his sister, then tucked him in and gave him a kiss.

"Daddy, I don't want you to fight. I'm scared."

Max whispered, "How many sides does an icosagon have?"

Simon smiled. "Twenty."

"Good job. When you're scared, recite the names of all the shapes you know, from the least sides to the most sides. It'll take your mind off whatever's scaring you."

"Okay. I love you."

"I love you, too. Don't wake your sister."

Max left the bedroom, easing the door shut so the sound didn't disturb Lydia. He continued his march down the stairs and to the study, threw the pillow down, and lay on the couch. Toby trotted up and launched himself into Max's lap, wagging his stubbed tail with happiness at the rare chance to sleep with his master. Max sighed and pushed the dog down to his legs, where Toby settled between his knees.

At least Max still had his children—and the damn dog. But the one person in the world who made him whole was slipping away, and he didn't know how to stop it.

Chapter Fifteen

Stacey tapped her foot and waited for Val at the Pothead coffee shop, excited and anxious to see her old friend for the first time in five years. When Val had responded immediately to Stacey's text to meet, she took it as a good sign. From what she'd read in the tabloids, Val and Max had two kids now, and had apparently avoided major controversy since the whole Blue Serpent thing. She still wasn't happy with Val for playing with her heart for most of their friendship, or for pretty much dumping her for a hot rich dude—oh yeah, and not telling her that she'd *fucking died*. But she had to admit Val had been through some seriously terrible shit. Even though her friend had rejected her support, she was still glad Val had ultimately gotten it from somewhere, and appeared to be happy now. At least one of them was happy. Stacey wasn't so sure about herself anymore.

"Stacey?" Val's voice said behind her.

Stacey's head snapped up, and her eyes widened at the sight of her friend looking almost exactly the same as the last time she'd seen her—unkempt red hair, no makeup, casual clothes, and yet still somehow a classic beauty. When she stood, Val embraced her in a tight hug. She pat Val on the back, but couldn't muster the same enthusiasm. Best to take things slow. Still, seeing Val after all these years brought home just how much she truly missed her old best friend.

"You look good," Val said as they sat down.

"You, too."

She scoffed. "Please. You're a terrible liar."

"Well, okay, I'll be honest—I thought you'd be wearing everything Prada or Donna Karan or some other designer brand, now that you're married to a rich guy."

Val glanced down at her hoodie and worn jeans. "Money doesn't give a person fashion sense. But it looks like you got some. Congrats."

"Yeah, well…" Stacey plucked at the arm of her gray pantsuit, an outfit Kat had picked out for her, and couldn't help cringing a little. The truth was she didn't really like it, much preferring to wear a flowing tie-dye dress with a hemp sweater, but that wasn't fashionable. She knew she looked better in the suit, and so she wore it, but it still felt as if she walked around in someone else's skin. "So, how are things?"

Val gave her a bright, fake-looking smile. "Oh, you know." Her smile fell away; turned out it was fake after all. "Not great."

Stacey frowned. "What's going on?"

Val drummed her fingers on the table. "Well, it's just—"

Her words cut off as she stared hard at something behind Stacey's head. Stacey turned and immediately recognized the problem. On the television attached to the wall, Delilah Barrister had appeared and was giving a speech at a press conference about how she vowed to help Seattle heal after the terrorist bombing of the Thornton Building. When Stacey looked at Val again, her face had darkened and she glared at the TV screen as if she might set it on fire with her eyes. Though Stacey hadn't been keeping up with Washington State politics, Val's expression said it all—her friend still had a major ax to grind with Delilah.

"I thought you would've taken care of her by now," Stacey said. Val had five years to extract her revenge on Delilah, and yet for some reason she hadn't. She wasn't one to give up easily.

Val's gaze cut back to Stacey, and she seemed to swallow back a knot of anger, forcing herself to relax. "She threatened my family, so I backed off."

"Oh my God, I'm so sorry."

Val shrugged, looking at a loss for words as storm clouds gathered behind her eyes.

Stacey cleared her throat and tried to steer the conversation to something more pleasant. "I heard you had kids. Congratulations! And here I thought you didn't want children."

"I didn't. But they made it happen."

Stacey's smile fell. "They?"

"Northwalk. The people pulling Delilah Barrister's strings."

Stacey felt the color leave her cheeks. Northwalk forced Val to have children? Kat never said anything about that. What else had Kat left out by omission? Maybe Val was mistaken, or jumping to incorrect conclusions. Stacey's mind began to race with possibilities, reevaluating their reason for being in Seattle. Were they really here for a succession ceremony, or did it have something to do with Val's kids? And how did Val's mom fit in? "Oh. That's—shitty."

Val shrugged. "It worked out in the end." She grinned. "Honestly, now I can't imagine life without my children. They're my sun and my moon. And Max is my ocean."

Of course he was. Life-long friendships could go to hell when true love came a-calling. She almost asked if Val was still fucking Sten on the side.

Knock it off, Stacey. She was the one who asked to meet with Val. Why immediately start shit? "What are their names?" she said instead of picking a fight.

"Simon and Lydia. They're fraternal twins."

"I'd love to meet them sometime."

"You can meet them if you're going to be around... How long are you going to be in the area anyway?"

Stacey let out an exasperated sigh. "Hopefully no more than a couple weeks—I mean, I say *hopefully* because... you know how my family can be." For now, she'd pretend she was there to visit her family for the holidays. No way was she mentioning dating Kat or working for Northwalk. Given Val still had a lot of unresolved anger toward the mysterious organization, she didn't expect her friend to understand the benign circumstances of Stacey's connection to them. Maybe they could talk about it later, if things went well between them.

"I do. My mom's in town and staying with us, if you can believe it."

"No fucking way," Stacey said, feigning surprise. Good thing Val brought it up so she didn't have to try to coax it out of her friend without giving away the source of her info. She wasn't a good liar.

"Way. She sent me a letter out of the blue, and I'm trying to figure out if she's legit, or if this is another Northwalk plot."

Stacey's best-friend reflex kicked in, and she found herself wanting to support Val despite all the times her friend had burned her. "Well, what do you think about having your mom around?"

"Honestly, I don't like it. Brings back shitty memories.

But...I don't know. The kids are already calling her Nana, and she's been nice enough. Maybe it'll be good. It's something I wanted for long time, but now that it's actually happening, it feels...not right." Val let out a mirthless chuckle. "But I don't know if it's my instincts or my decades-long seething resentment."

"I say trust your gut, and do what's best for your family."

"Those two things don't always align."

"So pick whichever one gets you the most free coffee."

Val laughed, and Stacey felt their old friendship start to thaw.

"We'll see. One day at a time, I guess." After a pause, Val asked, "Where have you been?"

With a faint smile, Stacey said, "Everywhere. All the places I've always dreamed of going, in the nicest hotels."

"How did you swing that?"

"I have a rich girlfriend—fiancée, actually."

"Can I meet her?"

"She's, uh, not with me now. She went to visit her own family this year."

"Oh." Instead of congratulating Stacey on her engagement, Val frowned. "You could have called. I thought maybe Northwalk got to you, and that they might have killed you."

"Please," Stacey snapped, and all her grievances poured out. "Who are you to talk? You started boning a rich guy and forgot I existed. And since when was I supposed to keep you in the loop on whether I was alive or dead? You certainly didn't keep *me* in the loop when I *fucking died*."

Stacey's hands shook with the raw hurt she'd thrown on the table. She hadn't wanted to start a fight, but there it was. At least it was all in the open now.

Val flinched at finally being called out on her decades-long secret. "I'm—I'm sorry. I should have told you a long time ago."

"Yeah, you should have!" Stacey threw up her hands. "I'm not supposed to be here."

"Yes, you are," Val said, a hint of desperation in her voice.

"According to *you*. You took away my choice in the matter. It was my decision to make if I wanted to fight the universe, not yours."

"You're right." Val's eyes turned wet. "I was selfish, and I'm sorry. I couldn't imagine a world without you. It's been hard these last five years, not having you around."

Stacey's anger waned. Now that she thought about it, it'd been hard without Val, too. Sure, she had Kat, but they weren't what she would call *friends*. Kat kept too many secrets for that.

"And—" Val took a deep breath, her eyes darting around the coffee shop as if she wanted to ensure no one could hear them. She leaned in close and whispered, "Max is like me, Stacey."

"He...what?" She couldn't mean what Stacey thought she meant.

"He's like me. He can *see things*, too, the same way I do. That's one reason why we're drawn to one another. We understand each other. He said I could tell you, but I never got a chance before you left."

Stacey closed her mouth after realizing her jaw was hanging open. Well, that explained a lot. *Of course* he was like her. Stacey knew Val wasn't the only seer—what Northwalk called people like Val, Cassandra, Delilah, Lucien, and now Max. Though, per Kat, they were extremely rare, about fifty of them in the whole world that Northwalk knew of, and the organization tracked them very closely. Weirdly, they tended to clump up, which messed with Cassandra's vision in some way Stacey didn't understand. Too many possibilities or something. Seattle was one focal point; Hong Kong another, where a rival organization called *Yongjai* ruled. Stacey tried to stay out of Northwalk business as much as possible—she considered herself Kat's fiancée above all—but she'd gleaned that much over the years. Why hadn't she realized before that Max was one of them? Seemed like something Kat should have told her.

"So you found each other, like the one male and one female Alaskan wolves who managed to follow the other's scent over thousands of miles."

Val smiled. "Kinda like that. But I think we would have loved one another whether or not we had this shared ability."

"Oh." Stacey struggled for words as her worldview began to change in the span of a few seconds. Not what she was expecting from this meeting.

Val glanced at her watch. "I'm sorry, I gotta go," she said as she stood. "I'm working a case, and I need to question a possible witness. I'm short on time."

"You're still working cases? I thought you'd retired."

"I have, but this one's special. It's—well, I'll tell you about it later, if you want to meet again while you're here. I mean, I'd love to meet again, if you can find the time."

"Yeah, I'd like that. I'll call you."

Val grinned. "Smell you later."

"Not if I smell you first, hot bitch," Stacey replied, and heard Val laugh on her way out the door.

Maybe they could be friends again, Stacey thought with a smile. But her mouth slipped into a frown when she considered their whole conversation. Everything her friend told her—assuming it was all true, and she couldn't think of a reason Val would lie about it now—were important things Kat *should* have told her, but didn't. Stacey always knew Kat could be slippery, and wasn't always one hundred percent forthcoming for a variety of reasons, but she trusted Kat loved her enough to tell her the truth about things that were important, like Stacey's previous death. As a result, she'd turned a blind eye to a lot of questionable shit, letting Kat run the show of their relationship and interactions with Northwalk.

And now it dawned on her—that had been a mistake. It was time for her to get her head out of the sand, starting with finding out what the hell Northwalk and Kat were really up to.

* * *

You'll sneak in through the back of the department store using the keys you stole the day before. Disarm the security system using the code one-one-eight-six-three. In the store's surveillance room, you will turn off the cameras. Now you'll be ready to proceed to the platform extended over the first floor, the one they erect each holiday season to showcase Santa Claus and the piles of toys privileged parents buy their greedy children. Using a set of wrenches, you will loosen the bolts on each support wire connecting the platform to anchors in the walls above. It will be difficult, and it will take you a long time. But you'll be finished and gone when the first morning managers arrive, and no one will suspect what you've done.

When their false idol and shrine to gluttony comes crashing down, it will take with it the bond that keeps the ebony fox and red raven together, those who defile my gifts, and soon the world shall be cleansed of their evil.

Chapter Sixteen

Val walked into Jones's and stood at the threshold, taking in the scenery of what used to be the Red Raven and was now a posh, overtly sex-free bar. She'd been to Max's former club only once before; she recognized the shadow of its basic architecture, though everything else had changed. He'd told her the private lounges were off the corridor to the far right of the entrance, and that was where she'd find Eleanor, if the woman was there. It'd be easier if Max had come with her, but after exchanging minimal words that morning, he'd run off to visit Michael in the hospital before work.

She'd apologize to him if she thought it would make a difference. He wasn't in a conciliatory mood yet, and neither was she. As long as he continued to ignore the fact their family was in danger, with Eleanor the likely cause, they'd stay locked in a stalemate. She wouldn't let it go until she knew beyond a shadow of a doubt her mother, husband, and children were safe.

At least her meeting with Stacey had gone well. Val figured all the drama constantly swirling around her life was the reason her friend had taken off to begin with—that, and all the times she'd broken Stacey's heart for what she thought was the greater good. Sure, she was married with kids now, but the last week proved nothing had really changed. She was still a chaos magnet. It felt great at the time, but maybe meeting with her old friend had been a mistake. She didn't want to mess up the new, happy life Stacey had built for herself. And how did she find out Val had prevented her death all those years ago? Kat or someone else in Northwalk must have told her. Goddammit, Val would never escape her sins. She'd been dying to explain herself, and talk more about her mother, and motherhood, and Max, and everything, but didn't want to unload it all right then. They hadn't spoken in five years, for Christ's sake. Probably the last thing Stacey wanted to hear was all about Val's never-ending problems. But she'd be lying if she said she didn't want Stacey to call again. Hopefully by then all this mess with Eleanor would be over, and they could truly reconnect.

Val approached the bar first, typically the "all-seeing eye" of any adult establishment. "Evening," she said to the bartender, a young brunette.

"Evening. What can I get you?"

"Some information." Val held up her phone, the picture she took of Eleanor during the memorial service on the screen. "What do you know about this woman? I'm investigating an insurance claim, and she might be able to corroborate the claimant's report. I know her first name is Eleanor."

The bartender frowned at the photo. "I don't know anything about her, except she worked here for a few months and quit recently."

"Really? The claimant says she was here only a few days prior."

"She put in her two-weeks' notice about two weeks ago. That's all I know."

What a coincidence that since Val had gotten wise to her, she'd suddenly made herself scarce. "Did she have any friends here? Socialize with anyone?"

"Nope. She kept to herself. Honestly, she's very pretty, but also creepy if you talk to her for more than two minutes. You'd know if you met her."

"Has she ever mentioned anything about her background, like where she's from or if she's got family?"

"Nu-uh."

"Any idea where she lives, or other places she might work?"

"No, sorry. But Mickey might." The bartender pointed to the kiosk set up in front of the corridor that led to the private lounges. A big dude in a suit that looked ridiculous on his hulking frame manned the desk as he poked at a tablet computer. Val thanked the bartender, then walked over to Mickey. He gave her a polite smile.

"Good evening, ma'am," he said. "How may I help you?"

"Hi there. I'm looking for Eleanor." Val flashed him the photo on her phone. "I heard she worked here up until a few days ago. Can you tell me where I might find her, like her home address or other places she works at?"

"Sorry, ma'am, we don't give out that information."

"I'm investigating her in connection to a recent crime. All I want is to talk to her, take her statement. You don't want to be responsible for obstruction of justice, do you?"

He cocked his head and gave her a smile with a hint of smirk. "I didn't know you were on the police force, Mrs. Carressa."

Dammit. The bartender might not immediately recognize her, but it looked like she couldn't rely on her anonymity anymore to pump people for info, now that she and Max were local celebrities.

"My Seattle PD application's under review. And it's *Shepherd*. Valentine *Shepherd*. But really, I need to talk to Eleanor. It's important."

"I still can't give out that information."

He wanted to play hardball, did he? She folded her arms and sized the man up. Given his spiffy duds and haute air despite a brutish frame and a jagged tattoo that peeked out from his collar, he might as well have screamed, "I'm overcompensating for an embarrassingly low-class background! Look at me rising above!" There was no way the bar owners would hire this guy to be the face of their most exclusive area unless he *was* the owner, or at least part-owner.

"A review from Max Carressa would carry a lot of weight for this place. Could do wonders for business—or turn people off. Suppose my husband gave your bar a one-star review because the staff was rude to him and refused to serve his wife. How do you think that might affect your fine establishment?"

The smirk wiped off his face.

"Or suppose he wrote a review about how amazingly accommodating Jones's was, how they catered to his every need and desire, never messed up a drink order, made extra sure his beer nuts were nice and warm, elevated his drinking experience to a Zen-like state of nirvana, *and* accommodated his wife? Which review would you rather have, *Mr. Jones?*"

Mickey Jones glared at her for a moment, then fiddled with his tablet before saying, "The address we sent Eleanor Fatou's paychecks to is 1614, 110th Avenue Northeast, Apartment 23B, in Bellevue."

Eleanor Fatou. At least now she had a name for a Google search.

"Thanks, Mr. Jones." She sent him a friendly wave on her way out. "Keep an eye out for Max's five-star review on Yelp."

As she plugged Eleanor's address into her car's GPS, her cell phone rang.

"I need evidence now!" Lacy screamed into Val's ear.

"And what is so special about now?"

"It's been almost a week! I'm tired of waiting."

"A bunch of people just died, Lacy. Sorry that's thrown off your timeline."

Lacy's voice turned to a whimper. "I have to see him every day, knowing what he's doing behind my back... You have to give me something. Anything."

Val sighed and glanced at her watch as she pulled out of her parking spot. "Okay, listen. I'll probably be home in a couple hours. Meet me there and we can talk."

"Fine."

When Lacy hung up, Val called Jamal. He still hadn't gotten on board with her shoot-on-sight policy for strangers trying to get into their house, though he had acquiesced to a strict no-entry-without-prior-notice rule.

"Lacy Zephyr's coming over in about two hours," she told him. "She's a high-maintenance blonde, a *Real Housewives* type. Fake everything. You'll know her when you see her. If she beats me home, you can let her in. Tell her to wait in the study."

"Yes, ma'am."

After she disconnected, Val tossed her phone into her tote with a curse. The last thing she cared about at the moment was Aaron's extramarital activities. But if she came up empty from her visit to Eleanor's place, maybe Lacy could give her enough info on Aaron's routine for her to follow him to Eleanor instead. Or possibly use him as bait.

* * *

Val tried not to finger her gun in its side holster as she climbed the stairs to Eleanor's apartment. It wouldn't look good on a police report if she immediately shot the woman, despite her gut's assurance that was exactly what she should do. She stopped in front of a plain brown door, set in a plain brown building in a totally unremarkable apartment complex. Stepping out of view of the peephole, she rapped on the door.

No answer.

She knocked again, then pressed her ear against the door. Silence. No one home. *Probably for the best*, she thought as she took her too-eager hand off her gun. After a quick glance to ensure no one was around, she took her bump key out of her pocket and slipped it into the doorknob's lock. Slowly she pushed the key in, feeling each soft click as the pins lifted and then dropped into the cut below, until she knew only one pin remained. Then she slammed the palm of her hand into the key at the same time she turned the knob, and the door popped open.

"Beautiful," she said to herself as she pulled the bump key from the lock and put it back in her pocket. Doing one more scan of the area to confirm she'd gone unnoticed, she stepped into Eleanor's apartment and closed the door behind her.

* * *

Eleanor pressed the button marked "Carressa/Shepherd" on the console next to the iron gate. The intercom buzzed.

"May I help you?" a man's voice asked through the tinny speakers a few seconds later.

Not Maxwell. Good.

"This is Lacy Zephyr," Eleanor said. "I believe Valentine is expecting me."

"Okay, come on in."

She heard a click as the gate's lock disengaged. Eleanor smiled and went inside.

* * *

Val walked through Eleanor's apartment, surprised to find it almost completely bare. No furniture, nothing on the walls. She would've guessed Eleanor had just moved in, or was about to move out, except there were no packing boxes. In the tiny kitchen, she opened the refrigerator and the cupboards—no food, no dishes. Did anyone even live here? Maybe she had the wrong place.

She walked to the apartment's only bedroom and finally found signs of occupancy. A mattress adorned with simple blankets and a pillow laid on the floor. A neat stack of five books, small slips of paper laid on top, sat beside the crude bed. A clear, crumpled wrapper lay on the floor. Val picked it up and sniffed it—somebody was a candy cane fan. She leaned over the bed and spotted a few stray strands of yellow hair. This was the right place after all.

Val picked up the papers on the books—ferry tickets, from Seattle to Bremerton and back, all at various times in the evening, all on Saturday. What was on the other side of the Puget Sound that required a weekly commute?

Pocketing one of the tickets, Val riffled through the books—all different versions of the Bible. Flipping through a couple, she noticed the same sections highlighted in each—no, Eleanor had highlighted the *differences* in the same sections of each version. The woman was obsessed with how the ancient stories changed depending on who told them. Weird thing to obsess over.

She dropped the books back on the stack. What other bizarre hobby could Eleanor be hiding? Val lifted a corner of the mattress and heard a soft thump. Lowering the bed, she saw a notebook on the floor, which must have slid out from underneath the pillow. She picked the book up and flipped it open. A journal.

"Bingo," she said.

* * *

The door to Valentine's condo swung open, and a preppy black man in his early twenties greeted Eleanor.

"Evening, Mrs. Zephyr," he said with a polite smile, "I'm Jamal, Ms. Shepherd's and Mr. Carressa's nanny."

"Please, call me Lacy," Eleanor said.

"I'm sorry, Lacy, Ms. Shepherd's not home yet. She was expecting you a little later, but you can come in and wait in the study if you'd like." He held the door open for her and stepped aside.

"I'd love that, thank you."

Eleanor entered the condo, walking slowly through the entrance hallway and stopping at the juncture between the kitchen, the living room, and stairs that ascended to a second floor. As Jamal kept walking, presumably in the direction of the study, she took a moment to look at all the things they had. Original art on the walls. Oakwood furniture. Designer curtains. Crystal tchotchkes, like the cat-sized stag on an end table in the corner—with an antler snapped off.

In fact, the longer she looked at their nice things, the more she noticed the flaws. Scratches on the artwork. Chips in the furniture. Stains on the rugs and curtains. An embarrassment of riches they treated with disdain.

They had so much to lose, and they didn't even know it.

* * *

Val read the first entry in Eleanor's journal:

Forgive me, Father, for I have sinned.

I looked upon another woman's husband and felt lust for him. I know I shouldn't feel such things, but sometimes I give in to temptation. I save myself for you, though, always for you. Through prayer I've removed the man from my thoughts.

She read the next entry:

Forgive me, Father, for I have sinned.

I saw a mother and her baby in the park today, and I imagined myself as that mother and the child mine, and the feel of its tiny body against my breast. Then I imagined wrapping a hand around its little neck and squeezing until its life was gone. I don't know why I thought of this. Is it what you want? Is it what you will me to do? I am forever your servant and await your instructions.

Val shuddered. Jesus Christ, this woman was crazy.

* * *

"Ma'am?" Jamal said to Eleanor when he realized she'd stopped following him. "The study's this way."

"Ah, yes. Sorry. Just admiring how nice Valentine's life is."

"Um, her *house* is very nice, true." His eyes narrowed a sliver, as if he sensed something wasn't quite right. No matter. What he thought of her was irrelevant. She wouldn't be there long anyway.

She followed him halfway through the living room when what she *really* came for appeared from around the corner of an adjoining hallway.

The children.

* * *

Val skimmed through the rest of Eleanor's crazy-person journal. Every entry began the same—*Forgive me, Father, for I have sinned*—followed by a few sentences to a paragraph of some mundane activity or sinister thought she felt ashamed of. None were dated, and none mentioned the bombing or the dead man in the cathedral's basement or trying to set the place on fire.

"Shit," Val muttered when she realized while the journal might be disturbing, it wasn't incriminating. Nowhere in it did Eleanor actually admit to committing any violent or illegal acts. She was too smart for that.

Letting out an annoyed huff, Val flipped to the last page:

Forgive me, Father, for I have sinned.
I know you've commanded me to bring the ebony fox and red
raven to heel, but I felt doubt when Mother told me of the

twin abominations who must be removed from your earth. You haven't shown me their deaths, or the source of their evil, even though I've asked to see it. I don't want to doubt Mother, but I can't help the temptation to see it for myself. Despite my sin of doubt, I am forever your servant. I love Mother always, and above all I love you.

Red raven? That was Val. Could Max be the ebony fox, and Lydia and Simon the twin abominations? Father sounded like a reference to God, but who was Mother? Could they be real people telling her to do evil things, or figments of Eleanor's delusions? If they were real, why were they commanding her to torment Val's family?

She read the final entry:

Forgive me, Father, for I have sinned.
Mother told me not to be tempted by someone else's sins, but I can't help myself. I want what she has, even though I know she only has them because she defied your will. I need your strength to set right the things that will go wrong without mourning what could have been. I want to look into Mother's eyes, and one day your eyes, and know I've done the right thing.

She read the passage again. *I want what she has, even though I know she only has them because she defied your will.* Sounded a lot like the letter she received just before the bombing. She pulled the now well-worn paper from her pocket and compared the handwriting. It might have been written by the same person…she couldn't tell. The letter looked composed with a steady, deliberate hand, while the journal contained quick scratches of words. The police could analyze it, though she wouldn't be able to tell them where she got it, or all the cryptic ways she thought it referenced her family. So really, giving it to the cops would be a waste of time. Well, there was *one* cop who would believe her, and wouldn't care about a little breaking and entering.

Val snapped the journal shut, then texted Sten and asked him to meet her for coffee in twenty minutes. She did one more walk-through of Eleanor's house to be sure she didn't miss anything. Given how empty and mostly unused the place looked, she figured Eleanor didn't really live there; she used it as a crash pad, a place to sleep and take a shower if she had no other option, and an address to put on legal documents. A woman like Eleanor probably had lots of boyfriends, along with lots of hotel rooms and love nests to call her own—at least one in Bremerton. She might not be back to the apartment for days, even weeks. With Val's mom needing protection from a future murderer, and her always vulnerable children, and Max needing protection as well, there was no way she could stake out the place for that long.

Shit. What now? Val looked at the journal again. Father was probably God, but if Mother was a real person, then Val had at least two people to look for. There was always Aaron, her only other connection to Eleanor. And whatever help Sten could provide. She stopped in the bedroom one more time and grabbed the book with the smoothest cover—the one most likely to have Eleanor's fingerprints on it. Damn, it'd have to do.

* * *

The boy and the girl stood at the threshold of the living room, two tiny statues staring at her.

"Kids," Jamal said when he saw the children, "Why don't you go back to Nana's room and show her more of your drawings?"

"She's in the bathroom," the girl said. She looked at Eleanor. "You're not supposed to be here."

Jamal's startled gaze cut between Eleanor and the girl. "It's okay, Lydia, your mom's expecting her."

Eleanor took slow steps toward the girl, a perfect black-haired cherub with wide eyes full of something other than innocence. "What if I said you're not supposed to be here, either?"

"Of course we're supposed to be here," the girl said.

"We've always been here," the boy added from behind her.

"Kids," Jamal said, his voice getting testy. "Really—"

Eleanor ignored the nanny's protests and knelt in front of the girl. She watched Lydia's gray eyes study hers without fear—reading her soul maybe?—while the boy looked over his sister's shoulder, anxiety pinching his chubby face.

"What do you see when you look at me?" Eleanor asked the girl. "Do you see the things I've done?"

"I see some things you *could* do," the girl said, utterly calm.

"And we don't like them," the boy added with a hint of childish defiance.

It was true. Mother was right—they had the Sight. A stolen gift from Father, perverted and bestowed upon them by the one who defied His will, a gift they had no right to possess. When Mother told her the children needed to die, it'd given her pause; Father had not shown it to her, and she didn't like killing children otherwise. But they weren't children really; they were *creatures*, things not meant to exist.

"What am I going to do to you?" Eleanor asked them.

The girl cocked her head as if she didn't understand the question. She didn't know. They couldn't see everything. But could they hear her thoughts?

I'm going to kill you.

The girl blinked, but otherwise didn't react. Neither did the boy. The children might have the Sight, but didn't know their fates, or her mind. Good.

Eleanor stood, smiling down at the children. "I just love kids," she said to Jamal, never taking her eyes off them. "They're so strange and wonderful."

"Mommy will stop you!" the boy said, his voice quivering with uncertainty.

She threw back her head and laughed. Silly creature. "I'm sure she'll try. She'll fail—"

"Mrs. Zephyr, please." Jamal stepped between her and the kids, arms outstretched like he broke up a fight. "Lydia, Simon, go back to Nana's room *now*. Mrs. Zephyr, the study is this way."

"You know, I don't think I need to meet with Valentine after all. Thank you for your hospitality. I'll see myself out."

Forgive me, Mother, for doubting you, she thought. *Your will shall be done, and the children will die.*

Chapter Seventeen

At Tully's coffee shop, Val drummed her fingers against the side of her peppermint mocha, not sure if she should feel angry or relieved. "You really found nothing on my mother?"

"Nada," Sten said from the other side of the small table where they sat. He popped the lid off his cup, retrieved a flask from his coat pocket, and poured a shot of liquor into his black coffee. Pushing the top back on, he took a slurp. "She's been off the grid for at least the last ten years. Criminals are shit at staying hidden, but crazy people excel at it. Ironic in a way."

Val sighed, deciding to split the difference between angry and relieved and settle on annoyed. A dearth of information about her mother's past meant she couldn't corroborate or contradict Dani's story about where the woman had been for the last thirty years. "At least this means she doesn't have a criminal record."

"Not in Washington State, or at the federal level. She could've been naughty in another state, though. No offense, but I'm really not in the mood to make forty-nine phone calls to check."

"And your contact said my mother didn't have anything to do with Northwalk?"

He nodded. "Not sure I completely trust my contact on this one, but…we've always had similar goals."

Val rapped her fingers harder against the coffee cup. She must be missing something. Could her long-lost mother *really* have waltzed back into her life with no ulterior motive and no connection to the conspiracy that stalked her and Max?

"Maybe Grandma Shepherd's legit," Sten said, then shrugged. "If I were you, I'd shoot her in the head anyway, just to be sure."

"Murdering my own mother's off the table, but thanks for your advice."

He gave her his usual shit-eating grin. "That's what I'm here for."

She considered asking him what he wanted for his trouble, but decided against it. If he didn't bring it up, then she'd let sleeping dogs lie.

"I need to ask you for another favor."

He sipped his coffee and raised an eyebrow. "You can ask."

"I'm looking for a woman named Eleanor Fatou." Val showed him the picture. "I know where she used to work, where she sometimes lives, and who she occasionally sleeps with, but I've been unable to track her down. She moves around too much. With my mother and the kids, and Max, *and* Christmas obligations, I don't have the time to stake out her haunts or hit up her known associates."

"Is this woman a rapist, murderer, cult leader, or wild political animal to add to your fan club?"

"You know that club includes you."

"And I am your *biggest* fan!"

"She's responsible for the bombing at the Thornton Building."

His jovial demeanor fell away. "That was terrorists," he said with rare seriousness.

"It was Eleanor. She sent this to me on the day of the bombing, just before it happened."

Val handed Sten the cryptic letter. He took a few seconds to read the letter before looking at her with a pinched frown. "Assuming this means what you think it means, what's her motive?"

"She wants to hurt us—me and Max and the children. I have no goddamn idea why. If I could find her, I'd ask." Val laid the journal and ferry ticket on the table. "She takes the ferry to Bremerton on Saturdays. I don't know if she lives there, or is visiting someone, or what. Maybe you can see if she's got an address listed there. I also found the journal in her apartment. I can't tell if the handwriting matches the letter, but some of her entries definitely refer to Max and me. Whether she's got some deeper motive, I don't know, but she planted a bomb that killed eight people and was probably meant for Max, then murdered another guy in a church and tried to set it on fire to torment us some more. She's a psychopath who's obsessed with us for some reason, and I have no clue where she is right now and I don't have the resources or time to look for her and—" Clenching her jaw, she took a deep breath to control the rage beginning to boil over inside her. How *dare* this woman come after her family—and just when Val felt the most vulnerable.

"I took this book from her apartment, too." Val dropped the smooth-covered Bible in front of him. "It's probably got her prints on it."

"And yours now."

"I know that, but ignore mine. Just see if there's a hit on Eleanor's prints in the police database. If there's any inch of you that takes the 'serve and protect' part of your job seriously, you should find her before she kills again."

Sten flipped through the journal, scanning a couple pages, his face unreadable. She doubted he gave one rat's ass about Max, and probably not her children, either. But how much did he care about his "partner"? Probably not any more than what she could do for him.

He sandwiched the letter and ferry ticket into the journal, tossed it back to her, then picked up the Bible with a paper napkin as he stood to leave. "You know what I love about you, Shepherd? I love how your problems become everybody else's problems, and yet somehow it's not your fault."

She gritted her teeth. The asshole wasn't completely wrong. Fucking Sten. "So you'll find her?"

"And what if I do? You're telling me you just wanna talk?"

"No, I don't just want to talk."

Zipping up his ugly Members Only jacket, he cocked his head and looked at her for a moment in the way she recognized from when he'd arrested one of her rapists on trumped-up child pornography charges. He acknowledged her anger, her thirst for revenge, and somehow understood what she was willing to give—and give up—to protect her family. Sten knew her in a way no one else did, not even Max. He'd seen the worst in her, and recognized a kindred spirit.

"*Kerlaču şartsa*," he said, then turned and left.

She'd never heard him speak a foreign language before, didn't even know he knew one. Typing the phonetic spelling of whatever he'd said into her phone, she ran it through her Internet search engine. One result popped up: roughly "Happy New Year," in Chechen.

* * *

As Val drove around the corner of her condo complex on her way to the carport, she saw Lacy Zephyr get out of a sedan and walk toward the front gate. Val cruised to a stop behind Lacy's car and caught up with her before she reached the gate. Might as well have their unpleasant conversation away from the children. And maybe if they exchanged words in the cold, Lacy would be motivated to keep it short, or at least save her screaming fit for somewhere warm. She didn't strike Val as someone who tolerated being uncomfortable one second longer than necessary. This talk was the last thing she wanted to do right now, but she needed to coax information out of Lacy on her husband's future plans, and when he might meet up with Eleanor again.

"You've found something?" Lacy asked as Val trotted up to her.

"Yes. It's not much yet, but—"

"I don't care, just tell me!"

Damn, someone was itching for bad news—or good news, if Lacy wanted an excuse to divorce her husband.

"Aaron's definitely seeing someone else," Val said. "I'm not sure about the extent of their involvement, though, if it's physical or—"

"Give me the pictures."

"This is the only one I have so far." Keeping an iron grip on her phone so Lacy couldn't rip it from her hand and spike it into the ground, Val held it up with Eleanor's picture on the screen. Lacy grabbed Val's wrist and glared at the photo as if trying to blow it up with her eyes.

Her voice suddenly hoarse, Lacy asked, "Where are the pictures of her and Aaron?"

"I haven't actually seen them together."

"But *Max* has, right? Otherwise how would you know?"

Val didn't answer. Max made it clear he didn't want to be involved in the case, and his budding friendship with Aaron probably made that doubly true now. "I need to know where Aaron might be rendezvousing with her. If you can give me a schedule of his typical day, I can follow him and get the pictures."

Lacy scoffed. "I don't know where the hell he is every minute. He goes to work, then he usually goes to that bar I told you about. Sometimes he just disappears and doesn't tell me where he's been, or feeds me some obvious lie." She gritted her teeth, eyes filling with frustrated tears. "*You're* the goddamn private eye. *You* find them!"

Before Val could ask her more about where Aaron might be shagging his homicidal girlfriend, Lacy stomped back to her car. As she stepped into the driver's side, she yelled at Val, "And you might want to keep an eye on your own husband while you're at it, since Aaron and Max are suddenly best buddies. Birds of a feather flock together. Chances are your man will be fucking someone else any day now. Men are pigs." She disappeared into her car and peeled off.

Jesus, Lacy. She wanted Val's *help?* To hell with her and her stupid marital strife. The only reason she cared about Lacy's problems anymore was because Aaron's mistress happened to be a murderer who was targeting her family. If Lacy chose to stay ignorant of her husband's whereabouts while assuming the worst, then her marriage deserved to die. And philandering wasn't some kind of virus, so that if Aaron sneezed on Max, he'd catch the Roaming Dick disease. Max would never stray, not in a million years. Not after everything they'd been through together.

Val returned to her car and drove to the garage in the back of the condo. Max's sedan was still gone. She glanced at her watch. Where *was* he anyway? He should've been home from work by now.

She dug her cell phone out of her tote and queued up Max's number, then dismissed it with an angry shake of her head. What would she say to him? *Where are you? You're not cheating on me, are you?* Goddammit, she was turning into Lacy. Maybe Aaron's wife had passed on the Irrational Jealousy disease.

And she *still* didn't know where the hell to find Eleanor. She could follow Aaron, or stake out Jones's or Eleanor's apartment in the off chance she might return, or stalk the ferry to Bremerton every Saturday night, but those things took time she didn't have, not with her mother and children to protect. Besides, if Eleanor knew Val was on to her, she wouldn't return to those places anyway.

It'd be nice if she could ask Stacey for help, or at least talk about all this with her, but dragging her old friend into this mess wasn't a good idea. They weren't there yet. The only person she had to lean on these days was Max, and when he wasn't around, it became glaringly obvious how alone in the world they were without each other.

Well, there was also Sten. Fucking Sten. He had police resources at his disposal to track down Eleanor. She could lean on him, if she had no other choice. At this rate they *would* be partners, and she'd never be rid of him.

Val stomped up the carport stairs and burst through the door leading into the kitchen. She stood in the threshold for a moment and took a deep breath. *Don't be angry in front of the kids or Dani—or Jamal, he might wet his pants.*

She heard children laughing and Toby barking his head off,

coming from the living room. Walking over to see what the fuss was about, she saw Dani growling on her hands and knees, face-to-face with the dog in a mock standoff, while the kids watched in delight. Jamal sat on the couch, rearranging flash cards with Japanese words on them.

"Mommy!" Simon and Lydia said in unison when they saw her. They ran to her and latched on to her legs.

"Hey, kiddos," she said with fake cheer and kissed the tops of their heads. "Were you good for Jamal and Nana?"

Lydia gave her mother an impish smile. "Mostly."

Dani stood, leaving poor Toby in a state of agitated confusion where he whined and spun in circles; he wasn't in on the joke. She picked up a stack of papers off the coffee table.

"We drew pictures," Dani said. She showed Val a crayon drawing of the Eiffel Tower, "Simon" written on the bottom. "They're very good artists. I mean, *very* good." She held up another of the Sydney Opera House surrounded by rainbows. "I kinda can't believe a four-year-old drew this. If I hadn't seen it myself, I'd swear it was a hoax—"

Val snatched the drawing out of Dani's hand. "Sometimes kids have flashes of talent. It doesn't mean anything."

"But pumpkin—"

Don't call me that. Val yanked the rest of the pictures out of her mother's arms.

"Your kids are very special. Maybe you should have them tested—"

"They are not special! They are normal. *Normal.*" *Shit.* This was exactly why it'd been a bad idea letting her mother stay with them.

"Oh, okay…" Dani looked away, her eyes twitchy. Nervous or crazy? Both? Maybe Val should tell her to leave tonight.

"Nana's gonna make us chocolate chip cookies!" Simon said. The children unlatched themselves from Val and gave Dani a hug. She smiled warmly at them, still avoiding Val's glare.

Who was this woman? The kids had warmed to her, though they'd liked their grandmother even before they met her. Children wanted to love their family. Not even Val's *special* son and daughter understood how thin blood could be. When she was a kid, she'd dreamed of her mother's return, how sorry her mom would be for being gone so long and all the warm hugs and bonding that would follow. Now her childhood fantasy had come true, and it felt...wrong. Unnatural. Nothing good ever came without a price.

"Um, ma'am," Jamal said, breaking the tension. "Mrs. Lacy Zephyr—"

"I know," Val snapped. "I talked to her on my way in. You can leave now. I've got it from here." A second later, she added, "Thanks."

He pressed his lips together as if he wanted to say more, but bid farewell to the children instead and left for the day.

"Can you two go upstairs and put on your best cookie-baking outfits?" Dani said to the kids.

Before Val could tell her mother not to order her kids around, Simon and Lydia sprinted out of sight like a herd of baby buffalo.

Sighing about her shitty day—and her MIA husband—Val walked to the kitchen and pulled a beer from the fridge, popped the cap off, and took a long drink. She'd kicked her binge drinking habit when she and Max permanently united, but she still liked to imbibe a responsible amount on occasion...stressful occasions.

After a few seconds of silence, Dani said, "Your kids are wonderful. I love spending time with them."

"You do, huh? It only took thirty years to give a shit about your family?"

Dani flinched, tears welling. Great, more fucking crying. "I know I was gone when you needed me, and I'm sorry. If I could turn back the clock and do it over again, I would in a heartbeat."

Val took a deep breath, then another swig of beer. Now it was she who couldn't meet her mother's eyes. She didn't want Dani to see the emotional struggle she waged with herself, how vulnerable she actually felt. If she opened her heart to her mother and the woman left again...*crushed* would be an understatement.

"I thought you let me come visit your family because you wanted to reconcile," Dani said. "What do you need from me to make things right?"

Val met her mother's gaze, her eyes narrowing a sliver. Reconciliation wasn't her primary motive, actually. "Do you have any enemies?"

Dani's face warped from concern to confusion. "Do I have any what?"

"Enemies. Like people you owe money, stole from, or crossed in some way. Anyone who'd want to hurt you."

She looked around the kitchen as if searching for an answer in the cabinets. "I...I don't think so. But there's a lot I don't remember, so I guess I don't know. Why?"

Maybe Dani's mental health issues would make her more likely to believe a woo-woo explanation for Val's concerns. "I have a feeling someone's going to try to hurt you."

Dani's eyes widened, and she held Val's gaze for long enough to make Val wonder if she was thinking something she didn't want to say out loud. "What kind of feeling?"

"It's...just a feeling."

Dani didn't know what Val could do, did she? Val always wanted to ask her mother about it when she was young, naïve, and confused about why her sexual experiences didn't match other girls' stories. Now that she had the chance, she couldn't bring herself to take the risk. But maybe her mom could do it, too, and was waiting for a cue to broach the subject?

What were the odds Val inherited her visions from her mother? Max and Val had passed their curse on to their children, so she figured there must be some kind of hereditary component. Max doubted it, though, telling her if that were true, Northwalk would've established a breeding program decades or even hundreds of years ago, for at least as long as the organization had been in existence. The world would be a very different place, he'd said, ruled by future-seers, like some kind of crazy, sexier *Dune* thing. She supposed he was right. He was always so logical. According to his reasoning, they might have had lots of children, and none of them would be Alphas. But of course, they immediately had two Alphas right away. Their own children were an unfortunate exception he couldn't explain.

She watched her mother's face for any sign of recognition or flash of insight into what Val referred to, but there was none. Val closed her eyes and finished off her beer, wishing alcohol would numb the sinking feeling in her heart for hoping for something so stupid.

"I don't want to bring negative energy into your family," Dani said. Val saw the flash of coldness in her eyes again, the one that'd been there when she first arrived, and just as quickly it disappeared. She'd done things she was ashamed of, Val guessed. Though Dani seemed open about her past, Val noticed her mother often skimmed over details, claiming she couldn't remember on account of her mental illness. Could be just an excuse.

"I don't think I have any enemies." She looked at the floor and said in a small voice, "Except, um, maybe you…"

Val knew she could be emotionally manipulative at times; now she saw where that trait came from. In any case, Dani had so far been a perfectly pleasant houseguest, and seemed genuinely interested in making amends. Maybe Val should cut her a little slack.

Sighing, she said, "I'm not your enemy, Mom."

Dani's eyes filled with tears again—happy tears this time. Val stiffened when her mother embraced her in a hug.

"Oh, thank you, pumpkin, thank you."

Pumpkin—she thought her mom used that nickname for her when she was a child. She closed her eyes and tried remember.

Would you like to bake a cake with me, pumpkin, for Daddy's birthday? I'll put the ingredients in the bowl and you can stir. That's it, teamwork! Love you, my little baker.

Like a warm blanket, the memory enveloped and soothed her. Val bit her lip and swallowed a lump in her throat, then slowly hugged her mom back. Some risks were worth taking. Hopefully, this was one of them.

Chapter Eighteen

Stacey took a deep breath of fresh December air and tried to calm her nerves as she waited for Northwalk to arrive. Mr. Rodgers's shady construction company had finished work on the forest mansion only a few days ago, and the smell still lingered—paint, sawdust, metal welding for the steel doors and other reinforcements, and the sharp, acrid odor of wires that made up the extensive security system electronics. Standing next to Kat and dressed in a stylish black wool coat—fancy for Stacey anyway—she glanced behind her at the guards manning the entrance. More took up positions inside, while still others patrolled the outside area around the mansion. Almost two dozen private security guards total, all in black suits with rifles slung across their shoulders and pistols at their hips. When six service sedans materialized through the trees, cruising up the long driveway toward them, she felt as if she were starring in her own spy movie and was about to rendezvous with the hero…no, the villain.

The sleek cars looped around the expanse of gravel in front

of the house and came to a stop a few feet away from them. The driver of the head car jumped out and opened the back passenger's door. A blond woman in a blood-red pencil skirt and ebony fur coat stepped out, a pair of bug-eyed sunglasses covering half her face even though it didn't seem terribly bright to Stacey. From the following cars, others began emerging to scan the surrounding forest and crane their heads up at the huge house. Together the Northwalk council, at least some of whom were Kat's kin, consisted of three men and four women, all so finely dressed in shiny suits, cashmere blouses, and shoes that probably cost more than most people's monthly mortgage, they put Stacey's attempt at high fashion to shame. From the fourth car, a woman clad all in white with black, silky hair emerged from the dark hole of the sedan's interior like an angel stepping out of Hell.

Though Stacey had never met or seen pictures of the lady, she knew immediately who it was—Cassandra, Northwalk's prized Alpha Seer and the woman who'd foreseen Stacey's death years ago, before Val had stopped it from happening. The way she moved, almost as if she floated, was a dead giveaway.

Like a couple clown cars, a gaggle of people in more sensible business attire popped out of the last two sedans and immediately began shouting orders at the drivers and chattering on cell phones. They must be the help. As footmen hurried to unload luggage, the council walked toward Kat and Stacey, their expensive heels crunching against the gravel as they went. *Oh Jesus*, Stacey thought as they neared, *I hope they like me.*

It didn't really matter if Kat's family liked Stacey, but it would still be nice to get on the good side of her future in-laws, even if they might be not-so-nice people. The woman in the red skirt and black fur coat took point, placing one hand on her hip and surveying Kat from behind her huge sunglasses.

"Mother," Kat said with a polite, cold upturn of her lips. Kat's mother held out her arms, and the two exchanged kisses on the cheek.

"Stacey, this is my mother, Honora."

"Very pleased to meet you, ma'am," Stacey said with a smile.

Honora removed her sunglasses, revealing the same ice blue eyes as Kat set in a rigid, expertly painted face. The Arctic stare she leveled at Stacey, as if her daughter's girlfriend were a fly who'd landed in her wine, was enough to wipe Stacey's grin away. Honora turned her attention back to Kat, apparently having decided Stacey's presence wasn't worth acknowledging.

"I trust you've made all the necessary arrangements?" Honora asked in a smooth English accent.

"Of course."

"Our agent in the field is doing her part. She's confirmed our assets have manifested and are ready for extraction. Are you doing your part?"

"Yes, Mother."

"Because we wouldn't want a repeat of what happened last time."

Stacey knew Kat well enough to spot her girlfriend's eyes twitch a fraction of an inch—a major show of unease for Kat.

"That wasn't my fault."

"No, it was. It really was. But your Uncle Poland was always a bit of an idiot." She checked the slim gold watch on her wrist. "Enough talking. We have a meeting in forty minutes. After I freshen up, show me to the boardroom."

Without another look at Kat, Stacey, or the rest of Northwalk, she brushed past her daughter and walked into the mansion, a half-dozen assistants trailing after. How would Honora know which of the twelve bedrooms was hers? Oh yes—that would be the biggest one. After Honora disappeared, the others finally moved. Each exchanged bland, seconds-long pleasantries with Kat before going inside to claim their own bedrooms, probably by size according to their respective rank, however they figured that out. Stacey would have been insulted Kat hadn't introduced her to the rest of the family, but the subzero reception she'd received from Honora convinced her it was probably for the best.

The last Northwalk man approached Kat with Cassandra at his side. Stacey met Cassandra's wide eyes and was nearly swallowed by the infinite azure within them. Those eyes saw Stacey die—probably saw *everyone* die, including those who hadn't been born yet. Put Val's ability to shame, really. Forcing herself to look away, she did a double-take at the man's blue eyes, blond hair, and shockingly handsome face—like a male version of Kat.

"Sister," he said with a grin that was almost warm, which compared to the others, made him seem downright cuddly.

Kat mirrored his smile. "Brother," she replied with more ease than she'd shown any of her other family members.

"Tracy, was it? I'm Julian."

"Stacey. Nice to meet you," she lied.

"Claire has always been good at picking assistants. She's an excellent judge of utility."

"I'm not her assistant. I'm her girlfriend."

"Oh," he said with mock surprise. "Of course, of course. Same thing." He looked at Kat. "We missed you in Prague."

She snickered. "I didn't miss you in Beirut."

"Ever the bitch." He reached into his pocket and pulled out a small white chunk of rock. "I got five while in Prague." Julian admired the rock for a moment, and Stacey's stomach dropped when she realized it wasn't a rock, but a tooth. "This one's my favorite. He was feisty. You?"

Kat rolled her eyes as if he'd made a joke, and not implied he'd murdered five people and taken their teeth as trophies. "Sorry, I keep the ears of my kills in my other purse. Didn't go with my outfit today."

"Liar. Severed ears go with everything." Dropping the tooth back in his pocket with one hand, he threaded his other arm through Cassandra's. The Seer didn't react, or even look at him. She seemed almost drugged, like her mind was in another world. Stacey had always assumed Cassandra held a place in Northwalk's top echelon. To see Julian leading her around, clearly Stacey had been mistaken. The Alpha seemed more like a prisoner than an insider.

He glanced at Stacey, then back to Kat. "Don't be too long, hmm?" With a sly grin, he added, "You know how I hate to sleep alone."

Kat looked at him with her typical unreadable expression, an amused smile on her face that might have been sincere, or not. Julian led Cassandra inside as if she were an invalid child.

After he'd gone, Stacey rounded on Kat. "What the *fuck* was that?"

Kat shrugged. "I told you they were strange—"

"You did *not* tell me they were rude, creepy, and incestuous."

"Julian's just messing around." She turned and began walking back toward the mansion's entrance. Over her shoulder, she said, "Don't take him seriously."

Stacey marched up behind her. "You neglected to tell me about your perverted, psychotic brother. So thanks for keeping me in the dark on important information, again. Oh yeah, and when they were treating me like shit, I couldn't help noticing that you stood by and did nothing."

"You saw them, they don't care about anyone but themselves. Fighting with them would've been pointless."

"You didn't even try!"

Kat stopped and turned toward Stacey. In the blink of an eye her expression morphed from steely determination to compassion and concern, like she'd flipped a switch on her face. Putting a tender hand on her girlfriend's cheek, she said, "Baby, I'm sorry. You're right. I should have tried. I'm so used to accepting their odd quirks, I don't think about how it might affect other people."

Stacey slapped her hand away. "You mean other *assistants?*"

"I told you, don't listen to my brother. He's trying to get under your skin. He has a sadistic streak."

Stacey snapped, "Like brother, like sister."

She marched into the mansion before Kat could launch into the usual routine of sweet-talking her way back into Stacey's good graces. Why did she keep falling for this crap? She should have known Kat's love was too good to be true. Promises of marriage, a future together…bullshit. Not with a family like that.

Feeling tears building in her eyes, she hurried past the throng of Northwalk staff, who ran around like ants putting everything *just so* for their masters. After climbing the stairs to their room on the second floor, she sat at the edge of the bed and put her head in her hands. She loved Kat with all her heart, but this wasn't working. Jet-setting around the world performing innocuous tasks was one thing. Diving into the dark heart of an evil empire was another. At least before, she could tell herself the odd jobs they did for Northwalk were trivial, even if it was for a morally ambiguous organization. She and Kat never hurt anyone. Now that she'd had an up-close-and-personal taste of what their bosses were really like…She wasn't cut out for this life.

But in my other life—in another universe maybe—I'm dead. What am I doing with my second chance? Whatever doing the "right thing" is supposed to be, this definitely isn't it.

She heard the bedroom door open and close, then Kat's hands touched hers. Stacey glanced up and met her girlfriend's stare. Despite the ice blue of her eyes, Kat could melt any man or woman with that look in the span of a heartbeat. Stacey wished she was immune, but she wasn't. Kat sat next to her and planted a deep kiss on her lips, and her anger began to wane. Damn, her girlfriend was a good kisser—a good *everything* when it came to sex.

No. Kat always did this. Whenever they fought, she'd turn on the charm until Stacey relented. And it always fucking worked. Not this time.

Stacey pulled away. "Stop it."

"I know I've been bad." As she unbuttoned Stacey's heavy coat, she said, "Let me make it up to you."

Stacey scoffed. "How? What're you going to do this time, Kat? Shove your tits at me and hope I stop complaining?"

"Yes to the first part." She slipped off her own coat, tossing it to the ground before straddling Stacey. Breath hot against Stacey's lips, she popped open the buttons of her silk blouse and unhooked the front of her bra so her creamy breasts spilled out. "But I'm also going to be honest. Ask me anything."

Unable to resist, Stacey cupped each soft mound in her hands, running her fingertips across the smooth skin, thumbing her girlfriend's nipples into hard points.

"Anything?" Stacey asked, her anger subsiding at the rare opportunity to get a straight answer out of Kat, along with the sudden heat between her legs.

"Anything, baby." She pushed Stacey down onto the bed, unzipping her girlfriend's slacks before slipping a hand into her underwear and sliding two fingers between Stacey's legs.

"*Mmm*," Stacey moaned as a fire roared to life in her belly. God, this bitch knew exactly how to play her. Despite knowing full well Kat was manipulating the shit out of her, she still loved every second of it. At least she'd make Kat follow through with her end of the bargain. "How are all the people in Northwalk related to you?"

"All cousins, except my mother and brother, who you met."

"Do you have any other siblings?"

"No. Just Julian." Kat's fingers slipped deeper into her, pressing harder until bolts of electricity shot down her thighs.

"What happened to Uncle Poland?"

"Hit by a bus."

"How is that your fault?"

Kat let out an annoyed sigh. "I put him up in a hotel, and then he was…well, goaded into running into the street, I guess you could say. Mother thinks I should've babysat him better."

"How long has she been in charge of Northwalk?"

"Oh, about seventy years, I think."

Seventy years? Honora didn't look nearly that old. Before Stacey could ask how that was possible, Kat sat up so her torso was level with Stacey's face. Stacey greedily accepted one nipple into her mouth, sucking on the delicious flesh as wetness pooled between her legs, threatening to explode into Kat's hand. Desperate to be inside her girlfriend, too, Stacey pulled Kat's pants down to the mid-thigh and entered her. As she stroked Kat's insides, enjoying the warm, wet feel around her fingers, she thrilled when Kat's head arched back and a wild moan escaped. The air seemed to thicken as they burned each other's fuses, getting closer and closer to combusting.

"How does your mom look so young?" Stacey mumbled against Kat's breast.

"Special drugs. They're all on them." She let out a tight chuckle. "Julian would have died a hundred times over if not for the drugs."

"Are you on them?"

"Sometimes." Kat's tits bounced to the rhythm of Stacey's hand, and her voice became strained as pleasure began to overwhelm her. "But only…if I have to."

"What does Northwalk really want? Are they trying to take over the world?"

Kat laughed. "Hardly. Northwalk wants what everyone in power wants—to stay in power. They don't want to take over the world, but they want to *control* it—and live forever to enjoy the bounty, of course. Being able to see the future is an incredibly powerful tool to that end, for lots of obvious reasons. And the Alpha is an extra special tool. One they won't give up easily."

"Do they control all the other seers, too, like Val and Delilah?" Goddamn, she was close, so close, but she needed answers. She had to hold out just a little longer…

She scoffed. "Do you really think anyone can control Val? That's one tiger I wouldn't want to grab by the tail. Delilah willingly worked with Northwalk for a while as a free agent, in exchange for help climbing the political ladder. She doesn't work for us now, but we still keep close tabs on all the seers and manipulate them as necessary, with or without their consent or knowledge."

"When do you—*ahh!*" Stacey couldn't finish before an ex-

160 Shana Figueroa

plosion of ecstasy ripped through her body. At the same time Kat's insides tighten around her fingers as her girlfriend came, crying out as if begging the room for relief.

When the earthquakes in their bodies passed, Kat cupped Stacey's head in her hands. "I love you. Remember that."

"I love you, too." Holy shit, did she ever. At that moment, if Kat asked her to set herself on fire and jump off a cliff while declaring fealty to the Devil, she'd have done it without thinking twice. She'd been too quick to give up before. So what if Kat had a crazy-ass family? Lots of people did. They could make their relationship work. When Kat assumed control, she wouldn't be her mother's errand girl or brother's verbal punching bag anymore. Together, they could turn Northwalk into a force for good, and not...whatever the hell the organization was usually up to.

Sliding off Stacey, Kat stood and quickly set her clothes back in place. "Time to prep for the boardroom meeting in a few minutes." She sat down at a cherry wood desk that doubled as a vanity table and popped open her laptop. "I need to make sure the Northwalk cells in Dublin and Cairo are ready for the video teleconference. We still have a lot to do before the big succession ceremony in a few days."

"When your mother will hand you the reins of the organization?"

"Yes." Kat grinned at Stacey, the same smile she used on marks—the *I'm telling you what you want to hear* smile. "And you'll be at my side."

A shiver ran through Stacey's spine, killing the warm afterglow of their lovemaking. *Would* she really be at Kat's side? How much of what Kat had told her was the truth? Honora didn't look old or unhealthy enough to make stepping down a necessity, so why would she abdicate to her daughter after seventy years of what Stacey assumed was iron-fisted rule? Unfortunately for Kat, even the most amazing sex in the world couldn't patch over the holes in her story.

Stacey steeled herself and forced out a grin she hoped Kat wouldn't suspect was fake. "You know it, baby."

Apparently satisfied, Kat swiveled back to the laptop and turned it on. They'd always trusted each other; Stacey because she loved Kat, and Kat because she knew Stacey loved her. For the first time, Stacey subtly craned her head over Kat's shoulder and watched her girlfriend type in the password to unlock the computer. Stacey hoped she was being paranoid. She hoped Kat loved her and told her the truth about everything.

But to quote a saying Val learned in the Army and had imparted on Stacey when they'd been Valentine Investigations partners: *Trust but verify.*

Chapter Nineteen

Max took a long drag off his joint and blew out the smoke in a slow exhale. From the leather couch he lay on, he watched the gray tendrils float up and disappear into the ceiling of Aaron's private room at Jones's.

Sitting in the loveseat next to Max, legs propped on an ottoman, Aaron said, "I'll admit it"—he took a hit off his own joint—"I didn't know you could hang."

Max chuckled. "You don't read the tabloids?"

"They exaggerate and lie. I assumed none of that shit was true."

With a snicker, he said, "Most of it is true."

"Hell of an exciting life you lead."

"That's one way to put it."

Max checked the time on his phone—quarter past seven. He should get home soon, spend some time with the kids before they went to bed. Strange that Val hadn't called wondering where he was. Probably too wrapped up in her goddamn obsession with Eleanor to notice he'd been gone. She might want to talk about what happened two nights ago—but probably not.

Hell, she might even ask for a repeat performance, and there was no way he was going to do...*that* again, whatever he'd done. It made him sick just thinking about it.

Running a hand through his hair, he let out a weary sigh. He couldn't help her. He didn't know how. She wanted to jump into danger again, face off with a deadly force destined to kill her—the yellow hyena, whoever or whatever it was. Maybe Eleanor, maybe not. What use could he be to her? To anyone? It's not like he could use his money to build a secret lair and amass cool gadgets to fight crime with under the cover of darkness.

Actually, he *could* do that, if he really wanted. His ability basically gave him access to an infinite supply of monetary resources. What would his superhero name be? The Fucking Fighter maybe? Sex Samurai? Magical Man-Meat Man—

"Jesus, I've had too much weed." Max sat up and rubbed the bridge of his nose, trying to pull his thoughts together, until a snickering cackle broke loose from his chest.

"What?" Aaron asked.

"Magical Man-Meat Man," Max said when he caught his breath. "That's my superhero name."

"That is really fucking weird." Aaron thumped his chest. "Mine's Count Doctopus."

"How is that not weird?"

"Count Doctopus has so much going on. It's a touch of aristocracy, a touch of intellect, and a touch of eight-legged freakiness for women who like that sort of thing. It's definitely better than Magical Man-Meat Man. What the hell is that even?"

"It's when...your dick can see the future."

Aaron nodded. "Ah, the all-seeing eye—the all-seeing One-Eyed Willie."

Max spit out another uncontrollable laugh, and they cracked up together until they ran out of breath.

"Oh my God," Max said, wiping tears from his eyes. "I need to get out of here." He was getting way too wasted, and too friendly with a guy he barely knew. But damn, it felt good. Too good.

He dropped his joint in an empty glass at the foot of the couch. Leaning over to reach the end table abutting the sofa, he pressed the intercom button on the phone perched there. When a waitress's smooth voice answered, he said, "Can I get a glass of water, please?"

"Of course, sir. I'll get that for you right now."

"Thank you."

Max fell back into the sofa, legs and arms splayed in a way that felt immensely comfortable but probably looked not so gentlemanly. The waitress would be scandalized. He'd sit up nicely when she got there. He'd try anyway.

Aaron's phone chirped. He had lots of friends who *holla*-ed at him often, though his annoyed sigh tipped Max off that it was the missus calling.

"Shit," Aaron muttered, confirming Max's suspicions. He let the phone fall in his lap and sank in his chair, head drooped to one side. "I gotta go. Lacy's going nuclear again."

"She thinks you're cheating on her." Max should keep his mouth shut, but he couldn't help himself. Aaron deserved to know if he didn't already. "She's hired someone to find out if it's true."

Aaron lifted his head off the loveseat. "Who?"

"I dunno." Max looked away.

"*Val?* You've got to be shitting me."

"I can't confirm or deny it."

"Goddammit, Lacy." With a heavy sigh, Aaron pushed himself off the chair, retrieved his jacket from the hook near the door, and began threading his tetrahydrocannabinol-addled arms through the sleeves.

"*Are* you cheating on her?"

Aaron scoffed. "You've met her. What do you think?"

"I think if the love is gone, you should end it."

"It's not that simple. And hell, I still love her. I can't resist a difficult woman." He glanced at Max and smirked. "Neither can you."

Wasn't that the truth. Though a more accurate term for Val would be *complicated*. Resistance was futile. He'd love her until the day he died. He hoped she felt the same about him, but her lingering anger with the people that stalked them—and with the whole goddamn world and every perceived injustice in it, for that matter—made him question what she really valued, and what she was willing to sacrifice for vengeance.

"You're not worried about her father?" Max asked, remembering that Lacy's dad was rumored to have ties to the Mafia, or actually be *in* the Mafia. He'd heard different versions of both scenarios.

Aaron shrugged. "A little." He smiled. "But you only live once."

Max supposed so, but he'd still rather not take the risk of crossing a mob boss. Then again, all those poor people living safe, uneventful lives who'd died in the bombing probably thought they had plenty of time to do something risky just for the hell of it.

A light knock on the door announced the waitress with Max's glass of water. She poked her head in and smiled politely at him as he still lay sprawled on the couch. Oh, right—he was supposed to sit up before she saw him like that. Damn. Despite how it pained his sluggish limbs to move, he forced himself into a proper sitting position and returned her polite grin as she handed him the water.

"Thank you," he said, and drank half the glass at once.

"Anytime, Mr. Carressa." She watched him for a moment as he chewed an ice cube. "Would you like another?"

"No 'ank 'ou," he said around the cube in his mouth.

She kept staring at him. Did she see something he didn't? He wiped his chin with the back of his hand to make sure he hadn't accidentally drooled on himself.

"Okay, well, if you need anything else, please let me know. Anything you need, really. My name's Annie. I'm just a phone call away."

"Yup, got it."

Finally she left. As soon as she was out the door, Aaron burst into snickers.

"What?"

"Holy shit, dude, you are a *fucking chick magnet*. How do you *not* cheat on your wife when beautiful women practically throw themselves at you?"

Max took another gulp of water. "Val's the only one who can handle my magical man-meat."

"Whatever, man. If I were you…look out, womankind." As he threw on his thick overcoat, he said, "A group of guys at my gym get together on Thursdays and play pickup games of basketball. Wanna join us?"

Play a *team* sport? That was a new one. Since he was trying new things lately, might as well give it a shot. "Okay. But I've never played basketball before."

"Seriously?" Aaron laughed. "Who *are* you?"

"A man who secretly fights crime with his penis."

Aaron waved dismissively at Max on his way out the door. "See ya at the office, Magical Man-Meat Man."

"Later, Count Doctopus."

As he left, Aaron called from the hallway, "My superhero name is better!"

Max shook his head. Aaron was right—his superhero name was better. He finished his water, set his glass on the end table, and rubbed his legs as if the stimulation would help him sober up. He could hang, but he was embarrassingly out of practice. It'd been decades since he had a real platonic friend—if he could call Aaron a friend. He definitely enjoyed the analyst's company, but they hadn't known each other for long. Then again, he'd known Val only a couple weeks before he'd realized he loved her. Whatever he had with Aaron seemed like friendship anyway. He'd spent the vast majority of his life keeping people at arm's length so they wouldn't discover his secrets. Spending time with Aaron, he began to realize what he'd been missing. It felt nice, having someone to be irresponsible and goofy with.

Standing, Max braced himself against the sofa's armrest, then sat again as the room slewed to the side a bit. He'd hoped the water would help him sober up enough to drive home, but it looked like that wasn't happening. Great, he'd have to call a cab and come back to get his car later. Val would be ecstatic.

He used the intercom again. "Can you bring me another glass of water, and call me a cab, please?"

"Right away, Mr. Carressa."

"Thanks," he said, rubbing his cheek. Maybe he'd take a nap there before he left.

A minute later, Annie came in. She carried a tray in her arms, on top of which was a glass of water and a package about the size of a hardcover book. She set her burden down on the end table and held his drink and the package out to him.

"This came for you," she said, shaking the object wrapped in plain red paper.

He took the water, then the package; certainly felt like a book. "Who sent it?"

"I don't know. Mickey said someone dropped it off. You must have a secret admirer! Probably lots of them…"

Max didn't like the sound of that. "Secret admirer" was another name for stalker. Shit, Eleanor hadn't sent this, had she? The last thing he needed was confirmation of Val's paranoia—or that Eleanor was the yellow hyena. He frowned at Annie, suddenly repulsed by her fawning over him.

Her smile slipped, as if she sensed he wanted her gone. "I'll let you know when your cab is here, sir," she said, and hurried out the door.

Setting the water down, Max set his jaw and unwrapped the package, praying he'd find something innocuous. It was a hardcover book, as he's assumed by the feel of it—a classic version of *Alice in Wonderland. From Val*, a sticky note on the front read. He turned the book over in his hands, fairly certain it wasn't actually from Val. For one thing, she didn't know where he was at that moment, though she could've traced his phone and found out if she really wanted to. But more importantly, she wouldn't send him a random gift with no explanation. If she wanted to apologize—which she probably didn't—she'd tell him to his face. Subtlety wasn't her style.

He flipped the book open, and something fell into his lap—photographs, he realized. Picking them up, he looked at them. They were—no. They must have been doctored. He looked at each one—five total—over and over again, cycling through them as if they might change with each viewing. The pleasant buzz he'd had disappeared, and his body went numb. Part of his brain disconnected, a terrible scream of rage trying to rise in his throat.

He heard somebody gasp, and tore his eyes away from the photos to see Annie in the doorway, staring at shattered glass amid a pool of liquid and ice at her feet. It was his glass of water. He'd thrown it.

* * *

Val awoke to the familiar sound of Max getting ready for work. So he'd returned home after all. She hadn't heard him come in; rolling over, she saw his side of the bed undisturbed. She'd hoped after three days he'd be calm enough to clear the air about what happened between them the night of the memorial service, but if he'd slept in the study again last night, he must still be pissed. Val sat up, stretching and kicking her legs over the side of the bed as Max yanked a tie from the closet and stomped to the other side of the room behind her without making eye contact.

Yep, still pissed.

After taking the kids—and her mother and Jamal by default—to visit Santa in the morning, she planned to spend the rest of the afternoon pounding the pavement for Eleanor. Since it was Saturday, she could go to the ferry terminal and ask if any of the employees working there knew Eleanor. It was a long shot—the boat commuted thousands of people back and forth across the Sound every day—but worth a try. She'd stake out the ferry all night if she could, but Max was prone to wandering off without telling her lately, and leaving her kids alone with her unstable mother was out of the question. She needed to conduct her investigation in small chunks.

She'd already questioned Eleanor's coworkers at Jones's and gotten nowhere. That left Aaron as the only person with a connection to her, and Max would be even angrier if Val jacked up his friend. Hopefully it wouldn't come to that, but mending bridges ahead of time would be a wise move.

Taking a deep breath, she closed her eyes and thought for a moment about what she should say. She needed to extend the olive branch, even if she thought she'd only done what was necessary.

"I'm sorry about what happened the other night," she said. "I shouldn't have asked you to—"

She heard papers slap against the bedspread next to her. Opening her eyes, she saw Max standing in front of her, his arms folded and face a mask of cold fury.

"What are these?" he said, his voice calm but words so sharp each one might have been a tiny dagger of dread stabbing her in the heart.

She looked at what he'd thrown on the bed at her side, and her breath caught when she recognized photos of her and Sten. Feeling the blood drain from her face, she picked up the first one, a shot of her and Sten through the window of his apartment as she straddled him on his bed, mid-coitus. The next one was the same location, same situation, but a different position—Sten had her pinned against the wall in this one. Underneath that picture, a wide shot telescoped in as he went down on her in the back of his police cruiser. Then one of her entering his apartment, when she'd gone there to ask him about her mother. The final shot was of her and Sten sitting across from each other at Tully's coffee shop, the date—this month—clear on a chalkboard to the side of them advertising peppermint mochas.

Oh God. How many more of these were there? Who took them? The first three had been taken during their twisted fling five years ago, but the final two were from the last few days. Someone wanted Max to think they were all recent, and she was cheating on him with his enemy.

Val's mouth hung open as she stared at the pictures shaking in her hand. "It's—it's not what you think—"

"Then what is it?"

"I—I—" She swallowed, her throat so dry she could barely speak. "This was—it was a long time ago, when we weren't together. I mean, I went to talk to him recently, but—but just talk, to ask him about my mother, if he knew anything about her, because he's connected to Northwalk and he would know, and nothing happened then. Of course nothing happened."

He was silent for a moment, destroying her with his withering glare, arms still crossed over his chest like a shield as his fingers tightened against his biceps. "If nothing happened, why didn't you tell me?"

Laying the pictures facedown on the bedspread, she put a hand over her mouth to keep from hyperventilating. Oh Jesus. Why did he have to find out like this? Could Sten have slipped him the pictures? What did he have to gain? It must have been part of Eleanor's harassment campaign against them. But where had she gotten the pictures?

"I knew you'd be angry," she said, barely able speak. "It's Eleanor. She's trying to hurt us. I don't know why, but she is. I was in her apartment. I found her journal—"

"That doesn't explain why these photos exist."

She choked out the only response she could give. "It was a long time ago."

He turned away, walked to the closet, and jerked a suit jacket out with such force the hanger it'd been draped on boomeranged off the rack and bounced against the wall before falling to the floor.

"Let me know when you think of a good excuse for fucking the man who tried to kill me twice," he spat as he shoved his arms into the coat sleeves.

"Max, please—"

He stormed out of their room before she could say any more, his heavy footfalls filling the silence he'd left behind.

Chapter Twenty

I haven't had one of these in years!" Dani said as she chewed on a miniature candy cane. "Almost forgot what they tasted like."

Waiting in the mile-long line to visit the FAO Schwarz Santa Claus in downtown Seattle, Val ignored her mother as she held Simon and Lydia in place with an iron grip, both children pulling in opposite directions. Mentally, she was too busy fighting the permanent sick feeling that lingered in her stomach after her fight with Max that morning, and the memory of those horrible pictures he'd shown her. It took all her concentration to focus on anything else, and she would've paid a small fortune not to be surrounded by screaming children, blaring Christmas music, and her mother's idiosyncrasies.

Val sighed as the line inched forward for the first time in ten minutes. After advancing two feet, it stopped.

"Oh, *come on*," Val mumbled under her breath. "Pick two things you want from Santa and move on, Jesus. How hard is that?"

She should have hired a Santa Claus impersonator to come to

their house and made up an excuse about Saint Nick getting lost on his way to the North Pole. It's not like she and Max couldn't afford it. But no, she had to drag them to the toy store to get the "real" experience, as if having her mother around spurred in her a need to show her kids how normal parents acted. Big mistake.

In fact, she should've canceled the ill-advised trip all together. She pushed back another wave of anxious nausea. How could she explain her involvement with Sten to Max? She hadn't actually cheated on her husband, but she'd violated his trust by having any kind of relationship with Sten, sexual or not, without telling him. Maybe she could convince him to sit down with her at a private dinner at home, sending the kids to bed early and bribing Dani to stay in her room with a pile of candy canes—

"I wanna look at Santa's workshop," Simon whined, pointing to a play area off to the side of the extended platform the whole Santa operation was set up on. The workshop included toys and games to keep kids busy while their parents saved their spots in line for two or more hours.

"I won't be able to see you from over here," Val said. With the crush of holiday shoppers all around them, she could barely see five feet ahead of her.

From behind her, Jamal said, "I'll take them."

Val frowned. It was one thing to leave the kids alone with the nanny in the safety of their own home, but quite another to let them wander off in a public place. Eleanor was still out there, being crazy and doing God knew what evil things.

"Please?" Simon and Lydia said in unison, their big puppy-dog eyes appealing to her softer side.

She knelt in front of them and asked at a volume only they could hear, "If I let you go over there, what will happen?"

"We'll play," Lydia said matter-of-factly.

"Then what? Will you be safe?"

They looked at each other, then back at her, meeting her gaze with blank stares as if they didn't understand her question. Despite their preternatural abilities, they were still only children. And they couldn't see every future event—yet. Thank God for that.

Simon smiled. "We'll be okay, Mommy."

It was the best response she could hope for. With some reluctance, she nodded at Jamal. "I'll text you when I can actually see Santa. Come back if there are any problems at all. And don't let them out of your sight."

Jamal nodded back an affirmative. He knew the drill by now. Val let go of the twins' wrists, and they shot like cannonballs into the crowd toward Santa's workshop, Jamal rushing after them. Glancing at her phone, she considered calling Max. The ambient noise was too great for a conversation, unfortunately. They really needed to talk. I'm sorry, she texted him. I can explain. Plz call me. I love you.

Sighing, she was about to shove the phone back into her coat pocket when it rang in her hand. Her heart lifted—thank God, Max wanted to talk—then sank when she saw it was from "Asshole," her call sign for Sten. Maybe he called to gloat about those fucking photos.

She turned away from her mother for as much privacy as she could get. "What?" she snapped as she held the phone to one ear while plugging the other with a finger to damp down the background noise.

"Why are you always so full of holiday cheer?" Sten said. "It's like Santa shoved a candy cane of happiness up your ass."

"*What* do you want, Sten?"

"Thought it might interest you to know we got a hit off Eleanor Fatou's fingerprints. Multiple hits, actually."

Val gasped. *Yes.* "And?"

"Katie Lee Edwards, picked up for prostitution in Michigan fourteen years ago, then again three years later as Donna Lords in Montana. Questioned in the disappearance of a couple of her Johns, but never charged. About seven years ago, as Julie Mars, police questioned her in connection to a nightclub fire that killed twelve people in California. Then six years ago, questioned again about a commuter bus crash in Chicago, three people dead. Four years ago, Lisa Higgins, questioned about a boating accident off the coast of Florida, three people drowned. Two years ago, same drill: Rachel Peirce, two guys found in a Dumpster behind the restaurant where she worked."

He took a breath, as if rattling off the long list of Eleanor's alter egos had left him winded. "And there you go. Never charged with anything. No known family. No history of terrorism. Just always in the wrong place at the wrong time, poor girl. Kind of like you."

"Don't compare me to her." That woman left a trail of destruction wherever she went...which *was* kind of like Val. But the big difference was Val never caused any of it, whereas Eleanor definitely did, whether or not it could be pinned on her. "So you're going to pick her up for the Thornton Building bombing?"

"That was terrorists, remember? I don't have an excuse."

She scoffed. "Bullshit."

"You're welcome."

"Bring her in."

"One, we don't have a current address for her on file. Two, I don't work for you."

"Who *do* you work for, Sten? People who like to take pictures? People who like to torture Max and me for fun? Is that what you want from me? To see me suffer?"

He responded with silence, a rarity for Sten. After a few seconds, he said, "You have yourself a fun family day," and hung up.

Rubbing the bridge of her nose, she slipped the phone into her pocket and tried not to scream. Eleanor had literally gotten away with murder, over and over and over again. How was Val supposed to stop a woman who really *did* seem protected by a divine force? Be nice if Max could help her figure this out, but of course he wouldn't, not with those fucking pictures still fresh in his mind. The second she got out of that damn toy store, she'd find Max, force him to sit down with her and talk about all the things that had driven them apart recently. She just had to make it through the next hour or so of picture-line agony.

Tapping her foot, she glanced at Dani finishing off her candy cane. "You really don't remember what mint tastes like?"

Dani shrugged. "I had a bigger one a few days ago, but they taste different than the tiny ones. I don't remember a lot of things. I don't recall the last time I celebrated Christmas. I do remember when I got you and Chloe matching My Little Pony dolls, though. Always had to get you girls two identical things. Otherwise, you'd fight over the same damn one." She smiled and shook her head as if recalling a fond memory. Touching Val's shoulder, she said, "Remember that, pumpkin?"

"I spend a lot of time trying to forget the past, actually." Val took a breath and tried to calm her anger at her mother's selective rose-colored memories. Of course Dani remembered the good things and ignored the bad—because she'd *caused* a lot of the bad ones.

Dani's grin fell away. "Oh." She bit her lip and cast her gaze downward. "I wish you'd tell me what I can do to make things right."

"What do you want me to say, Mom?" Val tried to keep her voice down so the crush of people surrounding them wouldn't get an earful. "You disappeared for thirty years. Your own daughter committed suicide and you couldn't be bothered to go to the funeral. How do you make that right?"

Dani blinked away tears, but thankfully didn't burst into sobs in the middle of the store, as was her usual MO since waltzing back into Val's life.

"I went to Chloe's grave once," Dani said with a trembling voice. "I wasn't on meds yet, so moments of lucidity were few and far between. But I had one, and then I learned one of my children was dead. So I found out where you and your father laid her to rest, and I traveled there to see it for myself."

Val looked into her mother's wet eyes, trying to gauge Dani's sincerity, but all she saw were her own eyes, the ones she'd inherited, staring back at her. "When?"

"I don't remember exactly. Ten years ago maybe? It was raining that day, a soft sprinkle. The air smelled like dead leaves. The ground felt mushy under my feet, but the grass sparkled. And I remember thinking I could easily dig into the soft ground with my bare hands until I reached the casket, opened it, and lay inside, then covered myself up with dirt, and no one would know what happened. No one would miss me. I wouldn't miss me.

"I actually started grabbing fistfuls of earth until a cemetery worker caught me and told me to leave. Then after that, I don't remember. But if I'd been in my right mind, that's what I would've done—lay down with your sister and never left. That's where I'd be today."

As "Deck the Halls" played through the intercom above them, Val imagined what it might be like to wake up from a coma only to discover one of your children had died. Falling back into the coma might be preferable. Her mother's story made sense. In the same situation, she doubted she'd act any differently.

"I'm glad you didn't do that," Val said, her words soft, "and you're here with us now instead."

"Oh, pumpkin, you don't know how happy it makes me to hear you say that."

For the first time in thirty years, Val smiled lovingly at her mother.

"Sometimes I imagine I still have two daughters, like opposites, and you just don't know about each other—"

"Can you two move up, please?" an irritated voice said behind them.

Val turned to see a balding middle-aged man scowling at them as he held a fussy little boy in place. In front of her, the line had advanced another two feet.

"Yeah, yeah," she muttered as she stepped forward to fill the gap. She looked back at the man again, something about him tickling her memory. He looked familiar…Where had she seen him before?

Then she remembered—her last vision with Max. He'd been one of the people she had seen die, falling to his death before being buried by debris.

With her heart suddenly in her throat, she scanned the crowd around her. There was the Asian man who would be crushed to death, twenty feet behind her. The woman who would hit the ground so hard she'd bounce lingered to Val's far left, chatting on a cell phone. And eight groups ahead of them, the man wearing the Rudolph sweater with the nose that lit up stood with a family of four in matching outfits.

The platform they all stood on was about to collapse.

Chapter Twenty-one

Barely able to breathe, Val grabbed her mom's arm. "We need to get out of here *now*."

"What? Why?"

"We just need to go!"

Oh God, the children. Where were the children? Val raced toward Santa's workshop, shoving her way through the thick crowd, ignoring people's cries of surprise and angry glares. Frantically aware of every second that ticked by, she burst through the periphery of the endless line, where kids of all ages entertained themselves playing with toys and activity books or pawing at a row of touch screen video games. Spotting Simon coloring at a table in the corner, Val sprinted to him and scooped him up.

He yelped as crayons fell out of his hands. "Mommy, I'm not done yet!"

"Where's Lydia?"

"Is there a problem?" Jamal asked from where he stood supervising a few feet away.

"Where is Lydia?"

"She was over by the video games a second ago. I just saw her—"

"Lydia!" Val screamed when she didn't see her daughter near the touch screens. "*Lydia!* Goddammit, Jamal, find her now!"

Jamal gaped at Val for a second, panicked that he'd failed to do his one job but also confused as to why it was suddenly an emergency, until he pointed behind her. Val turned to see Dani round a corner, clutching Lydia in her arms as she hurried toward them.

"Get to the exit!" Val yelled at Jamal and Dani. "*Run!*"

Without knowing why, they did as they were told, crashing through the throng of holiday shoppers in a mad dash to reach the edge of the platform. Val tried not to look down so she wouldn't see a little girl with a big red bow in her hair, a toddler in a tiny suit, a woman pushing a double stroller with twins inside. Jesus, all these families. She had to get them off the platform somehow. If she started screaming about its imminent collapse, people would either think she was crazy or a mad panic would ensue, or both.

She'd pull the fire alarm. That way, everyone could assume it was a false alarm while making an orderly exit off the platform and out of the building. It would work.

But her own children came first. *I'm sorry*, she thought as she forced her way past other people's children. Tears stung her eyes. *I'm sorry. I'll save you, too. I promise.*

Ahead of them, the exit sign beckoned like a life raft; below it, the fire alarm. Three more steps…two more steps…one more step—

When her hand touched the fire alarm, she heard a crash behind her so loud she thought the entire building had come down around them. She hit the ground, shielding Simon's body with her own as the rumblings of disaster seemed to go on forever, a freight train of terrible noise that drowned out all rational thought. Finally it stopped, and then the screaming began.

"Simon," Val said, lifting her head so she could see his face. He stared back at her with terrified eyes. "Are you all right?"

He gave her a succession of quick nods. "Mommy," he whimpered.

She looked up, taking in the total chaos around her. "Lydia," she called. To her left, she saw Jamal slowly sit up, his face pale and frozen in shock, eyes glassy. A cacophony of shrieks rose around them. "Lydia!"

Ten feet away, strands of dark hair made a trail that led under a body covered in dust and small pieces of debris, lying askew on the ground where the floor that connected the platform to the main building had bowed downward under the strain of the collapse.

"Mom?" Val choked the words out. "Lydia?"

The body stirred, batting away pieces of plaster, and Val recognized her mother lift her head. In a daze and sporting multiple cuts on her face, she coughed and pushed herself up. Lydia lay underneath her, unconscious.

"Lydia!" Confident her son was out of danger, Val scrambled to her daughter. She knelt next to Dani and caressed Lydia's cheek with a shaking hand. "Oh, no. No no no."

Dani grimaced and clutched her left arm. "Something hit us," she said, her words strained by pain. "I blocked most of it, but...I think it might've got her a bit in the head."

A sob borne of the most intense dread Val had ever experienced began to claw its way up her throat. "My baby..." She stroked Lydia's unresponsive face. "My baby..."

Don't panic. Do not panic. Her daughter was still breathing, still alive. *It'll be okay. Lydia will be fine. Simon said they'd be okay.* In case she had a spine injury, though, Val shouldn't move her—

The sob ripped its way out of Val's throat. She slapped a hand over her mouth to stifle the wails that followed, until her hysteria passed and she gained control of herself again. Her own cries were just one of many. Daring to glance down at the collapsed platform, she saw a sea of bodies, some moving, some not. From between the cracks in a pile of debris, Rudolph's nose blinked. Somehow the tiny light hadn't broken. It might've been the only thing that hadn't.

***

Val paced the area around Lydia's hospital bed while Max sat in a chair and held their daughter's hand. Though she was still unconscious, the doctors assured them Lydia hadn't suffered any skull fractures or cranial hemorrhaging, but they wouldn't know for sure if she was really okay until she woke up. She'd been out for four hours so far, brought to the pediatric clinic at the Harborview Medical Center along with dozens of other children who'd been injured in the "accident." The place was a freaking madhouse of panicked parents and family members. Max's sister Josephine had been kind enough to take an uninjured Simon home with her. After being treated for shock, Jamal went home, too, probably to retool his résumé for a new job. Thanks to Dani's heroics, Lydia had escaped relatively unscathed compared to most of the other kids—assuming she woke up.

Come on, Lydia. You're my strong girl. Fight. You can do this. Wake up. Wake up. Wake up—

Someone knocked on the door. A moment a later, a tired-looking doctor walked in. He gave Val a weary smile. "Hi, Mrs. Carressa. I understand you wanted an update on your mother's condition?"

"Yes—yes, please."

"Her ulna was fractured in two places, and her ribs were badly bruised. She's being fitted for a cast now. No life-threatening injuries, thankfully." The doctor smiled again, and Val got the sense he was happy to give somebody good news that day.

"Thank you. When she's ready to go, please let me know. I'm her ride home."

The doctor nodded and left. A television on the wall showed the local news, dominated by the toy store tragedy. "At least twenty-nine people dead and sixty-four injured," a somber reporter said. "Sources say the company that erected the platform is fully cooperating with police to understand how the structure could have collapsed, though authorities suspect a flaw in the platform's design is responsible…"

"Bullshit," Val said to the TV. She turned to Max. "It was *her*. I know it."

Max met her gaze with exhausted eyes, his face pale and grim. For the moment, it seemed, he'd put aside his anger with her to focus on their children. "Why would she do this?"

"Because she's a fucking psycho! I was in her apartment a couple days ago and found a journal of her crazy-ass ramblings. We're talking Kevin Spacey in *Seven*-level nuts."

His gaze wandered back to Lydia. "Why us?"

"Because she's obsessed with us, and she thinks God and somebody named Mother are telling her to torture us. Because for some reason we attract evil people. Because the fucking universe hates us!" She resumed pacing, stomping in circles like a caged animal, hot anger scorching through her veins. "I'm going to kill that evil bitch. And if they're real, I'm going to kill Father and Mother, and then Northwalk and Delilah while I'm at it. Every single one of them—"

"We should leave," Max said. He looked at her again, a dull sheen over his eyes—worried and tired, but not angry.

Val scoffed. "You *still* don't believe we're her target?"

"I believe you. And we should leave."

He couldn't be serious. After everything that'd happened to them, he wanted to just *leave*, as if Eleanor wouldn't keep hounding them for the rest of their lives?

"I am *not* running," she said through gritted teeth. "If you want to, take the kids and go."

Still gripping Lydia's hand tight, he gazed at his daughter's still face for a moment, then back at Val. "I can't leave without you."

She slammed her hands down on the foot of Lydia's bed. "Why do you have to do this? It doesn't matter what happens to me! Evil people are doing evil things, making the world a worse place, and somebody has to do something, Max! And why am I the only one who's angry, huh?" He'd killed his own father in a fit of rage and almost beat her rapist to death, for Christ's sake. He was capable of fury so intense it sucked the air out of the room. "Why aren't you angry?"

He didn't answer, just looked at her with weary, sad eyes.

"Daddy?"

In unison, Max and Val snapped their heads toward their daughter. Lydia blinked as if waking up from a deep sleep. Val ran to the bedside and knelt next to Max, putting her hand on top of her husband's holding their tiny daughter's hand.

"My baby girl," she said with breathless relief. "How do you feel?"

"Okay," she replied with childish uncertainty, not sure what the right answer was. "Where's Santa?"

"He...um—"

"Does anything hurt?" Max asked. "Your arms? Your legs? Belly?"

Lydia shook her head. "Is Santa okay?"

Val laughed through her tears. "He's fine. He flew back to the North Pole."

"I didn't get to tell him what I want for Christmas."

"He'll get the message, honey." Letting out a long exhale, she lay her head on Max's shoulder as the vise around her heart finally relented. Their children were okay—for now. *We'll be okay, Mommy*, Simon had told her right before the collapse. He'd been right after all.

"Ah, excellent!" Val heard the pediatrician say as she walked in the door. The doctor stood at the foot of the bed and smiled at Lydia. "You had a long nap. How you feeling, kiddo?"

Lydia smiled back. "Good."

"That makes me happy to hear. I'm going to check some things on you, okay?"

"Okay."

Val and Max stood and backed away to give the doctor space to take Lydia's vital signs. Things seemed under control at the hospital—for *their* daughter anyway. Other innocent children still struggled for their lives, thanks to Eleanor. How long until she struck again? Would she blow up the hospital? Their home? Each act of terror brought her closer to killing them. How long before she finally succeeded?

She wouldn't—if Val got to her first.

Max threaded his fingers through hers as if he sensed her intentions. "Don't go," he said. Despite how she'd betrayed his trust, he still wanted to be with her—his love trumped his anger.

She squeezed his hand and looked into his beautiful eyes as they pleaded with her, warm hazel with starbursts of green at the centers. Simon had inherited those eyes. He'd gifted both children with his genius-level intelligence, though their abnormal abilities made them seem even smarter than they actually were. Max had passed on the best parts of himself to his children, and together they formed a family she would kill to protect.

"I need to go to Jo's and check on Simon," she said.

"Then you'll come back?"

Val looked at him for a long moment, then said, "When we're safe from Eleanor Fatou."

Their entwined fingers slipped apart as she turned and walked away from him, out of the hospital, and out for blood.

* * *

You will wait until the final whistle notifying everyone to prepare for debarkation at Bremerton. Take care, child, for the red raven is hunting you, just as you intended. You'll walk through the crowded ferry, then descend the stairs to the control room. Before you go through the door, you'll screw the silencer onto the muzzle of your handgun. Then you will burst through the door and quickly kill all three officers in the control room. Find the throttle in the center of the main console. You'll push it all the way forward, up to maximum. After the crash, you'll find the red raven, a fly caught in your trap.

Do this for me, my child. Do not question. Obey your Mother and Father, and all your sins will be forgiven.

Chapter Twenty-two

Max knocked on the half-open door to Michael's hospital room, then stuck his head inside when he heard the old man answer.

"Max, my boy!" he said with a warm smile. "Come on in, I want to show you something."

Max pulled up a chair next to Michael's bedside. Each time Max visited him, the Carressa Industries CFO was in good spirits despite having lost his left arm below the elbow in the explosion. "I finally have an excuse to not go to work," Michael had told Max in his typical tongue-in-cheek fashion. If only Max could borrow some of that bottomless joy.

Michael held his phone up for Max to see, on its screen a picture of a prosthetic arm with a gold hook for a hand. "This one is made by a guy in Belgium. Nothing says 'classy yet humble' like a simple artisan prosthesis. I could have gone with the diamond-encrusted hook, or the hand made of white rhino horn. What do you think? Does it bring out my eyes?"

"It's nice," Max said with as much enthusiasm as he could muster, which was none at all.

Michael took a good look at Max for the first time since he'd walked in, then frowned. "Holy shit, boy. What the hell happened to you?"

Max swallowed hard as he felt something begin to unravel inside him. "Lydia was hurt in that toy store accident today."

Michael's face contorted from mild to deep concern. "Jesus Christ. I'm so sorry. How is she?"

"Some debris hit her in the head and knocked her out for a while, but she's awake and okay now. Well, she's asleep at the moment, but it's normal sleep. The doctors say she'll probably be fine."

Michael put a comforting hand on Max's slumped shoulder. "You have shit for luck, you know that?"

"It's not bad luck. Someone is coming after us."

"If you think that's true, you should go to the police."

"We don't have any real evidence. They won't believe us, and we don't trust them." Max rolled up his shirtsleeve, running his fingers over the Julia fractal tattoo. "The Julia set of equations changes drastically with only small perturbations in variables—it's chaotic. But there's an opposite set, which repeats and doesn't change when the variables change—the *Fatou* set." He rolled up his other sleeve and looked at the Davis-Knuth set—the twin dragon. Their vulnerable children. "Val thinks she can deal with it herself, but I don't think so. Not this time."

"Why don't you help her then?"

Max's throat tightened as tears built in his eyes. His hands fell to his lap. "I can't help her," he said, the words like little razor blades in his mouth. "She's so angry. I can't convince her to prioritize saving *us* over hurting our enemies, and I'm losing her. She asked me why I'm not angry like she is. I'm not angry because I'm scared. I'm losing her and I'm scared." A sob worked its way up his throat. "I'm scared—"

Uncontrollable sorrow spilled out of him, and he buried his head in his hands and cried like he hadn't done since his mother died twenty years ago. Everything he'd been holding in came out—the pain of those poor people who'd died in the Thornton Building explosion, the devastation of Michael's horrific injury, the shameful brutality he'd leveled on his own wife in their bedroom after the memorial service, the humiliation of having those pictures of her and Sten dropped in his lap when he'd had no clue, his terror at Lydia and Simon's brush with death, his exhaustion with the unending chaos of his existence. He couldn't face his painful life without her. She was the glue that held him together, the piece of his soul that grounded him in this world. Now he felt himself coming undone, reverting to the man he'd been before he met her, the one who'd existed in a black hole of despair, eager to die.

Without another word, Michael pulled Max toward him, and Max sobbed into his shoulder.

* * *

Parked on the side of the street, Val watched Aaron pull into the driveway of his McMansion-style house in Bellevue. Her whole body trembled with anger as she jumped out and stalked to Aaron as he got out of his car.

Idly sipping a cup of coffee, he did a double take when he saw her walking toward him, then yelped when she grabbed him by his lapels and slammed him against the car, coffee cup flying out of his hand.

"*Where is she?*" Val growled into his stunned face.

"W-who, Lacy? She's probably in the house—"

"The woman you're fucking on the side. *Eleanor.* Where is she?"

He gawked at her for a moment, probably deciding what was more important to him—keeping up the façade of his happy marriage or his physical well-being. Val jerked him toward her and then shoved him into the car again, to make the decision easier for him.

"I don't know!" he spit out. "She's gone. She said she had to leave, and didn't tell me where she was going."

"Don't fucking lie to me. She just killed a bunch of people at the toy store in Seattle, so obviously she's not gone."

"She did what?"

Val's fists tightened against his lapels. "What does she do in Bremerton on Saturdays? Where does she go when she's there?"

"I don't know. I've never met her there before."

"How do you contact her?"

"I leave a message on an answering service, and then she calls me back."

"Call her now. Tell her to meet you somewhere."

"She's not going to respond. She's gone—"

"Just do it!"

He gawked at her with wide eyes, not moving. He thought she was crazy.

"Eleanor just tried to kill me and my children at the toy store. She tried to kill Max with a bomb in the Thornton Building."

"She couldn't have done those things—"

"I will kill *you* before I let her kill *us*. So you'd better call her and tell her to meet you. Now."

The only response he gave her was a slight shake of his head. He wouldn't do it; he probably thought Val was angry enough to kill Eleanor, which was true.

With a snarl, Val slugged Aaron in the face. He pitched sideways and hit the ground. That's what he got for protecting a murderer. She heard him groaning as she walked away. Max would never forgive her for roughing up his one friend. But she had to try any way possible to get Aaron to talk, her only tangible connection to Eleanor. Now she had none.

* * *

After the hospital discharged her mom, Val picked her up and went home. Leaving Dani to her own devices, Val ran upstairs to change out of her Santa photo-op clothes of a cashmere sweater with leggings and into her ready-to-kick-someone's-ass outfit of jeans and a hoodie. She knew Eleanor took the ferry to Bremerton on Saturday evenings. If she staked out the ferry, she could intercept Eleanor, and make sure one way or another the woman never had another chance to hurt her children. If Eleanor thought she could rely on Val's moral compass to give her an edge, she picked the wrong fucking opponent. No one hurt Val's family and got away with it. *Nobody.*

As Val pulled on her boots, her cell phone rang—Stacey. She answered, the need to hear her friend's voice, like a balm on her battered psyche, too strong to ignore.

"I heard a rumor in the news you guys might've been at that toy store collapse this morning. Please tell me it's not true."

"Yeah, it's true."

Stacey gasped. "Are you okay?"

"I'm fine. We're fine. I mean, Lydia was hurt, but she'll be okay."

"Can I do anything for you?"

"Uh…" They used to make a great team when they ran Valentine Investigations together. They'd each take a piece of a case, split up to pound the pavement for answers, then regroup to compare notes and eat chocolate together. That is, before Val went and blew it all up by being a shitty friend.

"Just tell me what I can do to help," Stacey pleaded. "I—I need to do something good."

What did she mean by that? "You're visiting your family for the holidays, that's good."

"It's not enough."

Val glanced at her watch. Shit, she had to go. She didn't know exactly when Eleanor would board the ferry besides being sometime in the evening, and the window of opportunity was about to open. As much as she wanted Stacey's help, she couldn't put her friend in danger… Well, maybe Stacey could give her a hand in a relatively safe way.

"Meet me at the Seattle ferry terminal."

"The ferry? Why?"

"I think someone rigged the toy store platform to collapse, and I think that same person is going to get on the ferry to Bremerton tonight."

Stacey gasped. "Are you fucking kidding me? Why the hell would anyone sabotage a toy store?"

"Because they're batshit crazy, that's why. Listen, I have to go try to stop more people from being murdered by a maniac. You don't have to help me or put yourself in danger—"

"I'll see you there." Stacey hung up.

Oh God. Val appreciated her friend's help, but if another of her loved ones was hurt trying to help her, she didn't think she could live with herself.

As Val ran down the stairs, she heard her mother ask from the kitchen, "Leaving so soon?" Dani held a cup of tea with her good arm, the other arm wrapped in a cast from fingers to elbow and propped on the kitchen table.

"I have to run an errand. I'll be back soon."

"Picking up Simon from your sister-in-law's house?"

"No."

Dani frowned at Val slipping on a shoulder holster. "Where are you going?"

"I…can't really explain right now. It's complicated, and I'm short on time."

"Oh." Dani stared into her tea, the pain of being kept in the dark plain on her face. "Maybe you should bring a knife. They're less…loud."

Val walked to her mom and put a hand on Dani's shoulder. When Dani lifted her gaze, Val said, "I'm sorry, Mom. It really is a long story. But I want to thank you for what you did for Lydia today. If you hadn't been there, she might have died." Val choked up at the thought. "I can't thank you enough. I mean that."

Laying her hand on top of Val's, Dani smiled. "We're family. You would've done the same for me."

No, Val wasn't sure she would have. Not before that morning anyway. Now maybe.

"I'll be back soon, I promise." Val threw on a leather jacket over her hooded sweatshirt and headed for the carport.

"I love you, pumpkin," Dani said as Val was walking out the door.

Val stopped and looked back. She didn't know what to say. *I love you, too, Mom.* The words wouldn't come out. It didn't feel right yet. Val lowered her head and walked away. For that moment, it was the only response she could honestly give.

Chapter Twenty-three

W iping icy rain off her coat, Val walked into the busy ferry terminal and headed straight for the ticket counter.

"Which of these ferries goes to Bremerton?"

The woman on the other side of the Plexiglas looked up from her computer. "The *Kaleetan*."

"Give me a ticket to that one." She shoved a twenty under the glass and checked her watch; the ferry would sail in five minutes. "*Now*, please."

The woman huffed. "Well, *someone's* an Anxious Alice." She took about a hundred years printing out the ticket, then slipped it to Val. "There you go. Have a nice—"

Val snatched it up and ran toward the loading ramp, ignoring the ticket lady's cries about her change.

"Val!"

She stopped and turned to see Stacey waving at her from the middle of the terminal. Stacey jogged up to her and gave her a quick, tight hug.

"What do you want me to do?" Stacey asked.

"I'm looking for this person." Val showed Stacey the picture of Eleanor. "I'm getting on the ferry to look for her, but if you see her come through here, text or call me. Don't approach her. She could kill you."

"Got it. I'm the lookout."

"Thanks, Stacey."

Her friend nodded, and they hugged one last time before Val took off for the loading dock. She crossed onto the ferry without a second to spare, the pedestrian ramp disengaging right after she set foot on the deck.

Okay, she'd made it. Now to find Eleanor—if she was even on this trip. Val knew Eleanor would be on a nighttime ferry ride, but this ferry had four more trips to make that evening. Val walked the perimeter of the ferry before she searched the interior, scanning for any sign of yellow hair or red lips. She repeated the process two more times on each deck, even the car transport area.

"Shit," she muttered to herself when she came up empty. No sign of Eleanor. The ferry was just too big for one person to effectively canvas the entire thing. She could ask Stacey to help her, but that would be too dangerous. Keeping an eye out for Eleanor at the terminal was a nice, low-risk task. Maybe today would be the day Eleanor decided not to take the ferry. If she was quitting her job and cutting ties with old clients, she could have left behind whatever brought her to Bremerton as well, and this was another lead that would go nowhere.

As Val stalked the ferry, growing more frustrated by the second, she saw a Native American man with a face carved out of granite, wearing an orange vest with the green "T" decal for Washington State Ferries on it. He walked a few feet, jotted something down on a clipboard, and repeated the process through the length of the ferry—some kind of inspection.

She approached him. "Hey, this boat is the *Kaleetan*, right?"

"Yup," he said without looking at her.

"Going back and forth between Bremerton and Seattle?"

"Yup."

Val showed him Eleanor's picture. "Have you seen this woman?"

"Nope."

"What if I told you she was the woman responsible for the toy store collapse this morning?"

Finally he looked at her, though his face didn't budge from its stony expression. "I'd tell you to report that information to the police."

"Let's say I came by this knowledge though a visit from my spirit animal—the red raven."

"That's offensive stereotyping, ma'am."

Sighing, she rubbed the bridge of her nose as hopelessness and exhaustion began to set in. "Sorry"—she glanced at his name tag—"Ed. I've had a long day. I think I'm cracking. Which deck is the coffee on again?"

"Deck One." He reached into his pocket and handed her a voucher for one free cup of joe. "You need it more than I do."

She smiled at the gesture. "Hey, you'll tell me if you see this woman, won't you?"

The granite of his face reshaped itself as one eyebrow lifted. Then he wordlessly resumed his inspection. At least he didn't seem to recognize her.

Val grabbed coffee from Deck One and sipped it as she circled the ferry, showing anybody who looked like an employee the photo. They all shook their heads. No one recognized Eleanor.

A whistle blew. "Attention, attention. Debarkation will begin in ten minutes. Please gather your personal effects and return to your cars. The *Kaleetan* crew thanks you for sailing with us today." As everyone filed off, Val lingered, scanning every face she could see, which was only a fraction of all the passengers.

When it seemed as if everyone had debarked, Ed approached her. "You need to get off now," he said with zero affect.

"Yeah, yeah." Val left the boat, immediately bought tickets for the next four round trips between Seattle and Bremerton, and got back on. When Ed saw her again, he blinked—his version of a polite greeting.

"Seen an evil-looking blond woman yet?" she asked him.

He walked away, probably officially sure she was crazy.

Once again she searched the ferry as best she could, and once again, no Eleanor. She repeated the process over the next two round trips, until her mouth tasted like stale coffee and her eyes burned with fatigue. As the last group of people got off in Seattle, she allowed herself to sit down on an upholstered bench in a quiet corner for a moment. Not long ago—a matter of days, really—she'd been happy. Mostly happy. The feeling wouldn't be complete until she wiped the evil people who threatened her family off the face of the earth. And that might never happen. *This* was her life—the frantic struggle, the constant worry, the burning anger. The years in between had been the exception.

Simon looks at me with tear-filled eyes. "Help me, Mommy! Please help me—"

"Attention, attention. Debarkation will begin in ten minutes. Please gather your personal effects and return to your cars. The *Kaleetan* crew thanks you for sailing with us today."

Val's eyes snapped open, and she sat up from where she'd been slumped against the bay window. Hadn't they just arrived in

Seattle a few minutes ago? Watching people pick up their stuff and shuffle toward the exit, it hit her—she'd fallen asleep. Son of a bitch.

Forcing her weary body to stand, she dug her phone out of her pocket and gasped, feeling the blood leave her face—three missed calls and four texts from Stacey. *I think I see her. She's getting on the boat. What should I do? Are you getting this?*

While Val had been *fucking asleep*, Eleanor had got on the boat. She was here somewhere.

A shot of adrenaline kicked Val's senses into high gear. She rushed up and down the length of the boat, fighting against the crush of people meandering toward debarkation and cutting off her line of sight. Could be Eleanor wasn't even on this deck. *Goddammit*—then Val saw it on the other side of the boat—the yellow hair, the red lips. *Eleanor.*

Val bolted after her as she disappeared down a skinny stairwell. Descending the metal stairs, Val stopped for half a second at a door marked "Control Room—Authorized Entry Only," which stood partly open. Eleanor wouldn't go in there; she'd be trapped if she did. So why was it open—

The sound of running footfalls farther down the stairs caught her attention. She kept going down until the stairs ended at a door that led into the car transport area, rumbling as people turned on their engines in preparation to drive off the boat. Through a gap in the vehicles, she caught a flash of Eleanor running to the other side of the ferry. Val took off after her, weaving through the maze of cars, and saw Eleanor disappear through another door, going up. Taking the stairs two at a time, she burst through a door on the top deck, ran halfway down the aisle, and stopped, frantically scanning for any sign of Eleanor. Where the hell could she have gone?

"Ma'am?"

She spun around to see Ed looking at her, the thin lips on his stony face turned down a hair in disapproval.

"Did you see her?" Val asked as she worked to catch her breath, her heart still hammering in her chest.

"Who?"

"The blonde! The evil blonde!"

"The ferry is about to dock in Bremerton. You need to proceed to the exit."

"She was *just here*…"

Ed turned away from her, suddenly distracted by the approaching city lights outside. "Strange," he said to himself. "Why aren't we slowing down?" Then his usually expressionless face warped into terror. He dropped his clipboard and sprinted away from Val, toward the other side of the boat…toward the control room. Something happened there. Eleanor had *done* something, and Val had been too busy chasing her to investigate, even though she had known the control room door hanging ajar couldn't be right.

I failed again, she thought as shock numbed her body. *I had a chance to stop her, and I failed. Now people are going to die.*

A terrible force jerked the entire ferry backward. Val pitched forward over a bench and landed hard on the other side, then slid along the linoleum until she slammed into the base of the next bench over. The loudest scraping noise she'd ever heard filled the ferry as everything around her shook violently. After about an eternity it stopped, and there was eerie silence.

Sucking air back into her lungs, Val pushed herself to her knees, then her feet. She stood in a daze for a moment, looking around the empty deck with sluggish eyes. All she could hear was the rasp of her own breathing. Was she dreaming again?

Something warm ran down her face; she touched it and saw blood on her fingertips. She must have hit her head at some point, though she didn't feel any pain.

What now? *Do something. But I don't know what to do. But I should do something. But I don't know what to do*… She walked onto the outer deck and stumbled to the railing, looking over the black waters and then to the lights of the shore, where a cacophony of screams and sirens began to rise. The ferry had rammed the dock.

"Val, look out!"

Was someone yelling at her? Still in a fog, she turned just in time to see Eleanor about thirty feet away, pointing a gun straight at her, as Stacey grabbed the woman from behind. Val heard the high-pitched *pew* of a bullet pushed through a silencer, and flinched at the clink of the bullet ricocheting off the metal railing a couple feet away. Shit, Stacey had followed Eleanor onto the boat after all, and she'd just saved Val's life. And now Eleanor was about to kill her.

At once, the world snapped back into focus. *Oh God, Stacey.* Val sprinted toward them as Eleanor wheeled around and easily kicked Stacey away. Stacey stumbled backward and landed hard on her back, then threw up her arms as Eleanor trained the gun on her. A fraction of a second before she could pull the trigger, Val tackled her. The two women tumbled to the ground, the gun falling from Eleanor's hand and sliding across the deck. In a murderous rage, Val punched Eleanor twice in the face, drawing blood from those evil red lips. On the third swing, Eleanor deflected Val's fist and followed with a palm strike to her jaw and a knee to her ribs. So Eleanor knew how to fight, too. Great. While Val was distracted for half a second by the pain, Eleanor took the opportunity to flip Val onto her back and land a couple punches to her cheek, then shoved a forearm into Val's neck and leaned in, choking her.

"You know what's in Bremerton?" Eleanor hissed through clenched teeth as she pinned Val down. "The deaths of all these people. *That's* what's in Bremerton."

Val reared up and slammed her forehead into Eleanor's nose. Eleanor cried out and jerked backward, and Val shoved the woman off her.

They both jumped to their feet at the same time. With blood running down her face from cuts on her cheek and nose and a furious snarl on her face, Eleanor lunged for the gun where it teetered on the edge of the boat only a few feet away.

"Stacey, run!" Val yelled, a moment before Eleanor got her hands on the gun, and pointed it at Stacey.

"*No!*" Val threw herself into Eleanor before she could pull the trigger, and the women tumbled off the side of the ferry together.

The icy water hit Val like a sledgehammer. The shock of it froze her for seconds that felt like years. From all sides, death tried to seize her in a cold embrace, until her arms and legs fought free and struggled frantically for the surface. Her head popped out of the water, and she gasped for air amid a barrage of lights and sounds, and something that might have been Stacey's screaming. She spotted a smear of color in the distance—the shore, too far away. *Swim*, she ordered herself. *Swim there, and don't stop.*

She flailed her numb limbs until her body started moving toward the dock, toward life. Slowly the sirens became louder, the flashing lights brighter. Her energy waned as if she were sprinting a marathon, sucked out of her through the barely above freezing waters of Puget Sound.

Keep moving, goddammit. Keep moving. Keep moving. Keep moving—

Her arms and legs thrashed against something hard, and she realized it was rocks against the edge of the waterfront. She'd made it. With the last bit of strength she had left, she pulled herself out of the water and collapsed at the base of the pier. Then she felt herself lifted somehow, over the edge of the dock and onto pavement.

"We've got another one over here!" someone yelled.

Val opened her eyes to see two medics leaning over her. One wrapped her in a thermal blanket, and she was lifted again, then set down at the edge of an ambulance with warm air blasting out the back. Feeling slowly returned to her body, and she began to shake so hard, her teeth chattered.

The medic held up his index finger and moved it back and forth in front of her face. "Follow my finger if you can," he said.

Val did as she was told.

"What day of the week is it?"

"S-S-Saturday."

"Where are we?"

"B-Bremerton."

"Good," he said, apparently satisfied she was in her right mind. "What's your name?"

"Jane."

"Do you feel pain anywhere, Jane?"

Val shook her head.

"Good. Sit here and warm up. I'll be back in a few minutes, okay?"

She nodded, and he ran off to join the chaos of injured people, emergency workers, and confused and panicking bystanders. Val sat at the edge of the ambulance until her shaking subsided and her mental and physical strength were replenished enough for her to consider her options. Reaching inside her coat, she wasn't surprised to find her waterlogged cell phone dead. She'd need to call and check on Stacey, though it looked like Eleanor hadn't been able to seriously hurt her friend before they fell overboard, thank God. At least she still had her cash and credit cards, soaking wet but functional. Eleanor was nowhere in sight, and Val wasn't in a condition to search for her. And she couldn't allow herself to be recognized at yet another disaster scene. What if Ed told the authorities what she'd said to him? They couldn't pin anything on her, but she didn't need the scrutiny.

Taking a deep breath, she dropped the blanket, walked inside the ferry terminal, and used a pay phone to call a cab.

"You one of the people in the ferry thing?" the cabbie asked in a thick Middle Eastern accent, looking at her through the rearview mirror.

"No."

After a minute, he asked, "Need to go to the hospital?"

"No."

Her whole body began to shake again, and she thought she might grind her teeth down to nubs.

First, Eleanor had committed an act of terrorism by blowing up the Thornton Building, almost certainly to kill Max. Then, she tried to burn down a church by somehow murdering an old man and making it look like a natural death, and the resulting fire an accident. Then she collapsed the toy store platform, knowing Val and her family would be there, on that day at that time…and then she crashed the ferry—

To lure me here.

She knew exactly when Val would be at the toy store, and she knew exactly when Val would be on the ferry. She knew exactly how to get away with murder. Holy shit, Eleanor was a *seer*, like Max and Val. She must be. How else could she always be one step ahead? But why was she targeting them? She couldn't be an agent of Northwalk; those bastards wouldn't risk the children's lives. Maybe Mother had sicced her on Val's family—but again, why?

Why was a question she could think about while standing over Eleanor's dead body.

She should have brought a knife for close quarters combat. Now Eleanor would kill again, to get at Val, and it would be Val's fault. Next time, she'd show no mercy. No mercy for anyone.

Chapter Twenty-four

Eleanor tightened the bonds around Aaron's wrists and ankles, checking to make sure the connecting straps were secure around the bedposts.

"I can't stop thinking about the ferry crash yesterday," he said, "and the toy store collapse, and the Thornton Building explosion. It's fucking terrible, like the city is cursed or something."

"Yes, terrible," she said. "The city *is* cursed."

"You know, my friend's wife thought *you* were responsible for the bombing and the toy store disaster somehow. Crazy, right?"

"Very crazy."

"I don't have the heart to tell him his spouse has lost touch with reality. She wanted me to call you and lure you somewhere. Got this fat lip for saying no." He frowned. "What happened to your face?" His hand twitched as if he wanted to touch her cheek.

"Another client." She wrapped a black silk scarf around his eyes, then kissed his forehead.

"That's not right. You shouldn't put up with that."

"I know. I didn't." Eleanor looped a length of nylon rope around his neck and lay the ends loose across his chest.

"Can you make it tighter?"

"Not yet."

She ran her fingers up the length of his naked body. Goosebumps sprang up in their wake across his skin, and he let out a trembling breath full of anticipation. Already she saw him growing and hardening, aching for release.

"Tell me what you feel," she said. It was obvious what his body felt, but she inquired about his soul. He knew what she meant. They'd done this before.

"Guilty."

Sliding her leg across his waist, she straddled him and caressed his chest. "Guilty of what?"

"Cheating on my wife."

"And what will you do about it?"

"Keep cheating. I can't help myself. I'm weak."

"We're all weak in some way." She took his manhood in her hand and stroked it into a solid spear, then pierced herself with it. He let out a rapturous moan and bucked his hips as if he'd changed his mind about their dominant-submissive agreement. Too late for that now. She was in control, and always would be. "Repent, and you will be forgiven."

"I repent," he said, his voice husky as she moved on top of him, piercing herself over and over again. "I repent. I repent."

"I forgive you." She grasped the ends of the rope tied around Aaron's neck. "Tell me what else you're guilty of."

"Misplaced pride." He jerked when he felt the nylon move across his skin. A shiver rippled up his body. "I lost friends in the Thornton explosion. I watched their families cry at their funerals. I felt horrible for them. But the truth is, I'm glad it wasn't me. I still value my life over theirs. I shouldn't, but I do." Though she couldn't see his eyes, she heard the tears in his voice. "I'm thankful to be alive while they're dead. I'm weak."

Looping the cord once around each hand, she slowly began tightening the rope around his neck. "Repent."

"I repent," he said, his words choked.

She thrust him into her harder and faster, until pleasure and pain were one. It was the only way she could reach Him. "*Repent.*"

"*I...repent...I—*" The rope around his neck was too tight to allow any more words to come out. He thrashed underneath her, fighting against his bonds.

"*Repent!*"

Finally he stiffened, and she felt his sin spill into her. She gladly accepted it as no one else could—it was the fuel for her divine journey. Ironic that man's sin provided her reason for living after she'd been born with nothing, forced to sell her body, and then discovered her holy gift. Before, she was a lost little girl with an alcoholic, horny stepfather, until she felt the rapture for the first time and He spoke to her. Then Mother found her, another agent of God who'd been told by Him of Eleanor's special connection, and guided her along God's path. She didn't always understand why God made her do the things He asked, or the things Mother asked, but she was forever their servant. Both of them wanted the red raven and the ebony fox to suffer. Mother said it was because only through their suffering would the children be vulnerable to Him, even though Father had not shown the children's deaths to her yet. No matter. She always obeyed. It was her *purpose*. She closed her eyes and reached for Him, her light in the storm, her real Father—

You'll stand at the busy intersection of Mercer Street and Fairview Avenue. He'll be across the street from you, in his fancy car and his fancy clothes. He'll spot you and his weakness will consume him. You will beckon him toward you. He will come, and his journey back to me and the path of righteousness will begin.

Come with me, child.

You will open your eyes and look down upon the man who brought you to me as he basks in your glory. You liked this one more than the others, but you must bring him to me. I have great plans for him. You will kiss him good-bye, then tighten the rope around his neck until he is with me.

Do not despair, child. Your quest is almost complete. Soon you will fulfill your destiny, and I will reward you with everlasting happiness.

Back on the wicked earth, Eleanor opened her eyes and looked down at Aaron. With the rope loosened, he breathed hard underneath her, a satisfied grin on his lips.

"Oh God," he said, breathless. "That was exactly what I needed. Thank you."

"You're welcome." She took hold of the rope again, gripping it with white knuckles. No matter how it pained her, she must obey. It was His divine will. "Go with God, Aaron."

"Wh—"

She jerked both ends tight, and the rope snapped taut around his neck. He struggled beneath her legs, bucking and thrashing so hard, he almost knocked her off. But she gritted her teeth and held fast until finally he stilled. She fell forward, exhausted from the effort. Pushing the blindfold off his face, she looked into his bulging, lifeless eyes, staring at the ceiling. Droplets of water landed on his cheek and trickled down his skin, and she realized they were her tears. She truly had liked him the most.

Eleanor leaned down and kissed his blue lips. "I've given you a gift," she said. "Walk with Him now. And when you enter paradise, remember me."

She slid off him, found her cell phone, and dialed.

"I need your help," she said when Mother answered. "Father ordered me to give him a man's life, and I obeyed. Now I have to do something with his body."

"I understand. Where are you?"

"My apartment in Tacoma."

"Take only what you need and leave now. I've got someone in the area already. They'll come by and clean up."

"Thank you, Mother. I love you."

"I love you, too, child."

Eleanor hung up, put on her clothes, and gathered her very few personal possessions. On her way out the door, she glanced at the husk Aaron's soul had left behind, and felt a pang of jealousy. Soon it would be her turn—after she purged the world of the evil that defied His will. Then Valentine Shepherd and her vile children would be in His hands, and suffer eternally in Hell, as they deserved.

Chapter Twenty-five

Stacey paced outside the Seer's office and chewed her finger-nails, forced herself to stop when she realized what she was doing, then repeated the process. Why would Cassandra want to see Stacey, of all people? Though she hoped to marry into the family, she wasn't really part of Northwalk. First and foremost she was Kat's girlfriend, not a Northwalk employee. Honora definitely didn't consider her to be anything more—when Kat's mother acknowledged her existed at all, which wasn't often.

It didn't help she was still worried about Val. She'd nearly had a heart attack when Val tumbled over the railing. After ranting like a madwoman to a cop about her friend in the water and the crazy lady who tried to kill her, she'd received a simple text from a number she didn't recognize:

It's Val. Cellphone is dead. Went home, am fine. Sorry I got you into this.

Val didn't know Stacey was *already* in it, though to what degree even Stacey herself didn't know for sure. But she vowed to find out. If anything, Val deserved to know if Northwalk was planning to fuck with her or her family.

She gave the two guards standing sentry at Cassandra's door a polite, weak smile. They didn't reciprocate. All business, these assholes. Seemed about a million of them stalked the mansion, a private army inside a virtual fortress. One would think if you had someone who could see the future, you wouldn't need protection because you'd always know when danger was coming, but apparently it didn't work that way. Since the Alpha could see all *possible* futures, she saw them being attacked and not being attacked at the same time. Which event came to pass depended on a bunch of variables Cassandra was quickly losing the ability to describe in ways that other human beings could understand. That was the gist of it anyway, as Stacey understood from what Kat explained. And since Northwalk had oodles of enemies, they traveled heavy, ready for anything.

As Stacey considered coming back at a time when the Alpha wasn't preoccupied, Honora burst out of Cassandra's office. Half a dozen lackeys trailed after, furiously taking notes.

"Fucking *Yongjai*," she spat at the grunt closest to her.

Stacey recognized the name as a rival organization based out of East Asia. She and Kat had stolen some of their mail in Hong Kong two years ago; why the mail had been important, she had no idea. At the time, she'd been happy to remain blissfully ignorant.

"I want to know how the hell they got those plans, and I want to know *now*. Find out which flight their agent is on and crash it into the ocean. That should send a message."

Noticing Stacey for the first time, she fell silent and fixed Stacey with a glare that could flash-freeze Hell. Stacey had never been the timid type, but at that moment she would've gladly crawled underneath a rock to avoid those eyes.

"I have an appointment," Stacey mumbled, pointing at Cassandra's door.

The awful glare continued for several more agonizing seconds, until Honora finally asked, "What are you again?"

The insult gave Stacey an injection of confidence. "My *name* is Stacey, and I'm your daughter's fiancée."

Honora cocked her head as if observing a lab specimen. Then the side of her face began to melt.

What in the actual *fuck?* To the right of her nose, from her hairline to her jaw, Honora's skin started to sag off her skull like melting wax. Frozen, Stacey couldn't look away. Was the Northwalk matriarch a *zombie?* Should Stacey run? What was happening—

A lackey hustled forward with a jet injector and shot something into Honora's neck. In a blink, the skin snapped back into place. Everyone acted as if nothing had happened—except Stacey, whose mouth still hung open. With the most dismissive little laugh, Honora turned from Stacey and continued her march away from Cassandra's office, entourage in tow.

Jesus, what have I gotten myself into?

"Come in," came Cassandra's breathy English accent.

Stacey sucked in a trembling breath, pulling herself together enough so she wouldn't be a total ball of nerves in front of the Seer.

"Um, hi," she said as she stepped inside the large, Spartan space. Besides the simple glass desk sandwiched between a couple steel chairs, the only other thing in Cassandra's office was a strange contraption shoved in the corner. The thing consisted of a laptop computer hooked up to some kind of machine made from thousands of wires and tubes. Beyond a huge window, miles of pristine evergreen forest fanned out to the horizon.

"Go with Julian when he performs his tasks today," the Seer said from where she stood behind the desk, staring out the window.

"Kat's brother?"

"Yes."

"Ew. No." That guy gave her the willies every time he looked at her. No way would she willingly be alone with him. Kat said he wouldn't hurt her, but she wasn't convinced.

Cassandra turned toward Stacey and looked at her with blue eyes as deep as the ocean. "You must pass a test. This is the only way."

"What kind of—"

"You must go with Julian. When you do, you will have two options—choose love, or do not. It is important you choose love."

"Why is it imp—"

"If you do not, you will lose everything you hold dear."

"Can I just choose love now?"

"No. Go." Cassandra turned away, staring out the window again.

Stacey frowned. All this cryptic crap was a pain in the ass. Why couldn't anyone be straight with her? This must be what Val felt like, ping-ponging between different people's master plans with little to no understanding of what the hell was going on.

She turned to leave, then stopped to ask the Seer one last question. "Is Val actually important to…whatever is happening here?"

Cassandra faced her again. "She is important to me."

She still didn't know what that meant, but it didn't sound good. No wonder Val was paranoid—though no one in North-walk had mentioned Val, Max, or their kids yet, at least one person still had Val on her mind.

Before Stacey could suppress her gag reflex and go find Julian, she swung by her and Kat's bedroom. Confirming her girlfriend was gone but Kat's laptop was still there, she stepped inside and locked the door. She flipped open the computer and typed in Kat's password with trembling hands, glancing at the door as if Kat would somehow come storming through it despite needing to unlock it first. Stacey knew her snooping was a major breach of trust, but Kat had started it, jerking her around for the last five years with omissions, half-truths, and outright lies. Maybe she wouldn't find anything incriminating. A part of her hoped that'd be the case, and she could go back to her blissfully igno-rant state. But she had to know what Kat and Northwalk were really up to, and if it was worth tolerating Kat's deceitfulness and her creepy family until the succession happened.

When the desktop screen materialized, Stacey began clicking through files as fast as possible, looking for any related to Val. Most files held information on Northwalk's business dealings, like meeting schedules, accounts transactions, travel itineraries, etc. All boring, innocuous stuff—until she reached one file la-beled "Insurance." Opening it, Stacey assumed she'd find life or property insurance policies consistent with all the other crap, but instead she found text messages, saved as a text file, between "Norm" and "Gino."

Could they be Norman Barrister and Giovanni Dinapoli, Delilah's dead husband and the man who'd supposedly stalked the Barrister family and killed Norman? Stacey knew the official version of events wasn't true—Val had killed Norman in self-de-

fense, while Gino had been working for Norman to swing the
Seattle mayoral election Norman's way. And these texts proved
it. Holy shit, if this got out, everyone would know Delilah's version of events was a big, fat lie. Her career would be ruined. Kat
must have kept the texts in case Delilah ever stepped out of line.

Insurance indeed.

Val would wet her pants with excitement over this information. She could use it to keep her family safe. Stacey would need
to come back and save the text file to a memory stick, along with
some kind of video also in the folder, but that wouldn't be hard,
now that she knew what she was looking for.

A knock on the door sent Stacey nearly jumping through the
ceiling.

"Uh, yeah?" she said as she scrambled to shut down the laptop.

"Claire's female friend, I'm leaving now," Julian answered
from the other side of the door. "The future waits for no one."

"Fuck," Stacey muttered, cringing at spending an entire day
with a psychopath, at the insistence of a crazy woman. The
sooner she got the hell away from these people, the better.

* * *

Val, I need to meet with you to talk about something important. So, I haven't been completely honest with you...I'm
engaged to Kat, who works for Northwalk. Before you get
mad, I found some info on her computer that I think you
should see—

Sighing, Stacey deleted the way-too-detailed text. What
could she really say? *Sorry I lied to you, I knew you wouldn't like*

the truth—kinda like why you didn't tell me I'd died—but com-
pared to the weird shit I'm dealing with now, it seems kind of petty.
We're still friends, right?

Speaking of weird shit, she glanced at Julian, dressed in designer jeans and a black leather jacket, as he drove the nonde-
script sedan to parts unknown. As far as she knew, all he'd been
told was that she needed to assist him in some way, and he
seemed to accept the order without question. Then again, Stacey
had no idea what his mission was or how she was supposed to
help him, so they were both in the dark.

"Are you going to tell me where we're going yet?" she asked
him, not for the first time.

"An associate's place in Bellevue."

"Why?"

"Housecleaning."

She didn't like the sound of that. Anything described as
"cleaning" by members of a probably evil organization couldn't
be good.

"Cassandra must think you're a whiz with a mop," Julian said
with a little sneer.

Stacey threw him some shade from the passenger's seat, but
stayed quiet. Best not to encourage him. The sooner this stupid
test was over with, the better.

He glanced at her. "Have you ever had sex with a man?"

"*Excuse me?* In what universe is that any of your business?"

"I'll take that as a no. Men have so much to offer. Pleasurable
ridges, free hands. You're really missing out."

"You make a very compelling case for the opposite of what
you just said."

He laughed. "I like you. You're feisty. Maybe that's why
Claire's keeping you around. She doesn't normally hold on to

her flavors of the month this long. Either that, or she's got plans for you."

Stacey looked away, cringing and seething at the same time. Kat claimed her plan was to marry Stacey when she took over the family business and turn it into a force for good, but fucking Julian was probably right. Kat had a plan, and it wasn't what she'd told her girlfriend.

"How many other flavors have there been?" she asked, knowing she wouldn't like the answer but unable to resist.

"Oh, you know how us *men* are. I can't count that high."

Fuck him.

Stacey stayed silent for the rest of the ride, loathing every second she was forced to endure his presence, until finally they pulled into a plain brown apartment complex. He parked, grabbed a small blue duffel bag from the backseat, and looked at her. "Coming in or not?"

She'd rather not, but she had a goddamn test to take, so she got out of the car and followed Julian like Cassandra had told her to. They walked to the second floor, where he stopped in front of an ugly brown apartment door. Giving the door a quick once-over, he reared his leg back and kicked it in. Stacey flinched as wood splinters from the jamb flew through the air, the door banging against the opposite wall. *Way to be subtle, Julian.* Anyone in their immediate vicinity would've heard the noise. She prayed they'd be in and out of there before someone came to investigate.

At first the apartment looked unoccupied, until she noticed a piece of paper on the kitchen counter. Picking it up, she recognized it as a ferry ticket from two days ago, when the crash had occurred.

"Whose apartment is this?" she asked Julian.

"That of a valued associate." He went to each room, ripping the smoke detectors off the ceiling and popping the batteries out. Then he opened his bag, pulled out a bottle of something, and poured its contents on the living room carpet.

"What are you doing?"

"Helping our valued associate." Plucking the ferry ticket off the counter, he used a cheap lighter to set it on fire. "Little slow on the uptake, are we?" He dropped the flaming ticket on top of whatever he'd poured on the floor. A small fire sprang to life and began to grow.

Stacey recoiled from the blaze. "What the—there are other people who live here! You could kill them!"

He furrowed his brow at her, as if she'd made a shocked declaration that the sky was blue. "You *are* slow. Feisty, but slow—"

"What in the world…" someone said from the doorway.

They turned to see a wide-eyed man looking back and forth between them and the fire. He opened his mouth as if he might yell, and a lightning-fast Julian grabbed him by the shirt and flung him into the apartment. Julian closed the door quietly behind him. The man scrambled onto his back and crab-walked backward, his face a mask of panic. Stacey jumped when something touched her back, and she realized it was the wall. She'd backed into it, desperate like the poor man to get away. But Julian blocked the only exit. All she could do was stand there and watch in horror whatever was about to happen.

Julian pulled a combat knife from the back of his pants and tossed it at the man's feet. With a hint of an evil smile, he said, "If you can fight your way past me, you can leave."

The man gaped at Julian, then picked up the knife with shaking hands and stood. Julian didn't prepare to fight or even move; instead he watched the man like a curious zookeeper. White-knuckled, the man gripped the knife in his hand, the tip of the blade facing up, and desperately lunged at Julian. With no resistance from Julian, he buried the blade in his antagonist's stomach. Julian grunted in pain but didn't move for a moment, apparently enjoying the man's confusion. Then Kat's brother pulled a switchblade from his pocket and plunged it into the man's neck.

Stacey stifled a scream as Julian drew the blade back and kicked the man's lifeless body away from him at the same time. She ran for the door, but Julian was there again, leaning against it as if he were chatting up a sorority girl at a frat party.

"And where are you going?" he said as blood oozed out the wound in his belly, the combat knife still sticking out of his coat. To her right the fire grew, licking at the dead man's body.

"Let me out of here now, you fucking psycho." Her whole body shook with anger and fear.

"Okay. But I need your assurance you won't overreact."

Barely able to breathe, she choked out, "I don't want any part of this."

"Really? Because you already have a big part of it. What do you think your girlfriend was up to while you waited around in fancy hotel rooms for her like a good little fuck bunny? She's left an impressive trail of bodies of her own. Should I clue the police into those unsolved murders, or do we have an agreement of mutual benefit, partner?"

Stacey looked into his ice blue eyes—the same as Kat's, and Honora's—unable to break his gaze, as if she were a rabbit being stared down by a snake. The right thing to do was to say no. Let Kat accept the consequences of her actions, if what Julian said was true. Leave Northwalk and the whole terrible family business behind. But despite all the lies, she still loved Kat.

Choose love, Cassandra had said. Shit, this was the test. *If you do not, you will lose everything you hold dear.*

Swallowing hard, Stacey nodded at Julian's request.

"Say it."

"We have an agreement, all right, asshole?"

With a cold smile, he said, "Good." He opened the front door. "After you."

She hurried out of the apartment, walking as fast as possible back to the car. Jumping into the passenger's seat, she forced herself to calm down and *think*, dammit. Okay, Northwalk was *definitely* evil. No question about that now. Whatever Kat's loyalties were to her family, they had to get out—together. If the upcoming succession didn't result in severing all ties with her girlfriend's psychotic kin, then...Stacey would have to leave.

Choose love.

She'd figure something out. She had done what the Seer told her to do. It made her skin crawl, but it must have been better than the alternative.

A couple minutes later, Julian slipped into the driver's seat and took a deep, satisfied breath. He admired a small lump of something in his hand before dropping it into his pocket. Stacey's stomach turned when she realized it was one of the dead man's molars. Goddammit, putting up with this freak show had better be worth it.

He put the key in the ignition with a trembling hand, his face pale from blood loss.

"As your *partner*, it's my duty to tell you that you shouldn't drive if you're going to pass out." Maybe he'd bleed to death and she'd be free of his particular brand of nightmare.

"Don't you worry." He pulled the knife out of his gut. Reaching into his small duffel bag, he took out a jet injector like the one his mother had used. "This is the best part." He picked out one of several vials of blue liquid in the bag, inserted it into the injector, and shot the stuff into his neck. He cringed and convulsed for a couple seconds, before relaxing and sitting up straight in his seat.

"All better!" He lifted the bottom of his coat and flashed his stomach at Stacey. Where there had been a deep stab wound was now smooth, unbroken skin. So that's how he got his rocks off—letting his victims seriously wound him, then healing himself with the weird miracle drug Kat mentioned earlier. It made him basically immortal. That was fucking fantastic.

After throwing the injector back in the bag, Julian checked his cell phone. "Pick up in Tacoma. No rest for the weary." He put the car into reverse, and they were off to cause more murder and mayhem.

Jesus, she had to stop him. But how, without sending Kat to jail? Shoot him in the back when he wasn't looking? She wasn't a killer. She didn't even know how to use a gun.

Then what am I doing with him?

I'm choosing love. Choosing love…

Stacey sent a text as Julian drove: *Val, it's Stacey. Can we talk?*

Chapter Twenty-six

The moment Val stepped into the Pothead, Stacey sprang up from a table in the back and embraced her in a tight hug.

"I'm so glad you're okay," Stacey said, eyes wet as if she held back tears. "What happened to that woman who attacked you?"

"Hopefully she'd dead, but I'm not that lucky." Val rubbed the back of her neck, exhausted and still sore all over from her plunge off the ferry and fight with Eleanor—and looking like shit again.

"I'm sorry, I can't stay long. I promised Max I'd meet him in a few minutes to take Lydia home from the hospital." She and Max were already on shaky ground, having never truly reconciled or talked about the horrible pictures. At least he finally believed they were in danger. Without asking her, he'd hired bodyguards to stand watch outside their condo. How was that supposed to help against a woman who could see the fucking future? But he'd just ignored her protests, not even bothering to fight about it. Now she had to tolerate a couple blank-faced goons lurking right outside their front door, and who knew where their true loyalties lay. So things were tense between them, to say the least. Failing to honor her promise to him now could result in a rift they might never be able to close. "What did you want to talk about?"

"Yeah, um, let's sit down."

As Stacey fidgeted with the buttons on her coat, Val sat and frowned. Whatever Stacey had to say, she guessed by her friend's nervousness it wasn't good. The last thing she needed was more bad news.

"So"—Stacey licked her lips—"so when I told you I was here visiting my family for Christmas, that wasn't really true. I'm actually here with Kat."

Did Val hear that right? "Wait—the Kat who lied to you, and then planted a bomb in your car that almost killed a bunch of people?"

"Yeah, but…she had to, okay? Her family forced her to do it."

"Her *family*? Who?"

"Uh…Northwalk."

Val sat frozen for a moment. *You have got to be fucking kidding me.* "And you're working for them?" she asked, a new chill in her voice.

"No. I'm Kat's girlfriend, that's all—her fiancée, actually." She scoffed at Val's angry glare. "Don't tell me you've never compromised for love."

"I've never done anything evil," Val spat.

"Really? Not even all those times you pretended to have romantic feelings for me? Or that time I *died* and you didn't tell me?"

Val gritted her teeth as a pang of guilt shot through her. "So this is your way of getting back at me?"

Stacey sighed and shook her head. "Look, I'll admit it. I did want to get back at you by running off with the girl of my dreams, like you'd run away from me with the guy of your dreams. But now I realize that was stupid and shortsighted. It was good for a while—*really* good—but there were strings attached that I'd been ignoring until now, because I *can't* ignore them anymore. I love Kat, but her family is up to some seriously evil shit, and I can't stick my head in the sand and do nothing anymore."

If Stacey thought her excuse about working with Val's mortal enemies in the service of true love would garner Val's sympathy, she was wrong. Those people had manipulated her and Max's lives as if they played with dolls, killing, hurting, and threatening everyone she loved to fulfill whatever their twisted agenda was—world domination or some other shit. Val thought she'd had her best friend back after five long years, but it'd all been a lie, probably to gain her trust and make her vulnerable. Maybe Stacey didn't even know she was just another one of Northwalk's puppets now.

"Where are they?" Val asked. Might was well squeeze her *former* friend for information while she had the opportunity.

"A giant house in the woods. The head of Northwalk is Kat's mother, and she's going to hand the organization over to Kat in a few days, in some sort of succession ceremony thing. Then Kat will make it less evil—I think. That's what she told me, but—I don't know what to believe anymore. I need to *choose love*, so I'm giving her the benefit of the doubt for now. But I found some info on a computer at the Northwalk compound, about—"

"Where's the compound?" Val's voice cracked, tears she couldn't control building behind her eyes.

"They're only going to be here for a few more days. Why does it matter?"

"Because I'm going to go there and kill them all."

Stacey's eyes widened. "Val, come on. That's crazy. Just wait and let Kat and me turn it into a force for good. Besides, the place is a fortress. There's an elaborate security system and guards everywhere—"

Val shot up from her seat, nearly knocking over her chair. "Fine, don't help me. And don't ever talk to me again."

She turned and walked out, ignoring Stacey's pleas for her to come back and curious stares from other people in the coffee shop. When she got back to her car in the parking lot, she slammed the door closed, took a deep breath, and let out a ragged sob. Wherever Stacey had been for the last five years, Val had taken comfort in the hope that they could someday work through their differences and reunite. They'd been friends almost their entire lives. Now, like a punch to the gut, she realized that would never happen. Her best friend was truly gone.

Her phone chimed with a text. Wiping tears off her cheeks, she prepared to immediately delete any texts from Stacey, though it could've also been an impatient prodding from Max, wondering where the hell she was. It surprised her to see the sender as "Asshole"—Sten. She'd come to realize contrary to Sten's laidback, smarmy demeanor, he never did anything only for shits and grins. There was always a method to his madness. He wouldn't text her if he didn't have something important to relay.

Had he sent those pictures of their past fling to Max? She couldn't think of a good reason why he'd do that; maybe he was about to give her an answer.

Dreading whatever it was he had to say, she read the message:

Got a big fan here down at the station dying to meet you. Better hurry. She won't be here long.

Val's breath caught. *Eleanor.* Hot damn, he'd caught her! Of course, there was a good chance Eleanor had allowed herself to be caught as another way to lure Val into a trap, but she couldn't pass up the opportunity to question the crazy woman terrorizing her family. She'd explain it to Max later. Val started her car and took off toward the Seattle Police Department headquarters.

Chapter Twenty-seven

Val flipped the hood of the door, but could not make out the words. She caught half of them and then all the rest as soon as the voice was in position. She was certain he would recognize her. She then heard the Seattle Police Department headquarters.

Val flipped the hood of her sweatshirt over her head as she walked into the police station, praying no one got a good look at her. Most people there, if not everyone, would recognize her. Hell, some of them had personally arrested and interrogated her after the Pacific Science Center shootout six years ago, and then the showdown with Lucien in the Westford warehouse nine months later. The whole goddamn police department was intimately familiar with both her and Max, thanks to the death and mayhem that constantly dogged them.

I'm here, she texted Sten, then headed toward the interrogation rooms in the back of the station. She moved with confidence, pretending she belonged there so she wouldn't look suspicious—until she got to the locked Interrogation Area door and had to stand awkwardly in front of it, waiting for Sten to let her in.

"Hey," someone's gruff voice said behind her.

She turned enough to get a glimpse of him out of the corner of her eye—a big man with close-cropped blond hair and a detective's cheap suit, walking toward her.

"What're you doing here?" he asked.

Head down, she mumbled, "I'm waiting for someone."

"Well, you shouldn't be in here. Go wait in the lobby."

When she didn't move, he gripped her arm and yanked her toward the exit. Just as Val was about to punch his grabby ass, the interrogation room door swung open and Sten stepped out.

"Where're you goin' with my crack whore, Kirby?" Sten said to the detective dragging Val away.

Kirby stopped and looked down at Val. She turned her head away, pretending to cower so he couldn't see her face. From beneath the sweatshirt's hood her gaze met Sten's, his dark, sharp eyes a stark contrast to his bored facial expression. He really was an amazing actor.

"She your informant or something?" Kirby said, still keeping an iron grip on her arm.

"No, I use the phrase 'my crack whore' as a term of endearment for all the ladies."

After a couple seconds, she heard Kirby give her a dismissive sniff before shoving her toward Sten. "Keep your informants on shorter leashes next time."

"She's on *crack*, Kirby. My instructions go in one ear and smoked out the other."

Gritting her teeth, Val stomped past Sten into the Interrogation Area. He followed, closing the door behind him.

Throwing back her hood, she slapped him in the face.

He flinched in surprise. "Hello to you, too."

"Did you send pictures of us to Max?"

Raising an eyebrow, he asked, "Pictures of us doing what?" After correctly interpreting Val's seething silence, he said, "*Oh.* Huh. We should've figured. I told you what would happen if you took your anger out on me."

With a grunt of rage, she slapped him again. She might as well have tapped him on the shoulder for all the pain she'd seemed to cause him. Instead, he took her aback when he looked at her with eyes smoldering with desire.

"You'd better stop that. I thought you didn't want to have sex again."

She felt her cheeks heat up. He was right; her unbridled rage and the need to take it out on somebody had been the genesis of those stupid pictures to begin with. Not that they'd ever fall into bed again, but—well, best not to tempt fate.

Confident by his response that Sten hadn't sent the photos, and reminding herself why she came there to begin with, she snapped, "Where's Eleanor?"

"Your second biggest fan is in Room Two. But we need to establish some rules of engagement first."

"*Rules of engagement?*" Val had one rule—that crazy bitch was finally going to get what was coming to her. She scoffed and turned away from Sten, ready to march into Room Two and start wailing on Eleanor's smug face. He grabbed her arm before she got more than one step away, twisted her around, and pulled her flush to him with a grip that made Kirby's seem childlike. With their chests pressed together, in a flash she remembered what his naked body felt like against her own. She swallowed hard and set her face to stone as he leaned down, his mouth a couple inches from hers.

"*These* are the rules of engagement," he said, his words cold but his breath hot against her lips. "She turned herself in for questioning in the disappearance of one Aaron Zephyr, because of her connection to him through Jones's bar. However, we've had her detained for three hours now and I'm all out of excuses to keep her here. I sent the other detective on the case away to do some bullshit errand, but he'll be back soon and he'll probably cut her loose. You have ten minutes alone with her, tops. I turned off the cameras, but if she walks out of here with a bloody lip, they'll blame me, and I am not dealing with that shit. Do you understand what I just said?"

Aaron had disappeared? Did Max know? Her husband hadn't mentioned it, though they hadn't talked for more than a few minutes since the toy store disaster, so she wouldn't know for sure.

Sten's hand tightened around her arm when she didn't immediately answer him. "I need an affirmative, Shepherd."

"*Yes*, Jesus." She yanked her arm away when his grip finally loosened, rubbing the spot where she'd soon have bruises in the shape of his fingers. "Why didn't you arrest her for the bombing, or the toy store collapse, or the ferry crash?"

"Because you need things like *evidence* and *probable cause* for that. Fuck visions and paranoid conspiracy theories aren't admissible in court. I thought we'd gone over how all this law and order stuff works before."

The police hadn't found *any* evidence of Eleanor's involvement in those tragedies? *Bullshit.* Mother was helping her cover her tracks, Val knew it. All the cops could do was hold her for questioning in her lover/client's disappearance, until she lawyered up or asked to leave. *Shit.*

"Fine," she said through a clenched jaw. "Just take me to Eleanor."

He walked past her in the direction she'd tried to storm down, and stopped at the end of the hallway in front of Interrogation Room Two.

Looking at his watch, he said, "Eight minutes," then opened the door for her.

In the plain white room with a one-way mirror on the far wall, Eleanor sat calmly at a stainless steel table. Her gray jacket slung across the back of her simple metal chair, she fingered a Styrofoam cup of water and eyed the new arrival as if she'd been waiting for Val the whole time. When Val took a step inside, Sten shut the door behind her, taking position on the other side of the mirror to watch the fireworks, she guessed. The corners of Eleanor's hideous red lips turned up.

"Welcome, Valentine," Eleanor said. "You took your time getting here. But I guess I shouldn't expect punctuality from an agent of chaos."

Val stared her down, imagining all the ways she could break every bone in Eleanor's body. Her fingers twitched with the need to exact justice right then and there for Lydia, Michael, Dani, and all the other innocent people Eleanor had killed or hurt. She had to ball her hands into fists to steady them. Never breaking eye contact, she walked to the chair opposite Eleanor and slowly sat down.

"Who are you?" Val asked with as much calm as she could muster.

Eleanor cocked her head and smiled. "I'm the opposite of you."

"Meaning?"

"I preserve God's plan and protect it from your perversity."

"What the fuck are you talking about?"

"You know what I'm talking about. God has a path we must all walk down, a grand plan you are disrupting. He sent me to stop you."

"So you think you're receiving messages from Father—from God?"

Eleanor lifted her hands up as if she were attending a revival church meeting. "When my body feels the rapture, He speaks to me, and I obey."

Val glanced at the mirror, relieved that only Sten was witnessing their conversation. So Eleanor thought her visions were messages from God that she had to make come true? As far as Val knew, every seer's visions were unique to them—Max saw numbers, Lucien had seen medical technology, Val saw murder and mayhem, and Eleanor saw—or heard—the "voice of God." Her reign of terror could be a murderous chicken and egg scenario—she acted out what she saw in a vision, but the only reason she saw it in a vision to begin with was because she'd already committed to fulfilling the vision in the past. Thinking about it made Val furious—and her head hurt.

"God is not talking to you," Val said. "You have a...condition. It's a physical response to an unknown phenomenon that hasn't been discovered yet." Those were Max's words. It was all the explanation he could come up with.

Eleanor laughed. "When faced with the divine, you can't accept it."

The truth was, Val *had* considered her curse might be some kind of divine punishment. But it definitely wasn't a force for good. At best, it was like a gun—its utility, for good or for evil, depended entirely upon the person who wielded it.

"If Father is telling you to do bad things," Val said, "what is Mother telling you to do?"

Eleanor cocked her head a hair, as if slightly surprised Val knew of the mysterious other woman, but not fazed. "Bad things? No. Mother tells me to listen to Father. She guides me in fulfilling his divine plan."

Val slammed her fist on the steel table. "Who is she?"

Eleanor's smile fell away, though she didn't flinch. She wasn't afraid of anything. That's what absolute certainty in your own righteousness did to a person. "You know."

"No, I don't actually. Why don't you enlighten me."

Staring at something past Val, Eleanor's eyes misted over. "Mother is also God's agent on this earth. She showed me the way when I was lost, and loved and cared for me when no one else would."

"Is she telling you to terrorize my family?"

"Terrorize? That's ridiculous. She told me about you, your husband, and your children, what you all were."

"*Why?* What does she want? Who is she, goddammit? Answer me!"

"She guides me in fulfilling his divine plan—"

"You said that already, and it's fucking stupid. You don't have to do what the visions tell you to. You didn't *have* to get on the ferry, you didn't *have* to bomb the Thornton Building, you didn't *have* to sabotage the toy store platform. You could have stayed home."

Eleanor glanced at the mirror where she knew Sten watched them. "I didn't do any of those things." She wasn't about to confess in front of an audience. "But those sad things, I'm sure, happened for a reason. It's His plan—"

"You are not going to convince me that *murdering children* is His plan!"

Eleanor's lips tightened, and the faintest hint of sorrow touched her eyes. "It's His plan."

Like Max, maybe she'd tried to change the future before and failed—because only Val could change what she saw. That must be what Eleanor meant by calling Val an agent of chaos. Now Eleanor rationalized her visions as something she had no choice but to do, in the name of the Father, Son, and Holy Spirit—and

Mother. Given her rough past, and the strong possibility she'd been abused or threatened by some of her previous Johns, Val guessed somewhere along the line, her visions had morphed into murder and snowballed from there.

"You don't have to be this way," Val said, a tiny iota of pity tempering her anger. "Fight for the future you want, Eleanor."

Eleanor flinched, a flicker of doubt in her eyes for the first time.

"*Fight!*" Val slapped the table as if she could break loose some sanity in the woman who'd clearly been driven mad by the things she saw but couldn't change.

Instead, the doubt vanished and that horrible grin returned. "Mother and I are doing His will, enforcing the future as He intended it to be. *You're* the one defying Him and changing his plan. *You're* the aberration—you and your children."

Val jumped up from her seat, knocking her chair over, the sliver of pity gone in a flash of rage. "The *only* reason I haven't killed you yet is because we're in a police station, you crazy, evil bitch."

Eleanor chuckled. "Are you threatening me?" She looked at the glass again. "Mister Police Man, please note that she's threatening me. You know what else I've seen? You and I at a Christmas festival, the one along the Seattle waterfront tomorrow night. Both of us go, but only one of us leaves."

Val leaned across the table toward Eleanor, planting her palms on the smooth surface as she drilled into the woman's cool green eyes. "You think you can scare me? That you can *break* me? Many have tried. All have failed. So *good luck.*"

Eleanor sneered in response. "I think, after the Christmas festival, I'll take your husband. He's a fine man, and I could tell at Jones's that he wanted me. Mother told me my connection to

God would increase when we felt the rapture together. He'd be quite useful. Where is he right now, by the way? Have you seen what will happen to him yet?"

Val would have laughed at Eleanor's ridiculous attempt to egg her on, but she felt too sick to her stomach to try. "If you think he'd *ever* touch you, then you're even more delusional than I thought."

Eleanor chuckled. "What is it rich people like to tell anyone who will listen? 'I am the master of all I survey and I take what I want?' I'll take what *I* want this time. Maxwell's trip to Him, very soon, has already been foretold. Doesn't feel so nice being on the other end, does it?"

Val was only vaguely aware the interrogation room door had burst open when she lunged for Eleanor. To hell with the police station venue or Sten's warning. Eleanor would die right here, right now, by Val's hand. An inch from reaching the murderer, she felt herself jerked backward by Sten's iron grip on both her forearms.

"Stop it, Shepherd!" Sten said. "Time's up."

"I'll kill you!" Val bellowed. "I'll kill you—"

"Jesus H. Christ!" another man's voice said from the doorway. "What in the holy *hell* is going on here, Ander?"

Oh shit, Sten's expression said for half a second, before he masked it with his usual bored confidence. "What does it look like, Cody? A girl fight, obviously, over who's hotter—Fabio or Kevin Sorbo."

Cody squinted at Val. "Is that *Valentine Shepherd?*"

"No. I think you might be projecting your fantasies on other people—"

"God*dammit*, Ander! I don't know what the fuck you're trying to pull here, but Miss Fatou is free to leave."

Smiling, Eleanor stood and slipped on her jacket. "I certainly hope you find Aaron, Officer Cody. Please let me know if I can be of any further assistance."

Val strained against Sten's grip as he held her tightly in one spot. "No," Val growled as Eleanor walked past Cody, then out of sight. "No!"

Cody blocked the doorway with his body, folded his arms, and glared at Val. "And what is your connection to this case again, or do you show up places to cause trouble for fun?"

Finally shrugging out of Sten's grasp, she said, "That woman probably killed Aaron!"

Cody raised an eyebrow. "How do you know that?"

"Because she was having an affair with him."

"Yes, we know."

"His wife hired me to take pictures of them together that she could use to take him to the cleaners in a divorce."

"Do you have these pictures?"

"I don't have any of them together yet. But she could have killed Aaron because she didn't want to be caught in the cross-fire."

She knew that wasn't true; by the skeptical look on Cody's face, he knew it, too. But she couldn't explain everything she knew about Eleanor without sounding crazy.

Ah, to hell with it. "And she's responsible for the Thornton Building bombing, and the toy store collapse, and the ferry crash. She's trying to hurt my family through acts of terrorism, and she's not going to stop until she kills us!"

Cody blinked at her for a moment, dumbstruck. Then he chuckled. "Did Miss Fatou kidnap the Lindbergh baby as well?"

Of course he'd say that. Every second she wasted talking to the clueless police was one more second Eleanor used to get away.

"Can I just go, please? Can I go right now?"

Cody turned his glare on Sten. "Why did you let her in here?"

"Well, the thing is…Okay, you got me. We're having an affair, and I was doing her a favor. Don't tell anyone."

"*What?* That is not—" With a howl of frustration, Val lunged past Cody and ran down the hallway before he could stop her. She burst into the main police station and did a frantic scan of everything she could see—no Eleanor. Barreling past people in her way, no longer caring if anyone recognized her, she flew through the exit and into the cold street swarming with people in heavy coats and holiday sweaters. She spun in a circle, searching for the gray coat, yellow hair, and red lips. Round and round she turned, gripped by an impotent fury that had no outlet, until tears welled in her eyes and all the Christmas lights blurred together.

Eleanor had escaped. Again.

Chapter Twenty-eight

Max tried to keep his head down while at the same time walking with the confidence of a man who was doing just fine, thanks. The concerned half-second glances he got as he dragged himself through the corridors of Carressa Industries told him he wasn't selling it, though. After sleeping poorly for the last two weeks, then not sleeping at all the last three days, he guessed he was starting to look like he did shortly after he'd killed his father—sullen, withdrawn, slightly unhinged. He figured the sunglasses he wore didn't help; if anyone asked, he would say he'd had an eye exam. Yes, it was an obvious lie, but still better than putting the dark circles rimming his eyes on display for everyone to see.

He need to at least make an appearance at the office—not because he cared about the minutiae of Carressa Industries' business dealings, but to check on the people there and make sure they were recovering from the bombing. After giving assurances the building was still structurally sound, authorities had closed off a huge chunk of it in and around the explosion's epicenter while employees tried to commence with work as usual. He and the board decided to pack all the displaced folks into temporary offices on the lower floors. It wasn't an ideal situation for healing and moving on, but it was the best of a bunch of bad options. Michael assured him he didn't have to go in—or *shouldn't* go in, given what a goddamn wreck he was—but he did. These people were his responsibility. And in a way, the bombing was his fault.

Anyway, he had time. After he'd received Val's cryptic text that she had "something important to do" and would be late meeting him at the hospital to take Lydia home, he'd decided to hell with it and took their daughter home by himself. Thank God for Jamal, who'd shockingly opted to keep working for them. Otherwise, Max would have to leave the twins with Danielle, and though she'd saved Lydia's life, she still didn't seem completely stable. Then again, neither was he.

So after a handful of caffeine caplets and a few shots of Scotch to ease his nerves, here he was at work, trying to make other people feel better while he himself felt like something worse than shit. Max walked into the area populated by the folks in Accounting, where Nihan Shah worked before being killed in the bombing. He spotted a coworker he knew had been close with Nihan.

"Hi, Leslie," he said as he approached the petite woman with thick glasses as she plinked away on her keyboard. "How are things?"

She looked up from her computer and flashed him a friendly smile. "Oh, hi, Mr. Carressa—Max, I mean! Didn't expect to see you around here so soon. How's your daughter?"

Behind his glasses, he flinched. Why did she have to ask about that? Great, everybody knew about his problems. This visit wasn't about him. "Lydia's recovering. But how are you holding up?"

"I'm getting on, thanks for asking. I miss Nihan every day. They'd better bomb the *shit* out of the terrorists who did this. Otherwise, things are okay here. Everybody's pulled together to support each other. It's nice to see. Have they found out who's responsible for the toy store collapse yet?"

"No."

"If I were you, I'd sue the *shit* out of that store—"

"Okay, well, it was nice talking to you, Leslie. I'm glad you're doing all right. Let me know if you need anything."

"Thank you, Max. I'll send up some prayers for your little girl."

Max faked a quick smile and hurried away. He snuck into an empty bathroom, yanked off his sunglasses, and splashed water on his face. Bloodshot eyes stared back at him through the mirror. Jesus, Michael was right. This had been a bad idea.

Pull it together, Max. You're a goddamn adult. Other people have suffered just as badly—some even more so. Stop acting like a fucking baby and do your job.

Mopping up his face, he put his sunglasses back on, took a deep breath, and marched to the new area for Financials, where DeShawn Joy had worked. At the threshold he stopped, distracted by a desk repurposed as a memorial to DeShawn.

"You are always in our hearts," one hand-drawn banner read, next to a fresh bouquet of flowers and a picture of DeShawn, arm in arm with his wife. Max had done several walk-throughs of the area and seen this desk, but someone had replaced the picture of the finance guru standing alone on a beach with one of him and his wife at a party. *In the end, our love is all we really have,* Max remembered he'd said at the memorial service. *It's the only thing that will never die—*

He nearly jumped when someone touched his shoulder. Spinning around, he saw DeShawn's supervisor, Vincent, standing next to him with brows furrowed in concern.

"I'm so sorry about your daughter," Vincent said. "It must be hard on your family, after everything you've been through."

Max's throat tightened. *Shit.* "I—uh, how are things here?"

Shrugging, Vincent replied, "Good as can be. This Christmas season is so bittersweet, you know? It's supposed to be a happy, festive time of year, but it's hard to harness that holiday cheer when it seems like we've had one tragedy after another lately. How's Michael, by the way? Is his arm all healed up yet? I heard he might have a big scar."

"His arm is actually—it's—" *Gone. His arm is fucking gone.* Max choked on his own words. Suddenly his mouth was too dry to talk. Swallowing hard, he forced out, "Excuse me. I need to go check on something." He pushed past Vincent and practically ran to the elevator, mashing the button to the new top floor, where his temporary office resided.

He couldn't do it anymore. Not that long ago, he'd excelled at hiding his true feelings and putting on a mask to suit whatever event he needed to perform at. Even when he'd been racked with guilt after killing his father, he'd held the façade together most of the time. But watching the yellow hyena hurt his family and tear his marriage apart was too much. It'd been a mistake to let people see him like this. He'd grab his work computer, then extricate himself. Maybe go home and stare at the walls for a while.

Max made one last stop at his secretary's desk, propped awkwardly against the wall next to his makeshift office. Light throbs of pain began pulsating on the left side of his head—the seeds of a migraine beginning to grow. Yet another reason to get the hell out of there as quickly as possible. Taking off his sunglasses so he could rub the bridge of his nose, he asked Nadine, "Got anything for me before I head out the door?"

"Yes." Through bifocals secured around her neck with a lanyard made of festive beads, she read from notes she'd scratched on a pad. "The board meeting's been rescheduled for after the New Year. Charlene would like to talk to you at your earliest convenience about the Quality Foods and Boston Scientific acquisitions. And Roger wants your opinion on next quarter's proposed portfolio; he e-mailed it to you this morning." She looked up at him over the rim of her glasses, and her face turned motherly. "But I'm sure all this stuff can wait. I'm so sorry about Lydia. How are you and Val doing?"

He responded to her question by staring at her for a long time. Honestly, he didn't know how to answer. Val wouldn't talk to him, and he wouldn't talk to her. Why did everyone keep asking him about his fucking feelings?

Nadine's motherly expression faded. Her cheeks grew a shade redder as she realized his icy silence was all the answer she'd get.

He slipped his sunglasses back on. "I'm taking my computer and going home," he said, then walked into his office before Nadine could try to comfort him anymore.

Collapsing into a plush rolling chair he'd salvaged from a damaged conference room, he took a few breaths to try and calm himself. God, he was tired. Very, very tired. With weary eyes, he glanced at the couple pictures on his desk—one of him and Val on their wedding day, the other of him, Val, Lydia, and Simon at the park. He looked at those pictures often, to remind himself why he bothered coming to work at all, or even went on living for that matter. His eyes lingered on the image of Val gazing lovingly at him on the beach where they'd married in Fiji.

Had she been cheating on him then with that piece-of-shit cop? She'd said it had been when she and Max weren't together, but he didn't know what to believe. Maybe if she'd told him about it before he had those fucking photos shoved in his face, he'd be more willing to take her word for it. She was the one who ranted *they* were always watching them, so why wouldn't she assume they'd know about her affair, and use it against her? And why did she have to sleep with the man who tried to *beat him to death*, and then *shot him*? How could she not care about that?

Gritting his teeth, he knocked the photo facedown on his desk. Eventually she'd give him some excuse, say she was sorry, and he'd forgive her, like he always did. He was a goddamn fool. His whole life he'd let people take advantage of him, and now it was his wife's turn. He couldn't live without her, and she knew it. Balling his hands into fists, a familiar rage growing in his gut, he knew he had to get out of there before he blew. He should grab his computer and go—

Where was his computer?

Max sat up and looked around his desk, then did a lap around his office. No computer. What the hell?

He stomped back out to Nadine's desk. "Where is my laptop?" he said, harsher than he should have. His nerves felt frayed to their breaking point.

"It's not in your office?"

He growled, "If it was, why would I be asking you about it now?"

She frowned and looked at him with wide eyes, nervous to be around him for maybe the first time ever. He'd never been so coarse to her, but he couldn't help himself. His self-control was slipping by the second. "I'm sure no one's been in there since you've been gone…" she said. "I'll call security."

As Nadine dialed, he ran a hand through his hair and sighed. *Calm down, Max. It's not her fault.* A rival company could have exploited the recent chaos and stolen his computer to access Carressa Industries' proprietary information, though he'd never seen such a blatant act of corporate espionage before. That stupid laptop also had one of only two copies of his stock prediction computer program on it—

Shit.

He ran back to his office, unlocked a desk drawer, and jerked it open. The backup disk was gone.

"Fuck!" He grabbed the orphaned keyboard off his desktop and slammed it into the ground in an explosion of plastic squares. Why would anyone steal his chaotic mess of code? It wasn't even close to working.

"It's a black Alienware laptop, signed out to Maxwell Carressa…" Nadine was saying over the phone as Max stormed out of his office again. She eyed him with a touch more nervousness. She must've heard him slamming things.

"Is Aaron in today?" he asked, ignoring her conversation in progress.

"Just a moment," she said into the phone, then put her hand over the receiver. "Aaron Zephyr?"

"Yes, that Aaron." Jesus, was he speaking Greek today? He needed to talk to somebody, *anybody*. Count Doctopus would understand.

"You…haven't heard?"

"Heard what?"

"Aaron's been missing for three days. His wife filed a report."

Max stared at her slack-jawed as a wave of dread washed over him. Not Aaron, too.

"I'm sorry, Max—"

He left before she could offer any more words of pity. Aaron—gone. Val—gone. Anyone he got close to—gone or maimed. This was his life now. Back to bleakness.

Max hurried to the stairwell and jogged up five floors to the cordoned-off section, barreling through the police tape until he reached the husk of his old office. He sat down in his original chair, charred from the explosion. If he'd been sitting there that day, which had been his plan before going to lunch with Aaron, he'd have surely died. A bitterly cold breeze raked against his face through the shattered window that used to be one wall of his office. At the remains of his desk, he yanked the bottom drawer open and spilled the contents onto the floor, then found what he was looking for—a pill bottle filled with OxyContin. He didn't know why he kept it around…No, he did—he kept it in case he ever needed to go numb, or wanted to try to leave this world again. He'd tried many times to kill himself, and it never worked. But if his purpose in life was to have children with Val, maybe fate would finally let him go.

Twisting the lid off, he dropped two pills in the palm of his hand and tossed them in his mouth. He closed his eyes and sat back, letting the familiar bitter taste linger as the medicine dissolved on his tongue, remembering how it had given him the strength to face the day once upon a time, without Val—

But every time he'd turned to drugs for solace, he had regretted it. Would this time really be any different?

What the hell was he thinking?

He sat up and spit the pills out. He gave up too easily; that was his problem. Max pushed himself up from the chair, poured all the pills in his hand, and threw them out the window like confetti. He had no idea how to solve any of his problems, but falling into a drug-fueled haze wasn't the answer. He had his children, he had his sister, and he had Michael. Oh yeah, and Toby. He'd get Val back from wherever she'd gone, no matter what she'd done. She was his, and he was hers.

Not happy but no longer completely despondent, Max left the building, returned to his car, and headed back to the condo. He'd go home and try to sleep, clean himself up a little bit, then go find Val and bring her home. If she was dead set on finding Eleanor, he'd help her—for real this time. They'd do it together. As a united front, they were unstoppable.

Speak of the devil.

As he stopped at a red light in a busy intersection, something yellow from across the street caught his attention. He took off his sunglasses and rubbed his eyes, worried for a moment he was hallucinating. But no, there she was—Eleanor, the yellow hyena, in the flesh, wrapped in a gray jacket and standing at the intersection across from him. And was she *looking at him?*

She knew he'd be there, at that moment. Val was right—Eleanor was like them. She could see the future, and she was using her ability to kill people and tear his family apart.

Cold fury prickled across his skin at the same time hot anger flooded his veins. Eleanor needed to die.

He punched the gas, tires squealing against the pavement. Let them throw him in jail for vehicular homicide, he didn't care. He should be in prison for killing his father anyway. At least then he could say he rid the world of two monsters.

Aiming straight for the yellow hyena, he made it halfway across the intersection before a truck T-boned his car, slamming him to the side in a shower of metal.

Chapter Twenty-nine

Val sprinted into the Harborview emergency room lobby and rushed straight to the receptionist desk.

"Where is Max?" she said between huffs, trying to catch her breath. "Maxwell Carressa, I mean. I got a call he was in an accident and I need to see him right now—"

"One moment, ma'am," the receptionist said as she picked up a phone, "I'll check with the doctor."

"I'm his *wife*. Why can't you just let me in?"

"I'm calling the doctor, Mrs. Carressa. He'll be out in a moment, I promise." She pointed at the lobby chairs. "If you wait over there, he'll come get you."

Her whole body shaking, Val backed away and stood uselessly off to the side. Even she realized storming the ICU would be counterproductive. She had no idea where he was or what condition he was in. Maybe it wasn't that bad. Maybe he'd sprained some joints, broken some bones. As he lay battered and bruised, she would put her head on his chest as she'd done after he'd been shot, and they would finally spare a moment to talk. Maybe he could come home tonight.

Eleanor had made a veiled threat that she would kill him. But she wouldn't try to make good on her threat so soon. Val had just seen her at the police station a couple hours ago—

"Mrs. Carressa?"

Val looked up from where she'd been staring at her feet. An older man in scrubs walked toward her. He held out his hand for her to shake. "I'm Dr. Carter."

She shook his hand for half a second, the barest gesture of politeness she could get away with. "Where's Max?"

He cocked his head toward the way he'd come. "Why don't you follow me?"

She trailed close behind as he walked through the ICU, past blue curtains and buzzing equipment. A few staff members glanced at her in recognition, but no one stared. They were all professionals here. When she and Dr. Carter reached the other side of the ICU, he led her through a door into another smaller lobby, this one empty except for a single receptionist behind a desk.

"This is the area we use for well-known people who might attract media attention, like celebrities," he said, then nodded toward the receptionist. "Justine will give you an access card for future visits, so you can come in and out this way, at your leisure."

"Future visits?"

His face hardened into a professional mask, serious yet empathetic, and her stomach dropped. He was about to give her bad news. Oh God.

"Your husband sustained extensive internal and external injuries from the car accident. He's in surgery right now to repair his major blood vessels and control the bleeding. Unfortunately,

I can't give you a prognosis until he gets out. All I can tell you is he's alive right now."

Dr. Carter went on about the specifics of Max's injuries, but his words floated away from her as her whole body went numb. This was serious. Very serious. Eleanor *had* gotten to Max. How could the woman get across town so quickly? She must have had help, probably the same person who spirited her away from the police station in the blink of an eye—Mother. And how did Eleanor cause the accident? Did she drive the car that hit Max? Could she—

"Do you have any questions, Mrs. Carressa?"

Val sucked in a trembling breath. "How long will he be in surgery?" she asked, her voice weak.

"About five more hours. You can either wait here or come back later."

"I'll wait here."

The doctor nodded. "Please let Justine know if you need anything. I'll let you know as soon as his surgery is complete. Then we can talk about a long-term prognosis."

"Uh-huh."

He gave her what was meant to be a reassuring smile and disappeared back into the ICU. Val lowered herself into the nearest seat. What should she do? What *could* she do? The children—they were alone with Jamal and Dani, protected by bodyguards, expecting their mother and father to return at any moment. Unless they already knew about the accident, which wouldn't surprise her. She wanted to hug them both tight, one in each arm. But she couldn't leave the hospital until she knew if Max would be all right.

Phone calls. She had to make phone calls. Should she call Michael? Yes—but not now. After she had more info on Max's condition. The poor old man had his own problems to worry about. First, she dialed Josephine and gave Max's sister the news about her brother in the simplest and least disturbing way possible, impressed with how steady her voice stayed through the conversation. She asked Jo to please swing by and check on the children after the nanny's shift ended; Jo agreed wholeheartedly, of course. Then she dialed Jamal, repeated what she told Jo about Max's condition, and asked him to pass the information on to Dani, along with a simpler version to the children. He offered to stay for as long as she needed him there, but he'd already nearly gotten himself killed by a maniac while watching her kids, for Christ's sake. She assured him Jo would pick up the slack and told him to enjoy some time off until she asked him to return. Why did he still work for them? It certainly wasn't Val's sunny demeanor that brought him back. Maybe he truly cared for the children. Or maybe he was another one of Northwalk's pawns, waiting for the moment when both Val and Max were out of the picture so he could whisk the twins away without their parents getting in the way. Perhaps he was the one who would murder Val's mother.

Dani's gray eyes widen as she stares in disbelief down the barrel of a gun Jamal points at her. Her red hair, streaked with gray, frames a delicate face lined around the eyes and mouth with age. "Don't do this, please," she begs him. Her lips tremble. "I have something to live for now. You don't understand—"

BOOM BOOM BOOM. Jamal shoots her three times in the chest. She collapses to the ground and spits up blood for a moment before going still—

"Mrs. Carressa?"

Val jerked awake. She'd fallen asleep in the chair somehow, and her mind had decided to torture her with terrible dreams. She hadn't realized how tired she was.

Rubbing her eyes, she saw it was Dr. Carter who'd awoken her. She jumped to her feet. "Is Max out of surgery?"

"Yes. Can we go to my office and talk?"

Val nodded, the pit of her stomach twisting into a tight knot. If everything was fine and dandy, would he still want to talk to her alone? Save for the receptionist, they were for all intents and purposes alone in the famous persons' waiting area anyway. It must be a formality. He could still have something good to tell her.

When they reached Dr. Carter's office, he shut the door behind him. The knot in her stomach tightened.

HIPAA concerns. It could still be good news.

She sat at the edge of the chair across from his desk and waited for what felt like an eternity for him to sit down and start talking already. When he took a deep breath before he started speaking, she regretted her impatience. She already knew this was going to hurt. It would hurt more than anything she'd felt in her life.

"We've managed to control the bleeding, and your husband is still alive and in a stable condition, for now. However, he suffered several fractures of his lumbar and upper vertebrae, which in turn have damaged his spinal cord to a degree we can't quantify yet. He also had some traumatic brain injuries. He's not responding to any stimuli, and his respiratory reflex isn't working."

"He…can't breathe on his own?"

"That's correct." Dr. Carter leaned forward, and with eyes

full of compassion he said, "We have a neurosurgeon flying in tonight to evaluate him and see what our options are, but I'm going to be honest with you. His long-term prognosis isn't good. It's unlikely he'll ever wake up."

All she could do was stare at him. He'd probably had this conversation with dozens—maybe hundreds—of other people, because everybody dies. Shit happens. Bad luck.

But this wasn't bad luck. This wasn't a random car hitting another random car on a random day in a random city. This was *her* Max, the love of her life, the father of her children, the man she was destined to be with.

And now Eleanor had killed him.

"I am so sorry, Mrs. Carressa. We'll have a better understanding of the situation after the neurosurgeon evaluates him, but I want to temper your expectations."

"Can I see him?" she asked, ignoring the tears rolling down her cheeks.

Dr. Carter nodded and stood. She followed him again, gripped by the sensation she had stumbled into a terrible dream as if he were the Ghost of Christmas Future, showing her all the terrible things to come unless she changed her ways. If only she'd stayed away from Eleanor when Max had originally asked. If only she'd left the city with him instead of insisting on facing their enemy. If only she'd managed to stop Eleanor on the ferry. If only she'd chosen to go home with Max and Lydia instead of joining Sten at the police station. If she'd done any of those other things, just one of them, maybe Max wouldn't be brain-dead and fighting for his life in a hospital bed right now. But she couldn't go back—only forward. They were slaves to the future, Max used to say. He was right.

The doctor stopped in front of a patient's room and opened

the door for her. When she stepped inside, she gasped. Max lay in the hospital bed with dozens of tubes protruding from his body while a machine beeped steadily in the background. His face looked waxen where it wasn't covered in black bruises, his body limp, his eyes closed. A gas bag pushed air into his lungs.

She'd seen this moment before. The morning she spent in his home—the guest house to the Carressa mansion—back when they'd first met, she had this vision. Val had seen him die a few different ways over the years, and she'd prevented them all—but not this one. She'd *caused* it this time.

Holding back a sob, she asked, "Can I have a few moments alone with him, please?"

"Of course," the doctor said, and left.

Val pulled a chair to his bedside and sat down. She touched his hand, and the sob burst out in one painful wail that racked her whole body. Slapping her other hand over her mouth, she forced herself into some semblance of composure, for the sake of not dying there with him on that spot—not then anyway.

"Well, you were right," she said to his placid face, still the handsomest one she'd ever seen. He could have been horribly disfigured and he'd still be the most beautiful man she had ever met. "I should have stayed away. We should have left, all of us. But I couldn't. You know me. I can't leave well enough alone."

She swiped away some of the continuous tears streaming down her face.

"I want to say I *tried* to do the right thing, but…So far I haven't stopped anyone, or saved anyone, and now here you are and…and you didn't deserve this."

Val looked at the gas bag, blowing steadily in and out to the slow rhythm of the heart rate monitor.

"I'm sorry I didn't tell you about my, um, time with Sten. It occurred during the months I'd been forcing myself to stay away from you, and it was tearing me apart. And Sten was there, also frustrated and unhappy, and it just happened. You have to believe me when I say I never cheated on you. I never will. I'm yours, always. Until the end of time."

She let out a dry laugh as though they were having an actual conversation. As she stared at Max's silent, immobile body, her smile quickly faded.

"What should I do now? You want me to leave, I don't even have to ask. Take the kids and run, that's what you're thinking. And I should leave you here, you're also thinking, because you believe you're not important. But that's not true. You're important to a lot of people. The kids need you." Her voice cracked. "I need you."

Another sob forced its way out. For several minutes she cried at his bedside, caressing his hand and wishing she could look into his beautiful hazel eyes with their starbursts of emerald green in their centers one more time, and be amazed at the unmatched brilliance roiling behind them.

Finally, she tapped into her steel core, the one that turned her anger into strength, and her tears abated.

"You *meant* something, Max. You were a force of good in this world, despite all the terrible things people did to you, and Eleanor took you away. So now I'm going to take something from her."

With a new determination, she stood. "I'll be back soon," she told him. "I'm going to check on my mother and our babies, and then I'm going to deal with our problem, once and for all."

She leaned down and kissed his cheek, her tears sliding off her face and onto his. Then she set her face to stone and left the hospital. Bright midmorning sunlight blinded her tired eyes as she dodged paparazzi out of the regular-people entrance to get back to where she'd parked her car, and drove home.

Eleanor implied she would kill Val during the Christmas festival at the Seattle waterfront that night. Now she knew where Eleanor would be, and when. All she had to do was show up, and change the future.

Chapter Thirty

Val stumbled through the carport door and into the kitchen, dragging her feet as if they'd turned to lead, so exhausted she could barely move. Toby trotted up and made a sound like a cross between a bark and a whine at her, maybe sensing something was deeply, irrevocably wrong. Dogs could sniff that stuff out, some people thought.

"Mommy!" The kids ran up and threw their arms around her legs. She knelt and hugged them the way she'd craved, and felt a lump grow in her throat again.

Don't cry in front of the kids, she told herself. *Stay strong for them—and for yourself, to face what's coming.*

Jo and Dani appeared in the doorway between the kitchen and the dining room, concern etched across their faces.

"Is Daddy okay?" Simon asked, the hazel eyes he'd inherited from his father wide with childish concern.

"He's, um…" Dammit, she felt more tears dribbling down her cheeks. She pushed them away and tried to smile. "He wanted me to check on you. He says he loves you very much, and…and he'll see you soon."

Simon cocked his head as if considering something, before flashing her a bright smile. "Okay! I can't wait to see him, too."

He seemed awfully happy. Did he know his father was close to death? Why couldn't he see it?

"Simon, Lydia, can you"—she glanced at the two adults still in the doorway and lowered her voice—"can you see what's going to happen to Daddy? Or what I'm going to do?"

The twins looked at her and scrunched their faces, their young minds struggling to put into words things they weren't old enough to understand.

"There are too many choo-choo tracks," Simon said. "They cross all over each other."

Lydia nodded her agreement with Simon's assessment.

God, they sounded like Cassandra, speaking in riddles. What they meant, Val guessed, was there were too many possibilities. Maybe she had a caboose somewhere on all those train tracks. Max could probably analyze the situation and give her a detailed theory on what it all meant. All she could do was take action.

She hugged the twins tight. At least the absolute worst hadn't come to pass yet. Her children were still safe.

Val pushed herself to her feet with unsteady legs. She might collapse on the kitchen floor if she didn't get some sleep soon. "I need to lie down for a little bit," she said to the kids, as well as Jo and Dani.

"Pumpkin…" Dani said as Val walked by, on her way up the stairs.

Val didn't stop, or even look at her mother. Her brain had switched to autopilot while her body went numb. She trudged up the stairs and lay down on the bed, buried her head in Max's pillow, and closed her eyes, letting the scent of him lull her into a fitful sleep.

* * *

She awoke with a start, shaken by nightmares she could only remember in vivid feelings of dread and hopelessness. She pushed herself up, touching moistness on the pillow—more tears, leaked out during her restless slumber.

Stop fucking crying, she admonished herself. *Crying doesn't help anyone. Crying is useless. Stop it already.*

Stripping off her clothes, she stepped into the shower and got to work. After scrubbing her skin and hair clean, she began rubbing her clitoris. She needed to see *how* Eleanor would kill her if she was to prevent it from happening. She'd avoided her own death before; she could do it again. Under the hot, soapy water, she touched herself and thought of Max, of his strong yet gentle caress…but all she could see was his bruised and battered body in that hospital bed.

Come on, Val, concentrate.

She rubbed harder, this time imagining herself as the lead in a porno film, some anonymous woman being rammed by an anonymous man and loving every minute of it. She pretended to moan in ecstasy because it felt *so good*, and this professional sex machine was going to make her come so many, many times for the cameras…But Val felt nothing. The right nerves weren't firing. The string that ran from between her legs and up her spine wasn't vibrating.

It wasn't working.

Fuck.

Val let out a primal scream of frustration and slammed her fists into the wall. Not only had Eleanor taken away her husband and sense of security, the woman had also taken away her best weapon.

Yanking hard on her wet hair, she forced herself to pull her shit together. Giving up was not an option. A gun and a knife were all she truly needed to face Eleanor. She'd play the rest by ear. There was absolutely no way Val would let that evil bitch get away again, no matter how much she knew Max would plead for her to run. Tonight, they'd see for sure if Eleanor's God really loved her. Mother couldn't help her this time.

Val slapped the shower faucet off and threw on a black hooded sweatshirt and a fresh pair of jeans, then jogged downstairs. Darkness through the windows told her evening had arrived; she'd slept through the entire morning and afternoon. She found Jo cleaning the table off post-dinner.

"I can stay longer if you'd like," she said, though the circles around her eyes betrayed her exhaustion, and likely worry about her brother as well.

"Nah, I'll be all right. I've got my mom, and bodyguards now. Go home and rest, and visit Max. Thanks for all your help, Jo. We couldn't have gotten through the day without you."

With a weary smile, Jo hugged Val, then Lydia and Simon. "Good night, kids. Be good for your mother and Nana."

After she left, Val addressed her children. "I have to leave again, kiddos. I'm sorry, but it's important."

"It's okay, Mommy," Lydia said. "We understand."

"I'll be right back, though." She teared up once more. "I *will* see you again." God, she hoped it was true. It had to be true.

"Don't be sad, Mommy," Lydia said. "I'll always love you. Daddy, too. If you love us, we're never really gone. We'll live forever."

Max's words from the memorial service.

"You're not gone yet, honey," Val said.

"I know," Lydia replied with a cryptic smile. *Not yet.*

Her heart tightened, not wanting to leave her babies. But she had to finish this. They'd never be safe until she did. And Max *would* be avenged.

She kissed and hugged her children—*not* for the last time, dammit—and left them playing with LEGO blocks in the living room. After slipping a leather jacket over her hoodie, she walked into the kitchen. Dani stood up from where she sat at the table.

"Oh, pumpkin," she said, and Val lost it. She burst into tears as her mother embraced her, bawling uncontrollably in the arms of the only person besides Max she had to confide in.

"He's brain-dead," Val cried, trying to keep her voice down so the kids wouldn't hear.

"I'm so sorry," Dani said as she stroked Val's hair.

"What am I going to do without him? How am I supposed to go on? The children…I can't do it by myself."

"Yes you can. You'll find a way. You're my strong Valentine."

She didn't know about that, but she had no choice. The only way she could go was forward. Still, Dani's words soothed her enough for her to pull herself together. Taking a deep breath, she lifted her head off her mother's breast and swiped her tears away.

"Mom, I need to go take care of the person who killed Max."

Dani's eyes widened. "Take care of who?"

"Can you please watch the children?"

"Of course. But…what are you going to do?"

"If I don't come back, please make sure the children are safe. Take them to Jo's place, or Michael's family. Those are the only people I trust—and you."

A slight smile touched Dani's lips and her eyes moistened. "Thank you. I'll make sure the kids are okay. But please be careful. Whatever you're going to do…come back alive, will you?"

"That's the plan." It was her only plan, really.

As Val walked away, Dani said, "I love you, pumpkin."

Val stopped, then walked back to her mom and hugged her. "I love you, too." Finally, the words felt true. She needed her mother. Maybe that had always been the case, but now Val was willing to admit it.

Her mother planted a sweet kiss on her scalp before she finally left. *This* was what she was fighting for—her mother, her husband, her children. Her family. Eleanor wouldn't hurt them again, not while Val was still alive.

Either Eleanor would die tonight, or she would. Time to face her enemy—for the last time.

* * *

Though the sky is black, Christmas lights will nearly blind you. They hang off the awning of every booth and shop along the main route of the holiday festival. You will hurry through the crowd, as quickly as you can without running. The red raven is following you, coming for you. She'll think she has the upper hand, but she does not. You are in control, and she is in your thrall. You'll lead her into an apartment complex on the festival path, up the stairs, and onto the roof. You will face off with her there, a grand struggle for life and death. Know that I am on your side, as always. My eyes cannot be blinded, my wrath avoided, my will denied.

You will plunge a knife deep into her heart and know that I have made it so. It is the end. It is my will. It is destiny.

Chapter Thirty-one

Val dodged happy Christmas revelers and their families as she looked for any sign of Eleanor. Decked-out booths selling warm food and holiday tchotchkes choked the Seattle waterfront while festive music from a live band wafted through the air. It would've been a nice place for her and Max to bring the kids—if Eleanor hadn't shattered her family.

With her hood pulled over her head, Val scanned the crowd and fingered the gun nestled against her hip, hidden by her sweatshirt. She would never fire into a crowd, but Eleanor had no reservations about killing innocent bystanders. Jesus, what if Eleanor planted a bomb at the Christmas festival? Was that how she saw herself killing Val? That evil bitch was capable of anything. She had to get Eleanor away from all these people.

Pushing forward, she kept her head down but shoulders square, trying not to look too suspicious. The last thing she needed was security harassing her. She cut through the crowd, heading toward a crop of less crowded buildings to her left.

Then she saw the flash of yellow—Eleanor. About fifty feet away, one corner of her blood-red lips crooked up, then she turned away and disappeared into the throng of people all around her. Val knew Eleanor was almost certainly leading her into a trap again, but *goddammit*, she would not let that woman escape again.

She snaked through the crowd toward the last spot she'd seen Eleanor. When she reached it, she stopped among the mass of people and spun in a circle, searching. Where was Eleanor? She'd been in that exact location only a few seconds ago—

Searing pain shot through Val's left forearm. She cried out and touched the spot that suddenly hurt, and saw blood on her gloves. Someone had cut her—*Eleanor* had cut her, in full view of everyone, and yet the woman had been stealthy enough that no one saw.

"You okay?" a man next to her asked, reacting to her cry of pain.

Val ignored him and whirled around, desperately searching for her attacker. Where was she? Where was she—

Thirty feet away, next to a booth of Christmas wreaths, a shock of yellow hair stood out among the crowd, moving away from her, then disappearing again. Val bound for the booth, trying to keep her eye on the yellow while ping-ponging through the thick crowd. Finally, she reached the spot she'd last seen Eleanor, and…nothing.

"Goddammit!" Val said, breathing hard and swiveling her head in every direction. "What the hell—*ah!*"

She grabbed her right forearm as more pain bloomed there. Another slice to her flesh, with Eleanor still nowhere to be seen. How was she doing this?

Passersby shot alarmed looks her way as she freaked out for

what appeared to be no reason. Then she heard a chuckle. *Where, where, where—*

There! Eleanor glanced over her shoulder as she hurried away with a smirk on her face. Val rushed after her, grimacing at the pain in both arms, but undeterred. In the center of a crowd next to a group of carolers, something sliced open her left calf. She pitched forward into another woman before hitting the ground.

"Oh my!" the woman said as she helped Val stand. "Are you all right, young lady?"

Val struggled to her feet, hopping on her good leg while a blood stain grew on the back of the other.

The woman propped Val up and cringed at the wound while curious rubberneckers looked on. "Looks like you cut yourself. If you want to sit down on that bench over there, I'll go get help—"

"No!" Val pushed the woman away, ignoring the Good Samaritan's insulted *hmmph*. She had to get out of there, away from these people Eleanor was using as human shields. Forcing herself to put weight on her bad leg, she limped toward the less populated buildings she saw earlier, somewhere Eleanor couldn't hide in the crowd.

In a dark alleyway, she pulled out her gun and slumped against the wall. Already she could barely stand, and she hadn't even come face-to-face with Eleanor yet. With a shaking hand, she touched the switchblade in her pocket, ensuring it hadn't fallen out after her tumble to the ground. She wasn't good with a knife, but at least she'd still have some kind of weapon if she lost control of her gun. Now Eleanor…that bitch was good with a knife. Shit.

Val pushed herself off the wall and trudged down the alley.

Ahead of her, a dark figure appeared, silhouetted against the festive lights of the street beyond. The dark figure pulled a black winter cap from its head, and yellow hair tumbled out.

Shoot her now!

Val pointed her gun at Eleanor the same time the psychopath cut left and into an open door, retreating into the building.

"*Fuck.*" Eleanor was definitely leading her into a trap, acting out her death as the "agent of God" had seen it in a vision. But what could she do? Run away and let Eleanor kill more people trying to get at Val and her family? Hell no. She'd face her fate—then change it.

Gun at the ready, Val followed Eleanor through the door and into the dark stairwell of what looked like an apartment building. Footsteps above her told Val that Eleanor was heading up. She climbed the stairs in pursuit, as fast as she could but still slower than normal due to the leg wound. Up they went, up and up and up, until she heard the heavy door to the roof open and slam shut.

Taking a deep breath to steady herself, she shoved the door open while keeping her gun pointed straight in front of her, ready to shoot the first thing that moved. Darkness permeated the roof, lights from the Christmas festival below casting an eerie glow around the edge. With small, deliberate steps, she inched away from the door, scanning the area where a half-dozen ventilation outlets and skylight outcroppings provided ample hiding spots. She remembered her Army training—move to the periphery, then circle the area while moving inward to flush out the enemy. On high alert, Val took quick steps to the roof's edge.

"*Bang!*" she heard Eleanor say.

Val wheeled to her left, the direction of Eleanor's voice. She saw nothing…No, on the ground ten feet away, a square, palm-sized glow—a cell phone. To project a voice recording.

That's when she heard swift footfalls right behind her.

Shit.

Val turned just in time to swing her arms down and block the knife Eleanor drove straight at her gut. Literally face-to-face, Val tried to shove Eleanor away so she could get a shot off. Before Val could get any distance between them, Eleanor used her own arm to lock Val's handgun-holding right arm in place while her other hand swung the knife at Val's neck. Val grabbed Eleanor's wrist and held off the blade, inches from her skin. For a few agonizing seconds that felt like an eternity, they stayed locked in a deadly stalemate, Val gritting her teeth with the desperate effort to stay alive while Eleanor sneered in demented delight.

Then in one sharp jerk, Eleanor popped Val's right shoulder out of its socket. Val shrieked as pain tore through her arm. Still she held on to Eleanor's wrist with everything she had as the blade crept closer, knowing if she let go, she'd die. Her strength quickly waning, tendrils of panic began to seize her. She had to do something. Anything.

With a scream, Val reared her head back and slammed it into Eleanor's nose. Eleanor stumbled backward as blood spurted down her crimson lips. Val tried to lift her gun to shoot, but of course, her goddamn arm wouldn't come up all the way now. As she wasted a precious second switching hands, Eleanor lunged at her with the knife. In a desperate swing with her left arm, she managed to barely block the blade from sinking into her gut again, but the force of the impact knocked her gun from her hand. It skidded away as together they slammed into a cement ventilation outlet next to the roof's edge.

Struggling to breathe, Val groped for the switchblade in her pocket as she kneed Eleanor in the stomach, but it wasn't enough. Eleanor had the upper hand, and she used it. Ignoring Val's frantic thrashing, she stabbed Val in the chest.

Val screamed as the blade sank into her flesh, just below her right collarbone. Every nerve in her body caught on fire.

Eleanor smiled. "This is how you die."

No. Val pawed at the knife and felt Eleanor's hand still on the handle.

"Just like this. There's no one here to help you this time. And after I kill your children, the world will be set right again. Mother and Father will be happy."

No! Through the pain, anger exploded, hot and bright. *"Over my dead body will you touch my children!"*

In one burst of energy, Val yanked Eleanor's hand off the handle, pulled the knife out of her own chest, and plunged it into Eleanor's—straight into the heart.

Eleanor sucked in a single, startled gasp. Her bloody mouth hung open, her eyes bulging as she stared at Val in disbelief.

"That's for Max," Val hissed in Eleanor's face. "And now it's your turn to die!"

Eleanor's lips moved as if she struggled to speak, to deny that her God could have forsaken her after everything she'd done for Him. Her weak hands grasped Val's coat lapels, and Val thought for a moment she wanted to fight again despite not having a working heart. Instead, she stared deep into Val's eyes as if desperately searching for something familiar—and finding it.

"*Mother,*" Eleanor rasped.

Mother. Eleanor looked into Val's eyes and saw the woman she knew as Mother.

I have Mother's eyes.

With a single word, Val's world crushed to nothing, and everything she thought she knew turned to shit.

Before Val could stop her, Eleanor fell backward and off the roof. She landed with a disgusting crunch on the pavement below, across the street from the Christmas festival. A woman shrieked. Heads craned up, looking in Val's direction. Fingers pointed at her. She stumbled away from the edge, out of their line of sight as the pain from wounds all over her body shot through her, only numbed by the panic coursing through her veins.

She had to go home. Now.

Chapter Thirty-two

Val staggered into the kitchen, panting from the effort of keeping pressure on her chest wound while also driving home with a dislocated shoulder.

"Lydia?" she called out as she shuffled forward, her blood dripping onto the floor. "Simon?"

She heard the jingle of Toby's collar and his high-pitched whining, before he appeared at the threshold of the dining room. He was limping.

"Lydia! Simon!"

Val shambled as fast as she could go through the dining room, then to the living room. She stopped dead in her tracks when she saw Jamal facedown on the carpet, a pool of crimson around him.

She rushed over and knelt beside him. "Oh, God."

A guttural moan came from beneath his body.

"Jamal?"

Another moan. Holy shit, he was still alive. She pushed him onto his back, and his eyes fluttered. He clutched a wound on his stomach, blood seeping through his fingers.

"Jamal, can you hear me? What happened?"

He groaned and looked at her with eyes open to slits. "She…stabbed me…"

"Who?" Val knew who. But she needed him to confirm her worst fears had come true.

"Your…mother."

Mother—Val's mother, and Eleanor's Mother. Stacey had said Northwalk was in town for a succession ceremony to hand the organization over to Kat. Bullshit. They'd come for her children, and Dani was their inside woman.

"I came back because I forgot my bag…and she was taking the kids out somewhere…I told her to stop, and then she stabbed me and left"—because knives are *less loud* than guns, Dani had told Val—"I don't want to die…"

Mother controlled Eleanor, and Northwalk controlled Mother. But Eleanor had wanted to kill the twins. Why would Northwalk risk it? Maybe…maybe because *they knew Eleanor wouldn't succeed.*

"Where did she take Simon and Lydia?"

"I don't…"

"Where?"

"I don't know. She didn't say. I don't want to die."

"You won't die here." She didn't know if that was true, but she hadn't seen his death in a vision, for what it was worth. With shaking hands, she fumbled in her pockets for her cell phone and called an ambulance. Then she limped to the kitchen, grabbed a hand towel, and pressed it to Jamal's stab wound.

"Help is coming. Keep pressure here." Val squeezed her eyes shut for a moment, fighting back blurriness growing at the edges of her vision. She needed medical help, too. But she couldn't wait. She needed to find her children first.

Struggling to her feet, she left Jamal and staggered through the front door. "Jamal's bleeding to death in there," she said to the useless bodyguards as she passed by. She'd told them to trust her mother, so they'd let Dani walk right out with her children. "An ambulance is coming. Go stay with him until it gets here."

The guards gawked at her for a moment, totally confused about what was happening, then ran inside as she walked away. She crossed the interior courtyard and went out the iron fence, stumbling onto the sidewalk. Gripped by panic, she dragged herself down the street, no idea where she was going or what she was doing. Her children were out there somewhere, with her mother, their nana, the traitor. She should have seen it coming—

A sedan roared up to the sidewalk and came to a screeching halt in front of her. The driver's side door flew open, then Sten got out and walked to her so fast he might as well have been running.

"Get in," he said.

She ignored him and kept shambling down the street. Whatever he wanted, it could wait. She had to save her children. They came first. Her children. God, her children, her children—

He grabbed her good arm and jerked her to a stop. She groaned as fresh pain spiked through her body.

"*Get in.*"

"No—"

Without another word, Sten dragged her to the car, threw open the passenger's side door, and shoved her inside. Too weak to fight with him, she sat hunched over in the seat and struggled to stay conscious as he punched the gas. A radio crackled with indistinct chatter in the console; they were in an unmarked police cruiser.

"An ambulance and a couple cop cars are responding to your 911 call," he said, sounding tense and annoyed at the same time. "They're also very interested to know if you had anything to do with Eleanor Fatou's dramatic death tonight at the waterfront Christmas festival." He glanced at her as he drove like a maniac away from her condo. "I'm going to guess by your fabulous makeover the answer is yes. Can't let my partner land herself in jail."

She leaned back against the seat as her head began to spin. "She took them," Val muttered.

"Who took what?"

"My mother. She took my babies."

Sten glanced at her again but said nothing, his rare silence a testament to the seriousness of the situation.

"I should have shot her in the head like you told me to. She played me. She *fucking played me*, and now I have nothing. Max is brain-dead, the woman I thought was my mother is dead, my children are gone...I have nothing to live for. *Nothing—*" A weak sob escaped her chest and cut off her words.

"Where did Danielle take them?" Sten asked, his voice gruff and somber.

"I don't know. Probably wherever Northwalk is."

His lips tightened, and deep anger twisted his features.

She scoffed. "What do you care? This was the plan all along, wasn't it? Why you helped Delilah bring Max and me together, why you fucked me and then declared us partners, why you *pretended* to check into my mother's background and verify with your contact she had nothing to do with Northwalk, you lying piece of shit bastard—"

"Shut up, Shepherd," he snapped. "I *did* check into your mom's criminal history." His face darkened further. "And my contact lied to me. Guess our goals don't align after all."

Val's cell phone rang. She thought about ignoring it, but decided the timing was too specific to be a coincidence. Fumbling it out of her pocket with weak fingers, she looked at her caller ID—an unknown number.

"It's them," Sten said. "It's what they do."

Val sucked in a trembling breath and tried to clear the fog from her head. Then she answered the phone. "Where are my daughter and my son?"

"With their nana, of course," Dani said on the other end of the line. The usual uncertainty and softness were gone from her voice, replaced with a sharp, ominous edge. "Congratulations on winning your bout with Eleanor. I wasn't sure which of you would come out alive. My money was on her, honestly, but I guess I underestimated you and that pesky ability of yours to change the future."

Tears born of both anger and sadness burned Val's eyes. "You goddamn bitch. I should have killed you when I had the chance—"

"But you wanted your mommy back too much for that."

Through clenched teeth, Val asked, "How long have you been working with them?"

"Oh, I don't know, a few decades maybe. They pay well, and have excellent benefits. You know, I really did suffer from serious mental illness before they found me. Most of what I told you about that was true. Then they found me and cured me, and I've been grateful ever since. I didn't know you were one of their seers until recently, though. Who would've guessed—my own kid! Well, I'm sure that's why they recruited me in the first place, which seems obvious now. Look at you, keeping important secrets from your mother. How did Max like those pictures I sent him of you and your other boyfriend, by the way? So many secrets you've kept."

"Where are my children?"

"I said they're with me. What you mean to ask is, 'What do I need to do to get my children back?'"

Val swallowed hard and rubbed her cheek, smearing her tears and blood together. She choked the words out, "What do you want?"

"My employers think your particular brand of seer ability could be very valuable, if harnessed correctly. You know their Alpha calls you the Omega? No other seer has a unique designation. You must feel special. They'd like to employ you, too. We could be a mother-daughter team, you and I."

Bile rose in her throat at the thought of working for those people, or seeing her mother alive ever again. "Why wouldn't I end up like your last partner?"

"Oh, Eleanor, that poor, confused girl. She was a lot like you, desperate for a mother to love her. I have to give her credit, though—she made an *excellent* distraction. Cassandra said the odds of us succeeding in taking your kids increased dramatically if you and your husband were separated. Boy, did Eleanor ever come through on that front, despite having no idea what her *true* purpose was. But now you're all alone. Why don't you take Eleanor's place? I think you've earned it."

"No."

"Are you sure, pumpkin? Because what you'd get in return is the assurance your children are safe and well taken care of. They're both Alphas. Either one of them could replace Cassandra. Northwalk only needs one."

Val felt the blood drain from her face. The world spun.

"In fact, having an extra Alpha around could be a problem, if *Yongjai* ever got their hands on it—"

"I'll kill you first! You hear me? If you or any of you evil fucking people even *touch* my children, I will kill all of you!"

Dani chuckled. "Sure you will, pumpkin. Well, think about it. We need to decide which one to keep and which to kill anyway—assuming you won't cooperate. I'll call you back when we've made our decision." The line went dead.

Val let the phone drop from her hand onto the floor. She rested her head against the cool glass and closed her eyes, her mind and body in so much pain, everything had gone numb. Maybe now was a good time to die after all. She'd dodged death before, but everyone died eventually. Perhaps what her mother—the old, fake Dani—had said about visiting her sister's grave and wanting to crawl into the coffin wasn't such a bad idea. She knew now that story was a lie, but it was still inspiring—

"Jesus, Shepherd, get your shit together!" Sten hollered from the driver's seat. Had she been talking out loud to herself? Yes, she had. "Your kids aren't dead yet. You can't die until you've at least tried to save them. And you still owe me."

"Whatever you want, just take it," she muttered. "I can't fight. I don't know where my babies are. I can't work for Northwalk."

"You can't give up."

"Just take what you want and let me die…"

Sten yelled something else at her, his voice growing urgent and…concerned? But she'd either lost too much blood or gone into shock, and his words floated past her like snowflakes in a windstorm.

Chapter Thirty-three

After a blur of time, her body slumped to the right, then she had the strange sensation she floated through the air. Opening her eyes a crack, she realized Sten had taken her out of the car, cradled her in his arms, and was carrying her somewhere. The dark December sky turned to soft interior lamp lights. Forcing her eyes to open wider, she saw a stained ceiling, then the plain twin bed she lay in, and finally bits and pieces of what looked like a shabby extended-stay hotel room around her. Couch cushions propped her legs up, she guessed put there by Sten to alleviate her shock.

"Where are we?" she asked weakly, unable to muster the energy to sit up and look around.

"It's called a safe house," he said, ransacking a cupboard in the kitchen. "It's cheaper than a beach house."

"Why are we here?"

"Because you're a fucking mess." Walking back to the bed with an armful of medical supplies, he added, "And if you're arrested, we'll both be in deep shit."

"I thought you only cared because I owe you."

"That, too." He dumped the supplies on a nightstand, then lifted her head and pushed a pillow underneath with surprising gentleness. "There are several reasons." After pouring three shots worth of whiskey into a mug, he held it to her lips. "Drink."

Val gulped it down. She closed her eyes and felt the liquor burn a path down her throat, a soothing sensation compared to the rest of her body. With the same rare gentleness, Sten rolled her onto her left side and took hold of her right wrist and elbow.

"This might hurt a bit," he said.

Slowly, he rotated her arm upward. Pain grew like water building behind a dam, until the dam broke and she cried out when her shoulder popped back into its socket. She let out a long exhale as her arm finally relaxed.

"Thank you," she mumbled, eyes closed and barely awake as a reprieve from the worst of her pain combined with the alcohol worked their magic.

Only vaguely did she feel him threading her coat and sweatshirt from her torso, rolling her onto her back, and slipping off her shoes and pants until just her bra and panties remained. She had no energy to protest, and God help her, she trusted him. Like it or not, she had no choice. They *were* partners. Shit.

He tenderly touched the skin around the stab wound on her chest. "You've got the luck of the Irish, or wherever that red hair comes from. Looks like Eleanor missed all your vital organs. Guess she didn't pray for your death hard enough." She heard him riffling through his medical supplies for a moment. "This is gonna hurt a bit, too."

Val jolted awake as her wound caught fire—he'd splashed disinfectant on it.

"Give me the liquor!" she rasped.

He passed her the bottle, and she gulped down a mouthful. When a needle punctured her skin, she worked to stifle a scream, clamping her teeth together and clutching the sheets with white knuckles as he sewed the cut closed.

"You're being a real baby right now," he said.

"Shut up."

"Ever try doing this on yourself? It fucking sucks. Especially when you've been shot in your dominant arm so you have to use your off-hand, and there's a kill squad actively looking for you, and all your mates are dead, and you're eleven years old."

After she took another desperate drink, she asked, "Why haven't you told me about your past before?"

He shrugged as he sewed, every pass of the needle through her skin a new agony. "Why would I? We were never really together."

They weren't now, either…Ah hell, yes they were. At the moment, he was all she had. "I'm sorry your childhood sucked."

"Oh, you thought I was talking about myself? I was describing a hypothetical. And anyway, once you've heard one sob story, you've heard 'em all. Just fill in the blanks of misery. Family member or members died when I was blank years old, henceforth abused or taken advantage of by blank, felt different synonyms for alone all my life, plus some unrequited or tragic love thrown in there somewhere. I've just described the life stories of ninety percent of the population."

"Jesus, Sten, shut up—"

The horrible needle stabbing stopped. "Look at that, all done." He'd been talking to distract her. She forgot—he never did anything without a reason. He dressed the stitches with gauze and medical tape, then lifted her arms and leg to inspect the gashes there. "You can probably get by with butterfly bandages on these—unless you want me to stitch them up, too."

"God no."

She whimpered as he poured more disinfectant into the three other gashes, then applied the bandages. Dropping the half-empty whiskey bottle on the carpet, she let blessed unconsciousness take her away, not sure she wanted to return.

* * *

Val woke up from what she hoped had been the worst dream of her life. As her surroundings came into focus and the pain of her many wounds screamed across her body, her heart sank—nope, the last two awful days had actually happened.

Tucked snuggly underneath a comforter, she pushing herself up on her elbows and took a better look around. Sten's safe house wasn't in a hotel room, she realized, but a low-rent studio apartment. It did, however, looked like a cheap hotel room…just like the one in her earlier vision, when she'd argued with Sten and he mentioned her mother—which had brought her to him in the first place. Great, they'd come full circle.

With a groan, she sat up and dragged her legs over the side of the bed. A small, thick cathode-ray television droned in the corner, showing the local news in oversaturated colors. Summing up all the calamities that had befallen Seattle in the last few weeks, an anchorman announced a special guest—ex-mayor and current Congresswoman Delilah Barrister. Val flinched when her face materialized on the screen.

"These terrible tragedies break my heart," Delilah said, contorting her face into what Val considered the fakest expression of sympathy ever. "Luckily, Seattle is strong, and I know we'll get through this. We're stronger together!"

As Delilah kept lying about how much she cared for the city, Val hefted herself off the bed, walked to the television where it sat atop a beat-up end table, and with one strong yank she tossed it to the floor. With a flash and a pop, the screen cracked and went black.

A moment later, Sten entered through the front door, dusting a light coat of snow off the shoulders of a black field jacket. He'd ditched his work suit and tie for a pair of faded denim jeans and military-style tan boots—his shit's-hit-the-fan outfit, apparently.

Cocking an eyebrow at the broken TV, he took off his jacket and smoothed out a bunched-up black wool sweater he wore underneath. "Finally, you're up. I thought you were going to sleep all fucking day."

Maybe she should have. What was the point of waking up anymore? Max was basically dead, her mother had betrayed her, an evil cabal had kidnapped her children and she had no idea where to start looking for them, and Delilah was using the city's chaos for her own political gain. She should've stayed blissfully asleep.

Sten walked to the kitchen, poured himself a mug of coffee he'd made sometime before Val woke, and took a long slurp. "Checked the police scanners. They've got an APB out for you, but no arrest warrant yet. Still, if they see you all banged up, they're gonna know you tangled with Eleanor, and into the slammer you'll go. That is, unless you can prove stabbing a woman in the heart and throwing her off a roof was all in self-defense."

"No, I went there to kill her." Despair wrapped around Val's heart and hollowed out her voice. Returning to the bed, she sat in a heap. "Eleanor was going to kill me, but I changed it."

He walked to Val and held out his coffee cup, offering her a drink. She ignored it.

"They want me to work for them, because I can change things."

"Makes sense. They want your kids, but they need you and Carressa out of the way—especially you. They know you'll never leave them alone until you get the kids back, but since you can change the future, they can't predict what you'll do. You'd give Northwalk a run for their money, and they don't want to deal with it. Since Eleanor failed to kill you, the next best thing is to force you to work for them, control you that way. A classic 'threaten a loved one to ensure compliance' move." He sipped coffee and frowned at the far wall. "I've seen them run similar plays."

Chugging the rest, he set the mug down on the kitchen counter and paced the tiny apartment, head down in thought. "This isn't as bad as it seems. You work for them for a little while, gain their trust, wait for your opening, then turn one of their little prophesies against them."

"I can't do that. I can't work for them."

"Yes, you can." He looked at her and sneered, "What, Eleanor sever your spine, too?"

He wanted her to get angry, but an overwhelming sense of hopelessness stifled every other emotion. She dropped her head in her hands. "I can't do this."

"Yes, you can. You'd be surprised how much shit a person can put up with when properly motivated."

"I think I'd rather die."

"It's really not that bad."

"Yes it is." She picked up the half-empty bottle of whiskey from the floor and took a long drink. "Yes it is."

Sten rolled his eyes. "Here we go with your goddamn hysterics again."

She ignored him to concentrate on drinking the liquor as quickly as possible. If she focused on breathing through her nose, she could shotgun it—

Sten grabbed her arm and yanked the bottle from her lips. "Stop it. It's not that bad."

"Maybe you can live like a slave, but I can't."

She must have hit a nerve, because anger flared behind his eyes. His grip around her wrist tightened until the pain became too much and the whiskey bottle dropped from her hand, thudding against the stained carpet at their feet. She whimpered but refused to ask him to stop. She'd let him kill her if he wanted. She almost wished he would.

He seized her other wrist and slammed her down on the bed, the mattress groaning underneath the force. Pain from her many injuries jolted through her body.

"I never took you for a quitter, Shepherd," he said, his mouth an inch from hers. "There are ways to resist. At the very least I thought you'd want to have one more quality meeting with your mother. Your efforts so far have been frankly pathetic."

Angry tears leaked down her cheeks. She wanted to spit in his face, but she wanted release more.

Show me where they are, she would say to him, begging for a vision he could focus like no one else, not even her own husband. The words were on the tip of her tongue, ready to slide into the world as she'd foretold and lead the way to them having angry, desperate sex. Maybe Sten would show her where Dani took her children, and she could go there and rescue them. All she had to do was give her body to him.

But she couldn't do it. She loved Max too much to let it happen. There had to be another way.

"Stop," she said, summoning the last threads of her willpower. "Get off me."

His black eyes stared hard at her, his anger replaced with something else—hunger. For a scary second, she thought he might take her anyway. Instead, he stood, backed up, and collapsed onto the couch.

He bellowed, "What *can* you do then, Val?" His smarmy, self-confident mask crumbled under the weight of his anger and frustration, revealing his own bald desperation, a surprising match for her own. "Because I can't live like this anymore either. You have to do *something!* Make a fucking decision!"

She sat up and clutched the sides of her head. *Think, Val, think. Come on. There's got to be another way.*

"What…what are the chances Northwalk is nearby?" she asked.

With his eyes closed, Sten rubbed the bridge of his nose as if trying to calm his passion down. "High. They wouldn't trust anyone else with their Alpha—or multiple Alphas now—for more time than absolutely necessary. They would insist your mom come straight back to them with the kids."

"Their Alpha…does that mean Cassandra's with them?"

"Most likely, yeah."

"I saw her in a vision a few days ago. She was in a big room in a house surrounded by a forest. And Stacey mentioned Northwalk is hiding out in a forest mansion that's been beefed up with extra security." She looked at Sten and sat up straight, her mental strength returning. "You can't just buy a fortress like that from Century 21. They must have hired a company to do extensive renovations—work they'd want kept off the books so it couldn't be traced back to them. They'd need to hire a construction company with no problem working without permits and breaking the law."

"The place will be a hard target," Sten said. "Getting in will be a challenge." But not impossible.

Val stood, nearly naked but finally energized, her mind sharpening like a keen knife. "Good thing I know someone with connections to a shady construction company who owes me a favor."

Sten met her gaze with an eagerness for vengeance that mirrored her own. The black thread that bound them together felt tighter than ever.

"Do you have weapons?" she asked.

He scoffed. "*Do* I." He walked to the kitchen and pushed the refrigerator out of the way, then popped open a panel embedded in the wall. In a secret compartment, he'd stashed at least a dozen guns—rifles, shotguns, and a few pistols, along with hundreds of ammo rounds.

"You never know when there'll be a zombie apocalypse," he said, "or when people who can see the future steal your kids."

"That'll work." She began pulling on her clothes with a new sense of purpose, fueled by a burning, insatiable desire to hurt those who'd hurt her as quickly as possible.

"I lied when I told Dani I'd kill them all if they touched my children," she said. "No matter what happens, I'm going to kill them all anyway."

Chapter Thirty-four

Stacey paced the room that she and Kat shared in the forest mansion, staring at the text messages she'd sent to Val on her phone.

I'm so sorry about Max.

Are u ok?

I'm still in town…do u need help?

I know you're mad at me, but I'm here for you.

Where r u?

The longer Val failed to respond, the more anxious she got. Though her friend had told her essentially to go to hell, when she saw news of Max in critical condition at Harborview Hospital, their nanny stabbed, the Carressa kids missing, and Val herself nowhere to be found, Stacey's panic reflex kicked in. How did Val always get into these goddamn situations? Some things never changed. Poor Val.

"Calm down, baby," Kat said from the bed, where she sat completely naked, toweling her hair down after a shower. "I'm sure the police are on it."

"Are you kidding me?" Stacey rounded on her girlfriend. "You're seriously telling me Northwalk didn't have anything to do with this?"

"Max and Val have a lot of enemies," Kat said, ignoring Stacey's agitation. "Didn't some newspaper get a tip a woman was stalking them?"

"So you know nothing?"

With a shrug, Kat shook her head, then shot Stacey her most innocent smile.

She's lying.

Stacey turned away so her girlfriend wouldn't see her crestfallen face. She didn't trust anything Kat said anymore. *Choose love*, Cassandra had said. *I'm trying, goddammit, I'm really, really trying—*

"Hey, come here," Kat said, tossing the towel to the side. She walked to Stacey and pressed her perfect body against her girlfriend's. "I've got a few minutes before my mother's meeting." Kat seized Stacey's lips in a long, deep kiss. "Why don't I help take your mind off Val's problems?" Her hands moved down to Stacey's pants, working the zipper free.

Stacey stepped away. For maybe the first time ever, she wasn't overcome with lust for her sex goddess of a girlfriend. "I need some air," she said. "I'm going out for coffee."

Kat frowned, a rare hint of shock in her eyes. "Okay. How long will you be gone?"

Throwing on her coat, she said, "I dunno. A couple hours or so."

"Bring me back my usual latte?"

"Sure."

Kat grabbed Stacey's arm before she walked out the door. "Baby, you know I'm on your side. I'd do anything for you."

"I know," Stacey lied. She wanted with all her heart to believe it was true, but she wasn't buying it anymore.

"I love you."

"I love you, too," she said truthfully, her heart breaking at the realization her feelings were almost certainly unrequited. Was Kat even capable of love? *Choose love, Stacey. Choose love…* "I'll be back soon."

Kat smiled, satisfied their relationship crisis had been averted. In reality, she had Cassandra to thank.

Stacey wound her way through the gilded compound toward the exit, ignoring the half-dozen silent security guards along the way. She hated this place. No amount of expensive wainscoting and designer wall drapes could make it feel any less like a prison. Every time she stepped outside, she felt lucky to have made it out, even though nothing physically kept her in. It took a key card and a thumb print to unlock the steel-reinforced doors at the entrance; maybe she'd pretend she lost the card and stay at a hotel that night.

As she walked by Cassandra's office, something shiny caught her eye. A metallic object the size of her thumb sat wedged half-way underneath the Alpha's closed door. Stepping closer, she recognized it as a silver cigarette lighter. It couldn't be…

She knelt and picked it up. Turning it over in her hand, she gasped when she saw the inscription etched on one side: *It's never too late to quit! Commit arson instead. Love, Val.* Holy shit, it was the lighter Val had given her as a gift for her twenty-first birthday. When she'd stopped smoking about a year into her relationship with Kat, she'd lost track of the damn thing, and thought it was gone for good. How the hell had it ended up here? Did Kat have it this whole time? Seemed almost as if someone put it on the ground specifically for her to find—

The door to Cassandra's office flew open, and a little blond boy ran straight into her. He bounced off her legs and landed on his butt.

She reached down to help him up. "Are you all right, little man?" What in the world was a child doing there? She'd never seen children in Northwalk's fortress before.

He looked at her with big hazel eyes brimming with tears. "Do something."

"Do...what?"

"Simon," an older woman with short red hair called from inside the office, "don't run away, darling. Everything will be all right. Come back to Nana."

Next to the woman, Cassandra stood by silently like a specter—as she always did—while Honora tapped her foot, her creepy plastic-like face contorted into an expression of supreme annoyance.

Head down, the boy shuffled back inside. Instead of returning to the woman, he embraced a little girl his same size with black hair and blue eyes the color of steel. She cradled the boy—probably her brother—in her arms as she glared at Honora with a surprising amount of defiance for a kid who couldn't have been older than five. In fact, the little girl reminded her of... *Val*.

Stacey's stomach dropped. *Sweet Jesus, please say those aren't Val's kids.* And that woman, with hair the same color as her best friend's, except streaked with silver...*And please say that's not Val's mother.* What in the *fuck* was going on here?

With her chin jutted out, the girl said to Honora, "My mommy's going to kill you."

Honora's lips tightened. She looked at Cassandra.

"She lies," the Seer said.

The Northwalk matriarch relaxed, confident in the Alpha's proclamation. Her gaze cut back to the children. "Seems like the girl is the stronger of the two." She smirked. "Interesting how it often works out that way."

Honora walked to the children and pulled them apart. They both started wailing. Stacey's heart clenched into a knot.

"Best to separate them now," she said.

Simon chanted to himself, "Monogon, digon, trigon, tetragon, pentagon, hexagon, heptagon—"

Honora slapped him hard. Stacey gasped and clamped a hand over her mouth. God, this couldn't be happening.

"Shut up," the Northwalk matriarch snapped at Simon. She looked at the girl. "You, too. Or should I hit him again?"

The girl fell silent, though angry tears streamed down her plump cheek.

"Smart girl. You won't even remember you had a brother."

Honora shoved the boy at their nana—Val's mother. He buried his head in the woman's leg while she caressed his head.

"There, there, it'll be all right," she said in a soothing voice, her face totally devoid of compassion.

"The girl will be your successor," Honora said to Cassandra. "We'll hold the ceremony tonight." She looked at Val's mother. "You keep the boy for now. We'll decide what to do with him when we hear back from the Omega."

The succession ceremony…for the *Alpha*, not Northwalk leadership.

Kat lied to her. *Of course* Kat lied. That's what she did. Stacey knew all along, but couldn't accept it. In fact, she might have continued not accepting it if she hadn't been standing in front of Cassandra's door at that exact moment, accidentally witnessing this horrific exchange…Ha, "accidentally." Bullshit. Someone wanted her to see it—probably Cassandra. Why? The Seer told her to choose love, and she fucking did that already. What more did the Alpha want from her?

"*You*," Honora said, noticing Stacey for the first time. "Fetch my daughter."

Too stunned by what she'd seen to argue, Stacey turned and walked away from the office, back toward her and Kat's room. *Do something*, the boy said to her. He was right—she had to do something. But what in the world could she do to help those poor children? Breaking them out of the Northwalk compound by herself wasn't an option—too many guards. Asking Kat for help was out of the question now, too. She was done forgiving Kat's lies, or trusting her with anything.

Stacey stopped in the middle of the hallway to swipe tears from her eyes. The walls closed in around her. She couldn't breathe. Where could she go? What could she do? Do something. *Do something…*

Looking at the lighter she still clutched in her hand, she read the inscription again. *Love, Val*, it said.

Choose love—

Cassandra told her to choose love, but she didn't specify what *kind* of love. Stacey had chosen romantic love with Kat—and she'd chosen wrong. She should've chosen the love of friendship, and love for herself, to have the courage and self-respect to do what she knew in her gut was right. Following Julian hadn't been her test—*this moment* was her test. Accompanying Kat's brother on his homicidal errands had just been the prep, so she had the perspective she needed when the real test came.

Sucking in a lungful of air, Stacey dropped the lighter in her pocket and stood tall. She knew what she had to do. Time to fight for love.

She walked quickly, but not too fast to be suspicious. When she reached Julian's room, she pressed her ear against the door. Hearing nothing, she slipped inside. Her heart thumped against her rib cage as she searched his room, looking under his bed and in his drawers. Pulling open the closet, she finally found it—the small blue duffel bag. She reached down and grabbed it at the same moment she heard the knob on the bedroom door turn.

Oh shit.

Stacey dived into the corner of the closet half a second before Julian walked in. If he found her in his room, stealing his precious drugs, he'd kill her—or worse. She held her breath as he moved around, catching glimpses of him through the closet door slats while he threw off his clothes. Glancing up, she stifled a curse when she saw a row of business suits hanging next to her. If he decided to change into something more professional, she was screwed.

She had to get out of there. One thing she could count on was Kat always having her cell phone within arm's reach. God forbid she miss a call from Mommy Dearest. With shaking hands, Stacey texted Kat: *On my way out, your mom said she wanted to see you asap—you and Julian.* She hit Send.

He began to whistle some awful tune as he opened and closed different drawers. A pair of underwear and socks landed on the bed, and when he walked into her field of view, she saw he was naked.

Hurry up, Kat.

He disappeared again, and a few seconds later a tie was tossed on top of the undergarments. Shit, he was preparing to don a suit.

Come ON, Kat!

She bit her lip as his approaching body blocked the light

coming in through the slats, a scream rising in her throat when he grabbed the closet's knob—

Someone knocked on the door. He stopped and turned away from the closet. *Sweet Jesus, thank you*, she mouthed.

"Finally got rid of the beard?" he said when he answered. "Or whatever the opposite of a beard is."

"Don't be jealous," Kat said. "It's unbecoming." Stacey heard the door close, then Kat walked into her field of view, a simple blouse and slacks hastily thrown on. "I'm sorry you don't understand love."

"I understand what a completely useless emotion it is."

"Get dressed quick. Mother wants to see us right now."

Was he still naked?

"Don't want to have a quick fuck first?"

Kat laughed. "Maybe after. Come on, let's go."

Were they joking? Who wisecracks about incest while walking around naked in front of their sibling? Ah hell, it didn't matter. They could screw like bunnies and have oodles of inbred children for all she cared. Would've been nice to know before wasting half a decade on a bed of lies. That was what she got for blindly following her heart—or more accurately, her vagina. Screw Northwalk, screw Julian, and screw Kat…Claire…Kitty…whatever her name was.

After more opening and closing of drawers and the rustling of clothes, Stacey surmised Julian threw on something less formal than a suit and followed Kat out of the room, shutting the door behind him. She exhaled a huge sigh of relief. Certain death at the hands of her *ex*-girlfriend's psychopathic brother—averted. Now all she had to do was slip out of the mansion without being seen, get to Harborview Hospital as quickly as possible, and perform a miracle.

Chapter Thirty-five

Val banged on Lacy Zephyr's door. A second later, Aaron's wife answered, eyes widening at the sight of Val. With a nervous glance over her shoulder, she stepped outside and shut the door behind her, wrapping an Afghan sweater around her arms to keep out the evening chill.

"What are you doing here?" Lacy whispered as if her house-guests could hear her through the walls.

"I need a meeting with your father. Right now."

"Why?"

"You can ask him after we've talked."

Lacy turned her nose up at that answer. "You're wanted by the police. Why should I help you?"

Val pointed at the unmarked police car parked on the curb, where Sten waited. "He's the police, so they know where I am." That was technically true. "And you owe me a favor."

"No I don't. You didn't get me pictures of Aaron with his mistress."

"She's dead now. I gave you a free upgrade. You're welcome."

Lacy's mouth fell open, and she scanned the area as if looking for signs of a sting operation.

"I'll take that meet-and-greet with your dad now, please."

With a tense sigh, Lacy said, "Fine. I'll text you the address where Daddy works, and let him know you're coming."

"Pleasure doing business with you, Lacy."

As she walked away, Lacy called after her, "Wait. Do you...know where Aaron is?" Her voice choked up. "I really miss him. And I still love him, despite whatever he's done."

The image of Max lying in his hospital bed, brain-dead, flashed through Val's mind. With hot tears and a cold breeze stinging her eyes, she glanced over her shoulder at Aaron's wife—likely his widow now. "You should have told him that when you had the chance."

* * *

Mister Rodgers's Lumber Yard sounded like a kid's playground. One would never guess there were probably bodies buried underneath the construction equipment.

Val and Sten drove to the main warehouse in the back, where Lacy's father waited for them. Sten followed her into the building's interior, to provide some muscle in case things went south. She didn't need him there, but the implication of a masculine threat went a long way with macho criminal types who might be wary of dealing with a member of the "weaker sex." And Sten was, in truth, an excellent killer. So was she, when necessary. A confrontation would be ugly. Best to get in and out of there as quickly as possible.

Sawdust tickled her nose as they walked through the huge building, passing lumber machinery and piles of wood in various states of processing. A half-dozen blue collar employees—working too late to be up to anything good—eyed them along their path through the warehouse. Finally, she spotted Mr. Rodgers, leaning over a wide drafting table while flanked by two big, expressionless men.

"Pretty late for a meeting, Ms. Shepherd," he said, "but when my baby girl asks for something, how can I say no?"

Skipping past the niceties, she asked, "Have you done work on a mansion in the forest recently?"

He cocked his head half an inch. "Why do you ask?"

"I know for a fact someone refurbished a house in the woods with heavy security—someone who had to work fast, and didn't go through the usual permit process so they could stay under the radar."

"I don't like what you're implying, Ms.—"

"Fine. If you're not the one who refurbed the house, I'll have to find out who did, and offer them a lot of money instead."

Lifting his eyebrow, he said, "Say, hypothetically, my team did in fact do some work on a mansion in the woods. What's your interest in the matter?"

"I need to get in there. Tonight. I assume you installed a secret back door to override the security system, just in case. Well, this is your 'just in case' moment. Give me the house's address, and access to the back door."

"What kind of compensation are we talking here?"

Val scoffed at his stupid question. "Do you know how much my husband is worth?" She planted her palms on the drafting table and leaned toward him until they were face-to-face. "Name your price."

A slow smile spread across Mr. Rodgers's face as he realized today was his lucky day.

* * *

Pulling off the narrow highway that would eventually splinter
and end at Northwalk's mansion in two miles, Sten parked on
the shoulder. He turned off the car, and they sat in darkness for
a moment, the vast expanse of woods east of Seattle known as
Tiger Mountain State Forest surrounding them.

"You know we'll probably die tonight," Sten said.

"I know. Do you have a problem with that?"

"Not at all. I've been waiting for this moment for a very long
time. Just need to make sure you're not going to change your
mind when our deaths become imminent."

She let out a mirthless laugh. "Max is dead. If I can't save Simon and Lydia, I'll be happy to be dead, too."

"All right, partner. Let's do this."

They threw open their doors and stepped into the chilly night.
Sten popped the trunk, where they'd stored their gear, and they
slipped on body armor and loaded up with as much ammo as
they could carry, rounds shoved in every pocket. Thanks to Sten's
extensive cache, they each carried an AR-15 assault rifle, a Glock,
and a .45 handgun. Before leaving Sten's safe house, they had
each downed a handful of muscle relaxers to blunt Val's current
injuries as well as the wounds they'd surely sustain during their
assault, and caffeine pills to keep them going. She could feel the
meds beginning to work their magic, dulling the agony of her
cuts and pumping adrenaline through her veins. Like a bull ready
to charge, thick puffs of air rose from her mouth as she slapped a
magazine in her rifle and racked a round into the chamber. If her
children were in the mansion, she'd get them out. If not, she'd kill
everyone she saw, maybe leave one alive to beat for information.
Northwalk's reckoning had come.

As ready as she'd ever be and itching to fight, she nodded at Sten; he nodded back. Together they trotted into the woods, in the direction of the mansion. After twenty minutes of jogging past evergreens silhouetted in the moonlight, sweet pine and cold mist filling her lungs, they reached the back door—a camouflaged metal case nestled at the base of a tree about a quarter mile from the house.

Val fished the key Rodgers had given her out of her pocket, and used it to open the padlock securing the case. Tossing the lock to the side, she opened the case and looked at the relay box inside, a red switch affixed to the left side, as Rodgers said it would be.

According to Lacy's dad, once Val hit the switch, Northwalk's security system would shut down and all the electronic locks throughout the house would disengage. An alarm would sound and emergency lights would come on courtesy of a generator in the basement, but there wouldn't be enough power to bring the security system back up, not without finding the breaker the relay box had cut into and disabling it. The only thing standing between Val and her children would be whatever muscle Northwalk had on hand—probably a tiny army. And they'd know immediately an attack was coming. The moment she flipped the switch, there was no going back.

Val looked at Sten; he raised his rifle and nodded, ready. She hit the switch in the relay box, then jumped up and sprinted toward the house, Sten right behind her. Less than three minutes later, they reached the periphery of the mansion and took position side by side, stalking forward, guns up. From inside the mansion, they heard yelling. Val ran to the entrance and shoved the heavy, steel-reinforced door open. Then the shooting began.

Chapter Thirty-six

"Natalie, please," Stacey said to the medical resident where they stood in the corner of Harborview Hospital's main lobby. "You have to sneak me in to see Max Carressa. It's important."

Natalie crossed her arms, blowing a piece of hair that'd escaped her messy ponytail out of her face. "Why, exactly, do I owe you any favors? You cheated on me!"

"A long time ago!"

"Not to mention I could lose my job if I get caught sneaking you into an area you're not supposed to be in. *And* it's unethical."

Stacey would've shoved a wad of twenties into Natalie's hand if she thought it would work, but her ex-girlfriend was too classy and honest for that. Dammit. "Listen, I know I fucked up when we were together, and I'm sorry. But this isn't about us. My best friend's husband is dying, and I think I can help him. I need to at least try."

Natalie's rigid posture softened a bit. Whispering to keep any undercover reporters from overhearing, she said, "He's suffered severe cranial and spinal trauma. He's unlikely to live through the next twenty-four hours, let alone regain consciousness. You can't help him. Unfortunately, nobody can."

"Then he has nothing to lose. Please, Natalie, let me see him, only for a few minutes. If what I try doesn't work, I'll leave immediately, and no one will know I was here."

Natalie sighed and shook her head. "Well…what is it you're going to do?"

"It's an, uh, herbal thing. With crystals. Ancient Chinese recipe. I just sprinkle it around his bed. I've seen it work before. It's like magic!" She gave Julian's duffel bag around her shoulder a slight shake for emphasis.

Natalie rolled her eyes at Stacey's description, no doubt thinking her ex-girlfriend had succumbed to some crazy medical fad similar to avocado colon cleanses or huffing rhino horns. "You absolutely *cannot* touch him, or any of the life support equipment he's on, or pour anything on his wounds or his skin, or give him anything orally, intravenously, rectally, or any other way you can think of. Understand?"

"Yes! Thank you, thank you. I owe you big time."

Natalie motioned for Stacey to follow her. "Just don't get me fired."

They wound through the corridors of the hospital's interior, Stacey keeping her head down to avoid drawing attention to their little smuggling operation. After a few minutes of serpentine walking, they came to a small room with about a million machines in it, all hooked up in some way to Max's lifeless body on a hospital bed. She'd never been the biggest fan of Val's husband, but damn, he did not deserve this.

An older man in a hospital gown looked up from where he sat at Max's bedside, his face taut with grief. "Hello?" he said, a cross between a greeting and a question.

"Hi, I'm Val's friend—Stacey, my name's Stacey."

"Nice to meet you," he said, though his voice sounded drained and his smile weak and fleeting. "I'm Michael, Max's…friend…dad…something in the middle."

Jesus, the poor guy was missing an arm, too. "I'm sorry for your loss," she said, unable to stop herself from glancing back and forth between Max and the spot where Michael's left arm should be.

Michael rolled his eyes. "He's not dead yet, and I've still got one arm, so all things considered, it could be worse. And your awkwardness is providing some much-needed comic relief, so thanks for that."

"Oh. Glad I could help."

"What are you doing here anyway?"

Natalie nudged her and nodded toward Max: *Get on with it already.*

Stacey walked to the bed. "I came here to pay my respects."

"I said he's not dead yet."

"I know, I know." She reached into the duffel bag and eased a vial of blue stuff into the jet injector. With a nervous glance up, she saw two doctors conversing on the other side of a window, gesturing toward Max and shaking their heads. "I wanted to, um, try something."

Stacey pulled the injector from the duffel bag. She didn't know exactly how they worked, but Julian and Honora made it seem simple enough—press the tip against the neck, pull the trigger, and watch a miracle occur.

As soon as Natalie caught sight of the injector, she was in Stacey's face. "What the *hell* are you doing?"

"Just let me try—"

"No!" Natalie seized Stacey's arm, and they struggled for a couple seconds over control of the hypo.

"Please! I've got to try—"

The sound of Max flat-lining broke them up.

"*Shit!*" Natalie lunged for a defibrillator on the wall while Michael pushed away from the bed, terror racked across his face.

It was now or never.

With Natalie distracted, Stacey pushed the injector's tip into Max's neck. "Please work," she said, and squeezed the trigger.

Nothing happened. Fuck. *Fuck!* She'd failed. She'd chosen love too late. What would she tell Val if she ever saw her friend again? How could she look her in the eyes, knowing how she'd let her down—

Max's hand twitched. Then his arms followed, and his legs. The heart monitor sprang to life with a torrent of chaotic beeps, a procession of jagged peaks flooding the screen. Twitches turned to spasms, and the hospital bed bucked and banged against the wall as his whole body convulsed.

Just when Stacey thought she'd somehow made him worse than dead, his eyes popped open. The convulsions winded down to thrashing as he cast a wild gaze around the room. He jerked his head up and yanked the tube out of his throat, gagging when the end came out, before sucking in a lungful of air.

Max looked at Stacey, then Natalie, then Michael, and then the horde of doctors who'd begun storming the room, every single person frozen and staring at him.

He gasped, "What...am I...doing here?"

For a moment, no one said anything, unable to get their jaws off the floor.

Oh my God, it worked. I can't believe it worked.

When Stacey's voice returned, she said, "You were in a car accident."

He blinked at her, still dazed. Hopefully, it wasn't permanent. "Was I? When?"

"Yesterday."

Touching his temple, he pushed off a bandage wrapped around his head, revealing smooth, unbroken flesh underneath. "But how did I—"

"I'll explain everything later, okay? Right now, we need to get the hell out of here. Val and your kids need your help."

Mention of his family seemed to snap him out of his confused state. He threw off his bed sheet. "Where are they?" he asked as he pulled tubes out of his body.

"A mansion in the woods. I'll take you there." She dug into the duffel bag and pulled out a pair of khakis, a sweater, and shoes she'd swiped from Julian's bedroom. "You can put those on. We have to go now."

He jumped off the bed and teetered as the side effects of Lucien's mystery drug seemed to hit him. After a few seconds, he found his balance and threw on the spare clothing. Less than a minute later, he was dressed and rushing out the door, pushing past the crowd of doctors too stunned to stop him.

Stacey shoved the duffel bag into Natalie's arms, her ex-girlfriend still standing by with the defibrillator pads in both hands. "Hope this is enough to make us square," she said on her way out, following Max. "Enjoy your Nobel Prize in Medicine."

Chapter Thirty-seven

Rifles at the ready, Val swept to the right while Sten took the left, shooting a couple guards they'd taken by surprise. They faced a long hallway that ended in a foyer, which branched off into half a dozen other hallways with connecting rooms, according to the plans Mr. Rodgers showed them. She had no idea where her children could be in the house; they'd have to sweep each floor as quickly as possible so Northwalk wouldn't have time to escape. Taking prisoners wasn't an option. These people forfeited any mercy she might have shown them when they killed Max and stole her babies.

Val taking point, she and Sten ran down the hallway. A siren like a fire alarm blared through the house, tiny emergency lights along the walls providing only enough illumination to see ghosts of the mansion's innards. Guards swarmed into the foyer and opened fire on the two as they approached, their guns flashing in the darkness with each *pop*. Val and Sten slammed their backs against the wall and took cover behind the hallway's corners, waiting for a lull in the gunfire before sending a volley of bullets back at the guards. A few Northwalk grunts crumpled to the ground while the rest dove behind expensive furniture for some semblance of cover, as if a three-thousand-dollar Italian leather sofa could stop rifle rounds. Val stepped out from behind the corner and shot through the couch and a couple end tables. Chunks of stuffing and wood splinters erupted into the air and coated the guards' bodies like volcano ash. Three more grunts jumped up from their hiding spot and fired at her, but their shots bounced off her body armor and only nicked her arms. She riddled them with bullets before they could do her any serious harm.

"Clear!" Sten called out with his back against hers, his rifle sweeping the area of destruction he'd created on the opposite side of the foyer.

"This way!"

They pushed farther into Northwalk's stronghold. The guards kept coming in waves as the two of them kicked doors open and swept each room they passed, not stopping for anything. They pushed relentlessly forward, clearing the first floor, then the second, mowing down anything in their path, letting bullets ricochet off their armor.

Sprinting up the stairs to the third floor, Val took down the guards waiting around the right corner of the connecting hallway while Sten went left. When the last goon dropped, she heard Sten cry out behind her. Wheeling around, she saw him drop to his knee, clutching his calf, blood oozing through his fingers. Val grabbed him by the arm and helped support him as they ducked into the nearest cover, somebody's bedroom. She propped him against the wall, and he slid to the ground into a sitting position.

"One of those bastards got me," he grunted, lifting his fingers to reveal a bullet hole clean through his calf.

She slung her rifle across her back, threw open a dresser drawer, and dumped out the clothes inside. Grabbing a long-sleeved shirt, she began tying it around his wound. "Did it go through the bone?"

"Negative."

"Then you're fine."

He choked out a strained chuckle. "Sure, I'll just walk it off—"

Something slammed into Val's side, sending her rolling across the floor. As she tumbled, she caught sight of tall, blond man whacking Sten across the face with the base of a lamp. Sten slumped over, unmoving, as the man lunged toward Val. She jerked out of the way a half second before the lamp base smashed into the floor where her head had been and splintered into pieces. With her rifle pinned beneath her back, she reached for the Glock at her hip. As she pulled it out of the holster, the man jumped on top of her, knocking it underneath the bed and pinning her arms down.

An evil smile spread across his face. "Valentine Shepherd, the Omega. I always wondered what you tasted like."

"Keep wondering, motherfucker!"

She kicked a knee up and he fell to the side, but he managed to keep hold of one of her arms. With her other arm, she pummeled him in the face and torso, anywhere she could reach, as they rolled around on the ground. A glint of steel caught her eye, and she grabbed the man's wrist as he swung a knife toward her. Goddamn Northwalk and their fucking knives.

He kneed her in the chest with enough force to knock the air out of her lungs. As she gasped for air, he yanked his wrist out of her grasp and stabbed her in the hand. Val shrieked as he smiled at his small victory. In her fury, she finally landed a solid blow to his nose with her free hand, pushing him back enough so she could kick him off. Gritting her teeth, she yanked the blade free and scrambled to her feet at the same time he sprang up. Before she could swing her rifle around or pull the .45 wedged in her back, he threw himself into her and pinned her against the wall.

He laughed as if they were just playing a rough game. "Now you're mine—"

The crack of a gunshot cut off his words. His head jerked to the side and he fell over, a bullet hole in his temple. Chest heaving, her eyes cut from the man to the shooter—and there stood Kitty, Max's old personal assistant and Stacey's girl-friend.

"Good riddance," Kitty sneered, her gun still pointed at the man. "I always hated my brother—"

Another shot rang out. Awake and sitting upright with a nasty gash across his cheek, Sten followed Kitty with his pistol as she stumbled backward, a circle of crimson blooming from her gut. When she hit the opposite wall, the gun dropped from her hand and she slid to the floor, clutching her wound.

Val dropped the man's knife and marched to Kitty. She grabbed the woman's shirt and yanked her close.

"Where are my children?" Val snarled into Kitty's face.

"They're in the boardroom...on the fourth floor..." Kitty forced the words out as her life slipped away. "Tell Stacey...I really did love her..."

"Your regrets are not my problem," Val said, letting go of Kitty so the Northwalk agent could slump to the floor and die.

She retrieved her handgun from underneath the bed, then helped Sten stand. "You okay?"

"No," he said, tightening the shirt around his calf. He

dropped the magazine from his rifle and slapped in a fresh one. "Let's go."

Sweeping back into the hallway, Sten limping but able to move forward, they rushed back to the stairs and climbed to the fourth floor. At the top, the short hallway took a sharp right. Val knew from the floor plan it ended at a makeshift boardroom, the last obstacle between her and her children. She looked at Sten. His face pale and pinched with pain, blood running down his cheek, he met her gaze with steely eyes and nodded. Together they stepped around the wall, rifles up. A hail of gunfire erupted as what was left of the guards put up their last stand in front of the boardroom's closed doors.

A piece of wall exploded next to Val's head, and the world went dark. When her senses returned, she heard Sten screaming at her.

"Get up!" he yelled in her face as sirens blared all around them. "Goddammit, Shepherd, GET UP!"

She struggled to stand, but her legs wouldn't hold her weight. Blood trickled down her forehead and into her eyes.

Sten pulled on her arm in frantic jerks, unable to drag her far on his injured leg.

This is where he dies.

"Get up—"

Forcing herself to move her heavy limbs, she grabbed Sten and yanked him on top of her. Bullets bounced off his armor as she blinked away blood, pulled out her handgun, and returned fire, killing the last of Northwalk's guards.

Sten rolled off her, and they lay on the ground for a moment, gasping for air. She'd saved his life. Maybe now they were even? Hell, it didn't matter anymore. They were partners, bound forever, no matter what happened.

He pushed himself to his feet on unsteady legs, then pulled Val up. Leaning on each other until they regained their balance, they stepped over the guards' bodies and walked to the boardroom. She tried the door; Northwalk had locked it. She almost laughed at the prospect a flimsy lock would keep them out after the gauntlet they'd endured to get there. Val kicked the door until the lock broke and it swung open.

"Stop," an older woman with blond hair said when Val entered. The woman stood in the center of the room, flanked by long, ornate oak tables occupied by five other people in designer suits. They regarded her and Sten with expressionless faces, fingers laced together with white knuckles the only hint of their unease. Cassandra stood to the woman's right, the first time Val had seen the Alpha in the flesh. As in Val's visions, the Seer was an ethereal presence, looking at everyone and everything as if she knew exactly what was about to happen and her singular interest was watching the future unfold. To the woman's left, Danielle stood with a deep frown on her face and fear in her eyes.

Tossing her rifle to the side, Val aimed her handgun at the woman. "Where are my children?" she asked, her voice deceptively calm.

"I am Honora du Lothgard, leader of the Northwalk," she said. "It appears we have a misunderstanding."

"Where are my children?"

"Your children are safe. They are very special, and we are not the only people who know of their existence. A rival group based out of Asia, the *Yongjai*, are also very interested in acquiring them. We can keep your children safe. We can teach them how to control their abilities. Isn't that something you want?"

Val stepped closer, the barrel of her gun pointed straight between Honora's eyes. "Where are my *fucking children?*"

Honora flinched away from Val's pistol, the first time she'd shown any sign of fear. Then she lifted her chin in defiance. "You can't kill me. It's been foretold. Cassandra sees *all* futures, and you don't kill me in any of them—"

Val pulled the trigger. Honora landed on her back at the foot of the oak tables, a single hole in her head. Half a second later, Sten opened fire on the rest of Northwalk. They screamed and launched from their seats, attempting to flee, but in less than five seconds their bodies were strewn around the boardroom. He took a moment to glare down the barrel of his rifle at Cassandra. Unfazed by the carnage around her, she stared back at him with piercing eyes as if looking into his soul.

Stop, Val would have said to Sten if she had any compassion left in her. From what she could tell, Cassandra was merely a tool of Northwalk's, another one of their slaves. But Val was all out of mercy. She wanted to take anything Northwalk-related and rip it to shreds.

Sten's lips peeled back from his teeth in a silent growl, and he shot Cassandra in the chest.

As the only member of Northwalk left alive, Val's mother cowered in the center of the boardroom. With her hands up, she backed away from her daughter.

"The twins are in the side room over there," Dani said, pointing with shaking hands to a door on the opposite wall.

"Open it," Val ordered, her gun trained on Dani's chest.

Dani nodded and backed up until she reached the door, then pulled it open. Lydia emerged first, followed by Simon.

"Mommy!" they yelled, and Val nearly collapsed with relief. They ran to her, and she fell to her knees and embraced them in a tight hug.

"Are you okay?" she asked, her words trembling.

"Yes," Lydia said. She looked at the scene around her. "Mommy, what happened—"

"Don't look," Val said. She pointed to the far corner behind her. "Wait over there and don't look."

They walked to the corner and held hands, their eyes wide and fearful.

Val turned back to her mother, and a flood of searing rage wiped away the happiness she'd felt at the sight of her children alive and well.

With her gun trained on her mother, she said, "I spent all this time trying to save you. I invited you into my home, let you get close to my husband and my children, because I wanted to stop your murder."

Dani backed away as Val stepped closer. "They made me do it," Dani said. "I didn't want to, I really didn't!"

"I thought no matter what a shitty mother you'd been, your life was worth saving because you were *my mother*. But I was wrong."

Dani backed into the boardroom table, unable to retreat any farther as Val closed the distance between them. "I—I love you guys. In fact, I didn't know what love was until I met you and Max and the kids. Northwalk forced me to betray you. Pumpkin, please don't."

"Now I know," Val said, "*I'm* the one who kills you."

"Don't do this, please," she begged. Her lips trembled. "I have something to live for now. You don't understand—"

"Val, stop."

Was that…*Max*? She whipped her head around, and there he was, standing in the boardroom's doorway.

"Max?" she breathed, staring in disbelief at his perfectly

healthy body. Stacey stood behind him, her face pale as she looked around the room with a hand clamped over her mouth.

"Daddy!" the kids yelled. They ran to him and wrapped their little arms around his legs.

"Come on," he said, waving Val toward him. "Let's get out of here."

He didn't want her to kill her mother. To hell with that.

"No," she said, keeping her gun trained on Dani. Despite her sublime shock at seeing her conscious, healthy husband, she hated her mother more. "She tried to steal our children. She deserves to die."

Max pushed Simon and Lydia behind him, trying to shield them from the imminent execution of their grandmother. "You don't need to do this—"

"Yes I do! She'll come after us again. I won't give her the chance."

"You'll never forgive yourself if you do this."

She gritted her teeth and glared at her mother, her anger and pain so raw it stung her eyes. "I don't care," she said as tears welled. "I hate her. *I hate her.*"

"But I love you, Val. I can't live without you. Come home with me."

Come home with me. She'd said those same words to him when he'd been committed to the psych ward after trying to kill himself. He'd wanted to stay and rot there, but she had convinced him to come home with her, because she was his home—and he was hers.

Her hand shook. She wanted to punish Danielle *so badly*. The woman had sicced a psycho on them, tried to tear her and Max apart, kidnapped and threatened her children—all while playing off Val's desperate need to reconnect with her mother. Every instinct in her body screamed at her to pull the trigger.

Amid a sea of blood will stand the ebony fox and the crimson wolf, Cassandra had told her. Now Val realized what her choice really was: kill her mother—the crimson wolf—and sacrifice her capacity for love in the process. Choose the ebony fox—Max—and sacrifice the anger that fueled her vengeance. She couldn't have both.

Her gaze cut to Sten. Dirty and bloodied like her, he lowered his rifle and looked at her. The anger she knew well still roiled beneath his eyes, along with a touch of sadness. She looked at Max again.

His voice trembled, a note of desperation in his words as if he realized how close she was to leaving him forever. "Come home with me, Val. Please."

All her injuries began to throb. Exhaustion pulled on her arms and legs. She looked at the carnage around her, what her orgy of anger had wrought. All she had to do was put three bullets in her mother's chest, and her fury would be sated...But would it really? *Yongjai* was still out there, and Delilah Barrister, and other seers with malicious intent, and everyone else who might hurt her or her family.

If she pulled the trigger, she committed to that version of the future. She could never go home again.

Looking into her mother's eyes—the same as her own—she held her breath and squeezed the trigger—then relaxed her finger and let her arm fall before a bullet could leave the chamber. She turned away from Dani and walked to Max. As a sob burst from her chest, he encircled her in his arms, pulling her into his warmth and love while she broke down at the unfairness of the world, the cruelty of people to one another, her inability to punish everyone who deserved it—and the fact she had to accept it, and embrace love as the only real way to survive the storm of life.

The gun slipped from her grip onto the floor. She leaned her head on his shoulder, took Simon's hand while Max took Lydia's, and together they left.

Chapter Thirty-eight

Sitting cross-legged on the bed in Val's guestroom, Kat's computer in her lap, Stacey stared at the screen and bit her lip. The white background of an e-mail stared back at her, the *Seattle Times* in the "To" field. Attached to the e-mail were the contents of Kat's entire "Insurance" folder—texts between Norman Barrister and Gino Dinapoli that proved they'd conspired to break the law, including murdering people. But the real gem was the video showing Norman, Gino, and Kat in a three-way sex session that had Stacey's jaw on the floor.

She wasn't surprised Kat would do such a thing; Stacey knew better than anyone the mastery with which her ex-girlfriend had used sex to trick people into making bad decisions. The real shocker was what the video represented—unequivocal proof Delilah had lied about her family's involvement with Gino. There was no way she could claim the Italian criminal had been terrorizing her family when her husband was caught on tape getting some backdoor love from that same criminal. It might not result in jail time for Delilah, but it would certainly ruin her career.

Her best friend had been gracious enough to let Stacey stay with the Carressa-Shepherd family, until she could rebuild her life from the wreckage left after five years lost in a fetid fantasy with Kat and Northwalk. The fact that Val trusted Stacey enough to invite her friend into her home, after everything that went down with her mother, brought tears to Stacey's eyes. She'd saved Max's life, Max had saved Val's life, and now Val was saving her life. And *that's* what Cassandra had meant by choosing love.

Too bad it couldn't have been true with Kat. Stacey's heart tightened thinking about all the things that could have been between her and the woman she had loved. Kat's own hubris had been her demise. At least she'd left Stacey one gift, if unintentionally, before she died—her laptop, blessedly untouched by the intense firefight in the Northwalk mansion. Stacey had grabbed it just before Sten burned the whole place to the ground.

Saying a silent thank-you to her dead girlfriend—the last time she'd ever do so—Stacey hit Send.

* * *

With the hood of her sweater pulled over her head to hide her identity—and the cuts and bruises on her face—Val sipped her latte and smiled at the television on the wall. She'd never get tired of watching the local news play shaky footage over and over of Delilah Barrister running away from the cameras, the caption "Ex-Seattle Mayor and Congresswoman Delilah Barrister Resigns over Husband's Sex Scandal" emblazoned underneath. Finally, Delilah was getting her comeuppance. Only a few days ago, Val would have insisted it wasn't enough, given the death and destruction the ex-mayor had left in her wake. But she'd had a taste of what unbridled anger and vengeance were like, and she didn't want any more. Delilah's humiliation and crushed political aspirations were enough.

It was definitely better than watching yet another news report on the latest freaky event to befall the Carressas. Val had told the police about the sophisticated criminal ring—of which Eleanor Fatou had been a member—who'd stabbed her nanny and kidnapped the Carressa children with the intention of extorting her and Max for money. But she took the fight to them, she explained, and got her children back herself. It was mostly true. The police bought her story in so far as it was so bizarre, they couldn't come up with any other rational explanation to contradict her. They hadn't connected the burned-down mansion in the woods to her yet; hopefully it would stay a grisly mystery. If anyone in the department was still on Northwalk's payroll and suspected the truth, they kept their mouths shut and quietly began updating their résumés for new illegal employment.

Danielle had disappeared, and Val doubted she'd ever see the woman again. That was fine with her. Val had enough family; she didn't need someone to call "Mother" anymore. As for Sten, he'd disappeared as well, but he could go anywhere he wanted now, finally free of Northwalk's chains. Despite all the terrible things he'd done, she was happy for him. She knew better than anyone the caustic effects of being forced to live a life you didn't want. Maybe now he could find some peace, and be less of an asshole.

Val checked her watch and hurried to finish her drink. She'd promised to meet Max and the kids at the hospital so they could visit Jamal as he recovered from his stab wound, and there was no way she'd be late this time. The twins insisted on giving their nanny pictures they'd drawn of him and his future wife, a doctor named Natalie, who currently tended to him. Val couldn't offer a plausible explanation for how the kids could know such a thing, but it didn't matter. Jamal was family now.

Groaning from her many injuries, Val pushed herself to her feet. Before she could step away from the table, a familiar voice behind her said, "Congratulations."

It took Val a second to register the woman sliding into the seat across the table from her as Delilah, nearly unrecognizable in jeans, a plaid shirt, and a camouflage baseball cap with a pony-tail sticking out the back. She crossed her legs and folded her hands in her lap as if she still sat in an executive leather chair in her Congressional office.

"I underestimated you," Delilah said, a tight, mirthless grin on her face. "I didn't think anyone could take down Northwalk, but rumor is they've suddenly gone silent, and I assume the world has you to thank, given what I've *seen*."

Val lowered herself back into her seat. "I used to see you becoming President of the United States and then starting a nu-clear war, because you shouldn't be in charge of a buffet line, let alone an entire country. Now you'll never hold political office again. So I really don't give a shit what you've seen."

Delilah leaned across the table toward Val, and her grin warped into a frown that radiated hatred. "I don't think that's true, because you know what I see in my visions? You. Always you. My entire existence has been dominated by *your* fucking life. I know where you'll be, what you'll eat, who you'll sleep with. I know everything you've ever done or will do, like a book you hate but are forced to keep reading."

For a moment Val was speechless. *That's* what Delilah saw? Made morbid sense, given how the ex-mayor had inexplicably outmaneuvered Val for the last five years. But she hadn't been able to stop the career-destroying video from leaking, because Val didn't know who'd sent it or where it had come from. For once, her ignorance had been an advantage.

Surprising herself, Val didn't feel a surge of rage or anxiety at Delilah's shocking revelation. Instead, she laughed. "You'd have to be a serious sex addict to see my *entire* life. I can't imagine the chafing."

Delilah's frown deepened at Val's dismissive reply. She leaned back and assumed her icy, prim posture again. "I might never make it to the White House, but I'm not the only person with 'Barrister' for a last name. My son is finishing up law school now. He's taken a real shine to politics and is talking about running for city council after he graduates. Are you sure I'm the President Barrister you saw in your vision?"

Aw, shit. Val hadn't considered that. The familiar, sickening call for action began its siren song in the back of her mind. As she stared Delilah down, imagining all the ways she could hunt and eliminate anyone with the ex-mayor's last name, the coffee-shaped clock on the wall caught her eye, and the song was silenced.

Val stood again, gathering up her trash and pushing her chair in with such nonchalance that Delilah's glare broke into a look of confusion.

"This chat's been nice, but I have somewhere important to be. If you want to keep obsessing over me, go ahead. But you're only wasting your time. The future doesn't care about you, Delilah. I don't care about you. Remember that the next time you make the beast with two backs—whatever you see has *nothing* to do with you."

Val turned her back on Norman's widow, tossed her empty coffee cup away as she walked out, and didn't look back.

Chapter Thirty-nine

Curled up on the couch underneath a knit blanket, Toby nestled next to her, Val watched the Times Square New Year's Eve celebration play out on television. Some band she'd never heard of, composed of five boys who looked only slightly older than her own children, performed a catchy pop song as a massive audience froze their asses off. The ball had dropped in real time almost three hours ago, but a delay in the broadcast allowed the Pacific Coast to experience the moment at their own stroke of midnight. Stacey had already called it a night, not in the mood to stay up late or party. Like Val, she'd been reflective and thoughtful of late, reining in her impulses until she got a better handle on who she wanted to be rather than giving in to whatever felt good in the moment.

Val, however, couldn't sit this night out. Glancing at the clock again, she scratched Toby's ears to keep her hands busy. She didn't particularly care for the New Year's Eve pomp and circumstance, but the prospect of things to come—in just a few minutes, hopefully—had her fidgeting under the blanket with barely contained excitement. That afternoon, she'd received a package from Sten, an unexpected token of his gratitude. On a single piece of paper he'd written "*Баркалла*"—"thank you" in Chechen, the only clue she needed to know he'd sent it. Inside, he'd placed two vials of a clear liquid, along with a stack of papers typed in French.

While Ryan Seacrest prattled on about resolutions, Toby launched from the couch and ran to the kitchen. A moment later, she heard the door to the carport open and close, followed by Max trotting into the living room. He tossed his coat and baseball cap on a chair and smiled brightly at Val.

"I got it," he said, holding up a small grocery bag. He cocked his head toward the stairs. "Ready?"

She nodded, threw off the blanket, and followed him up to the second floor. Tiptoeing past the kids' bedroom, they quietly shut the door to their own bedroom and sat on the bed. Max emptied the grocery bag on the comforter between them; a couple syringes sheathed in plastic, a rubber tourniquet, and sterile wipes tumbled out. Then he retrieved one of Sten's vials from the nightstand. He held it up, watching the liquid swirl in the warm light.

"You don't have to do this if you don't want to," he said to her. He'd used those same words right before they'd made love for the first time and sealed their lifelong connection. Now came another critical decision point—whether or not to accept Lucien Christophe's cure for their condition.

According to Max's translation of Lucien's notes, the cure wasn't permanent; it lasted only three to four hours before wearing off, though Lucien had been convinced he could develop a permanent version if he'd had more time. Of course, they had to assume Sten sent them the real cure he'd stolen from

Lucien and kept hidden from Northwalk, and not something poisonous, but Val was sure it was the real thing. After all they'd been through together, Sten wouldn't kill her now. Max took her word for it without a lot of questions, thankfully. He'd finally accepted her explanation about her and Sten's relationship, and seemed to let it go. Since they'd both nearly died giving in to anger and old grievances, it didn't seem that important anymore.

"Let's do it," she said. Max would hand one of the vials, along with Lucien's notes, over to a pharmaceuticals lab to replicate and increase the potency—if it actually worked. The only way to be sure was to test it on themselves. Hopefully, it was the first step toward a normal life for them, for others seers, and most important, for their children.

He slipped off his sweater and sat bare-chested on the bed, then tied the rubber tourniquet around his upper arm.

"You sure you know how to do this?" she asked.

Rubbing a sterile wipe on his inner arm, he raised an eyebrow at her. "I used to be a heroin addict, Val."

"Oh yeah. Forgot about that."

He unwrapped one syringe and used it to draw liquid from the vial, up to some amount he'd deciphered from Lucien's notes. Val held her breath and winced when he eased the needle into his arm and pushed the plunger down. He used his teeth to unbind the tourniquet, then flexed his fingers. She exhaled in relief when seconds passed and he continued to look normal.

"How long does it take to work?" she asked.

"Close to immediately."

"Do you feel any different?"

"No."

Val pulled off her own shirt and held out her arm. He picked up the tourniquet and looked at her. "You're *sure?*"

"It didn't kill you." When he still hesitated, she moved her arm closer to him. "Just do it already."

His lips tightening for a moment, he looked uncomfortable letting her take the risk on a mystery drug, but he tied the tourniquet around her bicep without any further argument. He injected the rest of the drug into her arm the same way he'd done to himself, then cleared all the medical paraphernalia off the bed until it was just him and her.

They looked at each other like two virgins on prom night. In a way, they *were* virgins. Neither of them had experienced the ecstasy other people felt at the height of lovemaking; they could only imagine what it might be like. Now, for the first time, they would know. Her heart raced as he touched her cheek and traced his fingertips along her jawline.

"What if it doesn't work?" she asked, pressing her hands against his chest and feeling his heart beating as fast as hers.

"Then things will stay as they are now." He kissed her, then traced a path with his lips to her ear. "Is that okay with you?"

"Yeah, it is. It should have been before."

"Don't think about the past, or the future. Just be here with me now."

She did as he said, and cleared her mind of the chaos and pain they'd experienced in the last month, and throughout their entire lives, and would surely experience again in the future. All her senses focused on him—the taste of his tongue, the caress of his hands slipping off her clothes, the warmth of his bare skin pressed against hers, and the feel of him sliding inside her. As she held him tight against her, she didn't try controlling her thoughts to avoid a terrible vision of death and mayhem.

Instead, she let him fill her completely, losing herself in the emerald and amber depths of his eyes, seeing a reflection of herself there, and choosing to be that person.

She felt the familiar fire growing from where they joined, gaining in strength until an inferno made of passion and love engulfed them. His breath grew haggard against her lips. He entwined his fingers with hers as something completely unfamiliar and frankly scary bore down on them.

Then with a gasp, he tightened his grip, and she cried out as whatever he felt hit her, too. Like the single, clear note of a brass bell, it vibrated through every nerve, so intense she could barely breathe. She clutched Max to her as his body shuddered with hers, consumed by a sensation so powerful and wonderful, she thought she might cry. Slowly it faded, until only the echo of it remained, like waking up from the most beautiful, nonsensical dream she'd ever had.

Wide-eyed and chests heaving, they looked at each other, at a loss for words. Then they began to laugh as giddy delight replaced their shock. They laughed until they ran out of breath, exhausted and excited at the same time. While strains of "Auld Lang Syne" wafted into their room from the condo next door, he wiped a tear from the corner of her eye and kissed her.

"I don't think I could have done that with anyone else," she said, and he responded with a smile so bright and beautiful, it gave her stomach butterflies.

Before that moment, she hadn't thought she could love him any more than she already did. She was wrong.

Epilogue

Claire du Lothgard sipped champagne and watched the earth pass by underneath her from her first-class seat. Not as nice as a private plane, but she needed to keep a low profile for a while, let *Yongjai* and the other seer-controlling sects think Northwalk was no more, before rebuilding the empire. What should the new name be? *Felyne Enterprises.* She chuckled. Amusing, but too obvious.

Absently, she rubbed the spot where Sten had shot her. Though Cassandra had told her it would happen, she hadn't expected it to hurt so much. Despite a life dancing with danger, she'd never been seriously injured before. If she hadn't hidden an autoinjector with a dose of Lucien's miracle drug in the back of her pants, she would have bled out in less than two minutes.

Too bad about Cassandra. They would've made a great team, if the Alpha could have endured her never-ending visions. But like every Alpha before her, Cassandra's mind had been disintegrating for years, and she couldn't take it anymore. Instead of outright stealing Lucien's cure from Sten and using it on herself, her odd altruistic streak compelled her to create an elaborate scenario where Sten gave the cure to Val, and Max re-created enough of it to give to any other seer who wanted it. A cure for everyone except Cassandra, how noble. The Alpha preferred to die, and Claire wanted to be rid of her family. Egging on the Omega had been a win-win for them both.

In fact, it surprised Claire just how well their intricate plan had worked out in the end, though she should've known any plan hatched by the Alpha would be foolproof. Even so, the wildcard of Valentine Shepherd seeded in her doubt she couldn't ignore. Now that everyone had played their parts to perfection, all the pieces had fallen into place, and both she and Cassandra were free of Northwalk, she could finally relax and enjoy her victory… Well, mostly enjoy it.

From beneath the seat in front of her, she pulled out Max's laptop and turned it on. When she logged in, the screen went black. After a moment, a simple prompt came up and a word appeared on the screen:

Ask.

She typed, *Will I ever see Stacey again?*

No.

Claire swallowed back a knot in her throat. She wished she hadn't needed to lie to Stacey, but it was the only way the plan would work. That was the price she paid for her freedom. Some futures weren't compatible with love. But maybe there was more the computer couldn't relay. When added to certain future technologies, Max's program would be the keystone she needed to create her own digital Alpha. In its current state and even with some tweaks Cassandra made before she'd died, it wasn't much more than a very fancy Magic 8 Ball—the only one in the world that actually worked, but still frustratingly short on details.

Ask, the computer prompted.

Will I see Valentine Shepherd again?

Yes.

Claire laughed. Of course. Some things were inevitable.

* * *

Savoring the fluffiest croissant he'd ever had in his life, Sten admired the Eiffel Tower, framed by a big bay window, from inside the swankiest hotel room he'd ever been in. He'd never been to Paris before, or Europe, or anywhere, really, that wasn't a shithole. Slaves didn't get vacations. Now that he was free, he figured he should take one. But where to go first?

He'd decided to follow his heart. Yeah, it was a fucking cliché. But everyone else was doing it, so why not him? His first day in Paris, he'd spent an entire day at the Louvre, loving every second. The day after that, he'd toured the Notre Dame Cathedral before hitting the Arc de Triomphe. He'd even bought a beret and sat at an outdoor café while sipping espresso, living the dream of every American-in-Paris stereotype.

And now here he was, in this beautiful room, picking from an exquisite selection of pastries, cheese, and fruit, laid out literally on a silver platter in the lounging area. If he wasn't careful, he'd get used to these luxuries.

He heard the master bathroom's shower turn off. Shoving the rest of the croissant in his mouth, he walked to the half-open door separating the bedroom from the lounge and pressed his back against the wall about a foot from the threshold. A moment later, he heard footsteps on carpet and the rustling of a towel, then a voice.

"I'm here now," she said. On the phone. "Thanks for the accommodations. If I'd known *Yongjai* was this generous to prospective employees, I would've contacted you a long time ago...Yes, yes, thank you...No...I understand, but *you* must understand I can't just tell you where they are. We're talking about *two* Alphas here." After a pause, she laughed. "If you thought I was lying, I wouldn't be here right now."

The door to the bedroom opened all the way. Wrapped in a white robe and using a towel to rub her red hair dry, Danielle Shepherd walked out. She kept her head down as she clutched the phone to her ear, breezing right past Sten as he pulled a silenced gun from his pocket.

Oops for her.

She walked to the table next to the bay window. Tapping a pack of menthols sitting next to the silver tray, she pulled out a cigarette and put it to her lips. "Listen, I can take you to them myself, but I'm not telling you anything until we meet face-to-face. It's too dangerous over the phone—"

Turning, she finally caught sight of him and gasped, the cigarette falling from her mouth. Her gray eyes—Val's eyes—popped to the size of saucers, half a second before he put a bullet between them. With the heel of his boot, he crushed the phone where it'd fallen to the floor, until only tiny, useless bits of it remained.

Sten pocketed his gun, brushed croissant crumbs off his gloves, put his beret on with the bill tilted over his face, and slipped out the way he'd come in. Yeah, it was cheesy, traveling halfway around the globe to do the girl you loved a favor, especially when she'd probably never know, but he figured he'd earned the right to be a silly romantic. Maybe he'd travel the earth solving problems with his fists, or his guns, or both, keeping the world safe from evil people who profited off the misery of others.

Eh, that sounded hard. Maybe he'd just settle down in Mexico, drink Coronas on the beach every day, and Google "Valentine Shepherd" on occasion, ready to drop everything and travel north if it seemed she might need his particular set of skills again.

Ah, the things people did for love.

Corruption. Greed. Illicit sex. *Murder*. Private investigator Valentine Shepherd thinks she's seen it all, and her strange ability to glimpse the future gives her an edge no one else in the world has. But when her fiancé is killed trying to exonerate his client, billionaire Max Carressa, Val makes it her personal mission to bring the people responsible to justice, no matter the cost. Convinced the two men are linked by more than attorney-client privilege, she enlists Max's help in her investigation and gets more than she bargained for…

Don't miss *Vengeance*, the first book in the Valentine Shepherd series. See the next page for an excerpt.

Val went to the Carressa mansion on Mercer Island first, figuring Max was most likely to be home in the early evening, but she was turned away at the gate that surrounded the property by a Mexican housekeeper over the intercom.

"Mr. Carressa is still at work," the woman said with a thick Spanish accent through the crackling speaker. "And he is not talking to reporters," she added, sounding personally annoyed for him. "So if that is who you are, then don't come back, please. Thank you."

Val half smiled—apparently Max had earned his staff's loyalty. Maybe he wasn't a stereotypical rich asshole with a penchant for murder after all.

She made the trip to the commercial district in Seattle, where Carressa Industries occupied the top half of the Thornton Building, a modest skyscraper. At the headquarters, Val exited the elevator and sidestepped a janitor sloughing a mop across the marble floor of the lobby. She approached a young woman in a pantsuit—either a secretary or an intern—manning the front desk. The woman looked up from a business textbook and greeted Val with a superficial smile.

She took in Val's casual clothing with a slight sneer. "Can I *help* you, ma'am?"

"I'm looking for Maxwell Carressa," Val said.

"He went home for the day."

"I was just at his house, and his housekeeper told me he was here."

"Well, he's not."

"Where else would he be, then?"

The woman frowned. "Are you the police?"

"Yes," Val said. "I'm investigating the murder of one of his lawyers, and I just need to ask him a few questions. If you know where he is, you should tell me. Obstruction of justice is a felony punishable by jail time."

The woman's lips tightened for a moment, then loosened with a sigh. She grabbed a sticky note, scribbled something on it, and peeled it from the pack.

"He's at this address," the woman said as she handed Val the note. "He goes there a lot after work to…blow off steam, I suppose. He owns the place, but it's not common knowledge. He likes to be discreet. I only know because I have a friend who works there, and she helped me get this job. I don't frequent the place or anything, really. Don't tell anyone I sent you."

Val lifted an eyebrow at the woman, then glanced down at the address. Another place in downtown Seattle, a much posher area than South Washington Street—though going by the woman's attempts to distance herself from Max's home-away-from-home, even the highest social elite couldn't bury all their dark secrets. Whatever he was hiding wouldn't stay hidden from her for long.

* * *

Val parked on Union Street, across the road from the address the woman at Carressa Industries had given her. She double-checked to make sure she was indeed at the right place. All that marked the existence of Max's hideaway was a single red door inlaid in a featureless commercial building, sandwiched between a jazz bar and a handbag store. No windows or signs gave a clue as to what the place might be. Tourists and locals alike walked by it without a second glance on their way to the waterfront.

Val approached the door, illuminated by one sole lightbulb,

and knocked. A rectangular peephole slid open to reveal Asian eyes surrounded by thick eyeliner.

"Yes?" a no-nonsense voice asked.

"I'm here to see Maxwell Carressa."

"And who are you?"

"Seattle PD. I need to talk to him about the murder of one of his lawyers two days ago."

The peephole snapped shut.

"Shit," Val muttered. She considered whether kicking the door down would be enough to get Max's attention until about a minute later the entrance swung open. A gorgeous Asian woman in a strapless leather dress beckoned for Val to enter. Val followed her through a corridor so dark she could barely see the outline of the woman's lithe form three feet ahead. They rounded a corner and came to another door, this one all black, a red neon sign with the phrase "Red Raven in Moonlight" scrawled in cursive above it.

Val crossed the threshold into what seemed at first like a posh, mellow nightclub, all blacks and reds set in a dim glow to smooth electronic music. A few dozen people in expensive business suits sipped drinks and chatted with each other at black lacquer tables. Val did a double take when she realized at least half the crowd wore black bathrobes. What in the world was this place?

"Wait here," the Asian woman said before disappearing through one of three corridors that led away from the mingling room where Val stood. Val did as she was told for a couple minutes, trying not to stare at the weirdoes in black robes. They unabashedly stared at her, however, casting furtive glances at her comparatively cheap look, someone who clearly didn't belong at whatever this place was supposed to be.

She turned away from their judging eyes until she faced a corridor where darker, faster music wafted through. Out of curiosity she walked toward the music until she reached the source.

The hallway deposited Val into a lounge area with black leather couches surrounding a small stage. A beautiful man and woman performed a sensual dance for the benefit of a modest crowd. Val's mouth fell open when she realized the man and woman, writhing against each other in time to the music, weren't actually dancing—they were fucking. Her eyes cut to the spectators; she now noticed at least half a dozen of them masturbating while two couples performed oral sex on each other.

Holy shit—I'm in a high-end sex club.

Val had never been prudish, but this level of immodesty shocked even her. It was one thing to watch people screw each other on a computer screen; quite another to be in the same room with them. She felt herself blush and tried to look anywhere but at the people engaged in overt sex acts. Her eyes rested on a man in an expensive-looking suit, lounging on a sofa as he swirled liquor around in a tumbler glass and watched the show. In the dim light he looked like a twenty-years-older and thinner version of Robby, with close-cropped blond hair and a boyish face. His eyes wandered from the performance like he was bored until he noticed Val staring at him. He smiled and tipped his glass to her.

"Miss." The Asian woman's voice caught Val's attention. She stood in the threshold of the corridor Val had come through, arms on her hips and tapping her foot like she was dealing with a misbehaving child. "I told you to wait in the other room."

Val shrugged her shoulders.

The woman rolled her eyes. "Mr. Carressa will see you now."

She followed the Asian woman back through the mingling

room, up a staircase, and into another dark corridor that ended at yet another black door. The woman opened the door and let Val enter Max's private office.

Val expected some kind of kinky setup with maybe a giant heart-shaped bed and chains dangling from the ceiling. Instead, bookshelves lined the entire periphery of the room, broken only by a ten-foot-tall Celtic-style tapestry depicting an ancient tree—Val guessed either the Tree of Knowledge or the Tree of Life—directly behind a huge mahogany desk piled with papers and more books. Through the cozy light that illuminated the study, she made out hundreds of tomes on advanced mathematics, interspersed with works by Shakespeare, Dickens, and many authors she'd never heard of, some in foreign languages.

A thin blonde in a skirt so short Val could almost see her vagina leaned against the desk. She regarded Val as if the disheveled PI were a new lab specimen. On the far end of the study a man in his late twenties stood next to a bookcase, head down as he leafed through a textbook. He wore the dark gray vest and slacks of a fine three-piece suit, the sleeves of his white dress shirt rolled up to his elbows. Thick, wavy black hair framed a Hollywood-quality face with a sharp jawline and rough-textured lips pressed together in concentration. Val heard the door close behind her as he lifted his gaze to meet hers. She'd seen him enough on the news that an introduction wasn't necessary, but he gave her one anyway.

"Hello," he said as he snapped his book shut, then put it back on the shelf. "I'm Max."

"Valentine Shepherd." The photos they used on television hadn't done him justice. He looked even handsomer in person, she couldn't help noticing.

Max gestured for her to sit down at a thick leather chair

across from his desk. The movement exposed dragon tattoos inked in bright aquamarine colors across each of his inner forearms. As Val took a seat, she tried not to stare. They weren't dragons, she realized, but fractal patterns, like the intricate designs on folders she'd had as a kid.

He sat across from her at the head of the desk. "Kitty," he said to the blonde, "please bring Miss Shepherd a drink." He looked at Val. "What'll you have?"

"I'm fine, thanks. And call me Val."

"Sure thing, Val." The words rolled thick off his tongue as if he'd made a clever joke. He popped open a silver cigarette case, pulled out a joint, and held it up in front of him. Kitty sashayed over with a lighter and lit it. She went back to the periphery of the room while Max took a drag and then let out a long exhale, his hazel eyes watching the smoke drift away from him and disappear into the ceiling before snapping back to Val. His gaze pinned her down with an almost scary intelligence.

"You are not a cop," he said. "Impersonating a police officer is a crime."

"Yeah, but I don't really give a shit," Val said. "Somebody's got to do their job. Might as well be me."

He cracked a smile and took another puff from his joint. "I'm curious why you think Robert Price's death was murder. I heard he was hit by a drunk driver."

So that was why he'd let her into his inner sanctum instead of turning her away—curiosity.

"Robby was run down in broad daylight as he was about to meet an informant. That's not a coincidence. I was there when it happened."

"And what was he to you?"

"My fiancé."

"You?" Max raised an eyebrow. "I wouldn't have figured that."

"Why not?"

"Because Robby was a bit of a dough boy." He took another drag. "And you're not."

Val gritted her teeth at his backhanded compliment. Whatever Robby had lacked in the looks department compared to Max, he'd made up for in spades through compassion and warmth, something this pretty boy who might've murdered his own father probably wouldn't know anything about. She forced herself to stay objective and focus on what she came for.

"Robby was meeting someone named Chet, who said he had information that could exonerate you."

"No kidding," Max said, and looked lost in thought for a moment.

"Do you know anyone named Chet?" she asked.

"Got a last name?"

"No. Just Chet. Might be short for Chester. Effeminate Hispanic guy, early to mid-twenties. Probably lives somewhere around South Washington Street."

Max bit the tip of his thumb and squinted his eyes as if he were scrolling through a mental Rolodex. "Nope, I don't know anyone named Chet or Chester who fits your description." He looked at the blond woman. "Kitty, can you think of anyone?"

"No," she said in a voice like black velvet.

"What about the information that Chet said he had?" Val asked, a hint of desperation creeping into her tone. "What could an anonymous person know about you that might help your case?"

Max shrugged. "I have no idea. I would help you if I could. No one is more invested in proving my innocence than myself obviously."

Val deflated in her chair as the chances of finding Robby's killer went from slim to anorexic. She could search every gay bar and Chinese restaurant within a ten-mile radius of where Robby died, but even with Stacey's help, that could take weeks. The longer she went without any leads, the colder the case got. And that didn't include the planning she needed to do for Robby's funeral, boxing up his things, deciding what to give to whom—if she even had the option to choose since they weren't married—and figuring out what to do with the house she couldn't afford on her own.

Val realized she'd been staring at the tree tapestry behind Max at the same time she noticed he'd been staring at her. She blushed a little while his warm hazel eyes studied her, as if he could see into her and read her thoughts like one of his books.

"I'm sorry for your loss," Max said. "Maybe it was just an accident. The world is cruel that way. Sometimes bad things happen to good people for no reason."

She scoffed. "Like how your dad accidentally fell off his balcony?"

His gaze hardened but he smiled. "Yes," he said in a tone drier than the Mojave. "Like that."

Val stood. "I'm sorry for wasting your time. I'll see myself out."

He got up anyway and followed her to the door. As she approached the exit, he reached around her and grabbed the brass knob, turning it slowly before pulling the door open. Standing barely a couple inches away, she thought she felt heat radiating off him like he hid an inferno underneath his expensive suit.

She should have stepped back; she didn't. Whatever possessed him to suddenly enter her personal space, she wouldn't give him the satisfaction of being intimidated.

Well, not intimidated exactly. More like…intrigued. Dangerously. A moth drawn to his hidden flame. With him so close to her, she could see the five o'clock shadow spread across his jawbone, the slight chap of his lips, the light dancing off flecks of amber in his intelligent eyes. Intrigue turned to longing, a *want* for him so singular and intense it took her breath away. She eyed the buttons on his dress shirt and imagined slipping her hand between them, touching his flesh underneath—

"Nice meeting you, Val," he said as he held the door open for her, voice as cool and calm as winter snow.

She blinked as if snapping out of a trance. Stepping back, she sucked in a breath after realizing she'd been holding it. He smiled, but she recognized it as a practiced fake. Everything about his demeanor spoke of careful control—everything except the fire she felt in him just below the surface, one that threatened to consume her as well.

Acknowledgments

I'd like to thank the usual cast of characters who allowed me to realize my dreams: my agent, Carrie Pestritto; my editor, Madeleine Colavita; my husband, Chris; my beautiful daughters, Clementine and Violet; my best friend, Kendall; my mom, stepdad, sister, pugs, in-laws, and the Western Ohio Writers Association crew. And last but not least, my Keurig, without which I wouldn't have been able to finish this book.

About the Author

Shana Figueroa is a published author who specializes in romance and humor, with occasional sojourns into horror, sci-fi, and literary fiction.

She lives in Massachusetts with her husband, two young daughters, and two old pugs. She enjoys reading, writing (obviously), martial arts, video games, and SCIENCE—it's poetry in motion! By day, she serves her country in the U.S. Air Force as an aerospace engineer. By night, she hunkers down in a corner and cranks out the crazy stories lurking in her head.

She took Toni Morrison's advice and started writing the books she wanted to read. Hopefully you'll want to read them, too!

Learn more at:

ShanaFigueroa.com

Twitter @Shana_Figueroa

Facebook.com/Shana.Figueroa.9

You Might Also Like...

Looking for more great reads? We've got you covered!

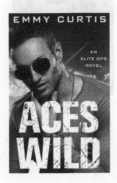

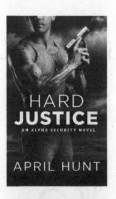